ANSWERS OF SILENCE

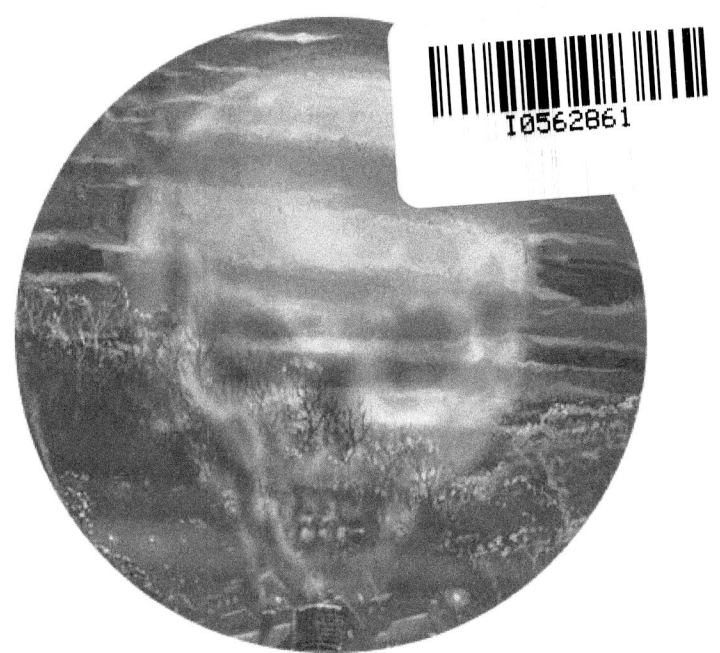

I0562861

GEOFF COOPER

deadite press

DEADITE PRESS
P.O. BOX 10065
PORTLAND, OR 97296
www.DEADITEPRESS.com

ISBN: 978-1-62105-196-1

Introduction - © 2012 by J.F. Gonzalez
The Questions of Doves - Originally published in an altered form under the title "Walking the Dogma " in Darker Dawning II: Reign in Black, 2002. This version appeared in Shivers III, edited by Richard T. Chizmar, CD Publications. © 2004 by Geoff Cooper
Incentive No. 43 - Originally appeared on Chiaroscuro. © 1998 by Geoff Cooper
Bleed With Me - Originally appeared in Shivers, edited by Richard T. Chizmar, CD Publications. © 2002 by Geoff Cooper
Gethsemane (Reprise) - Originally appeared in Bad News, edited by Richard Laymon, CD Publications. © 2000 by Geoff Cooper
Mo 3:16 - Originally appeared on Gothic.net. © 1999 by Geoff Cooper
Badgetree - Originally appeared in A Darker Dawning. © 2001 by Geoff Cooper, also in Cemetery Dance #49, CD Publications.
Latex: Like a Glove - Originally appeared in Bum Piss and Other City Scents, Dark Muse Publications. © 2001 by Geoff Cooper
The Sheriff of Pensie Avenue - Originally appeared in Bum Piss and Other City Scents, Dark Muse Industries. © 2001 by Geoff Cooper
Turning Leaves (An Autumn Romance) - Originally appeared in 4x4, Delirium Books. © 2001 by Geoff Cooper
For Whom We Mourn - Originally appeared in Masques V, edited by J. N. Williamson, Gauntlet Publications. © 2006 by Geoff Cooper
Mhz Minus Infinity - Originally appeared in Bum Piss and Other City Scents, Dark Muse Publications. © 2001 by Geoff Cooper
Strangers: Good Friends and a Bottle of Wine - Originally appeared in In Laymon's Terms, edited by Kelly Laymon, Steve Gerlach, and Richard T. Chizmar, CD Publications. © 2011 by Geoff Cooper
The Missive - Originally appeared, in altered form, as The Missive of Kenny Jeter of the Mons Olympus Colony - in Horror Horizons #1, Jobs In Hell Publications. © 2000 by Geoff Cooper. This version is the author's preferred and appears here for the first time. © 2012, by Geoff Cooper.
Jolerarymi's Rose - Originally appeared in Two from Zothique, and The Last Continent: New Tales of Zothique, edited by John Pelan, Bereshith Publishing. © 1998 by Geoff Cooper
One-Eyed Jack - Originally appeared in ...And Hell Followed With Them, Solitude Publications. © 2006 by Geoff Cooper
Answers of Silence copyright © 2012, 2015 by Geoff Cooper
Cover art copyright © 2015 by Alan M. Clark

All rights reserved. No part of this book may be reproduced or transmitted in any form or by any means, electronic or mechanical, including photocopying, recording, or by any information storage and retrieval system, without the written consent of the publisher, except where permitted by law.
Printed in the USA.

Acknowledgements

This book would not exist if not for the kindness, hard work, dedication, and perseverance of Paul Goblirsch, J.F. Gonzalez, Leigh B. Haig, David Ho, Brian Keene, Regina Mitchell, Jeff Burk and Rose O'Keefe—all of whom were instrumental in getting this thing into your hands.

It also would not exist if it were not for Gary Braunbeck, Richard Chizmar, Ray Garton, Rain Graves, Ryan Harding, Mikey Huyck, Matt Johnson, Richard, Ann, and Kelly Laymon, Tim Lebbon, Tom Monteleone, Jim Moore, Mike Oliveri, Norm Partridge, Tom Piccirilli, David Schow, Lee Seymour, John Urbancik, and Mehitobel Wilson, who believed in me the first time around.

ALSO BY GEOFF COOPER

Retribution Inc.
Bum Piss and Other City Scents
Shades (with Brian Keene)
4X4 (with Brian Keene, Michael Oliveri, and Michael T. Huyck Jr.)

*This book is dedicated to my children,
The Queen of the Universe and Bahbo.*

*Maybe in 20 years, you'll find a copy and be proud
of what your father used to be.*

In loving memory of
Jesus F. Gonzalez
and
Thomas Piccirilli

Rest well,
my friends.

CONTENTS

REVISION NO. 53
AN INTRODUCTION BY
J. F. GONZALEZ

Rumors of a long-awaited Geoff Cooper short story collection begin to circulate as far back as 2004. It has taken the better part of eight years to finally see that happen.

Those of you reading this should rejoice.

Many of the stories in this collection took a long time to be written. The reason for this: Geoff Cooper is a perfectionist. He will spend hours agonizing over a single sentence. He will rewrite the same story a dozen times, continually fine-tuning, polishing, refining, striving for perfection with each rewrite.

Reading Coop's material in preparation for this introduction has rubbed off on me.

It has taken me three goddamn weeks to write this introduction.

Before I continue, let me make one thing abundantly clear: forget about all the new-fangled writers who have emerged out of the woodwork of the horror small press in the last five years, especially the ones who are so eager to over-promote their work on every social media conclave. You hear the hype all the time: *Terry Dinkleheimer is a Master of Terror! Buy his novella The Creeping! If you enjoy Edward Lee and Richard Laymon, you will love Dinkleheimer!*

Of course we've all seen hyperbole like this. It's gotten worse since the advent of Twitter and Facebook. Some of these no-talents have more fans and followers than T.E.D. Klein (and if you don't know who T.E.D. Klein is, please correct that, like, *now*).

Geoff Cooper doesn't have as many fans and followers as the Terry Dinkleheimer's of the world on the social media pages he maintains, but that's okay. Long after Terry Dinkleheimer and others of his ilk are reduced to powder and

11

their works are forgotten, I am 100% confident that Cooper's work will still be spoken of with the kind of reverence and admiration people like me reserve for folks like Karl Edward Wagner.

Yeah, yeah, I know. The Terry Dinkleheimer's of the world don't know who Wagner is, either. Shit like that used to make me wail and gnash my teeth in frustration and anger. Now, not so much.

If anything, it makes me pity the fools.

What I'm attempting to do is draw a parallel between the works of those two men and the work of Geoff Cooper. That correlation: great things sometimes come sporadically. Sometimes they take months. Sometimes they take years. In the case of Klein, it can take decades.

You're holding this book in your hands. Point.

Most new readers and wannabe writers of the horror small press have very short attention spans, and not much of a comprehension for much of its rich history.

They discover the field much the way we all do; with wild-eyed amazement, usually drawn in by a brand name (Stephen King) or a big-time genre favorite (Jack Ketchum, Edward Lee, Richard Laymon, Brian Keene). For those of us who write in this genre, this love affair dates back to childhood. We are drawn to this material and seek it out for our entertainment—we attend horror films with our friends, we seek out the dark stuff for our reading material. We live it, breathe it. It becomes second nature to us. It becomes part of who we are as human beings.

Then we get the writing bug. And when that happens, we become a sponge.

We read our contemporaries. We seek works by new writers (sometimes indiscriminately). If we are discerning enough, we ignore the dreck and zero in on the diamonds in the rough. And if we know what is best for us, we soak up the works done by the Old Masters.

And we read lots of single-author short story collections.

Short story collections do more than preserve the short fiction by writers. It provides a time capsule; it provides a permanent home for those short pieces most readers miss as they fly by in magazines and anthologies. Most writers I know love working within the form, despite its limited audience. When a writer accumulates enough short story publications, the only way to seek greater immortality is to collect them in book form.

Most short fiction collections, especially those by journeymen writers, comprise of works cherry-picked by the author for various reasons; to select the best pieces from a particular time period; to conform to a certain overall theme. This is acceptable. After all, a dozen or so stories of varying length will quickly reach the word limit that most publishers deem acceptable for a book-length work.

Even fewer collections are compiled of all (if not most) of the author's works intended to provide the entire contents. These usually befall those who are less prolific, but whose works are of high quality: Laird Barron, David J. Schow, the aforementioned Karl Edward Wagner, and now, Geoff Cooper.

Geoff Cooper has never been terribly prolific. Among the dozen or so stories carefully selected for this volume, there are only another half dozen or so scattered throughout various out-of-print anthologies, small press magazines, or residing on disk drives from now defunct webzines. Coop has been at this game since 1997 or so. Fifteen years. Over a dozen stories and novellas. Again, T.E.D. Klein comes to mind. In fact, Coop just may be my generation's Klein.

I've been reading Geoff Cooper's fiction since around 1998, shortly before I formally met him in the flesh, in Monterrey, California, that same year. What has always struck me about his work is the obvious sense of influence; this is a guy who has read and absorbed the classics of our field, has done the same with its outlying genres of Science Fiction, Crime, and Fantasy, and then took these tropes to new dimensions, altering and warping them so much that they became uniquely *his*. Readers unfamiliar with the works of M. R. James may not see the slight nod to "The Ash Tree" in Coop's story "Badgetree: a Brackard's Point

Story," but I sure as fuck do. They will probably miss the tongue-in-cheek mention of M. P. Shiel's "Xelucha" in such works as "The Questions of Doves," too. Those are just two small examples of how Coop riffs on the genre's history— by bringing them to the present in contemporary terms, with his own narrative, characters, and themes, yet still finding a way to make those older works *resonate* through his work.

While Coop has a solid grounding of the field's rich history, he is a child of the splatterpunk era, to be sure. This is very much evident in such pieces as "Incentive No. 43," "The Sheriff of Pensie Avenue," and "Turning Leaves (an Autumnal Romance)." Coop will be the first to admit that David J. Schow was a big influence on him, but the works of Richard Laymon and Edward Lee reign high, too. In such pieces as "The Sheriff of Pensie Avenue" (and the very nasty "Latex: Like a Glove"), Coop's prose slips sinuously through you, leading you in with its hooks and enveloping you in every sensation. His descriptions of the inner city of his fictional Brackard's Point, New York, could be any inner city slum, but he makes it *his*. You *see* the decaying buildings, the bag ladies wandering with vacant expressions in their eyes, the street hustlers, the garbage piled along the mouths of alleyways. You hear it in the sounds: the police sirens, the crazy muttering of the homeless, the screams of the violated.

And to add to the sights and sounds, Coop assaults your sensory overload with the *smells* of this environment too.

Don't believe me? Try this random description from "The Sheriff of Pensie Avenue": "A few steps past, she heard someone lose their guts in one of the back alleys. Another smell wafted onto the street: Old English 800 and partially digested pretzels with mustard, sopped in stomach juice and malt liquor."

The reader is enveloped in this urban underbelly by the very nature of Cooper's prose. You feel it in your gut; you can smell it, taste it. A little further into the story, Cooper has you so acclimated to the squalor and filth of the setting of this story, that when you come across this line—"She passed

14

a small kitchen on her way to the bedrooms, and shuddered at the thought of the stench that would surely spew out of the refrigerator."—you immediately react. Go ahead. Read that story, and *don't* try telling me you didn't scrunch up your nose when you get to that line.

While Cooper's narratives are aimed squarely at the horror genre, much of his work transcends it. Witness "Mo 3:16" or "Jolerarymi's Rose." To be sure, horrific events take place, but they are window dressing for what are ultimately tales of human tragedy. "Jolerarymi's Rose" veers headlong into the universe of Clark Ashton Smith's Zothique, that fictional world of a future continent, where sorcery is a given and the machinery and science of our present civilization have long been forgotten. Originally written for the Clark Ashton Smith tribute anthology *The Last Continent: New Tales of Zothique*, Cooper managed the admirable feat of not only nailing the overall feel of Zothique, but he makes it his own. With "Jolerarymi's Rose," Cooper provided a bridge from the modern to a setting many find hard to wrap their heads around even on a good day. That both stories touch on the theme of the sudden loss of a loved one is the thread that binds them, yet both are set in two distinct universes: one complete fantasy, the other the very modern.

"Strangers: Good Friends and a Bottle of Wine" is an unabashed homage to his friend and mentor Richard Laymon. And while this shows in the prose style Cooper adapted for the story, it still has that inimitable Coop stamp on it. Not a simple pastiche (much like "Jolerarymi's Rose was not a simple CAS pastiche), Cooper takes "Strangers" to a place I never expected it to go. I had come to the story with certain expectations. Cooper blew them out of the water. 'Nuff said.

Never is this shattering of expectations so clear in "The Questions of Doves." Upon first reading the original version of this story (not included in this volume) on its first publication, I remember my heart skipping a beat and my stomach dropping the moment I read a certain passage—I won't spoil it for you by citing it here. Needless to say, I read the rest of the story with a sense of dread that was never really alleviated even after the story was finished. If anything, the dread was made greater upon re-reading the version included here. That a piece of fiction can still convey this in me even subsequent readings speaks volumes. More than just a genre potboiler, "The Questions of Doves" subtext is even more richly layered. It begs for subsequent re-reads.

Try evoking *that* level of dread, Terry Dinkleheimer!

One of the things that sets Coop's fiction apart from his contemporaries is its sense of locale. Brackard's Point, New York, is a fictional city, to be sure. It does to Rockland County, New York what Stephen King does to southwest Maine with his fictional Castle Rock or Derry, or what Gary Braunbeck does to Columbus, Ohio with his Cedar Hill stories. Many of the Brackard's Point stories share subtle links with each other. I won't tell you which ones. You need to dip in and see. Coop weaves such magic in this fictional city, that when you get to "Kenny Jeter and the Mons Olympus Colony," you aren't sure if the other Brackard's Point stories contain similar autobiographical elements. Coop certainly isn't the first to pen a piece of metafiction. Plenty of other writers have done this also, but Coop creates a careful fusion of fantasy and reality in this piece. It blurs the line. And in doing so, it accomplishes what the best horror fiction does.

It subverts.

The latest publication here (the aforementioned entry from *In Laymon's Terms*) was published just last year, but it was written well before that, and that's where my only rub lies with Coop. The man just doesn't write enough, goddamnit! On the rare occasions he *does*, he will spend months writing a few paragraphs. No wonder it has taken him close to sixteen years to produce enough fiction to fill only two average-sized volumes. I've produced scads more during that time—others with more pedigree and clout than both of us have produced even more. There have been rumors of novel-length narratives written by Coop, never published, but quietly worked on in secret. These rumors have been whispered amongst his friends for the last eight years. It's talked about it the way some people talk about

Bigfoot or Chupacabra. Will we get to see these gems? Try asking where T.E.D. Klein's second novel is [1].

Lately, Coop has drifted away from writing fiction for publication. The duties of career (Coop is an EMT) and family have demanded his time as of late. As an excuse for not being prolific, this is acceptable because family is important. Having heard his anecdotes of his EMT runs, I know there's a story or a novel in there somewhere. Maybe someday, this can provide grist for the story mill.

In addition to being a fan of the man's work, I've come to know him pretty well.

I consider Coop a friend.

Some introductions offer up personal anecdotes about the writer in question. I'm not going to offer up any of that in this piece. That's really none of your fucking business.

Know this, though. Coop is a good man, a wonderful father, and a good friend. I'm honored to know him.

As a writer, when Coop puts his mind to it and is inspired, he is one of the best writers I know. Period.

As a perfectionist, his dedication to the written word is amazing. It is infectious. It rubs off on you. Goddamn fucking hell, it rubs off on you. It's taken me three weeks to write this introduction. Normally, I can whip these things out in three days.

Three weeks!

---

1   T.E.D. Klein's first novel, *The Ceremonies*, was published in hardcover by Bantam in 1984. It became an instant classic and I hereby order you to locate a copy and read it. Klein followed this book up with *Dark Gods*, a collection of four novellas. A second novel, *Night Town*, was sold to the same publisher for publication in 1986. A provision was written into Klein's contract that for every month the book was late, he had to remit payment to the publisher. This clause was inserted in his book contract to provide Klein—even then a notoriously slow writer— to deliver. As of this writing, it has been twenty-six years. Either T.E.D. Klein had a great agent who managed to settle out of that contract, or he owes Bantam Books a small fortune. *Night Town* has never been published.

Hopefully, it won't take you three weeks to read through this collection. I seriously doubt that. I predict you will blaze through this in a day. Two days tops.

One thing I am certain of, though: these stories will remain with you long after you finish. Trust me on this.

Now, if we can only get Coop to finish that goddamn novel…

J. F. Gonzalez
Lititz, PA
May 1—25, 2012

THE QUESTIONS OF DOVES

It was warm enough to have the kitchen window open. Carma and I sat at the table, scanning the paper and talking over orange juice. Mourning Doves asked sorrowful questions from the cherry tree out in the backyard: *Oooh-weee? Ooh? Ooh? Ooh?...Oooh-weee? Ooh? Ooh? Ooh?*

They built a nest there, took turns watching over the eggs. They, like us, were starting a family. Perhaps they asked the same unanswerable questions we did of ourselves and each other at the time: *Is the baby going to be okay?—do we know what we're getting ourselves into?—are we going to be good parents?—will they grow up to despise us?—will they have a better shot than we did in life?* Questions, always questions. No answers ever forthcoming.

Carma threw the paper down in disgust, asked if I heard about the bank robbery.

I had. It happened less than a half-mile from our home, down at the bottom of the hill. Two tellers were killed. She passed me the paper. I scanned the article. No leads, nothing new.

"That's messed up," I said.

"Messed up? I'll say. What's it all coming to, if you can't even go to work without getting taken out?"

At the mention of the last word, our mutt, Rhea, stood up from under the kitchen table, placed her paw on Carma's lap and whined.

Carma laughed, rubbed Rhea's ears. "I wasn't talking to *you*, silly."

Now, of course, Carma *was* talking to her—and so Rhea began to bounce and grin and wag her tail even more. She ran, toward the door, then back to us. Then back to the door.

"Oh, God," I said. I had not yet finished my orange juice,

19

did not much feel like walking her. Of course, I would wind up doing it anyway.

Carma was five and a half months pregnant at the time. She *could*, of course, walk Rhea. The physical activity of walking the dog around for a few blocks would not put undue stress on her or the baby, but I felt an obligation to do trivial things like that for her—especially since she became pregnant. I am sure a shrink would read deep into my behavior and come up with some psychobabble one-hundred-eight-dollar-per-syllable diagnosis to explain my behavior. I had a simpler one: I loved her, and wanted to help out. Just not before I fully awoke.

"Can't it wait?" I asked the dog.

Rhea cocked her head at me, then came bounding back from the door again. She jumped up, placed both front paws on my lap.

"I'm taking that as a 'no,'" I said. "All right, fine. Fine. Just let me finish this and get my damned shoes on, okay?" I stood up, polished off the last swallow, and went to find my sneakers.

"Hey, why don't you take her down to Xelucha's?" Carma suggested as I tied my laces. "That way you can get one of your frou-frou coffees, and get her a doggie treat...."

"And oh...let me guess...get you one of the scones, right?"

Carma had developed a thing for Xelucha's scones right about the time she became pregnant. Going there was becoming a daily occurrence. Could be worse, I supposed. She did not ask for anything disgusting like caviar, pickles and ice cream, or asparagus. I could have fetched these things for her too, if she asked, but would have been less enthused about doing so.

"Well, being as you brought it up...if you don't mind. You know. While you're getting your frou-frou coffee and all."

"Ain't much frou-frou about a 20-ouncer with four shots of espresso slung on top," I countered. Carma was right, though. One of my friends in San Francisco got me started on this whole ridiculous latté thing. From time to time, I have spent five dollars on a single cup of coffee. But I didn't like admitting that. Not when you walk in to your average Starbucks and you see a bunch of 19 year old kids writing poetry on laptop computers. I tried to disassociate myself from such banality. But I still liked those quad-shot coffees.

"Whatever," Carma said. "But if you go, can you get me a scone?" Her scone. Already claimed. It was a foregone conclusion that I would return with one.

"Maybe," I tried to say with a straight face.

She pouted. "Pleeeeze?"

I would. Of course I would. She carried our baby. I could deny her nothing. She could have asked me to walk Rhea up to Buffalo and come back with some of the town-famous chicken wings, and I would have done so cheerfully. I was so incredibly happy with her, with us, with our life. But I still said, "maybe."

I wasn't going to admit I was completely pussy-whipped, even if we both knew it was true. I had standards to maintain, after all. I was shop foreman at this little 6-bay garage on the corner of Lake Road and Route 9W in Congers. The responsibilities were sometimes a drag, but after fifteen years in the business, it was finally starting to work out. I had to work Saturdays, because they were generally the busiest, but Sundays and Mondays off. No one else at the shop got two days in a row. At work, I was top dog—and the top is a nice place to be. It would have been great to be top dog at home too, but a guy could not have everything. So I was a little mushy—big deal. I had it good and I knew it.

Carma was the afternoon deejay at WHPL. *"The station that puts the* Rock *in Rockland County."* While on air, she was "Carmen Miranda" and always hung up on people after saying, "You have the right to remain silent." but at home, she was my Carma. And she was pouting at me to go get her a scone from the cafe.

"Of course," I said. "Anything else?"

"Nope." Her put-on pout evaporated into a grin. "Go walk. The Dogma."

Dogma...that was her name for Rhea. The Dogma. She was The Carma, the dog, The Dogma. Tacky? Silly? Perhaps, but it was our thing. You had to be in the relationship to appreciate or understand—only then would it make perfect sense.

As soon as I grabbed the leash, The Dogma bounded toward the door. I clipped her on, gave Carma a kiss, and stepped outside. It was unseasonably warm that morning, as if a late spring day got lost in the calendar's inexorable march, and somehow wound up on the 21st of October by mistake (wrong turn at Albuquerque?). We walked, listening to the constant questions of doves.

A little girl was walking in the same direction—toward the cafe. The girl followed The Dogma and I for two blocks as we made our morning rounds: *stop, sniff here, squat there.* I thought the girl must be meeting a friend nearby to walk with to the school bus stop. She was maybe eight or nine, with beautiful auburn hair and a pink jacket. Under her arm were tucked a few textbooks. In the other hand she carried a small brown paper bag.

Rhea saw her too, thought she was wonderful. The Dogma loved kids—boys, girls, no difference to her. To Rhea, kids (whether they were friendly or not, the loving, trusting fool she is) were cooler than a fresh puddle of St. Bernard pee. The girl was too far away to play, so Rhea let out a doggy sigh and continued on, every so often looking back to see if she had caught up with us and entered petting range.

We were halfway down to The Cafe Xelucha when it happened.

A sparrow swooped down from nowhere. Literally: nowhere. Not from the rooftops, or an overhanging tree branch; it was as if it materialized out of the very air it traveled through. I was watching the girl walk quickly up the sidewalk toward us while Rhea paused to sniff a mailbox. One instant, above her head, there was nothing—the next, a cruel little bird that squawked and chattered insanely as it nipped and clawed at tender skin.

I watched, momentarily stunned, as the bird looped back for another run. I could see its sharp little beak and black, shiny eyes honing in on her. Again, it attacked. The girl flung her books across the sidewalk to cover her face with her arms. The brown bag lunch sailed onto the neighboring lawn as she curled into a small ball. A small, auburn-haired little ball with a pink jacket that screamed.

Rhea let out a single "wuff," and her hackles stood on end. Her tail wagged slowly, sweeping the ground in a low, wide arc. Her every muscle quivered tight-wound spring at the end of her leash. *Unclip me*, her stance said. *Unclip me and let me get that bird.*

I'm not nuts. I've had my dog since she was a puppy—I know damn well what she wants when she wants it. If I have to explain, well...you've never loved a dog—it's as simple as that.

I unclipped her leash.

When she heard the release's metallic *click*, she lurched forward, then turned to look at me: *is it all right?*"

I snapped my fingers, pointed toward the girl.

The Dogma ran. Forty-five pounds of goofy mutt barreled up the sidewalk.

The bird swooped and dove, clawed at the little girl's neck and shoulders, ripped away small parts of delicate, pale skin. With each piece, it squawked in triumph. End the thrill off the chase. Begin the joy of the kill.

Allow me to say that Rhea's predatory instinct has long been domesticated. The Dogma has never won a fight—not with another dog, not even an ornery cat. She has never won because she *always* backs down. Aggressive? *Her?* The idea is laughable. At most, she would bark and growl and carry on like she's Queen Badass, until someone stands up to her. Then, she'll immediately duck for shelter, tail between her legs.

Rhea is a nice dog. She's a sweet dog, a good, loving dog, but she's a wimp. Once, when she was a pup, a cat rose its hackles and hissed at her. Rhea rolled on her back and peed herself as she whined pathetically. My old neighbor,

Tracy Phillips, had this tiny little pound and a half thing with pop-eyes and a ridiculous under-bite. I called it a rodent on a rope. Tracy, however, *insisted* the butt-ugly creature was a dog, even pointed out its picture in the AKC Book. It was a *pedigree*, she said, and was quick to offer the papers of its lineage up for my inspection. I declined, because to my way of thinking, that thing's papers did not make it anything other than an *expensive* rodent on a rope.

Regardless of its species, this…creature, I guess you would call it, growled at Rhea (who could, even then, chomp it down in one bite), and the big doofus hid behind me, thumped Morse Code for "Please don't hurt me" on the ground with her tail.

Considering her lack of aggressiveness, the way she launched herself at that bird, all four feet off the ground, a picture of grace and power in the air, impressed the Hell out of me. I nearly clapped as she snatched it in mid-flight, thought for a moment that I ought to paint her tennis balls brown and give them little wings, because she can never catch those: they'll *bonk* right off her head. It actually looked like she was a natural, there, for a moment—as if she knew what the Hell she was doing. That moment, she was Defender Of the Pack, saving The Pup from The Enemy.

The Enemy—the bird….

Birds are fragile—light, hollow bones. There's really not much to them.

Rhea killed it. Her jaws cracked the bird in half. When she dropped it on the ground, it lay folded back upon itself. She nosed it around. Her long tongue smacked against her rubbery lips, as if she had a bad taste in her mouth or a feather stuck between her teeth.

The bird did not move.

I turned toward the girl. "It's all right, honey. It's okay."

She did not rise. For a moment, she merely sat there, sobbed. Several scratches and small chunks of skin were missing from her neck. Against her pale skin, her blood was bright. Too bright. Too bright and too much of the wrong shade of red with her auburn hair and that glaringly pink jacket. All that red everywhere, but this shade—her blood—clashed horribly.

Rhea was sad because the girl cried. She whined, head down, walked in nervous circles. She crept forward, licked the girl's hand, until I heard this magical, soul-warming laugh.

"Yikes! It tickles!" the girl said. both her little arms flew out, clamped The Dogma in a tight hug.

Rhea yelped, backed away, tail between her legs, head down low. I thought the girl hugged Rhea too hard, maybe pinched her collar. I stepped around to soothe The Dogma's nerves with a comforting pat. Her muscles quivered beneath my hand as if she were afraid, all of a sudden.

Re-enter the wuss, I thought.

"You're dopey," said the little girl, and giggled when Rhea cowered from her high, sweet voice.

She was not telling Rhea anything new. I was just glad to see the little girl was all right. I clipped Rhea's leash back on. She did not notice at all. Usually, Rhea would look up at me when she heard the click of the latch, but not this time. She stared at the girl's face, and shook.

The girl's face rose toward mine. She looked at me.

The eyes Rhea saved...

My mouth went dry. They were *black*. Pure black, impossible to distinguish between iris and pupil. There was no white in them; they were two dark holes in the upper third of her face. I tried to look away. I wanted to look away. I could not. I had no choice but to look. To see.

Silence between us, as I stared into the dark windows of its soul. My lungs locked around the breath I took, would not let it go. I would have welcomed a shiver, but could not move.

It spoke: "I need my books."

There were two voices. The little girl's for the ears, and the one that resonated with irresistible power deep within parts of my being long thought vestigial and dormant. The command could not be ignored. I gathered the books from the neighboring lawn, the sidewalk. I straightened the pages and readjusted the dust covers before I handed them over.

"Good dog," it said.

Not to Rhea.

It laughed that beautiful laugh cleverly disguised as a little girl's, rose, and skipped down toward the bus stop.

It looked both ways before it crossed the street.

Two Mourning Doves asked their eternal question: *Ooohweee? Ooh? Ooh? Ooh?* From the power lines overhead. As that thing with auburn hair and a pink jacket approached, they asked again: *Oooh-weee? Ooh? Ooh? Ooh?*

Black, soulless eyes squinted at the birds overhead. It shifted its books under its arm and whispered a single word in answer.

They fell, dead as stones.

It looked back at me and said: "It's a girl."

Our baby. I knew she was talking about our baby. We did not know the sex. We didn't *want* to know. both Carma and I wanted to be surprised. They asked us when we had the ultrasound if we wanted to know whether we were having a boy or a girl. We told them no, we did not wish to know at the time. It was private question, one we often pondered, but did not want answered until its time came.

We certainly did not want it answered by this little bitch was standing over the corpses of two doves. Part of me wanted to strangle her, but that part was put in its rightful place by intense, irrational fear. I thought that if I touched her, my flesh would rot on my bones, if she chose it to do so.

"Going my way?" she asked, as she nodded up toward the cafe. Her body posture was nothing short of lewd.

Rhea and I started backup up a few steps. Going her way? Not likely. "The fuck are you?" I asked.

Rhea tugged at the end of her leash to draw me further away.

"Omega and Alpha. The last and the first."

That's backwards, I thought. *Isn't it the other way?*

Revelation came back to my head and realization flashed across my face. She saw the comprehension settle in my features and snickered.

"My God..."

"Not yet."

It snickered as I backed away.

Rhea's self-preservation kicked in, and by virtue of holding her leash I was to be taken with her, whether I protested or not. I did not, was merely too overwhelmed to react appropriately without a bit of assistance. She lurched, yanked my arm as she tried to flee. Her toenails scraped the sidewalk as she strained on the end of the leash, her collar dug into her neck. I cold hear her starting to choke, yet still she tried to drag me away.

By the time the thing's snicker became a full-fledged laugh, I had joined in with Rhea and bolted for the house. Having only two legs, I could not move fast enough for The Dogma. She dragged me along the side streets to the perceived safety of our home.

I hurried to the front door, Rhea looked back to see if it had followed. I could not bring myself to glance over my shoulder. I was afraid I would see it there. As soon as I opened the front door, both Rhea and I rushed into the living room. I slammed it, locked the deadbolt behind me—something I *never* do during the day. I stood, back to the locked door and tried to regain my breath as Rhea sat at my feet. We both panted—she less so than me.

"Back already?" Carma asked from the kitchen.

It took me a moment to catch enough wind to answer her. "Yeah," I said. "I...I didn't go. To the café."

I heard the tap water shut off. "Why not?" she asked as she entered the living room. After she looked at me, she asked, "What's wrong?"

"I just..." Just what? *Just ran into the weirdest frigging thing I've ever encountered and by the way, honey, we're having a girl? The antichrist told me so. Sorry about not having a scone for you, sweetie. It kind of slipped my mind...* I let the sentence die.

The more Carma looked at me, the more her face softened from annoyance to concern. "What happened? Are you all right?"

"Yeah," I lied. "Just kind of freaked out, is all." That's me: master of understatement.

"You didn't see *them*, did you?"

"Who?"

"The guys that robbed the bank?"

"The bank?" It took me a moment to figure out what the Hell she was talking about. I'd forgotten all about reading the paper with her—though it happened less than twenty minutes ago. "Oh! The bank! No. Don't worry. It's...nothing. Seriously."

She gave me *the look*. Every man has been on the receiving end of *the look* before. I don't care *who* you are—you've tried bullshitting your way around some sort of obstacle, and a woman—your mom, your wife, your sister, the chick at the return counter at S-Mart the day after Christmas—pulls her head back, points her chin down, arches an eyebrow, and looks at you with a stare so powerful, so sharp and penetrating, that it slices through your bullshit and taps on the guilt center of your brain. Only women can master this look. I've often wondered if they taught that stare at school, perhaps during sex education, when we were taken into another room and given a list of reasons for the toilet seat to be left in the upright position.

I did my best. I held my ground for 3.2 nanoseconds before I told her everything that happened.

Carma, of course, thought I was out of my fucking mind.

The rest of the day, conversation between us was brief in verbiage and shallow in depth. *"Do you really want a scone?" "No, it's okay." "What's wrong?" "Nothing."* Shortly after noon, she announced she had to do some errands. When I inquired *what* errands she had to do, she said, "Oh, just stuff."

I gave her my version of *the look*, but it failed. Instead of spilling the proverbial beans, she collected her wallet, checkbook, and car keys, and told me she'd be back around dinnertime.

Alone in the house, I sat on the couch and pretended to be interested in the television commercials and the shows that accompany them while Rhea curled up next to me and slept. I made myself a pot of coffee, and, as I went for the fourth refill, I felt a pressure building in my bladder that required release.

I left the toilet seat up.

After another half-hour of watching television commercials, Rhea nudged me with her nose. She wanted to go back out.

The Dogma apparently did not remember the events of the morning, I did, so I was less than enthusiastic about taking her for a walk. She, however, was persistent, and—I shit you not—gave me *her* version of *the look*. I'm telling you: it's a female thing. And Carma was—according to the thing with the pink jacket—carrying a girl. I was beginning to feel vastly outnumbered.

"Fine," I said, and got my shoes on.

Rhea tugged my arm, as usual, as soon as the door was open. We stepped out off the porch into the driveway. It had cooled down, almost October again. The doves had either tired of asking the unanswerable or received a response that satisfied their curiosity. I hoped it was one they liked hearing, if that was indeed what had happened.

Carma's Saturn was parked behind my pickup.

I froze.

She took her car keys. I remembered her taking them. I tried to think back, see if I remembered *hearing* the car depart. I could not be sure. I placed my hand on the hood. It was cool. I looked inside the driver's side window.

The keys were in the ignition. Carma's pocketbook lay spilled across the passenger's seat and floor, as if it were hastily cast aside. A tube of lipstick lay half-buried under a single smooth feather.

A thousand scenarios crowded my mind, choked out all thought. A thousand envisioned horrors flashed through my vision all at once, and my head began to spin, Numbness slid through my veins, sluggish and cold. I stood, dumbfounded, dimly aware of Rhea on the leash as she walked in nervous circles, holding onto the car's roof for support.

I stood there, head down, eyes closed, to steady myself. A moment or two passed before I opened my eyes and looked around. Should not have wasted the effort: my yard revealed no clues to Carma's whereabouts. I scanned the hedge, down along the fence, moved my head so I could see a little bit more of what might lie behind the cherry tree. There were no birds in sight, no sign of the thing in the pink jacket. I called for her, "*Carma? Carma?*" but knew as soon as I heard the question in my voice she would never answer.

Keeping an eye on my back, I led Rhea back into the house. Once there, I forced myself to calm down. I did not want to sound like a lunatic when I called the cops. I told the operator that my wife was missing—vanished from my driveway. I told her about the feather and the way the purse was scattered over the Saturn's interior. I told her Carma was thirty-one, pregnant, that she was five-eight and, at least before she was pregnant, a hundred and twenty-five or so (even if Carma owned up to only a hundred fifteen of them). I told her everything—almost.

The cops came and looked over the car, then asked their questions. They were suspicious, grilled me as if I were a suspect. Asked me if there was anyone—a former lover, perhaps—that I could think of that might abduct her. I told them no. They asked if I—or she—had received any threatening, anonymous phone calls. I told them no. They finally left me with a business card to use in case something came to mind (an insinuation I resented), and with the feeling that I had wasted valuable time.

By then, it was well past dark. Dinner time had come and gone. I paced all over the house, muttered to myself and wrung my hands. Rhea thought I was nuts and hid under the desk.

"She ain't coming back," I said to the dog.

Rhea peeked out, looked at me with large, sad eyes.

Then again, she looks at me with large, sad eyes when I'm holding a stew bone. She's a dog. They do that.

Thump.

My first thought was someone threw a rock at the window.

I ran over there—thinking it might be Carma, wanting to be let in and not having her keys, or that it might be the little bitch in the pink jacket, and I could get my hands around her delicate neck and start crushing. I was wrong.

A dove stumbled around on the outside window sill. It looked dazed, drunken. Large eyes pleaded with me from the other side of the glass. It opened its beak wide, and screeched. At first, I thought it would fly away soon after—that the screech was something out of pain, or that it felt threatened by me lunging for the window as I did, but it did not fly. It stood, favoring one leg, and continued to screech.

From the cherry tree behind, I heard a terrible cackling of chirps and caws. The branches hung heavily with thousands of grackles. As one, they left their perches and swooped down toward my window. Angry eyes and screaming beaks, lice-covered feathers obscured my view of my yard. I thought they would all attack the window, throw their bodies at it until the glass shattered and the house was theirs, but their plan was not that at all: they fell on the wounded dove, flybys with extended talons, dive-bombing beaks.

The hurt dove fell off the window sill to the yard below. I saw it scrambling on its back as it tried to right itself and failed. Its only protection was a few blades of grass. It had no chance. The grackles ripped it to shreds in moments.

The Dogma was going nuts. She stood on the chair, barked at the birds on the other side of the glass, teeth exposed, ears as erect a she could get them, her eyes intense and wide. The sense of *deja-vu* was beyond strong: it was overpowering. Maddening. Dog baring, birds screeching...a dead doves this morning and one mutilated by the beaks of its brethren in my yard, my wife and daughter gone, this thing in the pink jacket...

"Fuck it. Go get 'em!" I said, and ran across the room to open the front door.

She was standing on the porch, waiting for us. She smirked, giggled to herself. "May I come in?""

I growled. Rhea ducked behind me. "Where is she?"

"Oh. You want to discuss her, do you? Your girlfriend?"

"Wife," I corrected, but with the sense that I was being played. This little bitch knew I was having a girl—surely she knew Carma was my wife. "Where is she?"

The birds ceased screeching in the yard by now, and had all settled in behind her. An army of a hundred Grackles in neat ranks and files on my front lawn. A few could barely contain their bloodlust. With clips and chirps, they hopped from foot to foot. Blood spattered on their beaks. Bits of wet meat clung to their sharp claws. They tittered and cawed and each bird's black, soulless eyes were fixated upon me.

The only difference between their eyes and their master's was the skull that held them.

"Let me in."

That voice struck a chord deep inside my being. I took one step aside for her to pass, but Rhea growled and blocked my retreat. She would not let her in. I took courage from my mutt, who apparently found her backbone yet again.

"No. Where's my wife, you little bitch?"

"You kiss your mother with that mouth?"

I drew back my fist, and was ready to break this little girl-thing's nose, when the birds rustled their feathers as one. Rhea, from behind me, let out a single, low growl.

"Where's Carma?"

The thing in the pink jacket laughed. "Carma...*ha!* How adorable. This is your pet name for her, Carma, yes? Oh, how *quaint!* How *dear!*"

"Fuck you. What did you do to her?"

"I did nothing."

"Lying to me..."

"I repeat: I did nothing. I only gave her a dove and asked if she could love the dove as much as she did you. She lied. So she's gone. She did it—not me."

"Where did you take her?"

"I took her nowhere. She lied. *That* took her."

"Oh, fuck this," I said, and stepped toward her. The birds behind her rushed forward to meet me. The Dogma barked a barrage of canine fury and snapping teeth

Glaring up at me with those black eyes, the thing in the

32

pink jacket waved her hand, signaling her troops to fall in line. They obeyed.

"You want to find her?"

"What do you think?"

"Then take this," it said. "Take this dove and answer me: can you love this dove as much as you do your wife? Answer carefully, for that is the only way you have a chance of finding her."

I did not see the dove before, but I was becoming accustomed to such minute shifts in reality. Like the brown bird from this morning, it was not, then, it was. I wondered if the bird attacking her this morning was a friend of the doves somehow, or if it was all a setup.

The dove cooed, and fluttered toward me. I reached for it, but before it could land on my outstretched arm, Rhea leaped and snatched it in mid-flight. She chomped and I heard the breaking of hollow bones as she thrashed her head from side to side. Blood slung out of the dove's chest to stain wing, carpet, and muzzle alike.

"Rhea, no!" but instinct had her, and its command could not be dissuaded. I fell to my knees, tried to steady her by force, but she wriggled out of my grasp. Another moment later, she dropped the dove. I watched it fall from her mouth to the floor. There, I watched it shift from a matte grey to a dull black. It was no dove. My eyes had deceived. It was a Grackle, and it let out these tiny cries of either hatred or pain as the malevolent lights in its eyes faded.

I reached for the bird, but Rhea snapped at my hand. She'd never done that before. Ever. So shocked was I that I lunged backward at the cost of my balance. I fell backward on my elbows and stared at my dog in surprise. She leaned over her kill and panted, but showed no signs of aggression as long as I made no move toward the bird.

"Dumb fucking dog!" the thing in the pink jacket said, and stepped closer to the threshold of my home. "Let me pass."

Rhea snarled.

"I said *move*," the thing's voice lowered four octaves at

the last word, and rumbled with dark power. Legions of birds outside tittered and cawed.

They stared at each other—my dog and the pink jacketed thing. Rhea did not retreat. The little bitch did not advance. Three, four, five, heartbeats passed, and neither moved.

"Stupid animal," the thing said, and flipped its auburn hair back over its shoulder as it turned to face me. "Put her away and let me in."

"I can't."

"Can't? Can't? You can't even tell your dog what to do? Did your bitch wear the pants in the house or what? Let me *in.*"

Yes, Carma wore the pants in the family. I was only the Top Dog while at work. At home, I was there for Carma and our baby, and Rhea. Now that Carma was gone, I guess Rhea was top dog.

"You'll have to ask her," I said, and pointed to Rhea.

Rhea showed her fangs, dared the thing in the pink jacket to step through the door.

It did not get a chance. I slammed the door in its face and engaged the deadbolt.

It stood outside and screamed for a while, demanding to be let in, but I ignored it. The Dogma and I went back to the couch, to the television and the commercials, and increased the volume. I did not turn the sound up to drown out the thing on my doorstep. I did it so the thing on my doorstep would not hear me crying.

Rhea pissed on the carpet sometime that evening. I was not about to take her out. She did not even bother whining. Instead of sleeping on the couch with me, she curled up at the front door.

They were gone by morning. Only a few stray feathers and a bunch of bird shit on my pickup's windshield remained.

***

Carma—and my baby's—disappearance broke my heart. I've sat up countless nights since then in tears, wandered down every street in this town, most of Starson, Congers, and Nyack, too. Got jumped once on Franklin Avenue. Rhea bit the guy's arm. That's the fourth time she saved me.

It's been a year—she's still gone. Rhea is still here.

If I ever find my Carma (a hope that is dim, at best), I know the first thing out of my mouth would be: "What did you answer?"

I like to think I could believe her response. My Carma would never lie to me…would she?

Would she?

The nest in my cherry tree is abandoned. I do not know what came of the eggs. I wonder if the Grackles got to them.

Some days, as I'm having my coffee and petting The Dogma's ears, I hear the Mourning Doves. They call from trees, power lines, elsewhere in the neighborhood, but not my backyard anymore. It sounds as if they're asking a question.

Oooh-weee? Ooh? Ooh? Ooh?

It sounds as if they suspect the answer is not one they want to hear.

Oooh-weee? Ooh? Ooh? Ooh?

What did you answer, Carma?

What did you answer?

INCENTIVE NO. 43

Steel clanged against iron. Number Forty-Three struggled in the mattress-less iron bed frame, handcuffed shackled, gagged, her exertion voiced in muffled snorts.

Francis researched himself, previous kills scanned and saved onto computer. She was beginning to get antsy; he should have blindfolded her. She could see the monitor from the bed.

Shooting would not do—absolutely not—no style in it. Francis *had* used knives, nothing as garden-variety as stabbing. Numbers Four, Six, and Seven: amputation, evisceration, and decapitation, respectively.

Francis did not think of himself as a murderer. No, not a murderer—a connoisseur. Each kill superior to the last was his goal, but therein lay his dilemma: Francis Dwight Lundgren felt washed up.

What if he killed this woman, and did not surpass the forty-two before her? Where would he be then? Nervous knots of self-doubt tied up his faculties.

Francis looked over his shoulder from his desk chair at Forty-Three, could not decide. She was cute without being overly pretty—which was good. Pummeling a pretty face had its allure—pretty ones were so tempting to ruin: overdone, unstylish as arson.

In the end, it mattered little whether they were raw beauty or raw skank. They were all the same on the inside. Guts were still guts, intestines were intestines and livers, livers. When a stomach was ripped from the abdomen, the tough meat sac popped in a spray of gastric juices, it was impossible to tell if it came from a supermodel or a fifteen-year-old hooker junkie. Francis knew.

The latter, Number Twenty-Nine, was on screen. He

photographed her stomach acid and bile pooling in the abscesses of her arms.

But how to make Forty-Three special? Her hair was brown and curly, her body about average. He guessed she was within a year or two of his own thirty-six.

A plain gold wedding band encircled her finger. Someone loved her, or at least *pledged* to.

He had loved a girl once, back in junior high school. She was *Numero Uno*—strangled with used latex condoms she had shared with Number Two: the guy she had been fucking, (she never gave Francis the time of day, much less sex). Number Two's father worked for a chemical company in Brackard's Point.

Francis immolated Number Two with one of his father's products, a highly flammable solvent. When he was thirteen, he thought those two were inspired. Now...

They were shit.

Hindsight: maddening vision.

What to do with Forty-Three?

Francis stood from the desk, walked to where she lay shackled, inspected her, found her all around average. His first instinct was to compensate, make her death spectacular. Intriguing... but no. Unacceptable: almost *expected.*

He sat down again, continued searching his computer files. Every kind of death: slow, quick, painless, agonizing. He had starved a captive to death (Number Five), deprived another of water (Eight). He had cauterized a man's penis so that urination was impossible (Eleven), sewn a woman's anus shut (Twelve). The woman died faster.

He had poisoned three people: numbers Three, Nineteen, and Twenty-Two. In forty-two Deaths, Francis had used every method short of a firearm. No shooting. Shooting was not art. Shooting was gutless, akin to plagiarism.

Francis opened up more recent files, his masterpieces, his *Venus DeMilo*, his *White Album*, his *Ghost Story*.

Number Forty was dispatched with lye; alive as the caustic liquid dripped, steadily dripped. Five and one-half days it took to melt a hole in the man's chest. Francis remembered the man's screams. He had them on audio tape; pictures, time-lapse photography, every half-hour, clockwork. Art.

Number Forty was an engine of genius, a freight-train of originality followed. Forty-One was a woman; four pictures were taken as her Death stepped closer.

Picture one: the woman, with perfect fingernails, large, scared eyes, dressed in high-fashion business attire. She was half a decade younger than the one on the bed now.

Picture two, a pose with props: the woman's hand, a camping hatchet with a hammerhead, two ten-penny galvanized steel nails, and two severed fingers. Perfect nails.

Picture three: the woman's eyes, looking directly at the camera.

Picture four, zoomed: the woman's right index finger (and perfect nail, not visible) impaled through her large scared eye, which had become a runny mass of blood and yolk.

Francis bit his lip in memory. Getting the finger through the skull and into the brain was *very* tough to do. Ten-penny nails first, tapping, tapping a pilot hole in the skull, how hard they were stuck before the braincase cracked. Extraction was difficult, too, gently tapping the underside of the nail head, rocking them back and forth, loosening them. Then he used her fingers to pierce the brain. The thin delicate bones mushroomed after a few whacks of the hammerhead, the joints kept bending, but he persisted, reaching into the eye socket as he held the finger, keeping the joints straight as he whacked the finger into the brain. Oh, how glorious! To be in his work like that...

Fond memories. Art.

He was sure Forty-One was the best he had ever done, and would *ever* hope to do. That was until Forty-Two.

Forty-Two was a pregnant woman, eight and one-half months along. A shackle here, a handcuff there, she was helpless, her belly ready to burst. When he brought down his bathroom mirror, she did not know what to expect. She could not have imagined.

With care and precision, Francis nipped the corners of the mirror with a glass cutter, formed a point. Then she screamed.

He cut across her blossoming belly, angled the mirror so she could witness the Cesarean. She watched every phase of the operation: through the dermal layer, peeling back the skin, deflating, her belly evacuating in a wet gush. Several times Francis stopped, cleaned the mirror so she could see. He wanted her to see. That was *so* important.

She wept, cried, screamed. Francis imagined how she would handle labor, natural birth. He removed her baby, sucked the plugs out of the nose, knocked the plug in the trachea free, informed her it was a boy. It cried when he slapped its bottom. Its mother wailed. Francis cut the umbilical cord with the sharp glass of the mirror, pausing for a moment to show her the bloody wet screaming child. He did not think the placenta was strong enough to strangle her with; he was tempted to try.

Inspiration: he shoved the pointed mirror in between her ribs. She howled, thrashed around, twisting away from him. When she twisted in vain against the shackles and handcuffs, the mirror cracked inside her. When she moved, the shard wedged into her torso. Francis did not shrink back. He pushed harder with the part he held, deep into her, he dug around for a moment before he felt the spongy tissue of the lung yield.

Her last breath came not through her mouth, but through her chest. It made a wet phlegmy sucking sound, covered the mirror in a flecks of blood and a ghostly fog of steam.

Art.

As the child grew, Francis neglected his art in favor of surrogate fatherhood. The drive never left him. He was an artist; above all, that. A parent he was, but second. The torture of not practicing, temptation, but no, never yielding to it, until now, eleven and one-half years later.

Number Forty-Three was walking out of Schwartz's Drug Store on the corner of Harding Avenue and Bracken Street. She did not suspect the footsteps behind her, nor the blackjack that rendered her unconscious.

When she came to, she was in the back of his Chevrolet minivan, her hands, feet, and mouth bound in silver tape. He drove the minivan directly into the garage upon arriving home, dragged her to the cellar. Just like when he was good. Eleven and one-half years gone.

Now, he could think of no way to kill her. He checked his watch. Cory would be home from school in about ten minutes. It would not do for the boy to be home while he worked. Not at all.

Francis switched off the computer and scratched his chin, trying to think. Methods of destruction ran through his mind: Strangulation—done countless times, electrocution— Number Twenty-Eight—evisceration—been there, done that. Immolation—back to basics? Where the Hell had his talent gone?

Three twenty-one. Cory was going to walk through the door any moment.

Drug overdose—too close to assisted suicide, best left to Dr. Kevorkian. Drowning—Number Thirteen, a fish tank filled with semen. *Goddamn, that was good*, Francis thought wildly, remembering how hard he worked to fill the tank.

A diesel engine lumbered down his street, whined down to a grumbling idle, then rose in pitch, fading away. He froze, holding his breath. The damned school bus. Cory.

"Shit!" He ran up the stairs, leaving Forty-Three. Francis opened the cellar door, stepped through, shoved it closed against the thick foam weather-stripping, locked it behind him. Cory mounted the front porch steps; hollow thumps carried to the kitchen.

Cory opened the front door. Francis wiped the sweat off his palms and tried to appear casual.

"Hi, Dad," Cory said, and dropped his book bag on the kitchen table. He ran over and gave him a hug.

"Heya, slugger!" Francis hugged his son, removed the boy's Yankee cap and messed up the blond hair he inherited from his mother.

"Get any writing done today, Dad?"

"A little," Frank lied.

"Good. I'll get changed. You ready?"

"Ready? For what?"

"Today's Cub Scouts!"

"That's *today?*" Francis thought of the woman in the cellar. She would be all right if he left for a while.

"Yes, Dad," Cory said, in a tone Francis did not particularly care for. Cory had picked up the habit from school; Francis called it the *'Aren't you so fucking stupid, Dad?'* tone.

Francis hid his annoyance. "Get your stuff together, then."

Cory did as he was told. Such a good boy, despite the annoying habits learned from school. He emerged from his room a few minutes later, suited up and ready to go. Blue uniform, badges displayed proudly.

"Ready, Dad?"

Francis drove him to Rick Pelan's—the Cubmaster—house, amicably chatted about the Yankee game with the other fathers: Lee Garton and Tom Johnson, for a few minutes. When Francis was relating a bad call by the third base umpire, a dark blue Toyota truck pulled up the driveway. The men fell silent as the twins, Ryan and Mikey Taylor, poured out of the passenger's side, calling each other horrible names. The rest of the boys let them into the circle they had formed in the front yard, but said nothing. They were all scared of the twins. The men did not notice their sons all falling silent, because they all had their mouths open, and their jaws were scraping the concrete driveway, because Ryan and Mikey's mom, Lili, stepped out of the truck and was walking over to them.

"Gentlemen," she said in greeting, and took each one of them in her eyes. "Could one of you bring the boys home for me tonight?"

Immediately she had four volunteers. When the men had begun to argue about who should be the one to go to Lili's house at night, she slipped back into her truck and departed. Francis saw her slyly smiling through the windshield.

"You guys argue about it," Francis said. "I'll just bring Cory home." Then Francis bid them all farewell, and left.

It took nine minutes to arrive home. Assuming equal time to return, an hour and twelve minutes remained to kill the woman. He would wait until after Cory went to bed to dispose of the body. That, at least, required no Art. That was merely throwing out garbage. Every body he had ever disposed of was always done in the same manner: teeth removed with pliers and pulverized with a hammer, hands and feet removed and burned to ash. Limbs and torso chopped up, bagged, loaded into a large cooler, fed to the Hudson River. Ash and teeth particles were flushed down the toilet with his morning bowel movement.

There *had* to be something. He got out of the truck, entered the house through the door into the laundry room. His eyes flickered across the shelves: Bleach? Soap, lint, jeans, Cory's underwear. Bleach. Hmm... He picked up the bottle. It was very light. He opened the cap. A small amount, about half a shot glass worth, lay at the bottom. Not enough.

"Shit!"

Francis left the laundry room. The kitchen.

Knives? "No," he shook his head. Not again. Food processor? "It would take too long." Cast iron pots? Bludgeoning again. Under the sink—drain cleaner? Nope, contains lye. Remember Number Forty? Damn. Damn. Damn! He could not become a parody of himself.

One hour, three minutes.

Cleanser? Not likely. Dishwashing detergent?

Useless.

The bathroom. Rubbing alcohol? Hmm. Poisonous, but again, a fatal reaction would take too long, and not enough. Hydrogen Peroxide? Nah. Iodine? Not this time. First aid packages, gauze, cotton swabs, toothbrushes, toothpaste, bath bars, shampoo, conditioner, shaving cream, disposable razors? Nope, little blades would take too long anyway. Tweezers, hairbrushes, combs, dental floss, useless useless useless.

Fifty-eight minutes.

The living room. Magazines and throw pillows, stereo equipment, television? Hmm... The TV would probably be heavy enough to kill her if he were to smash it over her head, but then he would have to find a replacement before Cory got home, which would be in fifty-seven minutes. That was not good enough, but perhaps another time. Video tapes, cordless telephone, remote controls for both the stereo and television, and coffee table coasters. No, no, no, no and no.

Fifty-five minutes before he had to get Cory, he went to the cellar. He unlocked the door, descended the stairs.

Her head snapped attentively as he stepped onto the cellar floor; her hair had matted and sweated into a nappy, tangled mess. Her sweat smelled. She had soiled herself. The fecal reek hovered at nose level. The handcuff's pressure on her wrists reddened her hands; her veins stretched the skin in bulging blue tufts. Brown eyes pleaded sympathy.

Francis's fingers pulled at the bags under his eyes, and inhaled. *What to do with her?*

Fifty-one minutes. Tick. Tock.

What to do?

Francis walked over, reached for his medium's cheek. She recoiled as best she could, a shifting of angle of her head. Gently, he laid his hand on her face. Soft. Her jaw line was femininely round, her skin felt both feverish and grimy.

"Moof!" she said through the gag.

"Moof, eh?" Francis chuckled. "That makes a lot of sense. It's a bitch talking through that gag, isn't it?"

She did not know whether or not to nod.

Francis admired her for a moment, his hand running down her side as he might appreciate the fine body lines of a vintage Mustang.

Such a lovely chance he had here, to prove himself better than himself, to show that yes, he still *did* have the knack, and he *still* was an artist after all these years. No new annihilistic vision came over him as he stared at the subject, inspected it, concentrated on it like a single blank page, imagining the words.

Tick.

Tock.

Francis's frustration boiled.

Tick.

Still.

Tock.

Nothing.

He backhanded her.

"Mmeemph!" An inarticulate muffled voicing of pain and more than a little fear. It began.

She rattled the iron bed frame; the crisscrossed bars hummed in thin metallic voices.

Francis's hand stung from whacking her; he felt no better. It was not her fault he was frustrated, he knew that. So little time to do this properly. Normally, he would be fully involved in his work by now—carving or slicing or performing some type of surgery on the subject, but now...

nothing.

No adrenaline bum-rushed his system. Where was his Muse when he needed it? What would another artist do now? What would Arensberg or Clark or Boote do when they could not see beyond an empty canvas? What did Twain do when his paper was blank? What or whom did Lovecraft call upon when ingenuity had abandoned him?

Tick.

Tock.

"Meeummph!" The subject said under the gag.

"Shut up. You're breaking my concentration."

Francis raised his hand to strike her again, to enforce his word, and she immediately shrank back as far as the handcuffs and shackles would let her. An idea struck him.

He could scare her to death.

No.

No time. Forty-one minutes. Tick. Tock.

"Fuck!" He screamed, and smashed his fist into his palm. He cracked his knuckles. The subject meemphed and cried and quivered in her shackles and gag, thinking he directed the outburst at her.

"I told you to shut up!"

"Mmph! Mmmum!"

"Damn you, cunt! Would you shut your fucking yap so I can think? Jesus Christ! Can't you see I'm trying to work something out?"

"Mmumph?"

"That's it. You're fucking dead," Francis said. "But, you already knew that, didn't you? Yes, of course you did. I thunked you over the head at the drug store. Yes. Me. I dragged your unconscious ass down here, and chained your ass to an empty fucking bed frame. You. Are. Dead. I. Am. Going. To. Kill. You. Do you understand me?"

"Meemph! Muuimph mmph mmmm!"

She was still screaming/mumbling when Francis threw the computer desk chair at her. It cracked something as it smashed into her shoulder. She cried out in muffled pain.

"Still screaming? You want to scream?" Francis took the gag out of her mouth thirty-two minutes before he had to leave.

She wanted to scream, badly; she did not hesitate in doing so. Her voice shattered as her vocal cords crackled. The scream degenerated into a repeating mutter: "No, no, nonononono."

"No? Wrong answer. Yes, I'm going to kill you. Thing is, how? That's my problem. I'm having a damned hard time in figuring out how to do it."

"Kill me? I didn't do anything to you!" She screamed, and the effort apparently flared the wound because she winced and moaned.

"Neither did the rest."

"Oh, sweet Jesus," the subject whispered.

"Figures you would say something like that. When in doubt, pray. I've seen a lot of people pray who never would otherwise." Francis said, righting up his desk chair, placing it down next to the bed. He placed his feet on the empty rail and rotated them back and forth. "I can't figure out what to do with you. I need something original, something... beautiful," he began to gesture with his hands as he spoke. "Something *artistically unique* to separate your death from the others. Do you know what I mean?"

"You're crazy. Why don't you just shoot me and get if over with? You've already broken my collarbone, you bastard."

45

"Shoot you? SHOOT YOU? How cliché can you get? Twelve-year-old kids shoot people. I'm an artist," Francis pronounced. "Please, give credit to those deserving."

"You're insane."

He had lost track of the minutes, but was positive he had less than thirty. Maybe even less than twenty. He had to hurry, but still, nothing unique, no superior thought came to mind; he could think of no Death more exquisite than the last one, and nothing but nothing at all came to him. His inner sight, his third eye, his artistic Vision strained to see.

Myopic. Nothing. Closed.

He would never top Cory's birth, Cory's mother's death. He knew it. Should he abandon the Art entirely, go out on a high note, bow down at the peak of his career?

Retire?

No. He could not imagine it. He was cold as the concrete floor of his cellar, filled with moldy memories of better Deaths. He was not going to top the last one, and so, he was saddened. He thought about just shooting the bitch and getting it over with. It would save time, true, but was his dilemma strong enough justification? Did this give him license to whore out his morals?

No.

He felt the war in his core as he considered the option. Out of practice, but still... his dignity. The conflict assured him. Laymen would feel no conflict.

Decision:

He turned on the video camera.

His medium, the woman shackled and handcuffed to the bed, sensed something was about to happen, screamed.

He stood in front of the camera, looked straight into the lens. "*Incentive Number Forty-Three, In Black, Blue, and Red* by yours truly, Francis Dwight Lundgren. I shall begin now. Observe."

Francis calmly walked over to the woman, who redoubled her begs for mercy as he approached.

He felt a familiar sensation: every blood vessel in his body doubled in size, time ceased to exist, his senses melded into one, a greater sense.

Yes, the flow, the god-sense of creation.

Self-doubt disintegrated.

His fingers stretched, folded to a three-quarter fist: palm straight, first knuckles curled. Francis leaned down, and gently kissed the Number Forty-Three's forehead. For the moment, her screams stopped.

"Thank you," he whispered.

He raised back his arm, paused, looked into her eyes, smiled.

She screamed as his fist came down, cut off as his second knuckles crashed into her windpipe. Her trachea splintered, a hollow crunch/crack. Francis held her chin and shoulder, and twisted them in opposite directions, the shoulder down and to the right, chin up and to the left.

Snap.

She was dead.

Failure nagged his guts. It was not a good Death. Trite, incomplete, lacking his personal touch... He went upstairs to get the necessary instrument.

He leaned into the light. Three realizations came over him: first, he would hear the scalpel as it cut; secondly, if his eyesight were to fail, he would require contact lenses; thirdly, he would have to lie to Cory about the cause of his disfigurement.

Francis brought the scalpel around the back of his ear, his teeth clenched so hard he heard them crack, or was it tough cartilage being severed? Intriguing.

The blood flow was surprisingly modest, not what he expected, but significant enough to challenge his dexterity. It took longer to sever his ear than it did to kill the woman.

The telephone rang.

"Sorry, my fuel pump took a shit. Could you bring Cory home for me?"

"We were going to grab some pizza. Need him home right away?"

Francis smiled, "No. Not directly. I'm working now anyway."

"New novel?"

He flipped his ear up into the air, caught it. "Short story."

"Aah. Well, I'll drop him off afterwards, then."

"Perfect."

Holding gauze against his head, he went downstairs, walked to the corpse, dripped trails of blood. Francis propped his ear in the fleshy valley of her breasts. Back to the camera, zoomed in, five seconds focused on a visual cessation of sound—a glistening raw ear, silent heart—so symbolic. It was so beautiful, Francis wept.

He waited for his son to arrive. Cory would help bandage his ear; a good scout was always prepared.

BLEED WITH ME

Respect to Ulcer, and the Ft. Myers crew

"Come on, Mark. It ain't the end of the world, you know?"

He looked at me, eyes ablaze with emotion I had never experienced. It was pain, true, but more. Much more—hatred, self-pity, injustice, self-loathing, and rage so powerful it bordered on passion. My friend was crazy, driven so by his ghosts. He had been for months. Every time he started to recover, he would slide back down again. It did not take much to set him off: a word taken the wrong way or an allusion to a situation similar to his own would undo him all over again. The guy was a wreck.

I felt bad for him, but was powerless to help. I had not gone through his trials. My life had not blown up in my face, left me shattered. My sense of self had not been pulverized. I could just be his friend, be there for him, sift through the fragments, and pick up pieces not lost. Sometimes, though, he made it damned difficult for me to help.

"Listen to me," I said. "One day? This will all be behind you, and you'll be happy again. I swear, you will." I felt as hollow saying it as a campaigning politician promising no new taxes and a thousand points of light.

(*"Read my lips…"*)

Mark shoved back the stool, set his beer on the counter, and said, "You know? I've had about enough of your Pollyanna bullshit, Ron." He nodded over to Valerie, gestured toward his beer mug.

Val caught his nod, gave him the "Give me a minute" finger, finished washing some glasses. Mark looked back at me, eyes alight with madness and pain. "You want to know something?"

He wiped his mouth with the back of his hand. "Everything sucks."

"Oh, dude, don't even—"

"No, fuck you. Listen. Everything sucks, *all the time.* Just that sometimes you're too frigging stupid to realize it. That's how it *is*, man. That's how it's cut."

"Mark," I shook my head. "It's not always like that. Not *always.*"

"Whatever," he muttered, scanned the other side of the bar for Valerie and our beers.

"Mark, man, I know everything pretty much sucks right now, but dude, whether you like it or not? You're going to eventually move on."

"Not unless I die tomorrow."

He did not even turn to look at me when he said it.

From anyone else, I would have looked deeper into that statement. Mark would never. No way. I knew he *considered* it constantly. What happened over the next few weeks was his form of self-annihilation: he systematically killed the man he used to be. Through symbolic death, Mark sought rebirth. He found it.

***

The tattoo was the first I saw of it. Mark pulled up his jeans, took off his sneaker and sock to expose it all. The tattoo had a rose that stemmed from his Achilles' tendon, up the back of his calf. The bloom was in a woman's mouth. She bit down with a smirk both sexy and sadistic. Thorns pierced her lips, petals stuck out from between her teeth. Blood dripped, marred her chin.

I did not need to question the symbolism.

Valerie leaned over the counter to check out the new tat. "You're crazy, Mark," she shook her head. "You know that, right?"

"Yeah," he laughed. "Ain't it cool? Now how's about a beer?"

"You too Ronnie?"

"Sure," I said. "Why not?"

I was closer to the tattoo—I could see more of the detail: the grain of the stem's bark, the veins in the leaves, the cruelty of the thorns. I could see the familiar creases of the tattoo's lips (lips that once promised me pleasures—a secret I kept from him still). It was *her*, from the nose down. I remember being silently glad Mark did not use her whole face. I might have worried more, then.

He gauged me for a reaction. I became aware of him, inspected the art further, but saw nothing more. I had plenty of time to see it in its entirety. He was obviously waiting for a response, so I said the first thing that came to mind: "Jesus, that must've hurt like a bitch."

Stupid, I know. Stupid and obvious. Someone rattling needles on your tendons cannot feel good.

Mark grinned. "It didn't hurt enough."

Something in that smile disturbed me. I turned away, looked to the bar for Valerie and our beers.

"It was a certain type of unpleasantness," he continued. "I could have taken more."

"I don't get it. Why would you *want* it to hurt?"

"It's like life, man. It's supposed to."

Unwilling to argue, I shrugged.

"And, unlike *some* things I could mention—that bitch, for example—a tattoo is forever."

Cynical bastard. I wanted to smack the shit out of him

"This," he motioned to his leg, "is, though. *This* I keep with me. To remind me of the things that *do* last. Like pain. Like hate. Spite. Revenge." He pulled his pant leg back down, put on his sock and sneaker.

"So, you got a permanent image of her mouth for spite and revenge? Due, you're fucked up."

"No! Goddamnit! You're not fucking listening to me."

I did not mean to, but I jerked back in my stool. If I were someone else, I think he would have taken a swing at me. He still might have if Valerie had not arrived with our beers.

"Calm down, you two," she said. "You're giving the old men coronaries." She gestured toward the other side of the bar, where two of the regulars hunched over their ashtrays and muttered to themselves about us both.

"Ain't my fault Ron's thickheaded," Mark said.

"Talk about the pot and the kettle…"

"Oh, Jesus H. Christ in a chicken basket," Val said. She grabbed a bottle of Dewars' White Label from under the bar, and three shot glasses. "Now," she said as she poured. "Friends? All of us?"

Mark looked sheepish, and slowly raised the glass. "Yeah. Sorry dude."

"It's cool."

"Great," Val said. We clinked glasses and fired the shots down.

"Thanks," I told her after I recovered my breath. 86.8 proof has a nasty habit of burning a bit when taken raw.

"Don't sweat it," Val said, and gave my hand a squeeze.

"Why don't you two just bang and get it over with?" Mark asked.

I'm not sure who told him to fuck off first—Val or me. He was always trying to get us together, more so since his relationship went sour. I wondered if Mark believed he could have a relationship by proxy if he was to ensure Valerie and I hooked up. Val thought he wanted to live vicariously through us. I didn't like the sound of that because that would mean that Mark secretly—or not so secretly—wanted to sleep with her. That thought brought on the jealousy bug.

Okay, fine, I wanted her. Happy? But…we were friends. I didn't want to fuck up our friendship. Besides, cool as Val was, the girl had a couple of issues. She told me about them, sort of. Not nice things to think about. Sometimes, when I looked at her, I could see the emotional scars in her eyes. They were like ghosts, dim little reminders of past trauma.

She often said the same thing about me. Whatever.

"Oh, come off of it, you two. You know you want to—"

"Dude, drop it."

"Oh, come on."

"Mark," Val's voice was a warning. She game him a look, then collected the glasses and went to tend to her other customers. It was a few beers later before she returned for more than an alcohol delivery.

By then, both Mark and I had a good buzz on. We talked about the Yankees, and how nice it was of them to let Arizona have the pennant that time. We talked about the Bank of New York being robbed last week. We talked about a lot of non-subjects. Time-passers.

Once Valerie came back, we started having an actual conversation. Mark was precariously close to drunkenness at that point, so, at first, we both blew him off when he asked us: "You guys want to know how to deal with pain?"

I looked at Valerie, she at me.

(*Here he goes again.*)

We both said, "sure," or something similar. There was no stopping Mark now. If we declined the offer of his wisdom, he would have went on regardless. Mark did not notice, but both of us sighed, and leaned a little heavier on the bar. He also did not notice Valerie's arm and mine were touching (which is how we both knew he was smashed).

"The way you deal with pain, I mean, *real* pain, emotional pain?" He paused sipped his beer. "Is to make it physical. I swear, when they were doing those straight lines on my Achilles' Tendon there, I bit my tongue till I bled, I wanted to scream so bad. But now? I'm *glad* I suffered through it. I made it through, and now, I'm better for it. I've got something very cool. Very special. I mean, it's all *from* the pain."

"Kind of like catharsis," Valerie said.

I said nothing because it made sense, and I did not want to admit that Mark's sense and mine were in alignment because I knew Mark was as fucked up as a football bat about his situation and if he made sense to me, then, perhaps I was still fucked up. I liked to believe I was, as they say, *over it*. Yet, when I heard his theory, I had to admit—if only to myself— that it was, indeed, sensible. Damn him.

"Exactly!" Mark sipped his beer, set it down on the bar, then gestured with both hands as he clarified. "You take the deep pain—the shit in your soul, and put it in the flesh, where it heals faster. Once it heals, you have something tangible to remember *why* you suffered. You've got something that comes from *yourself*. You take *control* of the situation that way. Not someone else. *You*. You take control, to begin to heal. It becomes manageable."

"So, what you're saying is, whenever someone hurts you, get a tattoo?" I asked.

"Well…no," His brow darkened but his eyes and smile gleamed bright with something sinister. "It doesn't *have* to be a tattoo."

He slowly unbuttoned his shirt. Pulled it open.

Chrome flashed at us—reflecting the smoky bar lights. Metal studs with pointed ends shot through each one of his nipples. From his armpits to his waist, all the way down the ladder of his ribs, were a series of metal hoops, gradually growing larger as they descended.

Valerie gasped. I could only stare. It was everything I could do to keep my mouth from falling open.

"Jesus H. Christ in a chicken basket."

The piercings were out of character, but nothing I had not seen before. I just never expected to see them on *him*.

They did not bother me as much as the scars.

Shiny, grainy tissue crisscrossed his stomach: long, deliberate trenches carved into his skin. Above them were pinwheels, as if he poked something through his flesh and twisted until it ripped away. Mark's pectorals looked clawed, gouges torn outward from center. As if talons had dug into him. As if he tried to tear out his own heart.

"This," he said coldly as he held his shirt wide, "is what it looks like on the inside."

Empathetic hate surged within me. I closed my eyes. I turned to my beer, and swallowed deep so I would not speak. The beer had no taste. It could not wash away the bitterness on my tongue.

I thought about what he went through. Would I be that strong? Would I have survived? I could not positively answer yes. I did not know.

My thoughts grew heavier and my head dropped into my

left palm as I leaned against the bar for support. I stared at the bottom of my beer mug, slowly shook my head.

It was wrong, all so very wrong. Mark made sense. The tattoo and the piercings and the scars—the transference of pain—made sense to me. So help me, it made *perfect* sense. It was so simple.

"Ronnie?" Valerie's concerned voice, her small hand gentle on the back of my head. "You all right?"

I lied: "Fine."

I saw ghosts of pain in her. They identified with Mark's statements. With his shiny scars. She must have seen it in me, too.

Everyone has a haunting regret that causes sleepless nights decades after the fact, causes moments of remorse when we permit remembrance. Everyone has a ghost. Mine were not as bad as some, worse than others. It was only pain. *My* pain. My albatrosses to carry. At times, their weight hung my head.

I did not go to the funeral, but have visited his grave in Gethsemane Cemetery. Last time I was there, I could not bring myself to even mutter an apology to his stone. I merely stood, stared, read the dates that were far too close together. Where the flowers were supposed to go, I placed a kickball and hoped that was enough. Hoped the dead forgave easier than the living. At lest, easier than we forgave our own transgressions.

Hers was worse. I knew part of it—more than I ever wanted to, because I did not like picturing such things happening to a young girl—any girls—anyone—much less someone with whom I was friends: someone I cared about. It had to do with her mother's boyfriend, a bottle of Jack Daniel's, four short bungee cords, and a four-poster bed. Any questions?

"Val, I need another drink," I said.

"You're not even done with that one."

"I need something stronger."

She went to the shelves.

"Dude?" I began. I was deeper than intrigued. I wanted

55

to learn. *How…why…*Questions I didn't know how to ask. I understood only the answers: only half of the equation. Unacceptable. I needed more.

"Fuck," he answered—and waved any discussion away. "I'm done. I ain't talking about it no more. Not tonight. Val—give me one of those, would'ya?"

I have no idea what Valerie poured into that glass. I drained it immediately.

"So much for sipping whiskey," she muttered.

Mark chuckled.

I laughed as well, but the heat in my throat strangled the sound. "I'll sip the whole damned bottle right about now."

It sounded like a good idea.

***

Valerie stayed in my apartment that night. She was still there in the morning. I smelled her on my pillow when I woke up.

No. Not woke up. "Waking up" is what one did after sleep. I did not *sleep*. I *passed out*. Therefore, the correct wording would be "when I *came to*."

Physically, I felt the standard consequences of drinking to excess: bright light sensitivity, nausea, a headache and trembling that measured in the upper echelons of the Richter scale. The dirty sock fairy visited while I was unconscious, left each of my teeth encased in a small, well-worn woolen sock. Or so it felt. The back of my head had a monstrous lump. My hair lay matted against my head in a line of caked blood, but I did not remember hitting it on anything. A few bits and pieces, but little more. It was all very foggy. I decided I was better off kept in the dark. I did not want to know.

If Billy Joel was to give me one hint, honey I sure did put on a show. Yes, yes, I had to be a Big Shot, didn't I?

Valerie tried to be quiet as she rustled in the kitchen. I heard the coffee pot hiss and burp.

Coffee, I thought. *Thank God.*

I knew I loved that girl for a reason. I stumbled into the kitchen.

"How do you feel?" she swung a mug into my hand and poured.

"Like stir fried dog shit," I said. I meant it. The coffee was good: caffeine to offset the alcohol. What goes down must come up, and I had a long lonely climb to complete coherence. I needed all the help I could get. I rubbed my head. From inside my skull, Billy Joel still sang, a smartass *Ha-Ha! I'm-Not-Hungover* smirk in his voice: "*Go on and cry in your coffee; don't come bitching to me...*"

Fuck you, Piano Man—go ahead with your own life and leave me alone.

"You look it," Val turned her back toward me, vigorously washed her hands in the sink.

"Thanks."

Valerie asked me to hand her a dish towel.

"They're all dirty," I said. "All's I got's paper." I reached for the roll.

"Uh...all right. I guess."

"You guess? You want to dry your hands or not?"

"Ummm..."

I looked into the sink. Blood stained the white porcelain. Red on white screamed in my vision, such blatant contrast.

My system was already precarious, thanks to the hangover. Seeing the blood threw me completely out of synch. My lungs operated out of rhythm, refused to relinquish their grasp of the last breath. A glacier inched from the back of my neck to my spine, from my spine to my gut, as a burning lump of heat lodged in my throat. It tasted like beer foam and bile, and was difficult to swallow back down.

Blood dripped on the sink surface. Each droplet an entity, unique in shape and size. The only common factor was their content. They slid together and formed puddles, large enough to have ripples. Depth.

So entranced was I by the droplets of blood themselves, I did not think to look for a source, obvious as it was. Val's left hand. A deep cut between her thumb and forefinger—the web of her flesh gashed to the meat, if not the bone. Blood ran between her fingers, slipped under her rings, dripped off the curled knuckles.

"What did you do?" I asked.

"Nothing. I'm fine. I was just…" her explanation died on her lips.

I knew. I knew what she was doing. Mark's theory.

"What's wrong, Val?"

She said nothing as she took the towel from me and wrapped her hand. Her lips crunched in thought as she watched the stain spread.

I watched her. Held her. She was preparing not to answer, but rather to make a confession. Though my stomach felt toxic and my head pounded from the agony of being upright, I stood there, watched her think it through—how to word it for me. How much to omit.

I set the coffee cup down to hug her. Painful answers always come easier when spoken to the chest of someone you trust.

She did not speak. Not right away. She sobbed for a while, and I stood there, head pounding, guts churning on stale beer foam and whiskey, my mouth full of paste. Her tears and her blood soaked into my shirt.

"We should call Mark," she said after what seemed an eon. "See if he's all right."

I made to move for the phone. "I'll give him a—"

"But not yet," she squeezed me tight. "Please?"

Her voice. So small. Muffled. Needling.

I held her, felt her soft cheek against my chest. I looked down, saw the wetness on my shirt. Her tears. Her blood.

I held her, placed my head against hers. I held her, smelled stale cigarettes in her hair. I gently touched the puckered gash between her thumb and first finger, and wondered what pain she needed to purge. If it were me. If I was at fault. If I should even ask.

I held her tight. Held her until I felt a burning in my chest. Until I felt a scar form on my heart.

"You want to talk about it?"

"No."

"You sure?"

"Yeah, I'm sure, but…"

"But what?"

"Ronnie?"

"What?"

"Will you…" She abandoned speech, nuzzled against my chest again, hiding her eyes from me.

I breathed. Once Twice. She wasn't going to continue. I prompted: "Will I what, Val?" and held the third.

Her left hand found mine. Fingers intertwined. She looked at me with age-old hurt in her eyes, ghosts of bungee cords and rape, and saw the broken body of my childhood friend at the base of Hook Mountain.

Our ghosts recognized each other for what they were. They saw—thus, they knew: instant acceptance. Our pain did not like being lonesome. Our ghosts did not like being cold. Lonely.

Such distance, reaching across years to the woman that was already in my arms. Feeling her reach to me. Reaching from the deep well of memories we tried to forget, but in so trying, remembered far too often. Such distance traveled—from our childhoods to that moment.

By the time I exhaled, we had lived a lifetime together: we'd suffered. Agonized. Been betrayed by those we trusted, and abandoned by those we needed. Loved those that died and killed those we loved with hurtful words and good intentions. We'd both been wronged, and exacted revenge on ourselves—(*yes, we'll show them*)—we did so out of anger, out of rage, out of spite, out of pain: all the things that lasted.

We lived in that half-breath's lifespan. Lived together, and fell in love.

Hurt to hurt, scar to scar, ghost to ghost, we embraced.

She gurgled in her throat—a moan she tried to swallow down. Then, she spoke, answering the question I posed twenty seconds before. A lifetime ago.

"Bleed with me."

We kissed deeply.

Our lips did not break contact when the razor bit. When the pain flashed forked tongues of lightning across our eyes, when we stained the floor and table, we did not break. The exorcism weakened our legs, and we collapsed to the floor. The kitchen tile was cool, soothing against our flesh, raw from the gleaming razor's caress.

We remained locked, our lips slick with each other. We murmured promises into each other's mouth: of love, of truth, of eternity. Of shelter from pain, of warmth for our ghosts. Of acceptance and understanding (nothing that lasted).

We will never scab, for our lives are open wounds. We will never scar if we forever bleed.

GETHSEMANE (REPRISE)

The old man performed a song composed generations ago. He could not remember the words for his life. The elusive lyrics he substituted, hummed the melody: *da da de da da, dum, hmmm.* His audience did not complain. He sang to the dead. His throat was tired, his ass hurt from sitting on the small cooler he brought to his nightly ritual. Every evening, from an hour before to slightly after sunset, he performed.

The ground was saturated; too much grief shed in front of this tomb. Under the lush grass, footsteps squished—mud under the sod. Only he cried. No one else visited.

Pity-faced angels looked to the dusk-descending sky from atop the tomb, as if seeking higher authorization to transport the souls within. He hated those angels. He smiled every time a pigeon shit on one. The old man reached into his jacket, removed his pipe, tamped down a bowlful and lit it. He hummed all the while. He never broke meter, never went out of key as he slowly puffed aromatic smoke.

If he ever broke key, his family might still live.

He was a musician: was. He used to play First Baritone Horn with the State Philharmonic. He was away, playing a half-empty auditorium in Albany, when his wife and daughter were murdered in their sleep. Had he been home, maybe he could have done something. Maybe he would he with them now, one way or another.

The old man contemplated the *if onlys* and the *maybes* for nearly half a century. He had not touched his horn in forty-one years. Lucky for those damned angels they did not have trumpets. He would have snapped their sculpted concrete necks. He hummed as he smoked. In his cooler was a beer. He sipped, never disrupting the soft old lullaby.

Three young men approached from behind. They had

come to smoke a joint at their buddy Danny's grave, dead one year to the day. Accident. He fell off Hook Mountain. They watched him go: too fucked up to help. Danny's bones required a contact buzz on the anniversary. The old man heard their approach; he did not care.

Jammer pushed his Glock to the old man's head and said, "How about some cash, Grandpa?"

The old man continued to hum as he stood, reached for his wallet. He handed it over.

"Hey—how's about shutting the fuck up, okay?" Jammer flipped the old man's wallet over to Chuck, kept the nine at the old man's head.

The old man hummed: *da de daa, da de daa*, and shook his head. *No*.

"Are you mental, you old turd? I said to shut up!" Jammer's voice rose in disbelief, the old man told him—no, did not *even* tell him, but shook his head. *No*.

The old man continued to hum his song. Always the same soft lullaby in front of his dead family's tomb, under the angels he despised. He performed this number since before these kids, these punks, baggy pants and eyes glazed from pot, thieving hands and nine millimeter pistols, had been urges in their fathers' pants. He performed this song since their *fathers* were children.

Jammer looked to his buddies. "Do you believe this old bastard?"

Chuck looked up from the old man's wallet. "Bro, he doesn't even have enough for an eighth."

Ronnie helped himself to the old man's beer in the cooler. He offered one each to Jammer and Chuck.

Jammer opened it with his teeth, kept the pistol on the old man who continued to hum. "Am I losing what's left of my fucking mind? Because either I'm having flashbacks or this old fossil is *still* humming."

"Leave him, Jammer," Ronnie said. "We got his cash, his beer, let's get the Hell out of here."

Chuck agreed.

Jammer could not allow an old man to defy him. "Later

for that." He pushed his pistol's muzzle up under the old man's jaw. Pale, dry skin went white from pressure. "Shut. Up."

Hmm hmm hmmm hmm hmm de da, and a shake of head: *no*.

Jammer shoved. "Shut up, I said!"

The old man landed on his back, breath knocked out, *woosh*, as his lungs deflated. His piped bounced out of his hand, scattered sweet tobacco embers as it came to a rest, stem-down, in the mud.

The old man tried to hum with empty lungs, tried to continue the song.

The need for air overcame.

He hitched, strangled a note. The song died.

"Now? Now? Are you going to finally shut the fuck up now?" Jammer screamed and waved his hands: the weapon in his left, the stolen beer in his right. Amber foam flowed down the neck of the bottle, ran onto his hand. "You pain in my *ass!* Now look what you made me do, you damn old far." Jammer slurped at the spilt beer and foam.

The old man pushed himself up from the muddy wet ground, stains on his palms, elbows. He reached for his pipe before someone stepped on it. "Dumb punks. Couldn't you leave me alone?"

From within the tomb, there was a noise. Something heavy shifted.

Everyone froze.

Then, another sound. Stone grated against stone.

"What the fuck is that?" Jammer came close to the old man, body to his back, voice a terrified whisper.

The old man wept. Tears followed the deep creases in his face, but he did not answer.

Jammer held the gun to the back of the old man's head and grabbed him by the arm, backed up, hostage shield.

The old man did not resist.

"What's in there, Gramps?"

"It's a goddamned tomb. You tell me."

Jammer's grip tightened, the muzzle dug deep into the

base of the old man's head. Chuck and Ronnie drew their weapons, stood aside Jammer and his hostage. Chuck aimed at the tomb's door, shaky two-handed stance. Ronnie did not raise his gun, but watched, his finger coiled around the trigger like a python ready to strike. He alone still had his beer.

Pale smoky tendrils slipped through the cracks around the tomb's door.

"Holy shit," Jammer whispered.

"Dude?" Chuck looked toward Ronnie, took a step closer to him, placed one hand on his shoulder. Fear twisted his face, stained his armpits with sweat.

"Fuck," Ronnie said, not in answer. He raised his pistol.

The old man's tears streamed down his cheeks. He was smiling. "Donna." He tried to open his arms, embrace the ghostly wisps. Jammer's hand kept the gesture half-formed. "Stacy, baby." His tears were part pain, part love: stinging bitterness that cleansed the wound still wet after forty-one years.

The tendrils thickened, like ropes of smoke. They billowed out from the tomb without benefit of wind. The air was still, crystallized by fear and pain.

"Man, oh fuck, man, Jesus." Chuck looked over at Ronnie. "DO something, man! Make him make it stop!"

"What the fuck you want me to do?" Ronnie screamed back.

"Shoot him!"

"*You* shoot him! I ain't out to kill him, I just wanted to smoke a joint with Danny."

"Chuck—can it!" Jammer screamed. "Shit! Make this stop, Grandpa. Make this stop or I'll blow your fucking head off."

"My throat is tired," said the old man. "I prefer not to fight anymore." He turned and faced Jammer. "I miss them. Do you understand? I miss them so much…"

The ghostly ropes crept along the ground toward them.

Chuck screamed, backed up, his pistol forgotten as he tugged the hair over his temples. "Go away! Make them go away! Stop it! For fuck's sake stop this shit!"

Ronnie snatched Chuck's gun out of his hand. "Stupid fuck! You're going to shoot one of *us*, you keep this up!"

"Make it go away!" Chuck was close to tears.

"Let me go," the old man said to Jammer. "Please. I miss them." He pulled his arm out of Jammer's grasp. "Darling," the old man said as he stepped toward the tomb and the ghosts of his wife and daughter. "Baby…oh, I've missed you so much…"

Jammer aimed at the old man's back. Something flashed in the corner of his eye. He turned. Ronnie had his gun leveled at Jammer's head. "Not in the back, dude. We ain't no fucking Pearl River boys. You know better than that shit."

Jammer lowered the gun, spit on the ground. "Get back here you old fuck!"

The old man ignored him, spoke to the ghosts. "Sweetie…"

The misty creepers on the ground snaked up his legs, wrapped around him.

A woman's voice took up the melody he sang before,

Da da de da da, hmm, hmm…

Around his waist, torso and neck. The mist surrounded him, cocooned him like a spider's silk, up to his mouth and nose. They paused there, but never once did the song disrupt.

The old man inhaled. Down, deep into his lungs, he breathed in the ghosts of his wife and daughter, embrace most intimate beyond touch: souls to trapped soul. His heart burst as it touched them, forty-one years of beating without purpose ended.

From his chest outward, the old man's flesh disintegrated as the ghostly ropes intensified.

Back into the fold.

Together, they sang, slipped through the cracks around the door.

…HMM HMM MMM HMM HMMM DEE DAAA…

Three part harmony: father, mother, daughter.

"Yep, I'm gone. Later!" Chuck took off running. Jammer followed immediately, but Ronnie hung back a moment to listen to the song coming from inside the tomb. His sister, Tina, used to hum it to her kid when laying him down for a nap.

"Yo, Ron!" Jammer called to him.

Ronnie looked up. Jammer and Chuck were staring at him. Ronnie held his arms out, *what the fuck?"*

"Dude, come on! You got the papers!"

"Assholes," he said under his breath as he shoved his nine into his waistband, pulled his shirt down over the handle, and walked after them, shaking his head.

The sun went down on Gethsemane Cemetery; the song drifted through the still air of the graveyard. Atop the tomb, concrete angels listened, oblivious.

MO 3:16

11:53
...How do I say goodbye? Now ay...there's no way...I can't. I just...
...I...Mo, we...I was going to...
...Mo...
you'll never...We won't ever...Mo...
MO!

11:54
The nurse rested a comforting hand on my shoulder. Sympathy rimmed her eyes red. "She's in God's hands."

No cliché could have pissed me off more. "She *better* not be."

She said nothing in response, but made a face that disagreed with me. She stood respectfully silent. Her hand remained. I tried to shrug it off.

It was time for me to go, but I needed one last look. One long last look at the woman I loved.

Silently, I wept; tears dribbled inside, collected in my chest. I felt them settle there to burn: stagnant and acidic. It was over. Mo would never marry me. I wore her engagement ring on my pinky, could not stop playing with it, touching it. The sparkling diamond would have fit her finger perfectly. Mo never saw it, never knew it existed. She knew I loved her, but not *how* much.

How close she was to learning.

Two blocks away from her favorite restaurant, *Rick's-On-The-Hudson*:
Screech.
—Bang.
The other driver, the one who hit her, was Reverend

Sherman of the Brackard's Point United Methodist Church. He who would marry us. Would have, rather, had he not smashed into her. Would have, had Reverend Sherman's son *not* been killed in last month's horrible train wreck. Would have, had Reverend Sherman turned to his faith instead of the bottle. Would have, if he had not driven that day. If…

…*if*…

"If" began so many of my questions; damn near all of them. If I had chosen *The Bully Boy* in Congers instead of *Rick's-On-The-Hudson*, if I had just taken the trip up Congers Road to route 9W, a full what…ten minutes further?… could I have saved Mo's life? If Reverend Sherman's boss gave half a fuck about those devoted to Him and those who worked for Him, then maybe, *just maybe* could *He* have done something? If Mo did not drive insistently five miles an hour over the speed limit, if I convinced her into buying that Thunderbird instead of the Honda…if…

…*if*…

If only it were me instead of her.

Dark bruises spoiled Mo's pale freckled skin; black corruption surrounded her eyes jaw, nose, neck. Swelling distorted her beautiful face, repositioned her Celtic cheeks, drooped an eye and rearranged that delicate jaw line I used to trace with my fingertip while she slept. That always woke her up. She would try telling me to cut it out, but when Mo woke up, she was never coherent. We used to joke about it. We used to say she was fluent in Spanish the first five minutes she was awake.

Now, white tape held an ugly tube in her mute mouth. Another snaked around her face, up her nostrils. Some bastard had shaved half her head to access her scalp lacerations. Sutures bristled off her, small tufts of alien hair; her own soft, shiny brown hacked away, replaced with sporadic jagged lines of purple and green.

She would not wake up this time. No more three-quarters-of-the-way-asleep-Spanish for her. Or me. Ever.

I listened to the machine snap and suck and hiss as it breathed for her, watched the monitor, small dots of light on a dark screen, verify she still lived: the only way I could tell.

Mo's chest rose and fell.

The machines breathed.

11:55

The nurse tugged gently. *Come on kid, time's up*. The hospital and tradition both reserved Mo's final moments for her mom and pop.

I nodded to them as I exited her room. Her father would not look at me: normal. In six years, I could never remember seeing Pat Fullington's eyes. I had no idea what color they were. Her mother, crying, hugged me. "Jason, it's not your fault. We still love you."

"Than—"

Ants in my throat bit my response in half. I took a breath to say it again. Mo smelled like her mom. Same body wash.

"Thanks…a lot."

Mo's mother tried to smile. "I hope you'll—"

Pat placed an urging hand on his wife's arm. "Come on, Laura. There's not much time."

Mo's mother gave my shoulders a sympathetic squeeze, then followed her husband to say good-bye.

11:57

I walked to the stairwell, past the professional sympathy of on-looking nurses, a few scattered members of Mo's family whom I knew but could not remember or talk to now. I eased the stairwell door open, then ran down them, faster than the elevators could carry me. I tore past the surprised faces on the ground floor, exited through the Emergency Room, out to the parking lot.

Outside, I raised my face to the sky, screamed my heartbreak heavenward. My voice bounced off the concrete, stretched outward instead of upward.

I waited.

No answer. Stars twinkled in silence.

Three short beeps from my watch.

12:00

Midnight. A new day.

Seven floors up, they shut Mo off.

I looked to the night sky with tears on my cheeks. I had nothing to say, no words for the emptiness above.

Mo's engagement ring flamed with the cold white light of the parking lot, like a small star set in gold.

12:09

At every intersection I passed on my way home, I envisioned the accident: Reverend Sherman driving completely shit-faced, bypassing the stop-sign. Entering the intersection, crossing two of the three lanes, then—

BAM!

—his Grand Marquis slammed into Mo's driver's side door at forty-five miles an hour. Metal squealed, severed her legs as the little Honda's floor wrapped around them and pinched them off at the calves. I saw how Mo must have looked at Reverend Sherman, recognizing him as the driver of the car that hit her, realizing what happened an instant before her neck snapped.

Praise the Lord.

I spit out the window.

Amen.

12:32

I parked the car in the driveway, paused a moment, looked at the empty space where Mo's Honda should be. I looked at the dark windows of the house, but not for long. If I looked too long I might see a memory: her face in the window, her smile. If I saw, if I remembered, I would never enter.

I took a breath and forced myself from the car. I stepped up to the front porch, let myself in. I turned on every light I passed. Persistent shadows sulked in corners.

Drunken pastor. Man of God. Bullshit. No such thing. Sorry Pop, but you're wrong on this one.

I saw the answering machine's light:

Blink blink blink blink blink blink blink blink…
Blink blink blink blink blink blink blink blink
Eight messages. I did not press play. I did not care to hear sympathy from everyone, did not want to hear anyone tell me how sorry they were, how they wished…
Yeah, yeah, I wish too. Big fucking deal.

12:36

I tried to avoid looking at the photographs as I cried on the couch: Mo wearing goofy sunglasses and throwing a Frisbee; Mo on Hook Mountain; Mo at Nyack Beach; Mo and me at the Islanders game, matching jerseys, happy despite the Islanders' loss that night (no surprise there); Mo all done up on our anniversary last year, black dress, with homemade backdrop of our green top sheet hanging off the canopy of our bed…
She was so beautiful. I could not help but look. I tried not to. I tried. I tried not seeing her hair scrunchy on the table, tried not to notice her sweatshirt hanging on the deck chair's back.
I shut my eyes, leaned back, placed both hands over my closed lids. With my eyes closed, I saw myself getting the shotgun from upstairs, the barrel in my mouth, toe the trigger, my head inside-out. Yes. My solution…
No, impossible. I could never…
Life? Without Mo?
What for? Pointless. So pointless.
Death: *same thing.*

12:47

The telephone rang.
"Leave me alone," I muttered through the phone's shrill demand of "*Answer me!*"
The machine picked up.
"*Jason? It's me, mom. Are you there? …Pick up if you're there, Jason.*"
Great, I thought. *Just great. Figures she'd call now.* Though ma could not hear me, I talked back to her voice on

71

the machine: "Forget it, ma. I'm not picking up the phone."

"*I know this must be hard on you…*"

"You don't know shit, ma."

"*…but we* do *care about you…*"

"Shut up, ma."

"*…and you're in our prayers…*"

I snatched the phone off the hook. "Keep me *out* of your *prayers*, ma. I don't want to have anyfuckinthing to do with some supposed God that lets the peons who work for him drink and drive, okay?"

"I…Jason, please. Calm…"

"No, ma, I won't calm down." I was furious, almost screaming at my mother. I knew I was in the wrong, but I did not care. Nothing mattered to me anymore. "*Don't* pray for me. Or for Mo. I don't want you to."

Ma's voice was cold as she said, "I'm glad your father doesn't have to hear you talk like this."

I closed my eyes and shook my head. Pop was impossible. He would not stand for me badmouthing the Reverend Sherman. My father looked up to the Reverend, just like everyone else. "Pop doesn't need to…"

"Jason, if you think I'm going to tell him *not* to pray for you you're crazy. If you think for a moment that he *won't*, you're even crazier. God will see—"

"Fuck God."

"What? What did you just say?"

"Goodbye, mother."

"Jas—"

I hung up the phone, counted to three, then lifted it off the hook. Let her keep calling back. The line and me would both be busy: me suffering, the line open to…

…nothing.

12:51

I did not need prayer. I needed Mo. The only one to understand me and like me anyway. Love me anyway. The ring in my pocket…

I took it out. Through tears, the vision of the ring was

72

blurred, but brilliant: gold and cold stone, the diamond aflame as light reflected and refracted. How happy she would have been, how she would have smiled.

More tears: Mo's smile, never to be seen again. The smile in god's hands. The smile so brilliant and heartwarming Heaven had to take it from me.

Fate was cruel.

I did not *dis*believe. I believed. Believed enough to hate. Believed enough to feel guilt at the hate in my heart, but not enough to forgive, not enough to want to forgive. Believed enough to question my emotions' integrity—(*am I* wrong *to feel this way, considering*?)—but not enough to change them.

I believed in both right and wrong, but with Mo dead, I did not give a shit.

"What do I do?" I asked the empty room.

Like an angel's voice, I heard the advice Mo would have given:

"*Quit feeling sorry for yourself. Go for a drive, take a walk; do* something *to clear the garbage in your head out of there.*"

"Thanks, honey," I muttered. "I'll do just that."

I put Mo's ring on my pinky and left.

12:58

I drove with the window rolled down, my hand resting on the top of the door. Her diamond flashed all the colors of night: red and orange neon, brilliant white. Yellow sodium-vapor, deep purple. I drove aimless for a while, past the strip-joints on Seymour Street, through the construction down by the War memorial park and Gethsemane Cemetery, where the old movie theater used to be. When I saw the sign for Gethsemane, I slowed down. Mo would be buried there. I could not pass it. I could not see it. I could not accept that less than an hour and a half ago, she died. I turned up Central Avenue, past the new Pyramid Mall.

I saw the New York State Thruway on-ramp coming up on my right. I got on, headed north. Once past the regularly patrolled stretch between Brackard's Point and Nanuet, I dropped the hammer.

Problems have a way of disintegrating at a hundred miles an hour on an empty stretch of highway between towns. Not much matters then: only control of the car.

If a front tire blew at a hundred miles an hour, God help you.

Or not.

1:54

I sped across Rockland County, listened to the Thruway Song: tires thump-thump-thumped on sectional concrete, the engine steadily moaned. I stole wind from the still night; it fluttered through my open window. I turned off the Thruway in Suffern, Last Exit Before Toll—

(*...for whom the bell...*)

—I turned left off the exit ramp, then another, back onto the highway, heading south towards Brackard's Point.

The Thruway sang as I sped down it, *thump moan flutter*. I bypassed the first exit, which would have placed me at the mall again, then the second, which would have placed me near where Mo wrecked.

2:37

I exited the Thruway at the last Brackard's Point exit, right before The Tappan Zee Bridge, intent on turning around and heading back across the county for a third and fourth verse of The Thruway Song. I realized my mistake as soon as my headlights illuminated the line of hedges at the end of the exit ramp. I sat at the light, stared at the familiar structure.

The Brackard's Point United Methodist Church.

"Why me?" I asked as I waited for the light to change: *No Turn On Red*. I was about to run it when I saw movement in the headlight's beams. A shadow wove around the hedgerow to ascend the church's stone steps.

It's two-thirty in the morning. What in Hell are they doing *there?*

When I saw the bottle raise to the man's face, the glint of light reflected off the thick glass, I knew.

That son of a fuck. Reverend Sherman.

I did not look to see if the light had changed before I barreled into the church's parking lot. I aimed at a space, missed: both right wheels a foot over the line. I leapt out, left the door to hang open, ran toward the front of the church. The right signal blinked an orange glow on the asphalt.

Reverend Sherman leaned against the corner of door and wall. In his hand was a bottle. I saw the white label of the bottle first, then heard the Reverend speak from the shadows.

"I knew you'd come, Jason."

I paused at the Reverend's voice, shocked not only by the clarity of the words (he was not as drunk as I thought), but also at being identified.

The Reverend continued: "I expect you came to tell me how bad I am, how bad of a *person* I am, how I deserve death and damnation. You would be right, of course. Justified..." he paused to drink, "...in your hate. I hate too, you know."

I said nothing, looked at the Reverend, wondered what prevented me from ramming that bottle down the old bastard's throat. He was just an alkie with a funny collar. Just another drunk.

"Are you listening to me, Jason?"

"Not really. What the Hell are you talking to me for?"

"Isn't that why you stopped? To talk? Isn't that why you're here now? Or is it that you want to kill me? It must be one or the other," sip. "Because you're here, aren't you? You're here. There *must* be a reason for it. What is it? *Why* are you here?"

"Shut up, you drunk bastard."

"You want revenge, don't you? That's what you're after, isn't it?"

I looked away.

"Aah. I've hit a mark."

"Get bent." I walked down the stairs, away from the drunk son-of-a-bitch.

"Wait! Wait! I want revenge, too. That's what I'm trying

to tell you."

I stopped and fired my finger at him. "You!" I wanted to kill him, smash that fucking bottle of SoCo into his temple, stab him in the throat with the busted neck of it. "You want revenge? You are the one who killed Mo! *You* did it! *You* and that damned bottle of yours."

The Reverend tilted his head to one side, and asked: God had nothing to do with it?"

I stopped, mouth open to catch moths. *Was that* Reverend Sherman *saying that shit*? It surprised me, shocked me. The *last* person I expected to hear something like that from was the Reverend. "Say what?"

"Tell me you don't blame God for this."

I looked at the ground.

"I do," he drank, offered me a swig.

I refused.

He continued: "I blame Him for Jimmy's death as well as your Mo's. And I know how we can get revenge on Him. But I need your help. There is too many of them."

"What the Hell are you talking about?"

"It will take some effort. On both of our parts. I can't do it alone. Neither could you. *If* you were to want to try."

"Why don't you just tell me what you're getting at?"

He set the bottle down on the concrete, stepped away from the wall to stand on the top step. In the light, I could see his anger. His teeth and fists clenched, tight. Reverend Sherman was about to blow up. "I want revenge," he said. "On God. For what he took from me. My boy. My son."

I shook my head, kind of laughed at him. "You're nuts."

"I've started already."

"Started what?"

"Come with me, you've got to see for yourself." Sherman turned, grabbed his bottle, then opened the doors of the church.

Go with him? No, I did not think so. "Get bent." I started to walk away again

"Jason, quit being an ass." His voice carried with the door open, the empty church acted like a speaker box, all that reverb space behind him. "You have *no idea* what I'm going to show you."

"And I don't care."

"You will."

"Yeah? What is it?"

The bottle went up and the bottle came down. Booze slapped against glass. "God took my son. He took your Mo. I prayed I could take from him. I have faith. Just not in the same things anymore. My prayers were answered." The Reverend entered the church. He left the door open behind him.

I muttered something about his drunk stupidity, but followed.

The church was empty, save for the Reverend's footsteps ahead of me. They echoed through the cavernous expanse, but their origin—the Reverend—remained unseen, another shadow amongst shadows. Oppressive darkness watched and listened as I passed. I could feel its knowing presence around me, encasing me in dark arms that chilled me at their touch. As if it were a ghost—

(*Holy ghost…*)

—I shuddered, called, "wait!"

If he heard me, he did not acknowledge. His stride's meter continued unbroken.

I followed the sound of his shoes on the floor, jogged to catch up with him. Near the end of the hallway, he opened a door. I saw light briefly as it opened. His silhouette paused, looked in my direction.

My feet echoed in the hallway as I hurried to catch him. The dark enshrouded church creeped me out. When I saw that bit of light, I quit jogging. I ran.

The Reverend walked through the door, shut it behind him. Echoes amplified the hinge creaks. The light sealed inside.

I said something Pop would have smacked me for if he knew I said it in church.

I slowed down where I thought the door was. I found it by the hint of light glowing in the cracks. I opened the door.

The Reverend sat on the edge of a table, his bottle between him and a puddle of wetness. We were in the meeting room, where the Brackard's Point drunks held their AA meetings, where the old ladies would have their bake sales in the winter when it was too cold to have them out in the courtyard. He smiled a Southern Comfort-slacked smile at me as I stomped toward him.

"You mind telling me what—"

Drip.

The droplet caught me eye as it dropped through my field of vision. I thought the roof had begun to leak, but then realized it was not raining.

Drip.

Rain never fell red.

Drip.

I looked up.

Bound and gagged, wrapped in chains anchored to the far doorknob and through an eye in the ceiling was a naked figure. With wings.

The Reverend stood, then, and drank from his bottle. He passed it to me. I sipped without hesitation or thought, marveling at what I saw suspended from the ceiling. The chains ended in large meat hooks, skewered through the Angel's torso, hooked through its ribs. Blood trickled over steel and exposed bone. Gore splattered the white-feathered wings. "That's a…"

"Yes."

I drank again.

"Reverend, how did you?"

"I prayed."

I nodded, handed his bottle back to him.

The angel thrashed, its eyes met mine. They silently pleaded.

I thought of Mo, wondered if she had taken this angel's place.

The Reverend walked to the far corner of the room, where the chain was wrapped around the doorknob. Calmly, the Reverend unwrapped the links, and the angel began to descend.

Now he hung at a lopsided angle, the chains from which he hung on the second rib on his right side, the third on his left. Rivulets of blood coursed down his legs and back, channeling to drop through the crack of his buttocks. The Angel's body weight was ripping him apart.

"What are you *doing?*" I asked.

"Remove his gag, Jason."

"What?"

"Remove it."

"Why?"

The Reverend grinned at me. "Because I want to hear him scream."

"I'm not…."

"Fine," said the Reverend, and let the chain go. The Angel fell freely until the chain snagged on the doorknob, then abruptly halted with a jerk and a snap. His rib broke. The hook tore free, ripped away a large hunk of flesh as it broke loose. Through the hole in his torso, something pink and bloody sprang out and dropped in a messy trail.

I felt the swig of Southern Comfort start to come back up my throat. I gagged, doubled over as my guts clenched. Tears stung my eyes, but I could not stop looking. I was disgusted. I was amazed. I was sickened, repulsed, but fascinated. The Reverend stood amidst the scene, his face locked tight with fury. He seemed to glow with power.

The Angel's entire body weight was supported by the one chain, the one hook around his rib. He tried to flap his wings, lessen the fall, but it worked only to cause him greater agony as the chain began to twist. He spun; his flapping caused the chain links to jangle and clink as they slackened and snapped taut as they twisted till they bound, and then began spinning in the opposite direction. I heard muffled screams, watched the Angel thrash in pain. Blood dripped, marred its wings, slung off him from the centrifugal force; whatever was hanging out of the crater in his chest grew larger as it slipped out of him.

The Reverend walked up to the table, stood on it, and

grabbed the spinning bleeding Angel by the shoulder and hip to stop the dizzying spin. He slowly unwound the chain so the battered Angel would hang in front of him. Then he removed the gag.

I watched, dumbfounded.

"Don't *do* this," the Angel pleaded in a thick wet voice once the gag was off. "The consequences…"

The Reverend spit on him. "What makes you think we care of the consequences? What makes you think we care about *anything* anymore?"

"I can forgive you your sins," said the Angel.

"To forgive *is* divine," Reverend Sherman mocked. "How honorable. And big fucking deal." He grabbed the Angel's dangling, blood-streaked legs around the knees. He pulled. Something else tore in the Angel's body.

The Angel screamed.

It was a sweet scream, no crackling at full volume, no distortion from terror. It was pain made audible. Pure. Sent from heaven. The scream of an Angel: so beautiful. A pure soul, suffering.

I recognized that sound. It was how I screamed at midnight.

I could never scream like that again.

"Where's Jimmy?" the Reverend shouted.

"Who?"

"My son, my son! Where is my son?"

"He is among us," the Angel said.

"Call him."

"I can't."

I saw what the Reverend was up to now. I demanded to know where Mo was, if she was among them. She was, he said, but I do not know whether or not to believe him. I do not know if Angels can lie to try and save their own skins or if that is a mere human fault. I would like to believe the Angel. I would very much like to.

"What do you think?" the Reverend asked me. "Should we let him go?"

"Why?" I responded. "He's not going to make it anyway.

We should end his suffering. With mercy."

The Reverend smiled then slipped his hand into the Angel's torn ribcage, shoving aside the meaty masses that drooped out. His arm disappeared. He was trying, I think, to reach the Angel's heart.

The Angel screamed throughout, until the Reverend's searching expression changed to a sinister smile. Then the Angel wailed so loudly I thought my eardrums would rupture. It was a massive bellow of agony. No human could reproduce the sound. No human could suffer enough to mimic the anguished tone.

The Angel's scream lasted longer than he did. After the echoes died, all was silent.

The Reverend offered me what he tore from the Angel's body. "Eat," he said.

I took it. I do not know if it was the heart or not. It was warm and bloody.

Angel blood covered my hands in wet red gloves.

It tasted good.

"Next one is yours," the Reverend said.

I nodded.

"Let us pray."

Reverend Sherman took my bloody hand in his and lowered his head, shut his eyes.

I watched him a moment, then noticed the ring on my pinky. Mo's diamond burned brilliant in the light. More will come. Sooner or later, I will find Mo, and the Reverend will find his son. How many can there be?

I have faith.

Let us prey.

3:16

I shut my eyes.

BADGETREE

"Don't."

Jammer whirled around, Swiss army knife in hand. He was about to carve his initials into the tree next to him. He dropped the knife, and reached into his waistband for his gun.

"No need for the piece, kid." The man stepped slowly down the hill. "I ain't going to hurt you."

"Fuck off, man," Jammer said. "Besides, what makes you think I ain't going to hurt *you?*"

"Hey, you wouldn't be the first. Or the last. You want to come down here, smoke a joint, no problem. I ain't got a bitch with that—even though this is my property. I've known your friends and you have been coming here for years. I don't care."

Jammer's hand did not leave the nine.

"Cut the crap." The guy dismissed Jammer's pistol with a wave of his hand. "Have the cops *ever* shown up while you guys partied down here? Ever?"

There was no answer for Jammer to give: he was right. The cops never busted them here—even that time they had fifty people all hanging out, drinking beer, smoking pot, with a blazing fire going in the pit they had dug. This guy *knew* about that?

"Here, fine. If I smoke a bowl with you, would it make you easier?"

Jammer laughed. "You pop out of nowhere, want to smoke a bowl with me? With *me?* Hell, everyone in this town hates my guts, and you're here wanting to smoke a bowl with me. What the fuck is your deal, dude?"

The man pulled out a ceramic bowl caked with resin. He filled it, lit it and passed it to Jammer after taking a hit, who took his hand off his nine to hold the pot to his lips.

Good shit.

"So," Jammer said, "you're the guy who owns this place, huh?"

"Yeah. I'm that guy."

"Why ain't you ever called the cops on us, then?"

"Because I wasn't exactly a model youth, either. I don't care if you're hanging out here in my woods. But I just wanted to say, clean up the beer bottles—use my garbage cans at the end of the driveway—and please…PLEASE, don't carve up the trees."

"So, you're like some tree-hugging cast back hippie? Your wife doesn't shave her armpits, right?"

The guy took the bowl back, sucked another hit. He answered raspy-voiced through an increasing cloud of pot smoke: "I ain't married. I ain't a tree-hugger. Hell…" his lungs expelled the remainder. He coughed twice, and continued: "I used to own a tree company."

"So what's your deal with me carving my name in the tree, then?" Jammer tapped the bowl against his lighter before sending the last hit to his lungs.

"Just not my Badgetrees," he pointed at the two ugly, almost dead trees standing side by side. "Or the big Ash over there."

Jammer looked at the three trees the guy indicated as he sucked on the pipe. The Ash was huge: trunk stout enough to withstand hurricanes—surely it would handle a little Swiss Army knife. However, the "Badgetrees," as the guy called them, were nearly dead. It wouldn't matter if he carved his name with a toothpick or a chain saw; they did not look as if they'd survive the first spring storm. "Badgetrees, eh? Never saw one before."

"Doesn't surprise me."

"They look about dead anyway—why not just cut 'em down?"

The man laughed. "Oh, no…can't do that. You see, there's a reason I let them stand."

"You really like these two nasty things?"

"No. I hate them," the man said, and took back the bowl. "I can't fucking stand either one of them."

"So…what the fuck?"

"I'll tell you, but you've got to match me bowl for bowl as I tell the story, okay?"

"Yeah," Jammer said, "Why not?"

The man chuckled. "This might take a while."

Jammer shrugged. "I ain't got nothing to do but get baked."

"Fine," the man said. "Listen—"

***

All he wanted to do was size up a few trees, bid a job, and go home, but *Violation* toned her anguished wail; the woman's scream was rape.

Jake knew as soon as he heard it—he could envision what was being done to her. He leapt from the truck, grabbed a pole-saw from his pickup's bed, ran toward her screams. The closer he got, the more detail he heard—her attacker's deep male voices issuing brutal commands; closer still and he heard her whimpers. They were down the other side of the hill in front of him, in the wooded area where he was supposed to estimate the cost of clearing.

His flannel shirt worked out of his jeans as he ran across the unkempt yard; his shadow had a flopping tail. With his brutal-toothed saw at the end of its fiberglass pole, Jake looked like a peasant taking up arms in revolt against the tyrannical powers that be, prepared to fight against that which he despised.

Jake paused at the top of the hill, in the shadows of the very trees whose destruction he was to estimate. Adrenaline tightened his hands around the pole. He looked around—his quick eyes peered through the leafy shadows, his ears listening for her (whomever she was) to cry out again.

He heard only the gruff sounds of the men's exertion—tiny grunts as they abused her. He could not see them, however clear he heard the sounds; they must be close…

they *must* be. The trees concealed them, sheltered their crime from his vision.

Jake moved toward the sound, letting his ears lead him through the thick brush. Part of his mind filed the terrain away for reference—the part of him that estimated clearing the wood.

Movement in the undergrowth off to his right—near the base of one of the largest Ash trees he had ever seen. A blue Yankees hat nodded up and down in some sick rhythm, punctuated the grunts he heard.

***

"You mean here, right?" Jammer asked.

"Yeah. Right here. Now listen up, and pack the bowl, would you?"

Jammer did, hands on automatic pilot, face turned up to listen to the man's tale.

***

The pole-saw in both hands, Jake quietly crept forward through the underbrush. They were twenty-five feet away, but he could not see clearly; leaves and shadows blocked his vision. Stealthily, Jake moved forward, his eye on his step to ensure quiet progress. Slowly he advanced. His hands tightened on the pole-saw with every step. And with every step, his outrage increased.

(*Those sons of bitches*)

He got within five feet, saw the one wearing the baseball hat grinning and nodding as he watched his partner force himself into the girl. His pants were around his ankles, his hand stroking his dick as his fat friend grunted and shook on top of the struggling girl. Jake could not see what she looked like, only a glimpse of red hair tangled in branches and dirt under the fat guy's fist.

Jake lifted the pole-saw, rushed the watcher. He swung sideways like a bat, caught the man above his ear with the pole itself. Fiberglass cracked against skull. Vibrations shot up the handle, stung Jake's hands and wrists as the watcher's baseball hat flew into the branches of a small maple. The watcher toppled, his hands still wrapped around his quickly deflating erection. He rose slowly, his eyes askew; blood covered the side of his head. Dazed as he was, he tried to run, but his jeans kept tripping him. Unwilling to cease moving, he tried to pull them up as he tripped and fell away.

The man raping the girl stopped, said "What the fuck?" and tried to rise. Jake jabbed the end of the pole at the man's chest. The butt smashed into the man's solar plexus; his lungs emptied in a *woosh* and he fell backward. His mouth opened and closed on nothing as his lungs hitched for air.

Jake kicked him in the ribs. The fat man writhed in the dirt, tried to protect himself as he desperately struggled to breathe. He rolled over and clutched his chest. His jeans dangled around his knees. Jake saw the man's wallet ready to fall out of his pocket. He reached for it, opened it up.

Jake expected to find the usual inside—credit cards, money, driver's license.

He did not expect to find a badge.

Brackard's Point Police Department. Jake recognized the thing immediately. He saw the badge number, and the familiar logo on the side of every BPPD cop car: "*Pride in Our past, Faith In Our Future.*" He even saw the smaller writing in the center: "*Protect and Serve.*"

The guy—the cop rapist—finally sucked in air, coughed and spit and sucked in more air. When he could breathe again, his first action was to moan. "You're dead," the cop said hoarsely as he slowly pulled up his pants. "You fucked with the wrong two guys."

"You're a fucking cop," Jake said.

"No shit, Dick Tracy."

The cop started to rise.

"Don't you fucking move," Jake held the pole-saw's sharp jagged points next to the cop's tender throat. "Don't even."

"What the fuck are you going to do? Kill me? You can't

touch me, asshole. I'm a fucking cop. Who are you going to call? My buddies at the station?"

"I…" Jake shut his mouth. He *was* planning on calling the cops when he got a chance. Toss *that* idea out the proverbial window.

"Yeah," the cop said. "I thought so. Now, since you seem to realize that you're fucked, I'll let it slide that you attempted to kill my partner. And you're going to walk away. Forget that you ever saw anything here. As a matter of fact, you didn't even *show up* here. There's a Yankees game on right now—you were home, watching us beat on Boston."

Jake stood stupefied a moment, thought about becoming a lifelong Bosox fan before saying: "What about her?" He pointed to the girl, who sat in the dirt, swollen face and ruptured lips, her arms streaked with dirt. She bled and moaned softly as she tried to cover herself. Her skinned knees were pulled up to her chest, partially concealing small breasts. She stared at Jake, her face a distorted expression of fear, her eyes locked on the blade.

"What about who?" the cop asked. "I don't see anyone. Walk away, buddy. Walk away or I swear, your life will become a living Hell."

"I can't do that."

"How fucking noble," the cop said as he zipped his fly.

Thinking he was drawing a hidden weapon, Jake flinched.

The cop laughed. "See? You ain't got the nerves for this. You tried to be a hero, save the girl, ride off into the sunset, live happily ever after, right? Good ol' American dream. Can't fault you there. But you fucked up. Your nose is where it ain't supposed to be, *capiche?*" The cop smiled as he stepped forward.

Jake feigned with the pole-saw. The cop jumped back. "I told you not to fucking move."

"You stupid shit. You forgettin' who you're dealin' with?"

"You're a fucking piece of shit rapist, motherfucker. Don't move."

"What're you going to do? Chop me up into little bits

with the saw, there, tough guy?"

"I don't know yet."

Chok-chok.

The sound came from directly behind him. Jake smelled gun oil. Even if he had not smelled it, he could not mistake the sound of a shotgun jacking a round. The obscenely large muzzle shoved into his neck.

"I know," the voice behind him. "you're going to drop the fucking saw, dipshit. Right now."

"Protect and serve, right?" Jake said without turning around. He did not drop the saw. "How's your head feeling?"

"Nothing a few rounds at Callahan's won't take care of. Now drop the fucking saw."

The girl, thinking she had been forgotten, rose and scrambled around the trunk of the tree.

"Goddamnit! Get that little bitch!" the cop with the shotgun screamed. His partner started to run after her.

Jake swung around and chopped at the shotgun barrel. The impact nearly wrenched it out of the cop's hands. The gun went off and vaporized a patch of moss; a misty haze of loam hung in the area for a moment. The roar battered Jake's ears; he winced and swooned a moment. When he recovered his sense of balance and a fraction of his hearing, the shotgun was pointed at him.

The watcher pulled the trigger, and shot Jake in the stomach.

***

"Fuck. No shit?"

"No shit."

"You're Jake, right?"

"Yeah."

"Fuckin' A," Jammer said and passed the bowl back to him.

***

Jake felt the blast of pellets: a thousand points of pain. He screamed, wild-eyed, dropped the pole-saw and felt his stomach with his fingertips. The flesh he used to know was gone; his own body now alien: a ragged hole with his insides poking out.

The pain was a system of crippling agony that multiplied with every breath and increased with every movement. He fell to his knees. There, his knees soiled with dirt, his flannel shredded and bloody, Jake screamed until his lungs ran out of air. He refilled them only to howl again.

A bonfire of suffering burned in his belly; he smelled cordite and the raw, rank smell of his own guts. He felt the pellets work themselves deeper into him, tearing through tissue as he moved. He could feel them burning, still hot from the explosion that shot them into him. His hands came away sheathed in blood.

From his knees to his side, he lay in the cool damp earth, hoping to quench the burning in his stomach. From his side to his back, hands around his stomach, his mouth open, an endless scream pouring out of it. He pulled himself along the ground; cold greasy sweat stung his eyes. He leaned against a sapling, waited for the shot to finish him. The Yankees hat still hung from the tree. Jake stared at the blue on the green, wished the guy's head was still in it.

(*I am going to die here.*)

It did not come.

The cops had chased the girl through the woods, caught her and were dragging her back. She did not struggle much, except when she saw Jake bleeding into his lap. Then she fought against her captors to rush to him.

"Aww. Isn't that sweet. She's going to try and help *him*," the fat cop said.

"Why bother?" the cop with the shot gun said. "That fucking fucker is fucking fucked."

The other laughed at his friend's quip.

(*Fucking A. If I live through this, I swear, I'm going to*

bid this job so high…)

"Bastards," the girl said, though her swollen lips garbled the epithet. She gathered a few leaves, pressed them to his wound with light, thin fingers. As she did so, she murmured something Jake could not make out; by its cadence he assumed it was some type of prayer. Instantly, the intensity of the fire in his abdomen waned. He stopped screaming, looked into her face.

She was beautiful, her age impossible to determine— old soul eyes and girlish features; tiny, only five feet tall, and her hair, knotted with twigs stuck in it, was almost as long as her back. The expression on her face was the kind of look a parent might give a foolish but endearing child who did his best to try and help, but failed out of naiveté and ignorance. "Hold the leaves on there," she said, her voice soft but penetrating. "Do not let them go."

"Get away from him, darling," the cop with the shotgun said. "I'm about to do the poor bastard a favor. Finish him off. Unless you want to die now, too."

She looked into Jake's eyes and stroked his face. "Close your eyes," she said. She kissed his forehead with bloody lips.

Jake did as she asked. He shut his eyes, held the compress of leaves and moss on his wound. Cool comfort crept through him. Jake wondered if he were dying, if the comfort he felt was his rapidly approaching end. No, his heart beat too strong. Though the pain remained, it was dim, as if felt from a distance.

"Comfortable?"

Jake nodded in answer.

"Good," she said. "Now don't move. Just lie there, and don't let up on your hold. You've got to keep it on. Promise me. Whatever happens. It'll save your life."

"Okay," he said. "I promise."

She rose, faced the cops, and spoke in the voice of the forest: whispers of wind through treetops, rain hissing between branches. She spoke sounds so natural they seemed nearly blasphemous coming from a mouth so human.

In response, the leaves on the ground rustled. Their dry, paper-thin corpses, vibrated and twirled: tornadoes in miniature. Creepers rose from under them to sway in the air to the cadence of her litany like cobras from woven baskets.

"Holy fuck."

"Holy fuck."

Jake could not be sure who said it first: the cops or himself. The cops both seemed terrified by the lawless scene playing out before them; nature misbehaving.

But Jake thought that perhaps it *was* behaving, in accordance to a law more natural than man was ever intended to live under. He pushed himself off the ground, but there was immediate pain in his gut. Crippling, nauseating pain, and it was all he could do to clasp both hands on the moss and leaf compress and hold it there, through he noticed his bleeding had stopped.

The one cop tried to shoot, but the wooden stock of the shotgun had started growing; buds sprouted, branches erupted from the dead varnished wood. Sap flowed, and it took root in the hand that cradled it. He screamed, the shotgun now part of his arm, waving up in the air as his fingers disappeared and buds uncurled from his thumb. From his mouth a thin vine shot forth, stretching to the sky, greedily sucking up the sunlight. His voice choked and spasmed around the growing wood. His friend, the fat one, tried to run, but no, his feet were under the ground, his toes anchored nearly to the bedrock, and his ankles fused together; his movement stretched the thin bark, and he experienced the pain of a peeled birch, but voiced it as a man, a terrified, violated man, whose last sobs were of forgiveness, whose last words were curses, and whose last thoughts were of revenge: an egoist until the end.

Two new trees stood in the shade of taller ones. Their trunks were misshapen, gnarled, and their tiny leaves pale. The new trees would never survive. They were not fit. Over the course of years, they would slowly die, starved for water and light, eclipsed by those around them.

The girl looked at them with sadness.

"What the…?"

"Sleep," she said, touching Jake's face gently with her fingertips. "Sleep"

The dreams came quickly. In them, Jake thought he saw her melt into the living wood of the Ash.

***

"So then what?"

"Then? Nothing. That's it."

"Dude, you're full of shit. You're trying to tell me those two trees there are really people?"

"I told you what happened here, and that I'd prefer that you didn't cut those three trees, and why."

"You really expect me to believe that bullshit story? I ain't that stoned, man."

Jake sighed, lifted his shirt. His stomach was one massive scar of warped, rough skin.

Jammer looked at him strangely.

"Touch it," Jake said.

Jammer reached forward and touched the rough skin. Almost immediately, he pulled his hand away, clutched his finger and held it up to the sunlight.

"You believe me now?"

"Shut up, man." Jammer stared at the sliver of wood in his fingertip. "I got a Goddamn splinter."

The wind blew through the woods. The Ash creaked and the Badgetrees hissed their discontent.

LATEX:
LIKE A GLOVE

He came from behind as she walked through the Harborview Diner's parking lot and bludgeoned her with a tire-iron. The first hit leveled her. She rolled over; he swung at her face. Her nose crushed with the second hit. The third shattered her cheekbones, the fourth, her jaw: her face rearranged. Her blood clung to the tire-iron in sticky smears.

She had come for a cup of coffee and a doughnut. Inside, through the solid concrete wall, the kitchen staff cooked pizza burgers, French Fries with brown gravy. Drunks harassed the waitresses and shot toothpicks through the straws into the ceiling tiles. They left no tip.

The Harborview Diner's staff worked, sweated in the kitchen, mumbled about the assholes in section three, poured regular coffee into the decaf carafe. Outside, in the back of the building, separated from them only by two feet of concrete, the man wearing a *Caster the Friendly Ghost* mask beat her until his dick was hard, swollen…glistening with pre-cum. It looked *full*, ready to explode.

He rolled a condom down its length.

(*Oh God, he's going to…*)

She screamed for help (smashed face and choking blood muffled her desperation). None came. She begged for mercy. None came. She prayed he would not rape her. He did. She prayed for it to end soon. It did not.

He ripped through her as he thrust. His hot latex-sheathed hatred invaded her, his arms forced her to spread wider, close to tearing up the middle. The blood from her broken nose filled her mouth, and she spat it out to breathe.

"Yeah, oh fuck yeah. You like it, don't you?" Casper said, his innocent white plastic smile grinning with eyes behind that seared through her. Her need to live, to survive this and

93

endure was erotic to him, the bastard, the fucker, the rapist.

She could feel him coming inside her, the pulse of his cock like a rage-filled heartbeat. The latex swelled, caught his semen. At least she was spared feeling the flood spread within her.

He withdrew, zipped up his pants, left her lying there on the asphalt. He ran down toward Pensie Avenue.

She tried to rise, but could not without help. She crawled toward the dumpster used it to pull herself up. She almost went into the diner to beg for assistance, but decided against it—the people, the humiliation. Instead, she shuffled slowly to her car, locked herself inside, and wiped the blood out of her eyes so she could see.

The Hospital was twelve blocks down Harbor Street; home was four blocks away, down waters. She went home, driving slowly, because working the pedals and turning the wheel hurt. Timothy would be home. Timothy would taker her to the Hospital. All she had to do was arrive.

She parked on her front lawn, forgoing the driveway, minimizing walking distance. She opened her front door. Timothy was in the shower; she heard it running as she entered. The bathroom door was opened a crack.

She entered, called his name.

As she stumbled into the bathroom, something under his clothes cracked and crushed as she stepped on it. Something made of brittle plastic. She stepped toward the shower, passed the toilet: lid up, seat down.

A used condom floated in the bowl.

THE SHERIFF OF PENSIE AVENUE

She smelled bum piss. This was not Tracy's element. The air was tangible; it clung to her skin. Filth was everywhere. A wreck of a middle-aged woman muttered to a crack I the sidewalk.

"Cockgobbler, cock gobbler, gotta earn your keep."

Tracy kept one eye on the muttering woman as she walked past. A few steps past, she heard someone lose their guts in one of the back alleys. Another smell wafted onto the street: Old English 800 and partially digested pretzels with mustard, sopped in stomach juice and malt liquor. Puke, piss, refuse and pollution fought in her nose as trucks rattled by on uneven pavement and the sum began to close its tired, reddened eye on Brackard's Point. Far away in the concrete waste, a lone siren wailed. Streetlights flickered to life in the darkest corners of town.

Even filth had its evangelists—who preached that He was not only coming, but He was pissed. "Repent, sinner! And go unto Him with your Eternal Soul cleansed and pure! Receive Him into your heart and you shall be among the saved!" a man with a beard like steel-wool shouted, not to her, but to the street sign marking the intersection of Pensie Avenue and Waters Street.

The sign did not give a damn for its Eternal Soul.

The Muttering woman stood and confronted the steel-wool bearded bum. After a short argument, she slapped him across his filthy face, and he scurried down the street. She paused to console the street sign by petting its mast and speaking to it in soft, cheery tones. Then she ran down the street, following the steel-wool bearded bum, screaming, "Dark! Dark! Almost Dark!" She yelled down all the alleys, at the doorways, running with speed Tracy would not have suspected the decrepit figure could have possessed.

From the shadows they came, forgotten men and broken souls to follow her, all moving as best they could. Ten, twenty, more of them on every half-block. Tracy watched them assemble and move for a moment, then turned back up the grime-covered sidewalk, averting her eyes from those few she passed, pretending not to see their fetid misery. Their proximity made her feel dirty. Her reasons for being this close to them made her feel unclean.

She continued to search for her destination, walking past bums and panhandlers—the only other pedestrians—hoping that she would not have to be this close to them for a long time. (*He wouldn't have had it down here, in this hellhole. It has to be farther up.*) she thought, as she stepped over a piece of chewing gum flattened and blackened by feet not as careful as her own.

Few of the buildings saw a necessity to define themselves with clearly marked numbers. She passed the intersection of Pensie and Hudson without seeing a single marked structure, and then up another block past the intersection of Pier. Here, the buildings were mostly small warehouses, fenced in with coils of razor wire, rusted chains and stout locks sealed the gates. A third of the way down the block, she finally saw a warehouse with 837 painted in sickly yellow above the door, the door next to it painted to match with the number 839.

(*Figures. Not only am I going the wrong way, I'm on the wrong side of the street*).

Tracy crossed the road, and headed back the way she came. Every streetlight in working order cast dim ugly light on the sidewalks. Darkness was not kind to Pensie Avenue: every shadow was sinister, every heap of garbage looked like crouching predators ready to mug, maim, or rape, but the only thing that leapt out from doorways and from around corners were her own discomforting thoughts.

She walked down the cracked sidewalk—

(*Break your mother's back*)

—alone.

***

To her relief, her building had numbers. Carved into the rockwork above the door was the address: 528. In front of it were two working street-lamps. She took some pride at that; in this neighborhood, two sources of light was a sign of the elite.

The building itself was far from a status symbol. It was the runt of the block, four stories shorter and three decades older than any of the others. It squatted in the center of a lot that could have boasted a pretty yard, but had turned into a catch-all of dirty and loose litter. The ignored building was left out in the acidic air to die.

The poured concrete foundation was missing large chunks, where urban fauna—rats, roaches—settled in and claimed as their own to next and breed in the cracks and hollows. The lot was littered with crack vials, broken bottles, hypodermic needles, windblown chip bags, and cigarette butts—a garden of urban flora. A brown paper bag rolled across the side yard like a tumbleweed.

Tracy walked up to the building. No lights were on, though night fully claimed the sky only a few moments before. The building was soulless and grave-quiet. She was ashamed to look at it. What had she inherited?

This crumbling apartment building was her compensation for her father's fight with the creeping death that gnawed on his soft guts: prostate cancer. First came surgery and a degrading colostomy bag, then chemo, then more surgery, then more chemo. As the treatments killed him, so did the disease. He wasted away from within until he was merely loose skin over small bones. The disease finally had its way with him three weeks ago.

(*What did you leave me here, Daddy?*)
Some consolation prize.
(*Thanks, Cancer. You bastard.*)

Foolishly, she believed the garbage would remain outside the doors. When she entered the hallway, she felt ill. There were wine bottles (if Cold Duck could truthfully be called "wine") and brown paper bags, fast food containers with ants teeming on greasy corpses of fries. She looked at the bugs, and her heart dropped five inches in her chest. Bugs. How gross.

(*How could they live like this?*)

(*Where were the tenants, anyway?*)

She went to the first door and knocked. Nothing. Again, she knocked, pounded the door with her fist. The noise she made was the only one to be heard, save the delicate sound of ant carapaces bumping against each other as they tore off bits of French Fries to bring back to their next.

Tracy went to every door and pounded on it—no answer. No hinges creaked to see what the matter was. No feet shuffled but her own and the insects. A hill crawled up the tender skin of her thigh, brushed the razored hairs, leaving goose-bumps behind. "Get me the Hell out of here," she said, with no hesitation, she followed her advice. She ran out of the building and out into the street, and did not stop running until she saw a bus stop for the route heading back toward Snowdrop, back toward her house, her home, her nice, clean, spacious home where she could take a shower and get warm.

***

Tracy slipped the computer disk into her desktop PC and opened her father's files. He sorted by month and year—no subjects or other annotations. "This is going to take a while, I think," she muttered into a cup of coffee and clicked the mouse on the last file her dad left before he got too sick:—

```
RENT PAID:

1-A31March,  check# 15426378
1-B31March,  check# 15426379
1-C31March,  check# 15426380
1-D31March,  check# 15426381
1-E31March,  check# 15426382
```

"You've got to be shitting me."

```
1-F31March, check# 15426383
2-A31March, check# 15426384
2-B31March, check# 15426385
```

"What the Hell?" Tracy rested her hand on her chin. She opened an earlier file, and saw the check numbers all, again, sequential. They were obviously drawn from the same account, but that did not make any sense, either. Why would one person pay for every apartment, and why would they not use one check to cover them all? She ran her fingers to the bridge of her nose to pinch off an oncoming headache.

She called her father's bank, waded through fifteen minutes of blandly-voiced computer messages: "*Press one for credit card inquiries. Press two for savings information. Press three for checking information. Press four for loan information. Press five…*" before she got a live human being on the phone. The conversation went nowhere. Her father's account was closed, and they would not divulge any information, even to the next-of-kin, over the phone. This was policy, and they were not going to change it just for her. She felt stupid after she hung up to think for a moment that they would.

If she wanted answers, she would have to go to Pensie Avenue to find them. Somewhere in that building there had to be something that would shed some light on the subject. Maybe she would find someone to talk to, someone who could answer a few questions…she doubted it, because the place was empty.

At least she could get the place cleaned up, ready to re-rent. She hoped there *was* someone there, though. She did not want to have to find tenants for the forty-eight units.

***

By day, Pensie Avenue and all associated filth was not a nice place for an atmospheric stroll. The dirt stood out in crystal detail, the garbage—there was a lot, but not as much as it seemed by night—stank as the afternoon sun baked it into a cake of rancidity. The local vagrants went about their business: muttering to inanimate objects, preaching to the unsaved and uncaring, panhandling in practiced wheedling voices, picking scraps of food from overripe garbage cans like berries off a bush.

The building, she noticed, teemed with life. Radios blared from opened windows, people moved about; there was noise. She saw a little girl, perhaps four years old, plaing with a few dolls on the steps. Tracy could not tell which needed the bath more: the girl, the dolls, or the steps on which she played.

"Hi," Tracy said. "Do you live here?"

The girl nodded. She regarded Tracy with the disproportionately large eyes of a preschooler, but said nothing in response

"Is your mommy or daddy home?"

"Uh-huh."

"May I speak to them?"

"Uh-huh."

"Which apartment?"

"Six D."

Tracy thanked the girl and patted her head as she entered the building. The girl's hair felt like cold bacon grease on her palm. She wiped it off on her pant leg as she reached the first landing. She continued up the stairs and knocked on the door marked 6-D.

The woman who answered smoked a long cigarette; she reminded Tracy of a Chihuahua. Tracy glanced at the dress the woman was wearing. If it had ever been in fashion, its decade had long passed. The woman gave racy one quick head-to-toe look and said, "You ain't a cop or a Jehovah's Witness, so you've got about ten seconds. Talk quick."

Tracy was unprepared for a greeting like that. "I'm…I'm your new landlord."

"Landlord's a guy."

"That guy was my father."

"He dead?"

"Yes," she said, looking toward the ground, then back up to the woman's mongrel face. "He died recently."

"So now you own this place," the woman chuckled. "Okay, fine, Landlady, I'll give you another minute. What is it you want? Ain't trying to raise the rent, now, are you?"

Tracy was glad the woman offered no fake sympathy. She did not want to waste her graciously given minute of conversation with meaningless and false condolences. "No, I'm not, but I did want to speak to you about the rent. First, were you here last night?"

"Of course I was. Where else would I be?"

"I came right after dark. I saw no one, and couldn't get anyone to answer their door. I would have sworn this place was abandoned."

The woman chuckled. "Far from it. Just that no one will open the door at night for you—for anyone. Don't come here so late. We all sleep early."

"It wasn't late at all. I just wanted to—"

"Neighborhood ain't the best. Don't come here at night."

"Fine. I'll try to come during the day. But who is paying the rent?"

The woman's suspicious stare grew tighter, and she dragged her on her cigarette twice before saying: "We is. We all is paying."

"What do you mean 'we?' You and your husband?"

She held up her hand. "See any rings on these fingers? I ain't married. Girl's mine. Figured you saw her, huh?"

"Yes, I did. She's adorable."

"Always talking, that kid. What'd she say to you?"

"She just told me where I could find you, is all."

"So now you're here."

"Yes. I'm here."

"Wow," the woman said, sarcasm drenching the word like a sauce. "Nice speaking with you."

"Wait. I'm not done."

"You don't think?"

"No, I don't. I want to know who is paying the rent, and

I wanted to tell you, and everyone else, that if I come up here again and see the place looking like it does, I'll have you all evicted. This place is disgusting. I don't know how you permit your little girl down there to live in it."

"Fuck you, lady. Don't talk about my kid like you know what's going on. You don't know shit. Guess you'll find out who pays the rent sooner or later, now won't you?"

"I'd better not see it like this next time. I'll forward all cleaning charges to your rent after I take every deposit away."

"Playing hardball?"

"If I must."

"Ah. Yeah. I see. A new sheriff in town, eh?"

"Think of it that way if you like."

"I'll pass the word on," the woman said and slammed the door.

"White trash," Tracy muttered under her breath and went down the stairs. A few doors opened behind her; tenants stared at her back. When she turned, they shoved their heads back inside the doorways, like turtles sucking back into their shells, protection from predators.

She could wait. She could also evict.

***

At the end of the month, the rent checks came, all forty-eight of them. Attached was a note:—

Dear New Landlord,

Sorry to hear of your recent loss. Enclosed are all units' rent for 528 Pensie Avenue. I regret not being able to meet the new sheriff. You will receive a package like this the last day of every month

.

Yrs,
Aunt Connie.

"Aunt Connie?" Tracy said aloud, and checked the name signed to the checks. All were signed exactly that: Aunt Connie. Her name and address were imprinted in the top left corner: Aunt Connie, 528 Pensie Avenue, Brackard's Point, NY 10919. Whoever the Hell Aunt Connie was, she obviously had a chat with the lady in 6-D; the "sheriff" comment gave that away.

(*The Sheriff…*)

Tracy did not mind if that was how they thought of her. The image fit: bringing law, order, and cleanliness to the wilds of 528 Pensie Avenue.

"Okay, lady," Tracy said. "You'd better hope none of these bounce." She gathered them up and took them to the bank from which they were drawn. All forty-eight cashed without incident or delay.

***

Near the end of the next month, Tracy went to check on the building and see how it was holding up—if she would have to make good on the threats she conveyed to that bitch in 6-D.

On the way, she passed by Callahan's on Congers Road. As she walked by the large windows, she saw a pair of hands waving at her. She squinted through the glass. It was Gilly Tenebaum, sitting with some guy. Tracy looked at him twice, made sure they were actually sitting together. The way he was leaning toward Gilly left it doubtless. They were, indeed, together. Tracy was surprised, because Gilly, last Tracy heard, had sworn off men forever. The first time Gilly said that was in eleventh grade, when Joe DePuzzo—the asshole—dumped her for no good reason at all. Gilly took it hard, and rumor had it she had turned lesbian. Tracy knew she had not. Gilly had been hurt deeply, and it took her a long time to get over it. Even longer to be interested in a new relationship, which, like the first, ended in disaster. After that, Tracy heard Gilly swear off men entirely (again), but now she was sitting in Callahan's with a guy. Cute, too.

103

Tracy walked back up the sidewalk to the front doors of the pub.

"Tracy!" Gilly called out as she waved, "over here!"

Tracy walked over to the table, eyeing the guy with suspicion, trying to see something in his demeanor that betrayed a snake within his heart. She could see nothing as she approached, but that did not mean a damn thing. He had a dick: therefore, he was more than capable of breaking Gilly's unlucky heart. "Gilly! Good to see you!"

Gilly introduced the man sitting with her as Tim. Tracy noticed something familiar about him as he said hello. It was not his face; she knew she had never seen him before. It was his voice. She heard that voice before.

"What's your last name, Tim?"

"Hanover," he replied.

"You have a brother, don't you?"

"Yeah, Tommy. He's a few years younger than me."

"That's it, then. I kind of knew him. I thought you were sort of familiar. You and he have the same voice."

Tim smiled. "Yeah, my mom can't tell us apart on the phone."

"You want a drink, Tracy?" Gilly asked.

"Oh, just a glass of wine, maybe."

"I'll get it," Tim said, and rose to go to the bar, taking Gilly's empty glass along with him.

"Isn't he great?" Gilly asked.

"I don't know. I only said three words to him."

"We've been hanging out a couple of weeks. I really like him."

"Be careful, Gilly."

"I will. Don't worry." Gilly looked at the table. "I think this is the Right Thing."

"That's good. I hope so."

"Yeah, it is. I know it is. I can feel it."

(*That's what you said about Joe DePuzzo, too, remember?*)—"Sounds good."

"So what are you up to?"

"Well, I was going to check on the apartment building."

"The one your dad left you?"

"Yeah. The tenants are fucked up."

"Where is it?" Gilly asked. "I don't think you've ever told me."

Tracy said quietly. "Pensie Avenue," and paused, noticing Gilly's expression of surprise. She wondered if Gilly thought of her father as a slumlord. "Right by the intersection of Harbor."

"Eww," Gilly's nose crinkled in disgust. "I try not to go down there."

"Who does?"

"Down where?" Tim asked as he returned with a glass of wine for Tracy and a beer for Gilly.

Tracy told him about the building, and the tenants, but left out the weird parts—like the checks signed by Aunt Connie, and there seemingly being no tenants at all the first time she went there. As she talked, another glass of wine appeared in front of her, and it had been a while since she saw Gilly this happy, Tim seemed really nice, and the conversation was good so she stayed for a few more. She left Callahan's a little after dark with a little more than a buzz.

She found her building by the two blazing streetlamps out in front. The building was pitch black. Silent. Like last time she was here at night.

Tracy mounted the steps, slowly, because the wine made her legs feel a little too heavy and her head a little too light. She opened the door to the main hallway, and noticed another effect of wine: it makes your stomach a little too queasy when confronted with filth.

The place was gross again. The tenants seemingly went to dirtying the building up again right after the cleaning people came. A rat scurried away, squeaking into the darkened corridor. The ants that had been devouring French Fries last month were now marching single-file along the molding on the wall. New bottles littered the floor; garbage bags sat in the hallways by apartment doors. A long, thin, cigarette butt was squashed into the wood.

One like the bitch in 6-D smoked.

Tracy's feet, still heavy with wine, slammed on every step. They would hear her coming and boy, was she pissed. She pounded on 6-D's door. The sound carried through the walls, down the hall.

Nothing. No answer.

"Come on, you bitch!" Tracy screamed, her voice carrying in the empty buildoing with marvelous acoustic effect. "Open this Goddamned door!" She pounded again.

Still no answer. It was like last time. Dark, silent, and something eerily wrong about the lack of vitality. It was not as if all her tenants worked the seven-to-three shift. Tracy had not met any of the tenants but the bitch living behind the door on which she pounded, but considering the neighborhood, she somehow doubted she was renting to corporate America. Here, people did not fight to keep up with the Joneses: they fought to keep up with their jones.

Knowing it would yield nothing but noise, Tracy pounded again, and screamed for someone to answer her. Then she took out the large key ring, and tried several before one fit. She turned the key in the lock. The door swung open.

She entered, and shut it behind her.

No one greeted her; the belligerent woman and her red-haired kid were nowhere to be seen. The shades in the far window were drawn. All the lights were off. All Tracy heard was from outside—trucks rattling down 9w, cars driving through nearby streets, a motorcycle starting nearby. The smell inside the apartment was horrible: like a dumpster left unattended for three weeks in a New York summer. The reeking air was thick with mold and stale cigarettes. Tracy turned on the light, wondered how much it would cost her to get the place rentable again. Everyone in this building now was out of here, she decided. They were all going to go. She would get new tenants. It would be worth it. Better than having herself associated with this filth.

With the light on, she could see how bad the apartment was. The couch had seen better decades; its rusted skeletal springs poked through the rotting fabric, pale orange-yellow stuffing trailed behind the coils of metal. The walls were once white, but not since Tracy was born. Cigarette smoke and other grime stained them toward another color. Beige was inaccurate. Baby-shit brown was close. The carpet was low pile, tramped down and slick with what Tracy could only think of as funk.

"Hello?" She called, knowing she was wasting her breath. There was no one in the apartment but her. She felt as if she was intruding, almost like a burglar, but that was ridiculous. Who would want to pilfer anything out of this mess? If anything here *ever* had value, it had long ago been destroyed or spoiled. She passed a small kitchen on her way to the bedrooms, and shuddered at the thought of the stench that would surely spew out of the refrigerator.

She entered the first bedroom, turned on the light. The bed was smaller than hers by three sizes, its sheets grey by design, which thankfully concealed some of the stains. On the bed, a pile of loose garbage and litter lay covered by a think blanket, as if someone placed it there to cover a jailbreak. On the floor was more trash. She opened the closet. The dresses and outfits inside better suited for recycling. Well-worn shoes were on the floor.

She turned her attention to the pile of garbage on the bed. How the blanket covered it.

"I'm getting the fuck out of here," Tracy said, and immediately set to follow her own advice.

She ran for the door, reached for the knob and twisted. Her hand slung off it. Again, she tried the knob, and nothing. She tried to search for a lock, but it, too, was frozen. She pulled with both hands, tried kicking it down, tried using all her weight to get the knob to turn, but every attempt ended in failure. The fucker just would not budge.

Panic knocked its way to the front of her mind, and began to sober her up with a quickness. Sweat began a sticky trickle out of her forehead, between her breasts and under her armpits. "This is bullshit!" She screamed, and threw herself against the door. Tracy fought the stubborn knob and lock anyway she could think of, empowered by desperation. She screamed for help again, but of course no one answered.

What was another woman's scream in this neighborhood?

Escape was the only thing on her mind. She *had* to get out of here. Had to. What if they came back? What if she was discovered trapped in here because she could not open the door? It was just a fucking door, after all, not a marvel of modern science—hinges, handle, chunk of wood closing up a hole—but it was not allowing her to pass.

If the door would not allow her to pass—

(*I'm going to be caught in here*)

—the window.

She ran/leapt/climbed over the table encased in sticky grime and the rotting couch. She drew back the shades covering the smudged glass, suppressed the urge to smash it. As satisfying as the sound would be, there was no other need. She unlatched the window and looked…

…down…

…six stories.

She would never survive the jump.

(*Fire escape!*)

She ran to the bedroom again. She opened that window, stepped out on to the escape. With three quarters of her weight on her right foot, the rusted metal gave way with a dry squeak. Her foot went through, and she felt herself begin to fall. Blindly she grabbed at the window frame; her fingernails dug into the moist rotting wood. Then she heard the sound of the metal flakes hitting the ground below. Her ankle burned with pain—the diamond-shaped grating covered in flaky rot twisted around it, points of X's and V's trapping her foot like a crab in a cage.

She thought she would have to concentrate on holding on to the windowsill, but the pain did that for her. She squeezed so tightly as she stifled a scream, tried to extract her twisted, bleeding foot from the rusted metal encasing it. Every time she moved, she felt metal scrape deeper into her skin. Her sock was shredded. Blood pooled up between her toes at the end of her sneaker. If only she could use one of her hands, she could probably get herself out easily, but she needed to hang on. Or fall.

Sweat stung her eyes.

Slowly, Tracy tried to push her other foot through the grating and make the hole larger, but to push down with her other foot required her lifting up with the one already trapped, and the points dug deeper. So she hung, and tried to wiggle it out. Slowly, she recognized signs of progress: the pain from the digging metal was getting lower and lower on her ankle, and with her toes pointed straight downward—a maneuver that sent blinding sparks across her squeezed-shut eyes—she was finally able to snatch it free.

She inspected the wound, saw the dark chunks of metal in her torn flesh—

(*Tetanus...that shit is going to give me Tetanus.*)

—and tried to think of a way to clean it.

In this environment, she feared it was not possible.

With a whimper as she knocked her ankle against the sill, she pulled herself back inside. She limped on her good foot, held herself up by the dirty walls as she made her way to the living room. Her arrhythmic footsteps thumped through the silent building. She reached the couch, and, lifting her leg with both hands, propped it up on the table, taking care to only touch the tabletop with her sneaker, because whatever was coating the surface would surely infect her wound worse than the metal ever could.

"What now, Miss Sheriff?" She forced herself to keep thinking, to keep figuring a way out of the filthy apartment, with perhaps a stop-off at the Brackard's Point Hospital for a quick X-ray, a splint, a shot or two, and maybe a couple of Vicodin.

Hospital.

Ambulance.

Call an ambulance.

Clamping her mouth down to keep from shouting again, she lifted her leg down off the table. She could not gain enough leverage to push herself up from this position. Going down was easy: she had gravity to assist her, but now, getting across the room to the kitchen phone was a challenge.

She had to crawl.

Being this close to the floor, Tracy got an up-close-and-personal how-do-you-do introduction to the substance she previously thought of as funk. Funk, as an adjective, was inadequate, but, like the imprecise shade of the walls, close. She could not think of one word to describe the stuff. It had a certain consistency to it: like pizza grease at room temperature. It had distinct cohesion, and uncommon surface tension. To the fingertips, it was both sticky and slimy—like a mutant brother of the stuff covering the worst XXX movie theater's floor. There was a sucking sound as she lifted her hands from it, and it grabbed at the cloth of her pant leg, not wishing to let go. It smelled. As she crawled toward the kitchen, she smell was too thick for only her nose; it forced its way into her mouth, bringing a taste of rotten salad and rancid eggs, spoiled vinegar and oil dressing, sour milk with the overlying reek of stale cigarettes. She vomited when her hand landed in a particularly wet spot in the carpet, the wine from before stinging as it burned its way up her throat. The resulting smell created by her own puke and the already odorous floor was unique and devastating to mucus membranes. Her eyes wept from both pain and the burning stench.

This was not Tracy's element.

There was an old-style rotary phone on the counter. She grinned as she heaved herself up to call the three magical numbers to save her. She pressed the receiver to her ear.

Something squiggled.

She screamed, wiped her hand across where the phone had been, knocked something out of her hair. A large cockroach landed on the counter nearby and began to scuttle away.

"Fucking disgusting!"

She shook off the sensation of the squirming bug in her ear, but not too violently: she did not want to upset her ankle. She lifted the phone and looked closely this time. The cockroach had been inside the handset, the plastic hole for her ear was cracked, the speaker disintegrated. Antennae stuck out of the mouthpiece holes—more roaches were inside.

"Scumbags! Fucking bugs! Gross!"

Where were her tenants? She no longer thought of evicting. Her thoughts had turned more toward evisceration.

Back to the couch, the long, arduous process of crawling through the spunk of refuse. She was making herself sick again thinking of what it would have been, what combination of dirt and nastiness resulted in such a substance as that which covered the floor. She made it back to the couch and prided herself for not vomiting.

Using both hands again, Tracy propped her foot up on the table, and sighed, then coughed at the dust hovering in the air around her. She was defeated. Stuck.

(*Why me? Why did I have to inherit* this *place?*)

Self-pity displaced thoughts of escape. Nothing was working. No matter how creatively she tired to think, no matter how hard she tried to figure out new routes of egress, noting would work. She was stuck here until rescued. She hoped it would be soon, because her ankle hurt so badly. So, so badly. It hurt…

She let out another breath, a sign of resignation and defeat, and leaned back onto the couch. A spring poked her back, so she shifted to a spot where they had not quite worked their way through. With her shifting, a musty cloud of dust and mold spores and greasy germs reached from the cushions and covered her face with smell hands. After a few moments, the couch was again bearable. Barely.

Nothing else to do now but wait for help. Sooner or later, someone would come.

Tracy sat and waited. And waited. And waited some more.

She did not want to sleep in this disgusting rat-hole of an apartment in this shit-hole neighborhood. There were bugs in the phone—what if they crawled on her while she slept?—and there was funk on the floor. The couch, the very couch she sat on was *steeped* in grime, and unsavory scent clouded around the cushions like morning fog on the Hudson River. No, she was not going to sleep in here. She could not imagine anyone living in conditions like this.

Apparently, people did, day after day, month after month, and had Aunt Connie to pay their rent for them on time. Every month.

Noting made sense. After everything she went through, she wound up here, on this nasty-ass couch with her ankle torn to shreds, probably infected with Tetanus or some other nasty bacteria. She was tired, but did not want to sleep. The bugs might crawl on her, rats might nibble on her ears, shit in her hair. Things would move and breathe if she closed her eyes.

If?

She sat up, shocked that they were closed. "I'm NOT falling asleep in here," she stated firmly.

The garbage around her promptly ignored her heartfelt resolution.

Tracy again closed her eyes and drew in deep breaths through her nose to calm herself. In through the nose—

(*It stinks in here*)

—out through the mouth. She concentrated on a clearing her mind and telling herself it would be okay—

(*Nothing will ever be okay*)

—rather than thinking of the foulness that shared the space with her in it.

It was increasingly difficult to do. It took more than an hour, but less than a night, because at some point, she could not say when, she did not notice the pain in her ankle.

She slept until sunrise.

***

Tracy awoke to wet sucking sounds from the bedrooms. Startled from sleep, she sat up straight a moment to listen. Perhaps she was mistaken. She heard no other sounds like before, maybe they were residual noises from a dream she did not remember having.

Something, however, was moving in the bedrooms.

She tried to lean forward to see. God, how it hurt to move. As best she could, she craned her neck to see but the hallway blocked her vision. She rose, limped across the room, and peeked in the smaller bedroom's door. There were different sounds now: rustling, wet, rustling, like a damp rotting leaves and Styrofoam peanuts in paper bags. Tracy stepped closer, and smelled burnt hair, raw shit, bile and urine, sweat and thick saliva. She came to the doorway.

What she was seeing was not possible and far, far from natural. The garbage on the begun to take form. A small form, with little, dirty legs and greasy fred hair.

"Holy shit."

Slowly, the garbage on the bed solidified and the little girl she recognized took its place. Tracy's breath snagged on the lump in her throat, and her heart slammed out an tympanic rhythm in her chest.

The little girl stretched, and yawned. A sweet sound, in her young, high-pitched voice.

Tracy started to back away, and the girl heard her. Instinctively, she went to cover herself with the filthy sheet.

Their eyes met in the morning sunlight. The girl saw her, stared a moment, then shook her head sadly. Pure clear tears tracked down her stained cheeks, washing away some of the accumulated dirt. "Why did you come here? What did you have to come here for?"

"I…I wanted to—" Tracy collected her thoughts before continuing. "I wanted to talk to your mother again."

"Mama can't do nothing now."

"But I just wanted—"

"Just wanted what?" the woman's voice came from behind her. A lighter sparked around the corner. Tracy heard the grating of steel on magnesium, a cough, then footsteps approaching. The woman's voice said, "I told you. I told you not to come here after dark." She came around the corner smoking one of cigarettes, and regarded Tracy with both pity and irritation.

"But I—"

The woman waved her to shut up. "You stupid, silly, silly bitch."

Tracy made a noise of confusion and tried to turn away

from the noxious smoke. Pain grabbed her ankle and she limped back toward the living room. The woman and daughter followed. "I tried to get here earlier," she said as she hobbled toward the couch. "I had to talk to you. You weren't home when I came in. I thought the place was abandoned."

The woman laughed quickly, a spiteful outburst. "But we was here, wasn't we? We was here. You didn't see us is all. You never did. But you'll start soon enough."

Tracy shook her head. "No. You weren't here. There was no one home when I came in."

"Well, Sheriff, I ain't got time to argue with you right now. You's best be getting."

"Excuse me?"

The woman pointed to the door. "Bye, Sheriff."

"But my ankle's hurt. I need help!"

"You've got help, now get the fuck out of my apartment. Busy, busy day now."

"I can't walk. Please, can't you call me an ambulance, take me to the hospital? Do you have a car?"

"Are you serious? We ain't got no fucking car. And your ankle, well, it'll be better tomorrow. Sorry, but you've got to suffer it out for now."

"But—"

"But nothing! But…get the fuck out of here!"

Slowly, carefully, Tracy stood. Her ankle flashed silver reminders of pain and refused to accept its share of Tracy's weight. Her arms out to her sides to help keep her balance, Tracy hopped on one foot to the wall, used it for support, and went to the door.

The door turned easily.

"I don't understand…" Tracy said as she was leaving.

"You will," the woman said as she shut the door behind her.

Softly.

Tracy limped down the hallway, carefully negotiating the flights of stairs as she battled her immense confusion. Nothing made sense. She realized she was talking to herself when the hit the bottom. A misstep caused her to cry out, and her mumbling ceased—for the moment. She exited the building.

Outside there were few pedestrians, and those that were mostly locals—the Steel-Wool bearded man, the woman who continuously muttered to the sidewalk, a few others.

Down on the far side of the road, Tracy saw a man walking. He was in his mid-twenties, clean shaven and straight-backed tall. She limped toward him. "Excuse me," she said. "But could you please help me?"

"Get away," he replied. "I have no change."

"What?"

"You deaf? No change. Go away."

"I don't want change," Tracy said.

"Well, I ain't got not cigarettes, liquor, anything. My wallet's at home. Get a fucking job and quit bugging me, would you?"

"A job?" Tracy said, indignant. "I happen to own that building over there. I ain't a bum. I just need some help."

"Oh, yeah, sure you do. And I'm General Patton. Get bent."

He walked away.

She watched him continue down Pensie Avenue, waving the real bums, the real panhandlers away with a lash of his tongue or a flip of his hand. He smacked one.

Tracy watched, and felt pity for the poor son-of-a bitch that was slapped. Then she started to cry. A little, at first, but then in gushes. She felt overwhelmed, confused, in pain and dirty herself.

She found a payphone—one that worked—and tried calling Gilly on her cell, then at home. She did not remember Gilly's work number. Tracy then called 911 from the payphone, told them where she was and what the matter was, and that she was afraid her ankle was infected. The operator assured her help was on the way soon.

Tracy sat down and waited, wondered why everything was so screwed up. "Am I crazy?" she asked herself. "Why is everything around me fucked up? I ain't no bum, bag lady. My ankle is fucked up, I'm stuck on this Goddamned sidewalk, and no one gives a shit." If the asphalt of Pensie Avenue heard her, it did not answer.

She was getting hungry, but kept waiting for the ambulance. She would eat at the hospital.

An hour passed and the ambulance had not arrived. She called 911 again.

"You guys coming for me?"

"You're still waiting there?"

"Yes. The damn ambulance never showed up."

"Hold on, let me check."

"Okay."

Tracy heard switched flipping, keys being struck on a computer. The operator returned. "The ambulance reported in almost an hour ago. They said it was a prank call, that no one was there. Are you sure you gave me the correct address?"

"I'm sure. I'm at a pay phone at Pensie Avenue and Hudson."

"I'll let them know," the operator said.

Tracy hung up and waited some more. After another hour, she knew it was useless. She had to get something to eat. She was starving. She saw a small store, and got two bagels. The man at the counter kept staring at her as if she was going to steal something.

Morning turned into early afternoon, and Tracy's despair was only second to her confusion. She tried walking toward the hospital, but as the day wore on, she seemed to be getting nowhere. She was not sure where she was, only that she was somewhere a few blocks away from Pensie Avenue, which was back the other way. Some gnawing feeling kept pulling her thoughts back to the building. The woman in 6-D. The filth and the grime, the roaches that lived in telephone sets. Her answers were there amidst the carpet funk and the people who were trash as they slept.

The more the day wore on, she could think of nothing else. She kept looking back over her shoulder. The afternoon was wearing away fast, and she felt an instinct drawing her back. The more she tried to ignore it, the more insistent it became. She had to get back there. She had to get back to the building before dark.

(*Dark! Dark! Almost dark!*)

Tracy started limping back the other way.

Slowly, she progressed toward the building.

A man came up to her side and helped her along. "Got to get back before dark," he said.

"I know."

"First day?"

"Yeah."

"You'll pick it up. Not to worry, but the end of tomorrow, you'll know everyone's name, and understand everything."

"Oh, good," she muttered, thankful she would finally know *something*, even if she did not fully understand whatever it was she was supposed to know.

The girl was gathering things up off the porch, smiled at her approach. "You wanna talk to my mom again?"

"Yeah," Tracy said. "I think I'd better."

The little girl led the way up the steps. "She said you'd be back."

"No kidding," the man helping her along said. "You'd have to come back."

They opened the door and stepped inside. The hallways were alive with tenants, dirty, filthy smelly people that hurried to collect their things and get indoors. Footsteps echoed throughout ever hall, people called each other, urging each other to hurry.

"Dark! Dark! Almost dark!"

They scattered, waving to each other, wishing each other a good night, promises to see each other tomorrow. A few even waved at Tracy.

The crowds started to thin out as they reached the sixth floor. The man helping her brought her up to the door and said, "I've got to go on up now See you tomorrow, Sheriff."

"Thanks," Tracy said. "They call you Dormouse, don't they?"

"They do. See? You're learning already."

"I must've heard it somewhere."

"Who knows?" he smiled, yellowed teeth behind pale lips. "Maybe you did. But I've got to get a move on. Take care."

"Bye, and thanks again."

"Don't mention it," he said, and went up the stairway, to one of the floors above.

The little girl opened the door. Her mother was sitting on the couch, smoking a long white cigarette. "Don't just stand there like you're all stupid! Come on in," she said.

Tracy stepped inside. The little girl shut the door behind her, then carried her dolls and things to her bedroom and dumped them on the floor, and started getting ready for bed. Tracy was surprised. Tracy, at that girl's age, *never* wanted to go to bed, much less came in and started getting ready for it all on her own, without being told to by her mother. Tracy's mom had to threaten her with bodily harm before she would finally settle down and undress.

"So," the woman said. "What do you think?"

"What do I think about what?"

"About your day."

"It's been shitty so far."

"Figured as much. I suppose you got a thousand questions for me, don't you?"

"Yeah, actually, I do."

"Well, save 'em, because I ain't got to answer shit. Be a waste of my time anyway. Aunt Connie, she'll tell you. She'll tell you everything you need to know tonight."

"She's coming over? I finally get to meet her?"

The woman laughed. "Coming over? No. She's already here."

"Where?"

"You don't get it. Aunt Connie's in the basement."

"And she's coming up to talk to me?"

"If you've got to think of it like that, go ahead. But we've got to get ready for the dark right now."

(*Dark! Dark! Almost dark!*)

"I don't understand," Tracy said, her voice almost a whine.

"You will," the woman lit another off the glowing end of her previous cigarette. "You'll know everything you need to, like I said."

"When?"

"Aunt Connie will come and explain when you're asleep."

"Huh?"

"Unless you want to change right there, you'd better get on the couch here and lie down. Easier to come back together if you're lying down. Less gravity."

"Come back together?"

"Don't tell me you didn't see Francine."

"I…" (*The garbage on the beds. Oh m God…*) "I'm going to…?"

"Yes."

"What the Hell is happening?" Tracy tried to reach for the woman, then she quickly stepped out of the way.

"No use getting violent about it. Just lie down on the couch there. I've got to get into the bedroom."

"I don't want to—"

"Tough shit."

"You're going to make me?"

"No," the woman said. "I'm just telling you you'd be better off."

(*Dark! Dark! Almost dark!*)

"Just lie down," the woman placed the cigarette between her lips and used both hands to help Tracy to the couch and get into a laying position. "Trust me."

Tracy allowed the woman to get her down. It felt almost good, after hobbling around all day. She decided she would wait up for Aunt Connie, whomever she was, to talk to her.

"Now you just stay put, and I'll see you in the morning."

"I want to go home," Tracy said.

The woman looked as if she would reply, but said nothing. She walked into her bedroom. A trail of pale blue smoke dissipated behind her.

Tracy lay there a moment.

Almost…

119

...the sun set...
...dark—

***

The strangest sensation, her body quickly became rigid, loose, and light. Her joints felt weak, watery. There was no pain, but if there had been, Tracy thought it would be preferable because pain, at least, was something familiar. This, there was nothing like. She smelled burnt hair, and the fluids of her body, and heard them splash out of her in a wet gush. She looked down, and saw the flesh of her feet melting away, number ten envelopes beneath the skin. Her fingers were empty lipstick cases, her arms paper-towel rolls, her torso plastic bags. She never got to see what made up her face. Her eyes turned first.

***

She never felt herself reassemble.
She did not dream.

***

"Morning, Sheriff," the little girl said.
"Morning...Francine?"
"Yes," her mother said. "Aunt Connie visited you last night. That's how you know."
"You're Rhonda. Roundy-Round Rhonda, they call you."
The woman nodded.
"But...where is Aunt Connie now?"
"You tell me," Roundy-Round said.
The basement. Of course, she was in the basement.
It was time to earn her keep.
The Sheriff rose, prepared to limp across the room but was surprised to find her ankle no longer hurt. Aunt Connie had healed it, somehow, when she had changed.
The Sheriff stepped out onto Pensie Avenue, the sights

and smells of a brand new day invigorated her. She glanced over her jurisdiction, and saw that all was well. She walked up the sidewalk, eyes aware, keenly looking out for anyone violating The Law. The Law she was to uphold. It was her job. Aunt Connie had told her so.

Preacher Man and Dormouse waved to her as they set out to panhandle their way through another day. Muttering Marcie ran up the street, eager to converse with her special crack in the sidewalk. Leper Bob shuffled by slowly on his way to the War Memorial Park, but paused to tell her the news.

"Someone raped a girl last night."

Sheriff's eyes narrowed. "Where?"

"Behind the Harborview Diner."

"Harborview Diner? That's right in my back yard!"

"I know," he said. "That's why I told you."

"Thanks, Bob. I'll be sure to get his ass if he comes through our land again."

Leper Bob nodded, and slowly took himself up the block.

The Sheriff went and checked out the scene of the crime. She saw a used condom wrapper, and a bloody tire-iron in the dumpster. She inhaled, the thick juicy scents from within wafting up to her nose. "Yes," she said, the steel walls echoed her voice. "I'll get you."

She took the tire-iron and the condom wrapper with her, and prowled the streets, looking for him. Rapists were trash, filth, garbage…she would not allow them near her people. She carried the evidence up the road with her. She passed one man who looked at her as though she were insane. The Sheriff did not appreciate the guy's look but it was not him, she let him go. By Waters Street, she passed a man who did not look at her, but at the tire-iron and the condom wrapper. He ran into his house.

The Sheriff followed. She had her man.

He locked the door behind him, but Sheriff quickly ran around to the back. There was a porch, and she was up it and through the screen door quicker than he could get around to the other side.

"Get the Hell out of my house!" he screamed.

"You violated The Law," Sheriff said.

"What the Hell are you going to do about it?" he sounded amused. "If I did, that is."

"Bring you to Aunt Connie."

"What?"

"I do not judge. I apprehend. I am the Sheriff, and you, you piece of trash, are under arrest."

"Get the fuck out of here before I call the cops."

"No," Sheriff said, and swung the tire-iron.

He fell.

While he lay on the floor, she called the posse for help in moving him. They arrived, and grabbed his arms and legs. Every time he struggled, Leper Bob thumped him on the back of his head with the roll of nickels that was in his fist.

"This is the one?" Muttering Marcie asked as she peered into his face.

The Sheriff nodded.

Muttering Marcie grinned her black tooth grin, and said, "Aunt Connie's going to like him."

"We've got to bring him to the lot," Dormouse said. "To be judged."

The posse dragged and yanked the man out of his house and down the street, clamoring and whistling, excited because they were earning their keep. A few of the neighbors looked out of their windows, but quickly turned in again. No one wanted to become involved (a wise choice on their part). Soon, after dropping the captive a few times, and pausing to have Leper Bob thump him on the back of the head twice, they reached their lot, and they placed the man's face by the basement window.

They all backed away two steps. The Sheriff stood on her semi-conscious prisoner's back, pinning him to the ground. He was incoherent for a few moments, trying at first to wriggle away, but when he saw Leper Bob approaching, his struggles ceased.

"Look into the window," The Sheriff commanded, and held his face to the glass.

The man started into the dark window, little other choice

offered him. At first, he lay there, unblinking, his nose to the glass. Then he saw…

…and he screamed.

"He's guilty as fuck," Preacher Man said. "I ain't ever seen a son of a bitch as guilty as him."

"So what do we do?" Muttering Marcie asked.

The Sheriff looked at her, then up, around at the whole posse that surrounded Marcie's back.

(*Gotta earn your keep.*)

"Grab a rope," she aid.

The posse went wild, and several went off in search of something suitable. No one found a rope, but Preacher Man found a tie-down off a truck's bed. "That'll work," said The Sheriff, and nodded for them to lift the still-gibbering prisoner.

They carried him through the building. He tried to paw at the landings, but they ripped his fingers away. He tried to shake their hold, but dirty hands held on to him even tighter. Up, up, up six, seven, eight floors they went, and through the front door of Apartment 8-C.

The posse crammed into the two-bedroom apartment, smelly armpits and greasy elbows rubbing against each other as well as the grimy walls. The prisoner flailed about like a fish on the riverbank when he was dragged through the bedroom by angry, filthy hands.

"Thump him again Bob!" one of the women screamed.

The Sheriff held up her hand. "No." Her voice was soft, but edged with authority. "He's got to be awake for this."

No one questioned her, even the prisoner who stood dumbfounded and terrified, pale and sweating.

The Sheriff turned to face him. "Got any last requests?"

"I…I—"

"Fuck all that shit," Dormouse said. "Dangle his ass."

The posse murmured consent. The tie-down was placed around the prisoner's neck, and one end secured to the fire-escape. They counted aloud: "One…two…Three!"

They threw him over the edge.

He floated for a brief instant, arms and legs whirling in

circles to try to fly, fool gravity, but in the end gravity was not so easily duped, and its rule absolute. He fell. The tie-down became taut with a snap, barely audible over the loud crack of the man's neck breaking. The edge of the tie-down cut deep into the tender flesh of his neck, and lodged itself in the triangle of ear, skull, and jaw. Blood rained down on his shirt from his ragged throat.

He convulsed a jangling dance of violent spasms and dying nerves. His bowels collapsed with a loud fluttering, and his final orgasms dribbled out of his testicles. Shit rolled down one pant leg, and come stained the other.

"Nice job, Sheriff," Muttering Marcie said. "Aunt Connie will dig that wet."

"Yeah," someone toward the back said. "you ought to live a few month's rent-free for that one." The posse laughed at that—there was no such thing as free rent.

Slowly, after watching the man hang there for awhile, they dispersed and went back to their places on Pensie Avenue. The Sheriff walked down the sidewalk with a swagger in her hips, her eyes keen, her senses sharp, to protect and serve her people. As afternoon wore on, she went back to the parking lot of The Harborview Diner, and watched the whores and junkies, and waited for the next piece of filth to degrade her jurisdiction. When she heard Muttering Marcie's call of "Dark! Dark! Almost dark!" she went back toward the house, satisfied with her first day on the job. Only forty-seven more to go.

As the sun set, the metal on the fire escape gave way, and the hanging burden fell to the ground with a thud. After nightfall, a window opened in the basement of 528 Pensie Avenue, and a hand reached out, dragged the corpse in the yard through and into the basement. Aunt Connie held the dead man to her altar with two of her eight arms, and gobbled down his cock. She burped, and signed her name to check number 15426416.

"She's earned her keep."

TURNING LEAVES (AN AUTUMN ROMANCE)

I'm sorry, but I am who I am. Hate me for that, and I will hold no grudge. Love me for who I am not, and I just might.

Sure, I write, but you think *that* pays the bills? HA! Not! I am a mechanic during the day. My hands are roadmaps of grease-imbedded scars and swollen knuckles courtesy of broken cars that do not want to get fixed.

I'm an awful lot like those cars: I'm broken. I don't want to get fixed.

Like a '71 Ford pickup, I keep trudging along: two hundred fifty-eight thousand miles, oil leaks and overheats, bad shocks, misaligned, with all the creaks and squeaks and rattles.

I smoke. I drink too much coffee and do not eat right. I use such eloquent phrases as "Fuck it, that fucking fucker is fucking fucked," and "Slower than snail shit in January in Buffalo." Yes, I have been there, but no, I have not witnessed a snail defecating during my stay to verify the validity of my allusion.

I just think it sounds cool.

I am divorced. Surprised? Yeah, me neither. Blow me.

I am so far in debt it has become a running joke. (*Yeah, you're suing me too. Take a number and wait in line like everyone else.*) My nose is far too large for my face. I'm just the kind of guy no girl in her right mind would want to know. Why women talk to me at all, I never understood. I even cut my hair after my wife left to make myself uglier so women would not look at me.

It did not work.

Go figure.

***

An acquaintance of mine said at the Aegean: *never go to bed with someone crazier than yourself.*
  Words of wisdom.
  I wish I could abide by them.

***

I guess you'd say I have a lot of pent-up hostility toward women. I went through a particularly ugly divorce last year. My ex-wife (absolutely gorgeous woman, never understood why she even talked to me, much less married me) cheated on me (something I do understand) with the guy across the street (who is uglier than I am—go figure), moved in with him. Across the street. Talk about insult to injury. I had to walk out of my house and see the car in his driveway, see their shadows moving through the curtains.
  His front door was three hundred forty-two feet, nine inches from mine. Yes. I measured.
  I moved from Florida to Brackard's Point to get away before I did something stupid, like shoot him in the dick and my ex-wife in the mouth (would only have taken one bullet). A noble intention, if I may say so myself.
  A good intention.
  What better to pave the road to Hell?
  If sins are in the heart, I'm damned. Now look into my eye. Tell me if you see any giveafuck.

***

Marie looked like my ex-wife. She had deep brown eyes and curly blonde hair so thick you could hide in it, lose yourself in it as you searched for her neck. We met at the Irish place—Callahan's Pub on Congers Road. I was playing darts, noticed her watching me. Sure, I was flattered, but I figured she was probably crazier than your average patient at Swarthout Mental Health Center if she was checking *me* out. I've got a rule: if a woman is interested in me, she's obviously psychotic. It's usually a safe assumption, which is why I kick myself in the ass whenever I forget the advice offered to me at the Aegean.

Anyway. I was there with my friend Chuck, and his girlfriend, Denise (nice girl, mentally stable: hates my guts). Chuck and I were shooting. He was kicking my ass. After he won, I called to Marie; asked her if she wanted to play doubles, Denise and Chuck versus me and her. She came down, all curls and smiles and flashing eyes.

We played three games of doubles, then Chuck and Denise said they were going home. I figured it was about time to go, too, so we did: back to Marie's house.

To play singles.

It felt good to be with her, to feel her soft wet warmth all around me as I rammed my cock so far up inside her I could feel her spine crackling electric on the head of my dick. She came four times. Yes. Four. The first time she said my name over and over, the second she screeched, and the third, she said, "Oh my *God*." Between the third and the fourth, she was nothing but sweat and smegma, moans and thrashes replacing any intelligible words.

She was good.

She was a grabber—her nails found their way into my back. I twisted away. She did it again. Again, I twisted away. It hurt. I don't dig that shit.

She clamped on to the side of my neck with her nails. Tears filled my eyes. She kissed me hard. I tasted Guinness Extra Stout on her tongue. I threw her down, flopped out of her, then lay on top of her to re-enter, as well as to pin her to the bed. I did not want her to claw me again. I thought I felt a trickle of blood on my neck. I tried holding her arms. She struggled, but was more than willing to let me back in. She sighed as I filled her up again, made a cooing sound, and licked my nipple as she grabbed my ass. Then she tried to ram her finger in my asshole.

Fuck that. Exit only.

Next thing I know, I punched her in the mouth.

Her cunt twisted up around me and I came.

We came together.

When it was all over, when my dick dribbled out its last and began to soften in that steaming sauna pussy of hers, and the euphoria I always get from fucking a beautiful woman began to subside, I went straight down to the dumps. I felt like stir-fried whale shit for what I did. Horrified. Was that *me* who did that? My Christ, was it really *me?* For fuck's sake, I just hit this poor girl. What the fuck is wrong with me?

I must be the biggest piece of shit this side of an asshole.

"Enjoy that?" Marie simultaneously rubbed her jaw and wiped the sweat from the hollow of her throat.

I could think of several answers, but none I dared voice: *You were hurting me?* That seemed to me like the wrong thing to say. It was a little game, a little nasty sex, is all, a little bit of biting and nails. I obviously took it too far. What the Hell was wrong with me?

"I didn't mean..." I began to tell her the first lie. If she believed it, that would be the start of a relationship. Isn't that how they always begin?

"Yes, you did."

A small part inside me smiled, thankful she caught my line of bullshit. "I'm sorry, I don't know what came over me."

"*I* do," she said.

Silently, I collected my clothes, wallet, keys, cigarettes. That pack of Winstons' called to me; my lungs burned for one as soon as I touched the top of the box in my shirt, but she did not allow smoking in her house.

Fuck it. The fucking fucker was fucking fucked anyway; I didn't figure I'd ever be back here. I lit up, dressed in the dark, slowly smoking as I tried to feel if my underwear were inside out. I could barely see but I knew she was staring at me.

I could *feel* her hating me, everything about me, the way I made her laugh at the bar, the way I opened the car door for her, the way I licked her thighs, the way I walked, the way I smoked a Winston out of the corner of my mouth in her house—all she would ever know. I could not blame her. I hated myself, too.

I made my way through the shadowy apartment, left by the front door. As I stood on the porch, I heard her lock it and engage the deadbolt.

It was raining.

New York rain in Autumn is cold and steady. It seems determined to soak through your shoes and the collar of your coat to attack your toes and neck. I had my Mustang parked on the street out in front of her house. I started it, let the engine warm up to operating temperature, which takes a few minutes, especially in the cold. I smoked a cigarette as my engine idled, listened to the deep rumbling exhaust tone, the distinct loping idle I've got because of the cam I put in the engine. Once you hear my car, you never forget it. I gave her seven minutes of my engine idling outside her house. I revved it twice, and the motion light in her driveway flicked on.

Fuck it. If I'm going to be an asshole in her mind, let her never forget it, so she doesn't hook up with a shit-head (like me) again.

I dropped the Mustang into first, punched it. On the wet pavement, my tires let go instantly, and I went sideways. I cut the wheel, popped second, and fishtailed the other way. I continued up the street like that, the ass end of my car swinging back and forth, but I did not let off the gas. I was angry at her for making eyes at me in the first place—

(*Look at my schnoz, you silly bitch! What the fuck are you thinking?*)

—angry at myself for succumbing to them, and angry at her again for allowing me to pick her up and fuck her, but mostly angry at myself for hitting her. I could not believe I did that. I felt dirty, like some kind of stained-undershirt wearing, beer-gut having, oily-haired, balding motherfucker named Garth who smacks The Old Lady around when he runs out of Schlitz or Garcia y Vega cigars. Like a real scumbag. Like someone who should be shot.

I drove like a maniac. Anger rammed my foot to the floor as my car slid through the residential streets. I purposefully pushed myself to the limit of my driving abilities, not really caring if I lost it and crashed into a telephone pole or a brick wall. If I did, fine. I deserved it.

I jumped the curb over one lawn, then slid through the grass back onto the street; leaving deep ruts and rooster-tailing mud, splattering the side of the white house. On the way out, I aimed for a patch of flowers. Maybe they were pansies; maybe they were lilies, tulips, or marigolds.

I couldn't tell you the difference. All I know about flowers is they are fragile and pretty and smell good.

They're an awful lot like women, now that I think about it.

I wanted to destroy them.

The flowers, I mean.

When I splashed back on to the road, I cut it hard left, and punched it. The rear end started fishtailing again, so I kept my foot on the gas and tapped the brake pedal so the front tires would lock. They did. I launched forward like three hundred twenty horses straight out of Hell, careened down the roads of Brackard's Point, my tires pounding the shit out of the very best intentions.

I drove like a complete asshole the whole way home. I opened the door to my apartment, gave it an extra shove because it was raining and the wood always swells a bit when it's wet out, and slammed it behind me. From my bedroom I heard a thud. No worries: the pile of dirty clothes on the floor broke the fall of whatever went south.

It was about five-thirty in the morning, maybe closer to six, but I was pissed off, so sleep was as much of an option as me telling you what kind of flowers I ran over. I did not want to wake my neighbors up, but I needed to listen to something. I turned the stereo on low, but the CD that was in there could not be listened to softly. I put on my headphones, cranked it.

About nine in the morning, lack of sleep started to catch up with me, so I wandered into bed. I didn't have my head on the pillow three seconds when the phone rang.

"Yeah," I said, annoyed at someone calling me at this hour on a Saturday morning. If it was a solicitor, I was going to break out my personal copy of the riot act and read it *verbatim.*

"I couldn't sleep."

"Huh?"

"After you left, I couldn't sleep. Did I wake you?"

"Whoa. Wait a second. Marie?"

"Yes."

"I..." I babbled something that I'm sure sounded like I was choking. The last person on the face of the planet I expected to be on the other end of the phone was Marie.

"Are you all right?" she asked.

"I'm fine," I said, and thought, *how's your jaw?* "Listen, I'm sorry for... you know. I'm sorry I hit you. I never did that before. Ever. Believe me, I'm feeling like absolute crap because of it."

"You're silly."

"Huh?"

"Duh! Dipshit! Did you not realize I came when you did that?"

"I..." there I went again. She was throwing me for more loops than I could navigate at one sitting. "I figured you'd be calling the cops on me."

"What for?"

"Gee, I don't know, because I punched you?"

"Oh, God. Are you really that much of a prude?"

"What?"

"Why do you have to have such a closed mind?"

"What do you mean?"

"You are such a closet case. I thought you writer types had open minds about this sort of thing."

"Whoa. Hold time now. Just because I've published a few short stories and have a novel partial that's been "under consideration" for a year and a half means I'm supposed to feel *good* about punching a woman? You're fucking nuts! I feel like *SHIT* because of it. I can't believe I did that. But let's get one thing straight, okay? I do not...do *NOT* have a closed mind. Got me?"

"Whatever."

"For fuck's sake, this is crazy."

"Is it? Or was it just *really good* sex?"

"That it was," I admitted, "but still I can't believe I hit you."

"Don't worry about it. No damage done."

"I can't believe you called me."

"Believe it."

"This is nuts."

"So? Does that make it bad?"

"I don't know."

"You think too much."

Every woman in my life has told me that at one time or another. I think it was part of my wedding vows: *love, cherish, think too much until adultery do us part*. "I know."

"You sound tired."

"I am."

"You want to sleep?"

"Yeah."

"Alone?"

I *never* want to sleep alone. Who does? Asking if I wanted to sleep alone was like asking me if I wanted to come down with intestinal flu or suffer through an IRS audit, but I felt weird admitting it. It took me a moment to come out and say, "Not really."

"Can I come over?"

"Are you sure you want to?"

"I asked, didn't I?"

I gave her directions, told her the front door would be open, in case I didn't stay awake long enough to greet her.

I tried to lay down, be asleep when she came in, as if being able to sleep would somehow absolve me from it all. No solace: some worm in my gut kept twisting, tickling my throat. I was awake when I heard her come up the stairs. I opened the door for her. She had showered and looked great, her hair all brushed out and shiny, wearing red sweatpants and a floppy loose tee shirt, no shoes on. She carried a small bag and a pillow.

"I didn't know if you had an extra one or not," she explained. "Besides, mine is really lumpy and I can't sleep without it."

She looked great, but her jaw was kind of red.

She saw me noticing it, and touched the side of my neck where she clamped her nails into me. I could feel her fingertips traveling over the raised bumps on my skin.

"I did it to you first," she said. "Please don't think about it anymore."

"I don't want to think about anything," I said. "I want to go to bed. I'm exhausted. I've only been up twenty-nine hours straight."

"Come on," she said, "show me the bedroom."

I brought her in there, laid down on the bed. She laid her head on my shoulder, her leg across mine, her arm across my chest. It felt great to be wrapped up with a woman, to smell her, feel her breathing, her smooth skin, her warm, soft curves. She kissed the top of my head, and closed my eyes with her fingertips.

I thought about *petit morte:* little death. Accurate, because something in me died when I came with her. She closed my eyes with her fingertips, and something within me was reborn, a phoenix from the ashes in my mouth and the scars in my psyche.

I could not believe she was here, that after I knocked her in the jaw, she came over and wanted to snuggle, like normal people. Like my wife and I used to. It felt good. Better, maybe.

Being single is weird. You've got to have an open mind about a lot of things. Things you never had to consider before.

I'm getting used to it. Marie and I have been together a couple of months now and things are going well. We see each other a few times a week, have great sex, and talk just about every day. Sure, things are a little weird, for what I'm used to, but Marie has helped me keep an open mind.

And a closed fist.

FOR WHOM
WE MOURN

Gustav and Dimitri were close, once, before Dimitri opened Mother's grave and left behind an empty casket. After that, lumps of shame burned in Gustav's throat: rage smoldered in his chest, brotherly love twisted to rancor.

He held himself responsible for her desecration. If only he'd stopped Dimitri sooner. If he acted those years ago, he could have saved Mother much pain. He should have. He should have when he identified the darkness within his brother. Within them both.

Gustav did not because he was thwarted by an emotion most evil, sent upon his heart as a curse by some god the two had blasphemed. He loved his brother—as only men like himself could love—and hesitated pulling the trigger. In more lucid moments, Gustav understood Dimitri's actions. It was an addiction, One he knew well: the brain screamed, and the body reacted. *Feed me*, it cried, and it was hard not to obey... to find a book or ancient scroll and begin to read. Then the madness' thirst for darker knowledge grew insatiable.

If Gustav were in the grip of their madness, he would seek out the tomes, find the black incantations hidden between paragraphs mundane to unlearned eyes. Once the brain saw the secrets, it would recognize them in places most ordinary: proof of the madness in others. Sometimes he saw them still, but their meanings were never as apparent.

Dimitri understood what he had read, had learned. That's why he took Mother's remains. With them, he would seek the places of power. It was going to be a long journey. Gustav read a little before he gave chase. A little—enough to heighten the thinking, raise the consciousness. To tingle the brain. Tease it. The madness whispered within his mind. He stopped before it started to scream.

Before he left, Gustav checked his Makarov pistol—a good, Russian-made model. He packed extra ammunition, because it was scarce and expensive. He hoped he would not heed the weapon, but packed it anyway. Just in case.

***

He saw the old man wandering the streets in Istanbul, narrating events no one around him could see, asking questions no one but Gustav, Dimitri, and a handful of others could answer. The old man's left hand was a stump. Its bandages were new.

"You never saw him," Gustav said.

The old man turned. Gustav looked into his eyes. He Saw. Yes. He Saw too much. Saw that for which he was unprepared. Madness swam into and out of focus in the old man's stare.

"My hand. He stole my hand. And a bottle of my best brandy."

"When?"

"Two nights ago. I was asleep in my bed. The bed I made. I'm a carpenter. Was. My hand and my brandy—all that I needed. Why would he take an old, callused hand? Why would someone steal that? And to take my drink afterward, that was mean," the former carpenter sobbed. "That was mean to take my brandy after my hand."

"Show me."

The man led Gustav to his home, reeling from the Sight, asking far too many questions. Once there, Gustav demanded to be shown the bed, and inquired about the brandy. The man seemed oblivious to Gustav's tears.

"I hope you catch him," the man said. "I was a carpenter. I used to build houses. Now I see them falling. Falling down. He builds, too, doesn't he? He builds with bones."

Gustav nodded, placed his hand on the bed. Mother had lain here. The carpenter's eyes were heavy on him, patiently waiting an elaboration. Gustav wiped his hand on his coat. "You ask questions you do not understand."

"Teach me, then."

135

"Kneel down."

The old man's joints creaked as he knelt. He looked up at Gustav and clasped his hands, expectant. "I knew you would come," he said. "I Saw it." Gently, he placed his hand on the bed, where Gustav's own had set a moment before. He closed his cursed eyes and opened them again. "I Saw Her, too," the madman said, "I Saw Her through the eyes of the sphinx."

Gustav nodded—made sense.

"Will you teach me now?"

"Yes." Gustav leveled the gun at the old man's head, aimed through tear-blurred eyes.

"Thank you," the carpenter smiled.

The blast blew out his brainstem.

***

Gustav followed the trail of whispers through the desert to the Temple of Isis at Philae. Before he entered, he removed his boots and socks, his belt and weapon, setting them carefully in the sand outside the sacred boundary. From his pack he removed a book and fought the urge to open and read on the temple's stone steps, through his brain screamed. Not this time—too many men had died for this book. Its cover was the skin of a scapegoat slaughtered outside a Jewish settlement long ago. The goat would carry the villagers' sins out into the arid waste, but this one never made it: The Arab waited outside the Gomorrah on the eve of the ritual, and took the goat and its burden of sin to bind this book. Its words were enlightenment—and damnation.

Gustav lowered his eyes as he entered, holding the book before him. He made his way past hieroglyphs depicting Nectanebo II with offerings of incense to Osiris, to the inner sanctuary where the Waters of Life originated and Isis herself dwelled.

He dropped to one knee, raised the book over his head, shut his eyes, and waited.

"Is this…?" Not even Isis could bring herself to mention

the book's title.

"It is," Gustav said.

"This…" She stared at the book in amazement. "This is the original…complete?"

"Every page as The Arab penned it."

"You bring me this—a true offering. Much power is here. Won't you miss it?"

"Few gods—and no men—should ever read those words."

"But you have."

"Yes. Dimitri as well."

Isis grew angry at the mention of his name. "He was at Ghiza, looking for *The Book of the Dead*."

"I'm sorry," he said. "I had hoped to stop him before he reached your land."

There was nothing to say, so Isis smiled. "I would send you off with my blessing, but…"

"I know," Gustav nodded. He was too corrupt. "You cannot. I thank you for considering it."

She accepted his words with a nod, opened the book. A purple glow came from inside to cast an eerie light on her face. She began reading the ancient text.

Gustav watched her turn the pages in silence. As each moment passed, her expression changed—from awe to contemplation, contemplation to realization to disgust to horror. She shut the book after only a few pages, weeping.

Gustav's heart ripped in two. A woman's grievous tears were powerful in their own right. A Goddess's were far more precious. He accepted them as he could not her blessing, and felt unworthy of the gift. When he left, Isis knelt with her hand to her head. Gustav wondered for whom she mourned. He almost asked, but dared not.

***

Gustav followed Dimitri's trail of desecration across the desert. Holy cities were stained with his passing, the tombs of prophets and madmen opened, their remains drained of power and knowledge. Sometimes, he missed his brother by only a few hours. At other times, he lost the trail, and had to waste valuable days to recover it.

Dimitri slaughtered a sacred bull near Samrala, India. He and Mother's corpse had lain in the carcass. The villagers still wept when Gustav came upon them, but he left them to their grief, because he had only one way to cure it, and not enough bullets. Makarov ammunition was scarce in these impoverished lands. He refrained from expending any, until he reached Laos.

Eighteen of them were skinned alive and tied to bamboo stakes. Water dripped from buckets atop each onto their tongues; they could not dehydrate. When Gustav reached them, they all stared down at the small heaps of unusable flesh at their feet and watched leafy shadows creep across their skin. Dimitri had taken quite a bit with him: choice cuts.

Gustav needed no magic to see the root of their madness. They all babbled in their language, but Gustav understood nothing of what they said. He did not speak Lao, but could not mistake the pleading tone to their slippery, incomprehensible words. They reeked of deceit.

Flat tongues lingered maliciously over lipless mouths as they spoke, lidless eyes stared at his pale skin with hunger far deeper than sanity. They wanted to wear it. Like the crones sharing an eye betwixt the three, his flesh would be passed between eighteen.

Gustav shot them one by one. He paused only to reload and weep.

***

Gustav lost his brother's trail in Asia, but knew the general direction: north. There were many places Dimitri could go first, but Gustav knew where this journey would end: Lake Baikal. Gustav remembered how dreamy mother's eyes grew when she talked of Baikal: a dream never realized. Many her age wanted to make the journey at least once. Dimitri defiled her dreams and Gustav's soul bore the weight of shame at the mockery of the goals she never achieved.

***

Strange lightning came from Olkhon Island, where monks' bones lay unburied—not Dimitri's doing: it was the custom. Gustav thought of Dimitri amongst all those holy bones and his anger flared. He cursed himself for permitting this to happen, but another curse on his soul was redundant. The Siberian people believed Burkham, god of the lake, was angry, and families went hungry from the hoards of food and vodka sacrificed to appease Him. In the fishing towns on Baikal's shore, orders to sail were refused, and refused so often that they were no longer given. No one ventured past shore, much less to Olkhon to inspect the source of trouble.

When Gustav inquired of passage to Olkhon, he was met with skepticism and distrust. Some refused to acknowledge him because they thought him mad—(how correct they were)—while others looked at him suspiciously, as if he caused the strange lightning in the sky, as if he were responsible. How correct they were, too.

Unable to find passage to Olkhon, Gustav bought a small rowboat with an outboard engine. The man who sold it to him did not ask his destination. When the deal was done, the man took both Gustav's hands in his and said, "May Burkham keep you."

"And he you."

The depth of the man's stare betrayed his understanding. He knew. He knew and was not touched by the madness. He knew, and had a family. He knew, and held his humanity around him like a badge of station.

Gustav knelt before him as he had before Isis. The man let his shaking hands go, and bade Gustav to leave. When Gustav left the room and stepped outside, he wondered what god he had touched—if it were Burkham himself.

Outside, the weird lightning flashed soundlessly across the water. The lightning was green this time. Then purple.

Gustav looked across the massive lake to Olkhon Island, could barely make out its rust-colored rock from the cold, dark waves.

He hefted his bag of supplies down the ramp, loaded it into the boat, and draped a plastic tarp over the ancient texts to keep them dry. He was as ready as he could ever be for a confrontation with Dimitri.

It rained harder.

***

Silent thunder followed a flash of orange lightning. Unease quickened Gustav's pulse. Cold Siberian rain dripped off his beard to his neck, bleached his skin a frigid shade of white.

The waves grew, and as they slapped the boat's hull with muttering voices: *"Back. Don't. Back. Don't."* Each wave's voice was unique: like snowflakes, no two alike. As Baikal's water's roughened, the waves' voices grew proportionately louder: with meter-and-a-half seas, they were deafening.

Lightning flashed blue, red, and yellow, and the Siberian skies spit cold rain. The screaming waves tossed the tiny craft to and fro. Puddles sloshed about the boat's deck, soaked through Gustav's boots. His toes went numb. Gustav was no seaman, but he stayed his path as best he could: rolling with the waves, trying not to let the silent lightning or the loud voice of the waters distract his course or cause. *Nerpa*, the indigenous Baikal seal, regarded him with brown liquid eyes as he passed a group. Their expressions questioned his sanity: *Where are you going, man? This is not your element.* Gustav could almost make out warnings in their dog-like barks.

Cold wet wind collected in the wrinkles of Gustav's coat and boots, ran in rivulets off his brimmed hat, soaked through his gloves and froze his fingers. The boat bobbed and swayed across the ever-roughening waters, its small engine barely audible over the screaming waves. On top of the growing clamor, the nerpa joined in, calling him a fool and a failure, telling him to go back to shore, where he belonged. Gustav ignored the nerpa and kept his course, adjusting when could see the island over the rising and falling bow.

The boat shuddered violently as the water thickened to the consistency of molasses. The tiny engine strained, trying to propel the craft forward through water suddenly too thick. He gave it more gas, tried to raise the prop to ease the load, but nothing helped. The engine started getting hot. Gustav shut it down before it blew and left him stranded.

All was silent. *Nerpa* opened and closed their mouths mutely. The rain splashed on the water without sound. The waves flattened out. Dead calm.

The boat floated steadily toward Olkhon Island across a smooth silent span of water. Gustav took the Makarov out of its holster, jacked a round into the chamber, and let the boat drift. His spine shot out warnings to his system and his eyes darted from peripheral to peripheral. Something was happening, but he did not know what. Until he saw the billowing clouds on the water.

At first, Gustav thought it was merely a reflection of the sky above but these were not clouds of rain or snow; these were clouds of silt—

(*As above, so below*)

—from Baikal's bottom.

The water's surface bubbled and rolled without sound. Gustav smelled millennia of decayed fish in the Baikal mud. His nose attempted to curl back into his face to hide from the reek.

The boat began to sway. Bubbles from Baikal's bottom burped noxious gas. Mist loitered around him, shut down visibility. The unearthly lightning cast glows about the scene and threw distance and depth into confusion.

The boat lurched to port. Gustav fell to his knees, held on to the Makarov with his right hand, the boat's railing with his left. The stern spun around, kicked to starboard.

A hand-shaped wave smacked the bow. Wet fingers disintegrated, sprayed Gustav in the face, clung to his cheeks and beard. It tasted awful, smelled worse. His nose filled with methane reek and rotted aquatic life. He gagged from the smell. His stomach pitched its contents to the back of his throat. His eyes dripped stinging tears as he swallowed vomit. The boat lurched again, spun violently. Waves shoved against the starboard side of the bow—dirty, reeking waves, shaped like hands. They pushed. The small boat spun. Gustav held on, screamed demands for order, and in in anger called out his brother's name.

The hands reached over the deck, fingers stretched out, splayed palms. Gustav felt the cold wetness seize him, pull him toward the edge of the boat. He screamed as they lifted him over the rail. He splashed into the freezing water turned black by silt and mud. Watery half-formed arms reached for his ankles from the dark waves. Their grip was not tight, but he could not kick them away. They dragged him feet-first.

Rancid waves flooded his face. Water shot up his nose. They stripped his weapon away, and the Makarov sank to the bottom like a stone. Gustav fought the progress, tried to sit up, breathe, suck air, kick them away, but the wave-hands did not relent.

They pulled him toward the shallows. Olkhon's shore: jagged rock the color of dried blood, erupted out of the water before him. The hands gripping him dragged him ever faster toward the blood-red rock. Gustav screamed before they threw him against it—afterward, he could not: the force of impact expelled his breath from his lungs and ignited pain in his spine. Warm blood flowed over his cold forehead, stung as it dripped into his eyes, salty in his mouth. The waters of Baikal drank from the gash and the hands that assaulted him matched the color of the rock.

He was thrown onto the rocky beach. It hurt to moan. Even breathing caused pain. His fingers clawed at small pebbles cast atop the larger rocks as he tried to pull himself away before the water could grab him again, drag him back in.

Slowly his breathing stabilized. The flaring pain throughout his chest dimmed to throbbing. It hurt only when his heart beat.

He crawled up the beach for safety, groaned with every

aching movement and realized the silence had been broken. Besides his own voice, the first sound that registered was the hand-waves reaching for him. They smacked and slapped at the rock and behind him, the *nerpa* called him a fool, told him to come back to the water where it was safe, that there was nothing on the island good anymore, his element be damned.

Gustav turned toward the water. At first he thought the hands had left, but after a moment he saw their outlines skimming across the cove like the dorsal fins of mutant sharks. The seals congregated *en masse* out further, and continued to speak amongst themselves.

As he watched the seals and hands in the water, and thought about the lost pistol, the *nerpa* became restless. A visible wave of panic passed through them as the group scattered. The hands ceased to hide in the waves: arms shot out of the water, looking like a lunatic reeds. Their every movement was menace. Green lightning crackled across the sky.

He smelled the smoke. It wafted toward him from over the rise. He turned his nose into it, forcing himself to rise and trace it back to its origin.

The makeshift hut was dilapidated. No wall was plumb or square. Its roof leaned to the left, collecting rain in its deep bows. The thick smoke rose slowly through a chimney-hole to hang low in the damp air. Gustav recognized the smell: he could never forget the scent of burning bones.

He stepped over protective circles drawn in the mud around the perimeter and rapped on the door. It swung open.

The first thing Gustav saw was the glow emanating from the pyramid of skulls burning in the fireplace. Tongues of flame wagged and moaned. The monks' remains lamented their predicament and they cried out to deaf gods for mercy. The room they showed was impossible: its proportions too large to be contained inside the hovel. A harpsichord— Mother's favorite instrument—rested in the corner, amongst rich tapestries and original art in gilded frames. He saw a late sixteenth-century Dutch clock on the other wall, the type with only the hour hand. Dimitri must have worked hard to so alter the ramshackle lodging: such lengths were unlike him.

Gustav stepped over the threshold, calling his brother's name. He was answered only by the monks' remains in the fireplace, pleading with him to end their torment.

In the flickering shadows, Gustav saw an easy chair and endtable, a lamp, and behind that, a shelf of books, many of which were unique; handwritten copies of the unaccredited author's manuscript; most were in languages never meant to be spoken, and few were in any modern tongue. Gustav knew them all by sight. Many he had memorized in their entirety. His brain tingled as he saw them and his madness screamed. He approached the shelf, and from behind, heard the door to the hut slam closed.

Gustav spun, instinctively reached for his pistol, but his hand came up empty as he remembered the weapon was at the bottom of Baikal.

"What would you do with it if you had it?" Dimitri asked as he approached.

The question hung in the air between them, and Gustav let it hang. "Where is she?"

"So nice to see you too, dear brother."

"Where is she?"

"Where is who?"

"You know damned well."

"Mother," Dimitri called. "Gustav wishes to see you."

Gustav started a word of protest, but it fell from his lips when he saw her enter the room. She shuffled slowly and felt her way with one hand on the wall. In the other, she held a knitting-basket and several balls of yarn. Dimitri had resurrected her, repaired her flesh with that taken in Laos. Except for her eyes. They were absent from their sockets, but Gustav did not know whether that was Dimitri's omission or the logistics of rot.

Dimitri walked over to Mother, took her hand, led her to the chair. He did not bother turning on the lamp. Her hands drew up her needles. Their clicking was not the sound

Gustav remembered from his childhood, but there was no reason it should be. The familiar aluminum needles she used to use were replaced with fine, rune-carved needles of bone.

"What have you done?" Gustav asked his brother, though his eyes never left the shambling incarnation of his mother's reanimated corpse.

"I brought her back."

"Why, Dimitri? We know you *could* do it; that was never in question. What purpose could this serve? What benefit could come from it?"

"Mother can knit," he said. "I thought you would have remembered."

"Yes, of course, she could, but…" Gustav stopped as the significance overwhelmed him. One of the most ancient forms of magic, back to the Fates. How foolish of him to never have considered it before. Mother would be easy for Dimitri to control; the bond between mother and son does not stop with the cessation of life. With her resurrection, she could keep on knitting until Dimitri told her to stop, and that order would never be given. She could knit his fate, his victories and his accomplishments, his life everlasting. As long as he kept her secret—and well protected.

Dimitri whispered in Mother's ear. The harpsichord in the corner began to play. At first, the notes were random, then, as she started another loop of yarn, a melody took shape. Dimitri stroked her hair, smiling at Gustav.

"You've enslaved her," Gustav said, distaste on his tongue. "After all she did for us, you've enslaved her."

"All she did is nothing compared to that which she shall do."

Gustav looked at his mother's ever-moving hands. The flesh on her knuckles as thin, racked by fissures from which protruded blackened, drying flesh and bloodless veins. Everything those hands had worked for was gone, her life's work betrayed by her youngest son. Gustav glared at his brother as a surge of hatred renewed itself, a grudge held a lifetime. "I should have shot you when you were eight."

Click-click click, the needles tapped out the seconds.

Click-click click. Dimitri returned the glare with a parody of a smile, a sowing of teeth.

Click-click click.

"Then who would have taught her so much? Mother lived, died, and never realized anything outside of the mundane. She was unlearned, ignorant. She never got out of St. Petersburg, much less to the places I have taken her."

"You took her there for your purposes, not hers."

"Partially true. Why would I have come here? To Baikal? To come here and see it was *her* dream, not mine. I could have gone anywhere."

"If you wished her to see it, you would have given her eyes," Gustav advanced a step. Dimitri was within arm's reach.

"Go ahead," Dimitri said. "Do it. I see the thought in your mind. Anyone could. You wish to see me bleed. You wish to choke the life from me, the dangers to yourself be damned. Oh, noble, noble Gustav, you always were—"

Gustav could not control himself on longer. Rage flashed out his arms, wrapped his hands around his brother's throat. Hate clenched his fingers.

Dimitri's hands went up to block the attack, too late: Gustav drove him to the ground by his neck. He rammed his knee into Dimitri's sternum and pinned him, then lifted his head and rammed it into the floor. Dimitri's vision unfocused with the shock of impact. Again and again, Gustav slammed the back of Dimitri's head on the floor in perfect time with the mother's needles—

Click-click click

SLAM

Click-click click

SLAM

Click-click click

SLAM

—until Dimitri's body went limp. Gustav paused, wondered for an instant if he had killed him, but after a moment, he felt Dimitri's chest rise and fall. His tenacious will to live drove Gustav deeper into his rage and squeezed

Dimitri's neck, grabbed his larynx and twisted, until he felt the cartilage crack and splinter. He pummeled his brother's face with his fists and yet, Dimitri still breathed.

Click-click click

Wheezing, blood-wet, breath continued to draw past Dimitri's lips and in his mouth, his tongue rolled back, as if it tried to fan what little air it could into the ruined throat.

Click-click click

The raggedness of Dimitri's breathing grew fainter, the rhythm stronger. The blood stopped pooling in his mouth and the lips, ruined by Gustav's pummeling, wove themselves back together, drawing the smallest pieces of skin back from where they were knocked out of place.

Gustav's shock overtook his senses and he stared mutely at the magnificent transformation.

Click-click click

As he looked up to Mother, whose expression never altered, Dimitri began to laugh under him. Slowly, Dimitri pushed himself up off the floor. Gustav tried to hold him down with sheer force, but Dimitri was gaining strength. He crashed his fist into the side of Gustav's head and knocked him senseless, and while Gustav was dazed, he landed another fist to the underside of Gustav's chin, knocking his sense of balance askew.

Then Dimitri pressed his advantage, and heaved his body upward while pushing Gustav away. The next thing Gustav knew, he was being kicked in the ribs and screamed at for every perceived wrong he had committed toward Dimitri in all of his life, from the time they were eleven and seven, when Gustav first got hold of the black tome from grandfather's study and would not let young Dimitri read it, too; to the first grave they violated together, when Gustav asked the first and last questions of the corpse and claimed his right to do so was based on his being the older brother; to the girl Dimitri had a lust for when he was fifteen and whom Gustav had lain; and the meddling and foiling of countless schemes and plans and dreams, and with each accusation, another blow landed.

Gustav shrank back from the ferocity of his brother's assault, struggled to regain his feet, but Dimitri's kicks pre-empted such action. He curled on his side, tried to protect his soft throat and belly. Dimitri's kicks kept coming no matter what he did, so the only thing he could think of doing was scuttling away as best he could, rolling on the floor or crawling, whatever permitted an inch or two of safety from the ever-continuing barrage.

Click-click click

Gustav's retreat was halted by the wall: backed into a corner. He looked up through one eye, for the other had swollen shut. The skulls' flickering light from his left cast a dim glow on mother's back. Her hair was disheveled, fallen from her glamorous funeral style. She did not seem to notice. Instead, she mindlessly knit as they tried to kill each other, oblivious to all that occurred around her.

Dimitri's right leg kept coming in to his field of vision, a dark blur against the glowing backdrop that careened into his chest, his gut: a pendulum of pain. Dimitri saw his brother's predicament: against the wall, he could go no further. Lying on the floor, he could not rise. His tactics changed, then, and he rose his foot to stomp down with his heel.

The first landed in Gustav's midsection, its power explosive. He tasted the pain on his tongue, felt it roll with the waves of nausea through his torso. He doubled over, dimly aware that his arms that protected his face were useless against Dimitri's full weight should it come crashing through his skull. In his vulnerability, he became acutely aware of the cold, hard, unyielding floor beneath him, and how it would absorb none of the shock—the proverbial hard spot and the rock-hard boot heel, his braincase an egg between them.

Dimitri lifted his foot again, and Gustav reached up. His right hand missed, but his left caught the inside of Dimitri's pant leg, slowing the ascent long enough for the right to grab hold of Dimitri's ankle.

Dimitri shook his leg in an attempt to dislodge Gustav's grip, tried to shuffle back. Gustav held on, drew both of his arms around Dimitri's leg, pulled them to his chest. He felt himself pull away from the wall as Dimitri dragged him across the floor, felt the muscles in his brother's leg strain with the effort. Then he let go.

With Gustav's weight no longer restraining him, Dimitri's full-force back step betrayed him. He lurched in reverse, off balance, and his arms went out to try and stabilize himself as he went down. His right grasped nothing. His left grabbed the bookshelf. Instead of halting his fall, it tilted forward.

As the top books slid off onto the floor to crack their spines and tear the endpapers away, the light scrolls in cases crushed beneath the heavier, older volumes, Dimitri regained enough of his balance to leap out of the way.

Mother did not. The shelf smashed the lamp and table. Shards of glass and splinters of ancient wood cascaded to the floor, and the shelf came to rest on top of her frail corpse.

The harpsichord ceased its performance. The *click-click click* of her needles did not punctuate the seconds; passing. The sixteenth-century wall clock with the single hand melted into the wall on which it hung; the walls began to slide forward and lose their fine finish, fading to dilapidated wood that was neither plumb or square; the ceiling overhead faded to reveal the low-hung, bowed roof which let through columns of water through to collect in puddles on the earthen floor. The ornate hearth above the fireplace disintegrated, as did the bric-a-brac collected on its top, revealing a stone fire-pit. Smoke collected in the single-room hut and obscured vision: the skulls of holy men still burned and their tongues of flame softly lamented.

Gustav listened for Dimitri but heard nothing from his brother. The only sounds in the hut were the spattering of rain on the roof, the moaning monks and a tapping sound from the pile of broken books and crushed scrolls. Gustav labored to rise. His head spun, and he reached to the wall to keep himself upright. The nausea he experienced with Dimitri's crushing kick to his kidney returned. Every movement aggravated it further. His eye was swollen, blood was in his mouth every time he spit but he could not tell if it was from his lips, cheek, or nose—or any combination thereof.

Every breath was accompanied by a stabbing speculation of a broken rib. He moaned in chorus with the dead monks.

He leaned on the fallen bookshelf with both of his arms, hanging his head to dispel the nausea and drain the blood from his mouth. A sticky strand dripped off his lip to stain a page a hundreds of years old and partially obscured a passage regarding the elementary principles of creation, a destruction, and the manipulation of the two. Gustav remembered it from his studies, though he had not seen the book since he was a teenager and lost it to Dimitri in a wager on Olympic hockey. The corner of the book's spine rest in a growing puddle of muddy water stained the red shade of Olkhon.

After a few moments of recuperation, Gustav made his way around the bookshelf, leaning his weight upon it for he could not trust his own legs. As he approached the top corner of the shelf, it teetered: Mother's chair its fulcrum. The sudden weight shift surprised him, and he let go for a moment. Standing by himself, he could see Dimitri on the far side of the shelf as he lay crumpled on the floor. The wounds healed by mother's knitting had reopened, the magic fueling his chateau and life gone. All that remained were his creations: the shelf for the books, the chair, and mother's unnatural life. The rest he left to her to execute at his command. Dimitri had always looked for the easier way.

Gustav sighed. Part of him mourned.

Mother was closer, so he reached her first. She was pinned to the chair, her hands trapped on opposite sides of one of the shelves. Her eyeless face did not look at him, but against the wooden shelf as they tried to complete the loop she started when the shelf fell. She still wore her wedding band on her left hand. Gustav was happy to see it. It reminded him of her life, when she would turn it over on her finger as she thought of a suitable punishment for the boys for them when they were naughty.

(*Boys will be boys*)

Somewhere, a dark god laughed at the irony.

"Mother," Gustav said. "Can you hear me? At all? Mother?"

Slowly, her head turned toward him, and her eyelids opened to reveal black rot and Dimitri's shadow magic. There was no love in her eyes, no acceptance. Only the grave's empty wisdom, and that, he already knew.

Gustav wondered about the carpenter's mother, in Istanbul, whom he never knew. About Horus's—sweet, sweet Isis, and the tears she cried. About the mother of the Arab, about the mothers of the scholars and prophets…how these men all needed their mother's wisdom, how they all must have remembered mother's words in times of need. A single word from her would help.

"I'm sorry, mother," Gustav said.

The stare he received in answer was blank.

Gustav reached down and removed the bone needles from her hands. Despite their absence, she continued to try and complete the final loop. Gustav almost broke them over his knee, but the runes upon them caught his attention. To destroy these would be a sacrilege: he owed both Isis and the god at the lakeshore more than that.

The skulls in the fireplace muttered their approval.

Gustav reached forward, laid his hands on her face. He said something more, some small word of apology, barely muttered as he twisted her skull from her neck.

The *nerpa* outside wailed.

The magic powering her died, the flesh of the Lao fused to her own fell away. Gently, he carried her head to the fire. The dead monks within accepted her quickly, flickered their tongues over her face in passionate kisses. Within moments, her bare skull rest on top of the pile, and her voice joined the chorus. She did not speak, but she did sob.

Gustav almost asked her why, but dared not.

From the fire, he turned, and went to where Dimitri's corpse lay cooling in puddles of water from the leaking roof. Gustav kicked the books out of his way and crouched down before him. In death, his brother looked kind: how looks can deceive.

He sat there for a long time. The roof leaking on his face concealed that which ran from his eyes. His loss, guilt, and grief crushed all thought, overwhelmed most of his senses. He was aware of the wetness only because it reminded him of Isis, the tears she cried. He looked up, through the holes in the roof, and let the rain shower his face. As he cried into the grey sky, he wondered why, and for whom he mourned.

MHZ MINUS INFINITY

Woven between capillaries and arterioles, muscle, bone, and connective tissue, lay Dr. Tyler Egar's goal: the nerves—where man's world exists. He knows this intimately; they are his obsession.

"Nerves conduct to us our world," Tyler says. It is not the first time you heard it. "Is it too hot or too cold? Is the scent fresh bread or Pensie Avenue bum's-piss? Are you endangering your muscle structure by lifting something too heavy? Are your arms and legs being torn from their sockets?" You can almost mouth the words along with him by now, you've heard this so many times.

He continues: "Is the face before you beautiful or hideous? Is it your own? Nerves tell all," Tyler says. "But they can lie."

He would know. It is his obsession.

Tyler knows nerves lie when you trick them with repetition, patterns and colors. Nerves compensate for words on paper that should be, but are not; they reduce voices and traffic to babble and background noise. Your head fills with images and sounds when dreaming.

Tyler tricks his nerves often. He induces trances, has taken drugs, entered computer generated virtual realities. Everything he does is part of his experiments, every waking moment is a test. You fear he is beyond obsessed sometimes. You fear it might be contagious.

In his traces and hallucinatory states, he has described his visions to you. That is your job, as his assistant: to record his findings and assist with the experiments. You have recorded monologues of Tyler describing how he crushed monsters and ghouls, how he had intercourse with three-breasted women. His ejaculate was thick and seemingly endless. Tyler

153

said, when his nerves were tricked, his semen was caustic.

He describes to you his next test. It is the same as before, only minor changes. Again, and again, and again, he tries for something, but will not tell you what he is looking for. He merely says you will know when he gets there.

He sees you look at him.

He knows what you think. You think he is out of his mind, borderline psychotic. He knows what you think and he does not care. In a way, you admire him for that.

Tyler is paying you, so you keep your mouth shut, your thoughts to yourself. After all, you ate today. A roof is over your head; you can get from point "a" to point "b" if you must. True, you cannot afford *everything*, you do not have the multi-million dollar home and a new Porsche for every day of the week, but you aren't exactly dying of starvation and exposure, now are you?

Tyler looks worse for wear—his eyes are sunken, his hair greasy. He smells stale, as if he worked through many nights. He probably has.

"You've got to record this," Tyler says. His eyes are what you notice, sunken, but intense, excited. Insane.

Are you *really* that surprised?

He does not wait for an answer. You give none, but follow him to the White Room. You always thought this room should be black for some reason, maybe the movies you have watched: the mad doctor's room in the basement. Maybe it is fear of the experiments you monitor and record, what he pursues with such relentlessness and secrecy.

You're thinking of changing your profession, aren't you?

Wouldn't be the first time.

As Tyler enters the White Room, you take your place in the Control Room. You watch him through the banks of monitors, eight different camera angles of Tyler and the Surrounding room. The corner fluorescent lights cast soft illumination, white light bouncing off white walls. You begin recording both video and audio. The VU meter lights bounce at Tyler's footsteps. He asks if the levels are good.

"Of course they are," you say. You know what you're

doing. Tyler nods his head, and you start the procedure. Cut the corner fluorescents, turn on the overheads. You dim the overheads and change the color filter to blue. The White Room's soft walls and floor soak up the color and everything, Tyler included glows the color of an August sky. You begin the music: thick, watery chorus of noise. Water bubbles, gurgles through the speakers inside, waves break in Surround Sound. You decrease the temperature in there by fifteen degrees, dim the lights, dimmer, colder…

…dimmer…

You take a moment to check Tyler's vitals. His heart rate is slowing, respiration down thirteen percent. Soon, he will believe he is under fifty feet of water, and begin to dream, or hallucinate, of whatever the fucking whacko does in there.

You watch his body relax and continue to watch the monitors. This must be perfect to work: the timing is important. Slowly, you open the valve on the yellow bottle, and a sulfuric smell wafts out of the room's vents.

"Eggs," Tyler mutters. "Rotten eggs."

Dilute the smell with pure oxygen, then mix in compressed air while you change the lighting from blue to yellow, change the audio from water sounds to air: wind, leaves rustling on branches, twittering of birds both near and far. You increase the temperature twenty-five degrees and check his vitals. You allow them to stabilize.

"Egg," he mumbles, barely audible.

You flip off the color filter and spike the rheostat. Intense white light fills the room: Tyler's vital signs leap as his system tries to process all the new input to its nerves.

Did you do it too quickly?

His vitals are haywire, brainwave activity peaking, cyclic activity in the megahertz scale. The lights overhead sputter and spasm. The microphones in the room squeal through the speakers—feedback—you cut the gain, but the howling noise still screams out of every corner of the room. The lights continue to flicker, one of them shoots sparks, and for a moment, you see a rainbow aura around Tyler's head—

(Something prismatic? What could it be?)

155

—and all the light in the room seems to *bend* in his direction. Through the lights are fully on, shadows claim the corners, and all around Tyler is a ring of sputtering, flickering light, as if he were some magnet.

He slowly begins to rock back and forth in the chair, seemingly oblivious to the chaos around him. Amazed, you watch as the light warps and bends to follow his motions. A light bulb explodes, then another, raining glass down upon him.

He continues to rock, does not seem to notice, despite the crunching of glass at his every move.

His vital signs are surprisingly normal, with two exceptions: his blood pressure is low and his brainwave activity is still climbing, violent spikes of power on the screen, almost past the machine's range.

You flip on the intercom. "Tyler?"

He does not respond, continues to rock, rock, rock, and with every movement you hear the crunch crunch crunch of glass.

What the Hell is happening?

Wipe your mouth as you think. Okay, calm down. He is alive. It was probably just a...

Hell, it could have been anything—a power surge, a momentary increase of amperage. For the feedback? Same thing: harmonic noise generated by the surge.

Who are you bullshitting? You have no idea what the Hell happened in there, do you? *Do you?*

Tyler is alive. That much you know. His vitals are fine, though you hear through the monitors some static. It takes you a moment to realize it is FM radio.

You cannot help but think for a moment of the FCC trying to triangulate the source of the broadcast, what they say when they saw Tyler—but they would call him Dr. Egar. That would be funny. Sort of. Funnier if you were on the outside of the situation, but still worth a chuckle. Until they asked what was going on. That would be bad.

You never questioned the legality of experiments of this nature in a residential area, but you think the Brackard's Point

PD would have serious objections, especially considering that Dr. Egar lost his funding from the state, and that he was paying you decently. You never asked where the money came from. You didn't want to know, just wanted to do your job and get your check every week. That's all.

Now this.

Someone is bound to have heard something, one of the neighbors. If they call the cops, you're fucked. You must get him up, make him respond, help clean the shit up and get the story straight for when they come to the door. Worry about the whys and wherefores of the whole thing later. It's all recorded onto the computers and tape anyway; you'll have time to review it.

You let the machines roll as you leave the Control Room.

You open the outside door to The White Room, close it behind you and hit the button before you. You hear the hissing of air, then the door in front of you opens. You step through the airlock.

"Tyler?" you call as you approach. There is no reverberation in the White Room. The walls and floor suck your voice away as it leaves your lips.

Crunch, crunch, crunch.

"Tyler!" You are almost to him.

"Dr. Egar?"

His eyes are open but blank, vacant.

He whispers something, some soft round sound, *foo* or *ooh*, or *you*. You ask him to repeat it. He does not.

"Tyler, talk to me. Are you all right?"

Are you all right? HA! As if. The banality of your question makes you want to laugh out loud. He is sitting in the middle of an illegal experiment room in his cellar, rocking back and forth on crushed glass, the lights and sounds around him are behaving unnaturally, and you ask him if he is all right.

Faintly, you hear music.

"You're nearly a real treat…"

The rest of the song is lost in static as his head moves.

"Tyler! Come on! Stop it! Cut the crap! This isn't funny. We've got a real problem here!"

157

He looks at you. He smiles.

"*...but you're really a cry.*"

(*My God, he's made it.*)

Tyler holds out his hand, slowly, as if he wants help out of the chair. He is smiling serenely. Never, on the look of any man have you seen an expression more peaceful, more tranquil save for in a painting. It hung in the classroom of your Sunday School when you were a child. You take his hand, help him up.

He stands but does not move. Glass falls to the floor, almost noiseless; the manufactured acoustics of the room destroy all but the initial tinkle as it falls. You look to the seat. Small red dots of Tyler's blood stand out on the white leather. Some are smeared into thin streaks. You look at his back. Glass is imbedded into his neck, his shirt, pants. Several places are bleeding slightly. It must hurt, at least sting, but Tyler does not seem bothered. He does not attempt to brush it off.

"What happened?"

His smile broadens into a grin.

The song playing through his teeth continues: "*Ha ha, charade you are.*"

He holds his arms out wide to either side and steps forward to embrace you. He places his forehead against yours and you are lost in the magnificent stare of his deep eyes.

Hum-mumm mumm, hum-mumm mumm...

The noise in the background reminds you of engines on a ship, a constant steady rolling throb, as you rock easily back and forth, back and forth.

Tyler is next to you. Floating, dreamlike, he is smiling. He nods and you hear, "*Isn't it wonderful?*"

You hear him but he does not speak. Telepathy?

"*Exactly.*" He nods as if you spoke aloud. "*Cyclic transmissions! You did it!*"

He beams proudly at you.

You are unsure, confused. Where are you? Where is the room? Where is everything?

"*Why would you question such a good thing?*" Tyler's voice speaks in your mind.

Good thing? Everything is GONE! You're floating in NOTHING!

"*Yes,*" Tyler says. "*Isn't it great?*"

No. It is not great. It is horrible. Everything you knew, gone. You are frightened, confused. You want to go back, back home, were things are seen and touched and you have to open your mouth to speak.

"*No,*" Tyler says. "*You're here now. There is no back. There is no one to take us back.*" He sees your expression. "*I thought you would handle this better than you are.*"

He thought wrong.

"I'll leave you for a while. You will get accustomed to this I must go over there," He points deep into the rolling mists. "That's where my subjects are."

"Crazy bastard!" you think. "You can't just leave me here!"

He can and does.

"Son of a bitch!"

You stand a moment, trying to decide what to do when you see movement out of the corner of your eye. You whirl around, and see something scuttling low through the mists. Something short, brown, human…you think. Hope.

You sense something coming at you quickly from behind. You duck, and see your enemy. A huge double-bladed battle axe is in your hand. You swing.

With the shimmering of steel on bone, you cut the first one down. Here comes another. And another, and another, and another. You swing and dodge and blood flies off your axe blade. You handle it as a master, arcing it toward their knees, forcing them to step back or become legless. A reverse upswing catches one in the armpit, and back down upon another and you sever his arm at the shoulder. They have long, forked grotesque tongues, spine-like teeth, clawed hands and reek of dead flesh. You chop and hack the ghouls, who, despite their number, fall to your blade one after another, their blood slinging off the curved edge to sting your eyes and slick your hands. You hear, lurking between their wounded cries of anguish and mortal agony, the steady, droning noise.

Hum-mummm, mumm, hum-mumm mumm...

You must concentrate to hear it; your mind reduces it to background noise, like the mindless babble of several people speaking at once, or the steady noise of traffic.

Through the creatures you travel. None survive; you are a god. From the mists they spring, and back to the mists they fall, gasping gurgling gushing blood.

You see their encampment ahead of you, their captive humans tied to posts. You run into the midst of the camp with your bloody axe high. Your battle cry comes from deep within your chest, and as you scream out your bloodlust, the remaining ghouls scatter demoralized at the sight and sound of their conqueror.

The men and women you release are thankful. They caress you, merciful tongues and lips kiss you, licking and nibbling, biting and sucking.

From within your belly your orgasm explodes and one of your lovers cries out. Their skin drips off their bones, and they melt away before your eyes. Another eagerly takes its place. They die smiling. They are honored to receive your baptism, cost to themselves be damned.

Hum-mumm mumm, hum-mumm mumm
Rock, rock, rock...

They love you. Everyone here loves you.

Hum-mumm mumm, hum-mumm mumm
Rocking and rocking and rocking
Crunch-crunch-crunch-crunch

Another begs to eat of your body.

You will allow it.

Rocking and rocking...

STRANGERS: GOOD FRIENDS AND A BOTTLE OF WINE

"Can I help you?"

"Holy shit, he's got a gun!"

"Terry, no!"

John had no time to turn before he heard gunshots. Two, maybe three. Someone screamed, someone swore. Something fell. Glass shattered, footsteps crunched wetly through broken liquor bottles.

He hit the deck in front of the cooler, quickly scuttled to the end of the aisle, hoped the shelves would conceal him. He felt vulnerable, exposed. From his position, Jon couldn't see the men, but heard their exchange with the cashier: demands for money, hurry the fuck up, her pleas to not be hurt. The drawer dinged open. They demanded more, she had none, that was all—and she could not open the safe: she'd just started the job, was not trusted with a key. Over this Jon heard someone else crying in hysterics over Terry: "Please, Terry, be all right," she said. "Please, Terry don't die. Hang in there, Terry. Terry? You listening to me, Terry? Don't you fucking die on me!"

"Bitch, shut the fuck up before I put a cap in your ass too—you all whining and shit is pissing me off," said another voice.

Both men were near the register, their attention drawn by the cashier, the drawer, and whoever was crying by Terry. John wondered if Terry was going to make it—whoever the hell Terry was.

"You! Into the office—show me where the fuck that recorder is. I see those damned cameras. And hey, yo—keep an eye on this bitch and the door," he said to his partner. "I'll be back in a second." Jon heard them move, the jangle of keys, a door opening, then closing.

Jon wished he had his gun on him. It was illegal to carry in the State of New York without another special permit. He was lucky he had the gun in the first place: it as damned tough to get a pistol permit in this state. Since he bought it, he'd kept it at home, like a good boy, all the while knowing scumbags like this were everywhere, carrying illegally. He never dwelled upon it, put it out of his mind, hoped he'd only need a weapon while at home. Yeah. Right. Lot of good it was doing him or anyone else there.

There was only one robber in the front of the store now, threatening the woman crying over Terry. Jon figured this was the best time to move. But where?

Down at the end of the wall, there was a door leading into the cooler. If he could get back there, another wall between him and the robbers, he'd be safer. Unless they searched the store. He didn't think so—they were going after the security camera tape now, and would probably be gone in a few minutes. If he stayed here, there was a chance of his discovery, and these did not seem like the type of guys who wanted a whole bunch of witnesses. Terry—poor bastard—had already been shot. God knows what was going to happen to the cashier and the woman crying over Terry's body. Would they kill them, too? John didn't know, but wouldn't put it past these scumbags. Regardless, they wouldn't appreciate another witness—particularly a guy. He had to move: staying here was stupid.

The cooler door was fifteen feet away. Jon started to crawl as silently as he could. He reached the end of the aisle, looked down toward the front of the liquor store. Terry was wearing sneakers and jeans, lying in a pool of spilled Jose Cuervo and blood. He saw the pantyhose-covered leg of the woman—she was wearing white ones and they had a run, had soaked up the fluids around her and started to stain. He could not see the woman's face, or her upper body, only the profile of one leg as the knelt over Terry. He could not see the robber either: the shelves were in the way. He could, however, see the door to the office, and the back of the other robber as he blasted the cashier in the face with his fist. He saw a flurry of blonde hair as she went down past the view of the window.

(*Quit watching. Move! Move!*)

Jon hid himself behind the next row of shelves, paused a moment to catch his breath—he did not realize he had been holding it. He wiped his hands on his shirt, left two smears of dirt from the floor down his chest. His back to the shelves, he faced the cooler. He could see the reflection of the robber now, as well as the woman who cried, and Terry. Terry was lying on his back, but Jon could not see if he was breathing or not. The robber wore a ski mask, long-sleeved button-down shirt, and loose, baggy pants. He held a pistol in his hand, pointed it at the woman's chest. The woman had a black shirt on, skirt, and dark brown shoulder-length hair. Her hands were to her face as she cried and screamed for Terry.

Terry looked dead. *Those bastards*, he thought as he watched her at on her grief. *Fucking bastards*. If he had his SIG P-220, he'd be able to blast the scumbag in the chest if he stood up straight, drop him with two .45's to the chest, and end this nightmare. But he couldn't, because it was illegal for him to carry. As illegal as it was, apparently, to shoot someone as you robbed a liquor store.

He watched her for another moment before the thought dawned on him—that he was looking at her reflection—that, from this angle, if she or the robber—turned, they would see *his* reflection off the glass.

"Oh, shit," he said to himself. Time to move. From his sitting position, he tried to lean forward and get his knees kicked out behind him, ready to crawl, but without making any noise. It was difficult. He shouldn't have sat down. That was dumb. But he needed to catch his breath—not again. He'd stay ready to move until he reached the cooler, and got inside. Then, he could relax a moment and catch his breath—hell, then, he could even call the cops on his cell phone.

Christ, I hope no one calls in.

He reached into his pocket and shut it off, congratulated himself for his quick thinking. Now he just had to stay alive long enough to use it—and that would take more than quick thinking. Doubt curled his forehead as fear broke in a cold sweat. *Just make it to the cooler*, Jon told himself. *Make it to the cooler and call the cops. End this nightmare.*

He glanced at the cooler door. The robber and woman faced each other. He thought the aisle was long enough so that his movement would not register in their peripheral vision. Hoped it would be as he forced himself forward, to pause behind the next row of shelves, but only for an instant as he heard no gasp of surprise or shouts to stop, no gunshots, no footsteps, so he kept going to the last aisle, then reached up and slowly opened the door, just a crack, enough to slip his body through. Once on the other side, he held his hand on the cold metal, easing it shut so he would not be given away by its slam, or a creak of hinges. The door shut.

John heard only the hum of the refrigeration equipment, felt the chill of the air around him. His forehead and armpits were sweaty, and instantly, he felt cold. But alive. He was in better shape than Terry, at least.

John looked around the cooler. Boxes of wines and beer were stacked upon each other against the back wall, plenty of room for further concealment. He nestled between two stacks of boxes, and took the cell phone out of his pocket. He turned it on and dialed 911.

"Police operator. What is your emergency?"

"I'm in the liquor store on the corner of Waters and Seymour. It's being robbed."

"Waters and Seymour. We had reports of gunshots. Officers have been dispatched and are *en route*. Is everything okay?"

They're already on the way! Oh, thank God. "Uh…one dude's been shot. I think he's dead. How long till the cops get here?"

"Just a couple minutes. How many people are in the store?"

"Three—well, four, if you count the shot guy. Me, the cashier, and this gal. They don't know I'm here. I'm hiding in the cooler."

"The perpetrators don't know you're there?"

"No. I doubt they'd be letting me make a phone call, ya know?"

"How many perpetrators are there?"

"Two—that I saw."

"And they're armed?"

"They shot the guy. You tell me."

"Hold the line, please. If you can. I'm going to relay the information to the officers, okay?"

"Yeah, yeah, sure, sure, whatever. Call 911, get placed on hold. That's cool."

The operator sounded annoyed. "One moment, please."

Jon rubbed his hands on his arms for warmth while he waited, muttered under his breath. The dispatcher returned after a few seconds. "Okay. Are you still there?"

"Yeah."

"I apologize for making you wait—but the officers *had* to know that information, you understand?"

"Yeah. I guess."

"It's going to be all right."

"Tell that to Terry."

"Terry?"

"The dude that got shot."

"You know the victim?"

"No. I heard the gal screaming his name, is all."

"Medical personnel are also coming," the dispatcher said. "Wait—the officers are right outside. Can you hear them?"

"No. I'm in the cooler. I can't hear shit but the fridge thing running. What's going on?" Jon stood, stepped forward to look through the cooler door over the tops of the bottles of wine. He knew no one could see him in there: the liquor store was brightly lit, and the back of the cooler was dark. The glare hid him. He could see the robber, standing, his gun to the woman's head, and the other one holding the cashier in front of him like a shield. They faced the front of the store.

I could get them from here, Jon thought. The way the robbers were facing, he'd be able to drop them both and not hit the cashier or the other woman. *Damnit!*

165

"Where *are* they?" he asked the dispatcher.

"They're right there. Apparently, there's a hostage situation going on. Where are you, in the building?"

"In the cooler. Oh, man. I could make this shot."

"North wall, south wall?"

"I didn't bring my compass and protractor, ya know? Christ. Umm…The cooler's on the right, if you walk into the place."

"Okay. Can you see the perps?"

"Yes."

"What're they doing?"

"Backing up," Jon reported. "They're moving against the far wall. They've got the women with them.

"Fuck," Jon said. 'I've gotta go."

"Are they moving toward your position?"

"Yeah. Get someone *in* here already!"

"Stay on as long as you can—"

Jon killed the phone call, shut the power on his phone back off. What fucking good were the cops going to do if they never came inside? Jesus! Why hasn't someone *stopped* these fucking guys already? What were they *waiting* for, a written invitation?

Jon turned, looked for the largest stack of boxes to hide behind. He ducked behind them just as the door to the cooler was opening. He held his breath, afraid the ghostly vapors from his mouth would give him away.

"Please don't hurt—"

"I said get the fuck in there!"

"Just listen to him!"

"But what about Terry?"

"Terry's fucking dead, you stupid bitch! Now get the fuck in the freezer and be lucky you're walking in, instead of feet first, you hear what I'm screaming?"

"FUCK YOU! You killed Terry!"

Jon heard the fist hit her, the *uugh* as she crumpled to the floor.

"Now don't you fucking move!" one of the robbers told her. "This ain't over yet."

166

Jon saw a line of light sweep across the wall as the door opened and closed, heard the women start a debate. They spoke in intense little whispers. Jon could not hear much: their words were lost beneath the refrigerator equipment's constant low drone. He detected no tones of comfort—their sentences were focused verbal exchange, aimed at a specific goal, trying to connect with something almost tangible: survival.

Jon listened to them whisper back and forth, heard the frustration mounting between them as their voices rose. They were like synapses trying to connect in a shattered mind, endlessly firing in the wrong direction, progressing only into further insanity. If they kept it up, they'd get themselves killed. And him too.

He stepped from behind the row of boxes and said, "Shh—I've called the cops."

Both women turned and stared at him with blank expressions. They sat on the floor, knee to knee as they faced each other. The woman in the skirt had streams of mascara down her face, her white stockings soaked in blood and spilled gin. The cashier had one eye swollen shut, a dribble of blood from her left nostril from when the bastard hit her.

"Holy SHIT!"

"Shh! Keep it down—they don't know he's here," said the cashier. "Do they?"

"No."

"How long have you been here?"

"The whole time. I hid in here right after the shooting started. Called the cops from my cell phone."

"The cops are outside."

'I know."

"Why aren't they coming in?"

"I don't know," Jon said.

"I do," said the cashier. "This is now a hostage situation. They're afraid they'd get us killed if they were to barge in here."

"They're probably right," Jon said.

"That's what I was trying to explain to her," the cashier said.

167

"Those fuckers killed my boyfriend."

"Shit," Jon said. "Sorry."

"I'd like to rip their nuts off."

"Guess you won't be going Patty Hearst on us, then?"

"Who?"

"Never mind."

"I don't suppose you have a gun or anything, do you?"

"Not on me. You kidding? You know what you have to *go* through to carry legally in New York State?"

"It was a thought," said the cashier.

"Yeah, well, this is the *last* time I leave the house without it, I'm here to tell you."

"You have one at home?"

"Yeah. SIG P-220. Lot of good it does us here."

"My boyfriend has a Ruger .22 out in the car."

"Lot of good that does us here," said the cashier.

"I don't know how to use it. That's what he was going for when..." She started to choke up.

The cashier reached out and hugged her. 'It's okay," she said.

"No, it's not!"

"Listen," Jon said. 'I'm sorry Terry got shot—but you've gotta hold it together. Really. Because if these guys could get away with it, they'd—"

The door to the cooler banged open.

"SHUT THE FUCK UP!"

One of the robbers entered the cooler, a pistol in one hand, a roll of duct tape in the other. He looked at Jon—hate-blue eyes locked on him from behind the ski mask. "Who the fuck are you?"

"I...I'm—"

The robber took a step forward. "How the fuck did you get in here?"

"I've *been*—"

Another step. "Motherfucker!" The robber raised his gun.

Jon leaped behind the boxes as the shots rang out. Cold wine cascaded down upon him, drenching his face. The women screamed. The other robber came rushing in, gun at the ready. "What the fuck?"

"Another fucking guy in here!"

"Are you crazy? Fuckin' police outside! Trying to get us *killed*, dumb-fuck?"

With the door open, Jon could hear the cops on a megaphone: "*What was that? Is everyone all right? We heard shots. I'm telling you guys, if we don't see those hostages* right now, *we're coming in.*"

"Tape him up with the rest. Bring 'em all out here. Fuck. Another goddamned hostage. Shit. This fucking sucks. Goddamnit! I'ma go talk to these pigs. Get 'em ready."

The robber ripped off a strip of tape and put it over Jon's mouth. The tape blocked part of his nose, too. It was difficult to breathe, and what air he *did* suck in tasted like wine and adhesive. Then, the robber wrapped a length of tape around his wrists, locking them behind his back. He covered the women's mouths next, then led them out of the cooler, single file. Jon at the lead, Terry's girlfriend in the back. The women's hands were not bound, he learned when the cashier gave his hand a squeeze as they were marched to the front of the liquor store.

The light hurt his eyes; he had become accustomed to the darkness of the cooler, but was thankful for the relative warmth. Though he went into the cooler by choice, no, soaked with wine and the seat of fear, he was glad to be out of it—it was far too much like a cell. He heard the other robber speaking to the police.

"Hey, yo…Easy, man. Nobody's hurt. Just saw a spider, is all. My partner hates bugs."

"Very funny. Where are the hostages? I'm going to count to five."

"Easy, easy. We're bringing 'em out now."

"*One.*"

"Hurry the fuck up, willya?" said the robber by the door to his partner.

"*Two.*"

"I'm coming!"

"Three."

The robber gave all of them a shove, and they stumbled toward the front. Jon stepped even with the door of the liquor store, saw the cops outside in their riot gear, shotguns and pistols held at a low ready. When he stepped into view, most lowered their weapons a moment. Thank God. He'd had one gun aimed at him today, and that was more than enough.

Never again. I ain't ever leaving the house without that goddamned gun again. Fuck these democrats wanting to make me a victim.

Jon nodded to the cops. They acknowledged him with subtle movements of hand and head. They knew they were hostages in there, and would not risk them unnecessarily. Just seeing them there gave him an overwhelming sense of relief. He did not want the cops to come in shooting, have himself get caught in the crossfire, and end up like Terry on the floor, there, cooling in a pool of blood and cheap booze. *Terry. Poor bastard.*

Jon didn't want to, but he looked anyway. A fly landed on Terry's neck, right at the entrance wound, and was busily rubbing its front legs together as it flitted around his skin. Jon wished he could shoo it off—it was wrong for the fly to be landing on Terry like that. Jon was offended by its audacity until he realized that he had never met Tery when he was alive—Terry was dead moments after the robbery began. He looked over toward Terry's girlfriend—whatever her name was. She refused to turn to see Terry's corpse. Just as well. Jon wanted to offer her a word of reassurance and comfort, but the sentiments wilted in his mouth, for her, like the others, was a duct tape mute.

The robber forced them back along the wall after showing them to the police outside, back toward the cooler. Jon felt disappointment rise within him as he was forced through the door and back into the chill. The wine soaking him felt as though it was turning to ice. He looked at the flesh of his arms. It was running a mottled shade of red and white, goose bumps standing out from his skin.

Once the door closed behind them, the robber bound the

women's hands. He made Jon sit on the floor with Terry's girlfriend, back to back, and then wrapped tape around them both. He checked the window to the store. Apparently, the cops hadn't entered yet.

Then he held his gun to the neck of the cashier. Tears ran down her cheeks, and she shook her head, no, no, please, but could say nothing as the barrel traced down her chest, between her breasts. Her nipples were hard from the cold, and pushed out of her uniform shirt.

Oh, for fuck's sake, Jon thought. He's not going to. *Not with the cops outside*.

Yes, he was. He unzipped his fly and dropped his drawers. The cashier screamed as best she could from behind the duct tape. The robber ripped through the fly of her pants and yanked them down. She tried to struggle, kick him off, but with her pants around her ankles, she lost her balance and stumbled back into a case of white wine. Only one or two of the bottles broke. White mixed with the red on the floor: rose *a la* concrete.

The robber pinned her down and mounted her.

Jon stood, dragging Terry's girlfriend up with him. She was petite, didn't weigh a hell of a lot to slow him down. As the robber was forcing his way into the cashier, Jon drew back his right leg and kicked him in the ribs, just below the armpit. The robber cried out, then spun off the cashier, grabbing his weapon off the floor. He turned, aimed at Jon— for the second time—and fired.

Getting shot was nothing like Jon expected. He felt like he'd been hit with a baseball at the exact time he was burnt with the hot tip of a fireplace poker. The bullet was lodged in his shoulder. His left arm flared in pain, then went numb. If it weren't held in place by the duct tape, it would be hanging limp at his side.

The robber negotiating with the cops could not justify the second shot. They gave him until five. Then they came in shooting.

***

The bullet in Jon's shoulder sent him to the hospital. They operated, removed the offensive piece of lead, kept him for observation for 24 hours, then sent him home, where detectives from the Brackard's Point PD waited for him. Could he come in to the station as a witness? Make a statement? Of course, of course. They even offered to drive him—how sympathetic.

The cashier was leaving the station when he arrived. She recognized him, gave him a hug, careful around the wounded shoulder, thanked him for his intervention. He downplayed it, said he didn't do anything special. She insisted he did, threw the word "hero" about no less than three times in as many sentences. Jon didn't feel like one, and told her so. As they were starting to launch into a real conversation, the previously sympathetic and understanding cops became impatient and annoyed, urged the two to hurry it along. The cashier reached into her purse, wrote down her number and handed it to him. "Gimme a call," she said.

Jon took the piece of paper, looked at the name and number.

"Nice to finally meet you, Meg. I'm Jon."

"Gimme a call, Jon."

"You bet."

Jon replayed the entire ordeal for the detectives—all he could remember. He omitted nothing. They seemed most interested in the details surrounding Terry, which, for Jon, was a large blank. He hadn't seen it happen, only heard Terry's girlfriend screaming, a point he had to explain numerous times. He mentioned the irony of never knowing anyone else's name—only the dead guy's—then apologized for sounding callous. The detectives forgave him. The older of the two even laughed at the irony, once pointed out.

"I'd like to thank you for coming in," the detective said as the interview (Jon felt it was like an interview, even if they insisted it was "making a statement") concluded. "I realize going through this all again is difficult for you, but it does help us out a lot."

"I don't get it," Jon said. "I *saw* the guys go down as you came in. What's left to prosecute?"

"One of them is in ICU," the cop explained. "He might make it."

"No shit?"

"None."

"Which one?"

"The one who tried raping Miss Carter."

Jon's fists clenched. "Too bad."

"I can understand how you feel."

Jon looked the cop in his flat, cold eyes.

"No, you can't."

***

Jon and Meg's first date started at the Café Xelucha over double tall Americanos and scones, then progressed to Gethsemane Cemetery. They stood at the gates, but did not enter as a dark motorcade parade of limousines passed, lights on, through the day was as bright and the weather as fair as New York's geography permitted—especially in Brackard's Point, where Hook Mountain loomed over from the west to cast dusk early.

They didn't know Terry. Neither had the stomach to attend his funeral, yet both felt obliged to pay him *some* type of respect. They said their final words to the memory of a stranger in silence. They turned their heads and watched the hearse enter the cemetery, followed it with their eyes as it wound down the gravel path, twisting around through rows of tombstones and concrete angels.

From there, Jon and Meg walked for a while, no destination in particular, found themselves sitting on a bench at the War Memorial Park, sharing life stories as they watched the sailboats and ships out on the Hudson. She told him how she almost made it onto the television show *Castaways*, for the doomed seventh season, how broke up she was about it, yet thankful at the end, considering how it all turned out. He told her about his teaching job, how he'd been at the World Trade Center the day of the murders, leading his class on a field trip when the first plane hit.

After a lull in the story-swapping, Meg looked at Sing-sing, the state penitentiary in Ossining, on the Hudson's other bank. "You think they're gonna send that son of a bitch there?"

"I hope he gets the chair," Jon replied.

"You and me, both."

"You don't think there's any chance he'll get off, do you?"

"If he does," Jon said, "I'll be ready for him."

"What do you mean?"

Jon opened his jacket. Meg looked in, saw the handle of his SIG. "Illegal or not, no damned politician is going to force me to be a victim again."

"You ain't worried about getting caught with it?"

"More worried about needing it and not having it."

Meg nodded. 'I hear you there. I'm glad you have it on you," she said.

"Yeah?"

"Yeah. Feels a lot safer. After last week, I didn't know if I could ever feel safe again."

Jon didn't know what to say, so he held her. As she nuzzled against his neck and placed her leg over his, he knew he'd done the right thing. They stayed that way until the shadows from Hook Mountain grew long. The sun was two hours away from setting, but the cliff to the west darkened the streets early. With the sunlight almost gone, the wind blowing down the Hudson, they started to get cold.

"Dinner?" Jon asked.

"Sure—I don't live too far from here. I've got plenty at the house, couple steaks, some chicken I oughta cook up sometime soon. A few bottles of wine."

"You mean dinner at your place?"

"Yeah," Meg said. "It'll be safer." She patted his gun through his jacket, and stood. She led him up by holding his hand. Jon rose without understanding what she meant. He was going to ask, but decided that it didn't matter. Instead, he asked: "White or red?"

THE MISSIVE

The object was passed into the collector's hand in the dimly-lit corner of a twenty-four-hour convenience store. The kid who handed it to him was all lean muscle and danger.

"Where'd you come across this?"

"The Hudson," the kid said. "Down between Nyack and Piermont."

"I see," the collector said, nodded his head.

"So…You want it or not?"

"I do—if it's legit," the collector said. "But I have to be sure. We're talking a fair sum. I'm sure you can understand that I'd need to verify the authenticity."

"Okay," the kid said. "But how do I know you're not just going to bail?"

"A deposit," the collector said. "Half in cash. The other half a check, postdated two weeks."

"Like I'm going to be able to cash a check for a quarter-million dollars? Have you lost your shit?"

Despite the coarseness, the kid had a point…but the thing really looked like the real deal. The collector shrugged his shoulders. "Do you have another suggestion?"

The kid lit a cigarette. Exhaled. "Yeah. Half now. And your car. The rest when you get your results. I saw the thing fall. I know it's legit."

"My…car? Young man, this is a 1960 Porsche 356. No offense, but you driving this will attract a lot more attention than you trying to cash a quarter-million dollar check."

"Old man," the kid said, mirroring the condescension, "This is a Kimber .45 caliber pistol and it'll earn you a fuck of a lot of attention because you'll be the motherfucker with the huge-ass hole in his fuckin' head. You dig? So hand me the cash, hand me the keys, and let's get on with it."

"I don't suppose you'd be troubled to give me a ride home?"

The kid flicked his cigarette into a puddle. It hissed as the ember died. He grinned. "Sure thing," he said, and waited for the keys to be placed in his hand.

The collector surrendered them with reluctance, and concentrated on the cylinder throughout the drive. It broke his heart to glance over and see his car driven by this little fuck who couldn't fathom the significance.

***

Inside: a sealed vial of greyish/reddish soil, and the following:—

28 May, 2082
Mons Olympus Colony
4th Stone From The Sun
Solar System
Milky Way

Population of Earth
3rd Stone From the Sun
Solar System
Milky Way

FORWARDING ADDRESS REQUESTED (hahaha)

I'm sending off these canisters as a secondary measure via centrifugal launch; this is a transcript of the speech I made to Earth via satellite last night.
Just in case you missed it.
Kenny Jeter

Greetings From Mons Olympus!
How are you feeling? Warm? Cozy? In your home? Family around? Maybe you're at work as you watch this.
It's cold out here.

It's rough.

We want to come back home. To see the Earth again, to feel grass under our feet and swim in the water. To breathe the air. But we can't. Or won't when we get there. Thanks a lot.

Allow me to introduce myself. I'm Kenny Jeter. I was elected by default to send this message because I'm still alive, and can still speak clearly enough into the microphone to be understood.

I was on the third voyage of the Ursula to the Mons Olympus colony out here on Mars. The rough part had already been done: the housing set up, the permafrost layer tapped so water was flowing, the generators installed and on-line, the communication satellites in orbit, hydroponics farms operational.

We had air and water, artificial atmosphere, and we could even go outside with only a minimal suit—nothing like those big, bulky pressure suits the first crew out here had to wear so their blood wouldn't boil in their veins. We had it made.

You might remember us for having the first Martian wedding: in 2062, Billy Grader married that Russian gal, Natasha Markovlin. If you remember us for the wedding, congratulations: you're one of the good people left in the world. Mark your door with the blood of a lamb.

Most of you on that overpopulated cesspool of a planet wouldn't remember the wedding at all. Most of you were probably too busy polluting that Hellhole and making more kids to make it that much more unlivable. Most of you probably remember the story of the comsatellite taking a hit from an asteroid, and how contact with us was lost. All the computer-enhanced diagrams of the asteroid belt between us and Jupiter seemed to support that, didn't it? Of course it did. If we hadn't known better, we would have believed it, too. Well, obviously the asteroid story wasn't the case. No, the United States and Russian governments both found it beneficial to turn the comsats off when they found out what happened. That was fourteen years ago, back in '68.

We've been busy out here. We had a little meeting, and we all decided that this was how it was gonna happen: we'd launch our own satellites, control them from here. Sure, it took a lot of the energy that would have went to the life support, but with all of us dying off the way we were, we didn't need all that support on account of there not being as much life. Fuel to launch them we tapped ourselves, hydrogen mined from the ground here.

Oh, that's impossible you say, no one could do that kind of gas mining out there; the extreme cold and UV radiation would kill whomever in minutes, right?

Right. And that's what I'm getting to. We were dying.

There is life on Mars. It's a virus, which Dr. Alexander Wolcott identified and dubbed Mayflower. That's a joke, folks. He took one look at that thing, and knew we were in for it. I ain't no biologist, but this is how it was explained to me. The Mayflower is what we think made the Viking probe go nutty when it took that soil sample back in the 1900's, I forget when. I never was good at Early Martian History. Mayflower reproduces at an alarming rate when the temperature is above 20° Celsius. How it kills you is pretty neat: it doesn't do anything particularly nasty. You don't feel sick at all, other than a mild fever. It seeks out the bloodstream, and there reproduces through all your red blood cells. Within six hours, your entire system is infected. You breathe, but Mayflower-infected red blood cells cannot hold oxygen.

You choke. You fall down. Go boom.

This is when the comsats supposedly cut out on us. This is the part you, in your comfortable little air and water glob of pollution and overpopulation missed. Both the US and the Russian governments deemed it "inappropriate for the mass populous" to view, so they swept us all under the rug—the big, black rug of space, where no one's going to go check, where they won't send anyone to check, because, with a handy-dandy little asteroid story, it all seems perfectly plausible. Oh, yes, we know, we up here know they organized a mass grieving session, a few forked-tongued politicians made heartfelt speeches with their crocodile tears, and it's such a tragedy that the entire colony has been cut off from us, We Who Care So Deeply About Our Comrades Up In The Mons Olympus Colony.

We also know you all bought into it. You re-elected them, didn't you?

This is what you missed: You get back up a few hours later. The corpses of the folks killed by Mayflower do not stay dead. They reanimate.

Imagine our horror when the first few of them came a-walking after they've been tagged RHC. The first few we killed. Again. But that did not work either. We dismembered them, and that seemed to work rather well, but the pieces themselves kept moving, squiggling little blobs of human flesh, and the virus then seemed to spread even faster—more surface area to get loose, someone theorized, and I can't say as I disagree with them. We burned the bodies, too—and you must know how precious air is here for a mass-conflagration, but we were desperate—but the virus took to the air then, in the smoke, and we inhaled it and infection through your lungs is even faster than if it's introduced directly into the bloodstream through a wound.

Whatever we tried to do, we wound up killing ourselves quicker, and more of the Mayflower colonists were dying and rising again every moment. It was an epidemic—families were wiped out over the course of an evening: little girls biting their mother's breasts to get to the good, non-infected blood, and the mothers then infecting their sons, brothers against brothers, husbands against wives, and everyone basically against each other. A couple of the old military geeks tried heavy ordinance against them, but they, too, wound up taking the fall. I watched my father go nutty as my mom scratched our window every night until he finally locked me in the closet and went to her, tears in his eyes. He hugged her for a long time before she bit him. She returned the hug.

I did not want to set my ma and pa on fire, or cut them up in little pieces. So while she was biting him, and he laying in her arms, crying, dying, I instead ran and hid in the hydroponics farm, where a couple of others had hid themselves, too, but they found us there. We fought the dead. And lost. And the dead grew stronger as we grew weaker by exact proportion.

When there were a thousand or so of us left, after a month and a half of the madness, we arranged a meeting with the former colonists, the resurrected corpses.

Dr. Wolcott acted as their spokesman (he was infected a few days after he identified the virus by his assistant, who bit him hard and deep in the neck), and for us, it was Dr. Kelly Dunbar, daughter of the astronaut who led the first manned landing in the Great Rift.

We decided that the most heinous crime of all of this was not the spreading of the disease; after all, Mayflower infection is a disease, and those infected are sick, untreatable, but sick. Dead, but nonetheless, sick. The crime, really, was that we were sent out here into this hostile environment without being told, exactly, what that Mariner Lander found in that soil. They found Mayflower, and you didn't tell us. You sent us up here anyway, to give you a new planet to destroy. We don't belong here. Mankind was not supposed to tread these arid cold deserts, see Phobos and Deimos rise under a red sky.

Us and the Mayflower Zombis reached an agreement.

We're coming home. The dead manned the mines, assembled the panels and thrusters and all the things that, out here, would kill us live ones. We live ones hooked up the computers, electrical connections, and so forth because our better manual dexterity. We made the perfect team.

Once each man's job was finished, he joined the dead. His loved ones took him—it was easier to go unto those you love than strangers—and cared for him while he died, and kept vigil until he rose again.

The next launch window is in 5 days, 17 hours and 28 minutes. We're going the quick route: using a whole lot of fuel, but for us, it won't matter. It's not like we'll need Life Support.

As I said, I'm the last one left, and as soon as I step aboard the ship to carry us back to earth, they will bite me. I've made it clear: I want my ma to do it. You should have seen her as she took my father: I never saw her more happy.

I want her to be proud of me. I want to make her smile.

And when we finally reach earth—in about 7 months with our hydrogen ion engine—I hope you'll want to make us smile, too.

We're happy to come home.

***

The collector's phone rang. He glanced at the number before answering.

"Hello, Rigel."

"Yeah. Hi. What the Hell did you send me?"

"So," the collector said, "I'm assuming the soil sample is authentic?"

"Oh, yeah…it's authentic as Hell. I could care less about that. I'm talking about the microbe? What the Hell is it?"

"The future," the collector said. "It's the future."

The collector completed the conversation, and placed the sample on his shelf alongside the Mustard Gas, the VX, Anthrax, and Sarin, bookended between the injector nozzles from a V2. He sat in his leather recliner, dreamed of the day he would open them all, and smiled at the prospect.

He called the kid.

"You got the rest of my money?" the kid said.

"Of course. I do apologize for the delay."

"It's not a problem. I've been driving the shit out of this car…the chicks really dig it."

The collector managed not to crush the phone in his grip. "That's nice," he said, and glanced over to the shelf. "Why don't you come by and we can finish the transaction?"

"Be there in 45 minutes."

"I'm looking forward to it," the collector said. His eyes never left the vial. Not for a second.

181

JOLERARYMI'S ROSE

Zul-Bha-Sair's walls and towers loomed over the Celotian waste. Under Zothique's dying sun, the city's shadows and the Celotian's red sands congealed to dark clots. Irregular buildings protruded like fragments of bone from a wounded earth. Zul-Bha-Sair had one deity—Mordiggian—whose name and reputation (a demon, a ghoul of grandiose proportions and appetite) were whispered through the twisted maze of snakelike streets. Mordiggian claimed all Zul-Bha-Sair's dead; he was the only thing constant in the city. When the cooling ember sun winked out, and Zothique was cast into the nether-black, Mordiggian would claim all who died within his walls. His priests wore robes of black, their faces never seen; always, they hid behind masks of polished metal cast in horrible grinning skulls. They were walking servants of death. If the city had an anthem, it would be in minor key, its lyrics gloomy harmonies to murder smiles. It would be of fear, of death, of hopelessness. It would be a dirge.

If the sculptor Jolerarymi were to sing the song, his voice would be choked with dust from the stones he worked. He was not rich; his usual earnings were enough to buy food of questionable freshness. He always managed to afford a small token gift for is woman, the beautiful Sheleen, even if it meant he went hungry.

Sheleen made more in two hours on her back than he did at the stones all day. Her swollen breasts and sensuous curves fetched a high price in the marketplace. Sheleen's lips promised ecstasy. She always delivered. In bleak Zul-Bha-Sair, anything *close* to joy was worth paying for—at almost any price.

Of the two sculptors in Zul-Bha-Sair, Jolerarymi was the superior. But his competitor, Fetlicad, ruled the sculptor's market by both blade and coin. What Fetlicad would not buy, he could kill. The only place Jolerarymi sold his work was the one institution Fetlicad dared not intimidate: The Temple of Mordiggian.

Jolerarymi still shuddered at the sight of the skull-masked priests, Mordiggian's minions, but not without guilt. Their calling on him was work; it was money for himself, a gift for Sheleen, payment on completion. They kept him alive. He still shuddered.

He was working on a brazier-mount for their temple, one that had been broken under a rumor-shrouded incident. He asked no questions, did what he would eventually be paid for, kept his eye out for the newcomer or the out-of-towner that Fetlicad had not gotten to yet. Someone to pay him a retainer, enough for a meal and a small flask of Yorosian wine for Sheleen. They happened by sometimes. Sometimes: not often enough. He returned his attention to chiseling out the brazier-mount, throwing up chips of stone and dust that stuck to his sweat. It was then Sheleen walked in.

"My love," he smiled, setting down the chisel to embrace her.

"Don't," she said. "You'll get prints all over me. I'm going to the market." She was dressed for the part: coquettish curves barely covered, her lithe body lusting for attention.

"You need money? I have none."

"None?"

Jolerarymi shook his head.

"So what is that?" she asked, pointing to the work in progress.

"A brazier mount for Mordiggian's templ—"

"Stop!" she held her hands over her ears. "Say no more. I never want to hear that ghoul's name in my presence. Did they *pay* you for it?"

"On completion, my love."

She smiled at his affection. "But darling," she said. "I need money *now*."

"I cannot help you."

"Aah," her grin was wicked. "You can. You still have

the cot in the back, do you not?" Her leg wrapped around him, lewdly rubbed his groin. Her tongue licked his earlobe, tasting dust. He stood rigid. Her breath iced his nerves. She nibbled. "Do you not?"

His posture collapsed. "I really wish you wouldn't," he said.

"Do I have a choice?"

Jolerarymi did not answer. It was his fault they were poor. One day, she wouldn't have to do this for money.

One day…

He sighed. "If you must."

With a quick kiss, a flickering of tongue that sent him spiraling, she was out in front of his shop, brandishing herself to the men in the marketplace. Within one minute, she had a customer and had taken him into the back of his shop to ply her trade.

He gritted his teeth and tried not to feel jealous as he overheard the man's thrusting grunts, her moans, the sucking of air between her teeth. The hand holding the chisel went numb. He stood paralyzed.

(*It's your fault, you're poor. She deserves better. You make her do this.*)

She was, at least, kind enough to favor him before she left to spend the man's money on spices and perfumed oils. As she sunk to her knees where he stood, Jolerarymi tried to close off his thoughts when he shut his eyes. What relief finally came from him was insignificant to the distress he felt.

After her departure, he attacked the stone, hammer and chisel flying in anger. Each stroke he made, he thought of *them*, the sounds he heard. (*Were they false? Did she ENJOY it?*). Hissing in between her teeth, sucking in, her cries… He smashed the chisel one final time and stood, unable to concentrate.

He told himself he was going into the back to collect his thoughts, in case that rare out-of-towner walked in. It would not do if he were distraught talking to a customer. Bad business.

(*What business? There's more being made on that cot*

than from your hands!)

The smell of their sex hung in the air. The cot.

He looked. Stained. Several wet spots. They could not all be from the man.

He flipped it over so he did not have to look at the offensive sight of it; his fingers grasped a spot particularly damp. He slammed it to the ground. Again, again, and yet again, he smashed the cot. It splintered, bedding scattered, the supports cracked, fell to pieces. He kicked the larger chunks into the corners of the room. Then, having nothing left to break, he sat down on his workbench, placed his stone-dusted hands over his face and cried.

He heard a sound from the front of the shop: the shuffling of feet. Realizing that he had a visitor, he stood, made motions of eye-drying and regaining his composure. A man dressed in extravagant robes of orange velvet trimmed with brocade: raised patterns of rich shining yellow shot through blue silk. The robe hung heavily at cuff and hem; there was little doubt in Jolerarymi's mind that the brocade thread was pure gold. The man regarded him with a kind smile. "You *are* the sculptor Jolerarymi, correct?"

"I am."

"Excellent! I am Imecnis, emissary of King Dotuunet of Ehcac. The Emperor of Xylac shall be visiting our palace, and King Dotuunet wishes to impress him with, and I quote him, ' a statue from a foreign land fit for the Emperor's eyes to behold,' and so, I am here to see if you would be interested in creating such a sculpture."

"I would be interested, yes."

"Wonderful!" Imecnis said, and slyly added, "I do so much love to spend my king's money, because he is so loathe to part with it." The emissary laughed, and gave Jolerarymi a wink. "Good. Your retainer." The man placed not a purse but a *bag* of coin on the table. "I trust this will cover all expenses. Count it if you must."

"A retainer?" It seemed more as the entire fee. Never had he been paid so much. He looked at Imecnis, suspicious. "But we haven't even—"

Imecnis held his hand, silence. "This shall be one-tenth of your fee, no more. Will you accept my offer of my king's money?"

Jolerarymi could only stare at the bag, trying to fathom how much was in there. *If this is one-tenth...* His head swam. "I will, with thanks," the sculptor said.

"Very well then!" Imecnis smiled. "Deliver it to Ehcac within six months, and you may collect the rest of your fee."

"I surely will!" Jolerarymi licked his lips, opened the bag. It was more than he made the previous year, perhaps the one before as well. He dug his hands in, pulled up heavy handfuls of sparkling coin which fell, tinkling merrily. The sound was like foreign music, the weight, the *smell*, all too much for him. This money changed everything. Sheleen would never have to whore herself again; other men's moans would not longer haunt him. Happiness was his. "Thank you, my lord. thank you." On his knees in the dust of his shop, overcome with joy and gratitude, Jolerarymi wept.

Imecnis, himself embarrassed, told Jolerarymi to rise, grabbing him by the side, and helping him to stand. He smiled. "You are very, very welcome."

"If I may ask, how did you come about my name?" Jolerarymi asked as he wiped his cheeks. Aware of the spectacle he created, he felt like a fool.

"The priests in the death-mask recommended you to me."

"The priests of Mordiggian?" Jolerarymi looked at him in surprise. "You spoke with them?" He could not believe it. Men who lived their entire lives in Zul-Bha-Sair did not venture to the dread god's temple. They feared a visit in return. Mordiggian's name was death. To himself, the sculptor said, "I must thank them, then, as well."

"I'd not like to, either, but it is the right thing to do," Jolerarymi said.

Imecnis smiled, and said, "Noble artisan. Excellent! Conniptions! Dotuunet will pull his *hair* out when I tell him how much you cost!" The emissary bid him farewell, and left the shop, humming a happy tune from his homeland.

He did not want to go to Mordiggian's temple. Sheleen

would knock him senseless if she found out he had been *near* the place. Mordiggian terrified her. But guilt, the tugging guilt he felt... Mordiggian's priests had been good to him. They brought him business when he was starving. Now they had made him rich. Such kindness could not go unnoticed, un-thanked. Guilt. Remembrances of hungry nights, only able to buy the cheapest token gifts for Sheleen, horrible guilt, the disappointment in her face when she saw what he had brought. Guilt.

He filled both his pockets, having no purse of his own. Then, he buried the bag under the table, and closed his shop for the day. Jolerarymi squinted, noticed the failing sun's position in the sky, the red and purple shadows which were creeping across the marketplace. He had to hurry if he wanted to reach Mordiggian's temple before dark.

As he walked towards it, he asked himself if he honestly wanted to reach it at all. He felt compelled to thank the priests who recommended him, but was afraid of them, as all sane men were. Only fools did not fear death, only madmen dwelled on things worse. Jolerarymi tried not to think of any of them as he walked to Mordiggian's temple.

In the blocks approaching the temple, Jolerarymi saw fewer and fewer people. The closer he came, the less were his chances were of seeing a *living* being. Fear kept the streets empty and quiet.

The black polished pavement of the courtyard reflected his steps alone. Mordiggian's temple was a giant tomb, wide, low and flat. He knew the god was close. He could *feel* Mordiggian's presence. The god's power hovered about the temple like an invisible mist, grasping his spine with cold hands.

He began to ascend the steps. The darkness beyond the pillars front of him was so complete it was almost tangible. It was more than the *absence* of light; it was as if the place *repelled* it, banishing it to happier realms. There was no joy or mirth here—only the dead, the god which presided over them.

Movement!

Sound! A black blur leapt from behind a pillar, a flutter of wind through robes. Jolerarymi cried out in fright, stumbled backward, lost his balance on the steps. He fell, landing in an aching knot on the black rock. He looked up; one of Mordiggian's skull-masked priests stared down. Cold yellow eyes challenged him.

"I wanted to give thanks," Jolerarymi said as he got to his feet. "For recommending me to the outlander." He offered up a few coins, and began to approach.

The priest violently waved the coins away. In a growling/ hissing voice that snapped at the end of words: "Mordiggian has no need for your money. Go, sculptor. Thank him when you die."

Jolerarymi left immediately, with fright-accelerated steps. He looked over his shoulder, expecting to see a skull-masked priest pursuing, but there was none. Mordiggian and his priesthood had no concern with the living. They only cared about the dead. The closer he got to the market, the less frightened he was, and, once he *reached* the market and began to tell the whole tale, it had a macabre humor.

"You are mad for going near Mordiggian's temple," the silk merchant said, " to visit Mordiggian is to receive a visit in return, you know."

"Rumors," Jolerarymi said, lying to the merchant and himself. "Rumors for the ignorant."

"I believe them," said the silk merchant, but then congratulated him on his good fortune. Jolerarymi purchased the most exotic silks, whose price was always beyond his or Sheleen's reach. Then he went and visited most of the merchants in the market, telling the tale of his good fortune, buying the things Sheleen always wanted but could never afford.

In a city as dreary and as hopeless as Zul-Bha-Sair, good news was a commodity rarely offered in the marketplace. Through the city's narrow, winding streets, whispers carried Jolerarymi's name. His good fortune spread. By the time he reached home, Sheleen had already heard.

"You are rich," she grinned: greed barely diluted with

pride and adoration.

"I am, my love, and I've brought you these." He pointed to the cart full of things he had bought for her.

She kissed him passionately, swearing to *never* take another man to her bed, no matter *what* price he offered. She tried on the things he bought for her, smelled the exotic spices from Xylac and Cincor. Together, they drank the finest wines of Yoros. The silks he purchased for her were employed for more sensual pleasures than he ever imagined. Giddy, drunk, and drained, Jolerarymi lay in bed with Sheleen in his arms, convinced heaven was his. Her body was warm against his, their legs over, over, under, over, under, under: a lover's knot. He doused the oil lamp, then placed his arm around her to cross between her breasts, his hand finding comfort in the soft warm flesh. He took one final smell of her hair, and slept.

A sound awoke him in the middle of the night—someone trying to break in. He dressed, took with him one dagger, and went to chase them off. He came fully around the property, where two men dressed in slave's garb were trying to force the back door. They did not run as he had hoped, but rather moved in, splitting themselves to either side of him. These were not thieves. They were assassins. Like jackals, they attacked, drawing him towards one, while the other struck from behind. A tremendous blow to the back of his head brought him to his knees. Then, he noticed the third figure approaching. Fetlicad.

His rival grinned evilly. "It seems the priests of Mordiggian favor thee," Fetlicad drew a blade, and Jolerarymi saw its keen edge dripped poison; it smelled like decaying flowers. Fetlicad placed the knife against Jolerarymi's chest, and said, "You were to make a sculpture for a king, but you'll be a corpse for a whore."

The venom-soaked blade slipped between Jolerarymi's ribs. He had time to cry out once. Jolerarymi's final note of anguish echoed through the winding twisting streets, ricocheting off the high walls, rolling through the darkness; it died long after he did. When the poison touched his heart, it seized.

Sheleen woke to the sound of his scream. She lit the lamp, and reached for her dagger, but it was gone, he took it with him. She was looking for it when she heard Fetlicad and his two slaves enter, dragging Jolerarymi's corpse behind them. She screamed when she saw he was dead.

"Silence, whore!" Fetlicad smacked her. "I want the money. Where is it?"

She did not answer directly. Fetlicad turned the knife to her. He slipped it under her nose. "So you smell that?" he asked. "That is the poison which killed your precious Jolerarymi. Look at him."

She smelled it. She had no choice. Jolerarymi's blood, and another cloying scent—roses infected with festering mold; sweet, but sickly, deadly.

"Aah," Fetlicad smiled. "You do. That froze Jolerarymi's heart solid like a stone. It will do the same to you. The money? Where is it?"

Sheleen still said nothing.

Fetlicad pressed the blade a little harder against her nose. "The money, whore. Or do you want to join him? Mordiggian will have—"

At the mention of the god's name, Sheleen flinched, and finally spoke. "Do not mention that foul name in my house."

"Who holds the knife, whore? Where is the money? Tell me or I will summon Mordiggian's priests myself for you."

"Must you torture me?"

"The money!"

"In his shop! Under the table! No go. You've taken everything."

Fetlicad eyed her cleavage. Her fearful sweat shone in the oil-lamp's light. "Not everything," he said. The three of them had her simultaneously. When they had done, purple bruises marked her eyes, her lip was swollen and her throat red. The slave would have choked her to death if Fetlicad had not stopped him. She did not understand why she had been spared at first. He told her soon enough.

"Take his body out of the city," Fetlicad said. "Bury it. If Mordigg—"

At the god's name, Sheleen covered her ears, cringed. "Not in my house, damn you!"

Fetlicad grabbed her arms, and pinned them to her sides. She struggled, but he held her. He grabbed her chin, snapped her head to face him. Out came the envenomed knife. "If the priests find out of this, If I am even *questioned...*"

He did not have to finish the threat. His intention was clear. "I have no intention of feeding that monster," Sheleen said.

"Good," Fetlicad grinned. "Because you know the punishment for robbing our god of his sacred cadavers is death."

"He is not my god."

Fetlicad grinned. Sheleen knew he was mentally recording every word to hold against her. His word against hers. The word of a wealthy, feared man, or a marketplace whore. *Correction*, she thought. *Blaspheming marketplace whore*. Her loathing of Mordiggian was well known. Fetlicad had chosen his tactics well. She sneered as he left, and spit on the ground. Her saliva was tinged with blood.

When Jolerarymi's murderer left, Sheleen went out into the night, and traded herself for a camel and wagon. She returned, wrapped Jolerarymi's body in a blanket to hide it from view. If anyone saw his corpse they would detain her and call the priests; if the priests were called, as Fetlicad said, she was a dead whore. She filled the wagon with things for a journey: food, water, blankets for herself, her most precious spices and perfumes and wines; piling all of these on top of Jolerarymi's body to further conceal it. She stole out from the city, riding north through the wasteland desert.

She finally came to a small town near Ehcac. She set about earning money the only way she knew how, and did it with such fervor that questions of why finally arose. She told those that asked she was trying to earn money for a decent sarcophagus for her deceased beloved.

One man, who insisted she lay perfectly still while he mounted her, asked a question in return: "Why bury him?"

"What do you mean?"

"I am Dentril, a necromancer, and I propose a trade. Allow me your services for one week, and I will raise your beloved from his deathly slumber. What say you?"

Sheleen considered this. (*All the lovely things he bought me*). "And you can bring him back? Make him whole?" she asked.

Dentril said, "Whole I cannot make him, but animate? Yes. That I can perform easily. How will *you* perform in return? That is what I wonder."

"Perform your ritual first," she said, "let me see it done, and, if he wakes, then I shall do as you ask."

Dentril's smile revealed age-stained teeth. "Come, then, to my home."

***

At the necromancer's gate stood two statues whose cold-hewn faces stared at those entering. They appeared less of sentries of stone, but more of judges: condemning; damning. Sheleen tried to avoid their grave stares but they were always looking, always watching.

More statues adorned the necromancer's courtyard: grotesque idols of Thasaidon, Lord of Hell, lesser demons without names. Their horrible faces showed exquisite workmanship—hideous visages crafted by master artisans. She was both impressed and repulsed. Two men shaggily approached. Dentril instructed them to stable the animal, bring her things inside, and carry Jolerarymi's corpse to his study. Emotionless, they accepted their duty and carried it out. Sheleen knew they were dead. Necromancy made them slaves.

"Would they do everything you ask?"

"Everything I would ask them to, yes," said the necromancer.

A grinning rotted female greeted them at the door; her ribs were alive with maggots. The woman's smile was permanent—her lips had been removed. "My guest and I shall dine in my chambers in one hour," he said, and the woman turned to go. "But," he called after her, "bring wine to the study at once." The woman did not turn or nod acknowledgement, but mutely set out to carry out the order.

Sheleen followed to the study. Jolerarymi's body lay on the floor. She sat, and the woman who met her at the door brought her wine in a cup of silver. Sheleen did not thank the corpse, but rather its master. The woman left bloated maggots squirming on the floor—her passage marked by writhing white.

Sheleen watched the necromancer draw three circles around Jolerarymi's body. Then he chanted in a rounded, flowing language. Dentril called out powerful black beseeching entreaties to Thasaidon, and Sheleen felt a strange, knowing presence, like a cold mist, reach up her spine. Jolerarymi's eyes fluttered, his muscles contracted, relaxed, spasmodically shedding rigor-mortis, becoming usable, animate. No longer dead.

His eyes opened. He sat. Jolerarymi stood, and faced the necromancer, saying nothing.

"I don't believe it," Sheleen said. "Jolerarymi? Jolerarymi, it's me. Sheleen."

Jolerarymi looked at Sheleen, and said her name. She asked how he felt, to which he replied, "weary." Then, the necromancer resumed control, forbidding Jolerarymi to answer to any but him for the next week.

"You have your proof," Dentril said. "Now, the rest of our deal. Come. Both of you."

Sheleen and Jolerarymi followed the necromancer to his chambers. Jolerarymi always looked away, in the same direction, but was not distracted. He served Sheleen and the necromancer their meal. He wasted no movement, did as he was told, no more, nothing in his expression, his face always turned southward. It was his body, but it was not *him*. He was an animate slave. He did not laugh or smile, and it was hard to tell if he heard a thing that was said in front of him. He kept looking at the south wall. In the Dentril's chambers, it was the wall with the bed.

The necromancer stared at Sheleen's breasts while he

ate; he could not keep his eyes off of them. "Now," the necromancer said when he had finished, "my payment."

She performed: drawing her breath in hisses, wrapping her legs around him tightly—everything her customers usually expected. Dentril made her stop. Without surprise, he forced her to lie perfectly still, not respond at all. She played dead.

Jolerarymi watched from the corner of the room, all but forgotten. His face showed no emotion.

The necromancer was an old man, and his stamina low. The week that Sheleen paid off her debt—nightly, after Jolerarymi, who always looked southward, served them dinner—she lay down with her legs parted enough for entry, closed her eyes and did not moved. Jolerarymi's expression never changed in that week. He served, he waited, he watched the southern wall, the southern edge of the courtyard.

The last night of her service to the necromancer, she sighed with relief when he had acted out his necrophilia fantasy. When she was prepared to leave, the necromancer released his control over Jolerarymi. Sheleen told him to follower her out through the courtyard, and drive the camel-drawn wagon; they followed the road east to Ehcac. Jolerarymi, through sight of the grave, kept the wagon on the road somehow. He consistently looked over his right shoulder.

"The statues in the necromancer's courtyard," she said while the traveled, trying to initiate a conversation. " I know the images were vile, but I am curious; what did you think of the craftsmanship?"

"Excellent," Jolerarymi said without turning. He did not elaborate further.

"Are you feeling well?"

"I am dead."

His response unnerved her. The cold statement of fact, the lack of his normal voice inflection, the grim truth of it. "Do you thirst?"

"No," he answered, death-glazed eyes never leaving the southern horizon. The wagon never wandered on the road.

194

"What am I to do with you, then?"

"I do not know," He did not blink, his eyes needed no moistening. His preternatural sight was not as hers, in death, his body required no fluids, no comfort.

"Do you know what I have gone through, what I have *given* to have you back?"

"Yes."

"And do you care?"

"Yes."

"Then act like it."

"I cannot."

"You cannot love me?"

"No."

"What can you do? What of you has death not kept for itself?"

"Very little. Most things you command."

Sheleen asked him no more questions, for his answers were tiring her. She lay down in the back of the wagon, and slept. Jolerarymi drove, heading east, looking south, and when she awoke, she asked him where they were. "Nearing the city of Ehcac."

"Ehcac? Excellent! I must have audience with Dotuunet. To his palace."

Jolerarymi drove her there, saying nothing of the farmer's fields, or the stout walls of the city. He did not comment on the rolling green banks of the River Dusiin as it coiled like a silver serpent around the hills as it flowed westward. If Jolerarymi saw the rapids and waterfalls that were east of the city, he said nothing. If he saw the ships that traveled upstream, from the west through the wide-mouthed, slower moving waters, he kept it to himself. He did not look at the stone bridges. He looked south. Ehcac was a marvel for her to behold; its wide, regular roads and colorful banners so contrasted Zul-Bha-Sair's gloomy maze. Jolerarymi could not have cared less.

Ehcac's guardsmen, armed with ornate swords and wearing polished metal armor, stopped her at the city's gate. "That foul creature may not enter here," the higher ranking of the two said, and the younger asked when it became common for young beautiful women to employ the evils of necromancy.

Sheleen had not foreseen this problem and was angered. She stepped down off the wagon, snickering to herself as the guardsmen's eyes boggled at the glimpse of her shapely legs. She pulled her hair back, fully exposing her face as she approached them, and explained about Dotuunet hiring Jolerarymi for a statue. They did not believe her, but were so enchanted that the officer escorted them to the palace. None was surprised more than the guard when he learned that the dead sculptor had been hired, as he apologized profusely to Sheleen as he made his exit. The king could not be bothered with the details of Jolerarymi's death, but summoned his chief attendant to stand in his place. The attendant was the one who had made the trip south to Zul-Bha-Sair, and recognized Jolerarymi. He told Jolerarymi how sorry he was that all this had befallen him. He truly sympathized. To Sheleen's amazement, without her commanding him to the dead sculptor nodded acknowledgement, momentarily looking at the attendant rather than southward.

"We have come because we cannot stay in Zul-Bha-Sair," Sheleen explained. "For him to complete the work for which he was hired, we shall need a place to stay, and the materials for him to work." Then, aside to Jolerarymi, "can you see anything that does not lie south of you?"

"I can," Jolerarymi said, but did not prove it to her by turning.

Sheleen silently growled in frustration.

"It can be arranged," said the attendant, not hearing the private exchange. "Though it is forbidden for people no longer living to reside within the city's walls." to Jolerarymi he turned, and said, "no offence intended, but that is the law."

"I understand," Jolerarymi said without turning.

They were shown to quarters outside the city. It was a small, comfortable dwelling on the banks of the river, and it was seen to that he had large blocks of stone and tarps, and tools with which he would work. She settled in, made herself some food (the dead do not eat) while he stood, motionless, expressionless, like a statue in the shadows. When she had finished eating she wiped her lips and asked him why he responded to the attendant in the ways he never responded to her.

"He broke no promises to me," Jolerarymi answered.

"I've given *everything* up for you," she said. "You think I *wanted* to leave Zul-Bha-Sair? Do you think I *wanted* to have that foul old necromancer inside me? I did what I had to do. For *you* Jolerarymi."

"You did it for money," he said. "And you broke your promise."

"What promise?"

When Jolerarymi's voice changed, mimicking hers, as he breathed out the words she had said to him at her house when he returned with all those gifts for her. "Oh, my love, my darling Jolerarymi. Forever it will be you and I, never will I have another man." Then Jolerarymi's voice returned back to the dead toneless, inflectionless one. "Those promises," he said. He never once turned to face her.

"You don't understand," Sheleen said, coming around in front of him. "You weren't there. You didn't *do* what I had to do."

"You did nothing for me. You did it for yourself."

"Don't speak to me that way."

Jolerarymi fell silent.

"The necromancer and I worked a deal. You are to follow my instructions. Is that not what he told you?"

"It is," said Jolerarymi.

"Then do it. Make that sculpture for the king."

Slowly, without a word to her, he disappeared behind the tarp and began to work the block of stone. Over the sound of his steady hammering and chiseling, she heard him talking softly. She could not make out his words, but their cadence, their rolling fluid syllables reminded her of the necromancer's chanting magic. When she went to follow him he stopped staring at the wall. She had to align herself with his eyes to look at him, and when she did, though his face could hold no emotion, she could have sworn hatred lurked beneath his flat dead eyes.

She turned from him, and he continued to carry out the command.

Through the night he worked, through the next day as well. Every time she looked at him, he stopped and stared at the south wall, a silent challenge to look on his face. She never accepted. He continued to work, his hands crafted and shaped, but Jolerarymi never looked at the piece, only southward. His eyes never left that direction, and they did not blink. His forehead did not sweat. He did not breathe heavily with exertion or elation. He worked for weeks without stopping.

The dead did not rest.

One morning he was standing, silent, looking ever southward as she woke. He was filthy, having never stopped to rest or bathe. Dust covered his hands, his face, his arms and chest like a half-formed sculpture himself. The dead needed no hygiene.

"Is it done?"

Jolerarymi did not look at her, but nodded. She went out to the room in which he had been working. The statue was of her, her naked body gloriously rendered in rock. In her hands, holding it up as if to smell it, there was a single rose.

"I must tell the king!" She exclaimed, greed lighting her face. "Stay with the piece," she said. "The city will not allow you within its walls." Before she left, she stood and stared at him a while. She said nothing. She left.

"You're welcome," she said after her departure. His lips were set in a dead grin.

Dotuunet refused to leave the palace to meet the dead sculptor. In his place, he sent back with Sheleen his advisor Imecnis, two palace slaves drawing a cart laden with bags of coin, and four guards armed with bow and sword. Dotuunet took no chances with thieves.

"Excellent!" Imecnis said when he saw the sculpture, and stepped around to beam at Jolerarymi.

"I would be hard-pressed to find a more beautiful

rendition of the human body," the captain of the guards said, eyeing Sheleen. On cue, she blushed, and murmured her thanks.

"The money, then," Imecnis said with delight. He clapped his hands and the slaves laid the bags on the floor in front of the statue of Sheleen's likeness.

She could not help but open them. She lifted out a handful of coin, admiring it. She was grinning. A smell reached her nostrils. Rotting flowers. She turned to face the statue.

As she looked into her own stony face, and looked under Jolerarymi's perfect rendition of her nose, she saw the lips parting, slowly.

Jolerarymi turned, and for the first time in almost a month, Sheleen saw his face. He stared at her. Smiled coldly.

The guards backed up, their faces horrified, their swords drawn.

The captain screamed, "What is this? What sorcery is this?"

Sheleen could not answer his questions. Her mouth was locked open, and wider it opened, wider and wider. The statue's mouth as well opened wider, wider. It positioned the rose, the rot-riddled stone rose, the scent of poison in its mouth.

The scent was strong in Sheleen's nostrils, so strong. She tasted the rose, the teeth-shattering crunch of stone in her mouth, petals crumbling, their rancid smell pouring over her.

The statue chewed, biting, gnashing, tearing the rose to bits. It swallowed, stem and petal and thorn.

Sheleen cried—a piercing wail of agony that deafened the men in the room. She felt a weight in her chest unlike any she had ever known, so heavy, so solid.

Her hands went to her chest, and felt the coldness creeping out from its center. She looked at Jolerarymi with questioning sadness.

The statue, hands on its chest, wept a clear tear.

Jolerarymi did not attempt to dry Sheleen's eyes.

A sparkle on the statue's cheek, clear, brilliant: a flawless diamond against grey stone.

The chaos confused the guards. They looked to their captain, sought guidance from his rank, an order to fulfill. He hesitated, a moment of indecision; then pointed to Sheleen, "Kill her!" As if that would make a difference. The scent of rotting roses was strong, and she was collapsing.

The guards attacked as Sheleen crumpled. The first soldier's sword struck her neck with force enough to decapitate. It did not. With a clatter of steel scraping stone, shooting glowing blue sparks, the blade deflected upward. The guard was thrown off-balance; the weapon fell from his hands as he struggled to keep his footing. Bewildered, fearing reprimand, he hastened to retrieve it. The others stopped, again, looking to their captain.

Jolerarymi stepped forward, ignoring the guards' sword points. He stood in front of Imecnis and stared for a moment, then looked south, turning back to face Imecnis with flat wistfulness. Imecnis sadly smiled, nodded. the sculptor began to gather his payment.

The guards made to advance, but Imecnis raised his hand, stopped them. "Let him be," he commanded. The guards stopped; even their captain was silent.

Jolerarymi picked up the first of the nine bags, and handed it to Imecnis. The second he placed on Sheleen's corpse. He looked at her for a moment, bent down and touched her face. It was cold, hard as stone. Taking the remaining seven bags, he left the cottage, heading south, leaving the rolling green hills of Ehcac, the River Dusiin.

He walked southward, and when he finally saw Zul-Bha-Sair's towers and walls amidst the red-sanded Celotian waste, he smiled. He entered his city of birth, of death, his dead steps rose small dust tufts off the streets, his coins jingled in their bags. He reached the polished black stone of Mordiggian's courtyard, and, as always, it was empty. Funeral party of one. He entered the temple.

The priest in attendance said nothing, the yellow eyes gleaming from behind the mirrored skull did not challenge, they accepted. Jolerarymi walked past him, deep into the temple. He stood between two smoking braziers in sculpted-stone mounts, shifting the bags of coin in his arms.

Before him, the blackness shifted, writhing upon itself like serpents of smoke and oil. Mordiggian spoke, his deep voice both powerful and comforting, "Welcome, sculptor."

"Thank you," Jolerarymi took his money with him and entered the maw of the charnel god.

ONE-EYED JACK

"Out of every hundred men,
ten shouldn't even be there,
eight are just targets,
nine are the real fighters,
and we are lucky to have them,
for they make the battle.
Ah, but the one...
One is a warrior, and he will bring the others back."
—Heraclitus

"The situation?
The enemy is in front of us.
They are behind us and to our flanks
And they outnumber us twenty-nine to one
The poor silly bastards won't get away this time!"
—Lt Gen Lewis B. Puller, USMC, when surrounded by twenty-two enemy divisions.

He made it.

HEARTS

"In the absence of orders,
go find something and kill it."
—Field Marshal Erwin Rommel

We are all born for a purpose. Everyone can do something well. Most never find out what it is. They drift along in their existence, dissatisfied and bored, until time catches up with them and they pass on: lives wasted. A few, however, are lucky—or persistent—enough to learn their true calling and immerse themselves in it. Their lives and jobs are inseparable,

202

their names become synonymous with their vocations. Their accomplishments become the benchmark by which others are measured. History often remembers them fondly: Mickey Mantle, Galileo, Orville and Wilbur Wright, Sigmund Freud, Thomas Edison, Charles Schultz, John Lennon…men like that. I found my calling on the seventh of December, 1941: the day I officially died. The day I came alive.

My name was Jack Austin and I was a Lance Corporal in the US Marine Corps. That Sunday morning, I was fiddling around Ford Island, warming up for a game of baseball (which I believed was my true calling at the time, but the Yankees didn't agree) when the first wave of planes came in. They began strafing the ground, torpedo and bombing runs. I mounted a Bofors Quad AA gun and started shooting. I knocked six of them out of the sky when one came in from behind me. I knew he had me, so I started running like mad. The bomb exploded, and the concussion knocked me down. I struggled to rise, but moving was difficult: I had caught a serious amount of shrapnel. I tasted blood, I smelled blood, blood was in my eyes and dripping off my nose. It was welling up in sticky pools in the palms of my hands. It soaked through my shirt and pants. I kept moving.

Enemy planes continued to buzz overhead, strafing the ground with their machine guns and bombing the ships in the harbor. I heard several massive explosions. Smoke started to obscure the enemy overhead. Men were all running like mad, shooting, calling for medics and corpsmen, trying to rally together. Our ships' guns started booming. The men—those that had weapons—fired into the air with small arms: M-1 Carbines, M-1 rifles, a couple of Springfield '03's, a few BARs and a couple of Tommy guns.

I saw one marine standing in the middle of the airfield firing his .45 caliber pistol up at the approaching Zeros. Strafing fire kept hitting the ground around him, and he merely ejected the magazine, inserted another one, and kept plugging away at the Jap pilots. That one marine, it turned out, became famous—or his actions did. The George C. Scott movie, *Patton*, had a scene inspired by him, and recently, they interviewed one of the Japanese pilots that attacked us that day. The pilot said he saw that marine down there, firing his pistol up at the approaching aircraft. He had him in his sights, then, overcome with respect and admiration, he broke off the strafing run and gave him a wing-tip salute. The Japanese pilot called him the bravest American he'd ever seen. High praise, coming from the enemy sixty years later.

I wish I knew that marine's name.

We all should.

I tried to find my sergeant—Sgt Simmons—but ran into a corpsman instead, working on a sailor. I asked him for a towel as soon as he had a moment; I just wanted to wipe the blood out of my eyes so I could see well enough to shoot when I found Sgt Simmons. He said I should be dead and told me to get my ass to triage so they could start patching me up. I told him that wasn't necessary, that I didn't want to take the medical attention away from those that really need it. He told me it was an order. I obeyed. He was a sergeant. What choice did I have?

There were corpsmen, medics, civilian doctors and nurses all scurrying to assist the wounded. Some came in on stretchers, some were carried by their buddies or limped in themselves, like me. I remember seeing a sailor carry in a marine, pleading for someone to help the wounded man, who had been gut-shot and was badly burned. After two nurses came to tend to the marine, the sailor collapsed to the floor and died. He'd taken eight bullets carrying the marine to safety and did not even know it.

We should all know his name, too.

We don't.

"Get this one ready," said a civilian doctor as he glanced at me. "I don't want him dying waiting for surgery."

"I'm really not that bad off," I said. "I just got blood everywhere. Gimme a shower and a Band-Aid and I'll be fine."

"I'm giving you general anesthesia and a prayer that you live long enough to wake up," said the doctor.

Have you ever had general anesthesia? Where they totally

knock you out? It's awful, waking up from it. Everything is blurry and foggy, like you're on a real doozy of a drunk, then just when you think you're all right to move, you wind up puking your guts all over the floor. It's embarrassing, especially when the shoes your vomit splashed was a full-bird colonel's. I glimpsed his nametag. It was Ross. He wasn't *my* colonel; that was colonel Jackson, and he was with the *Indianapolis*, but he was a colonel nonetheless.

"I'm sorry, sir," I struggled to say as I wiped my mouth and tried to rise.

"What are you doing there, Marine?"

"Trying to salute you, sir."

Colonel Ross laughed. "You're wounded and still groggy from the dope they gave you. I think it's all right to let this one slide."

"If you say so, sir. I apologize for your shoes. I…couldn't help it. It wasn't intentional, sir."

"I'm sure it wasn't," he said, and wiped his shoes clean with a paper towel. He washed his hands in the sink afterward and then opened a folder. "You've been a marine for a little over two years, isn't that right, Lance Corporal Austin?"

"Yes, sir."

"According to your service record, you're well on your way to your next promotion. Could you see yourself as a Corporal, or a Sergeant?"

"I think I could, sir. I was planning on re-enlisting. I…I don't have much of a home to go to; I figure staying in the Marines is probably better than I'd get in civilian life."

"What makes you say that?" Colonel Ross asked as he flipped through pages in the folder on his lap.

All these questions. My head was pounding, my mouth was dry. I thought I was going to puke again. "My dad died in '29. After the crash, understand, my mother and I…we haven't seen eye to eye for years. I think she's glad I'm in the Corps; keeps me out of her sight." I wasn't sure I was making any sense. Had he been Sgt Simmons, I'd have begged off the questions until later.

Colonel Ross nodded. "I see. It says here that you were

in a bit of trouble as a youngster, is that correct?"

I lowered my eyes, partially out of shame, partially because I really wanted to lie down and go back to sleep. "Yes, sir. That's true, but times were rough then. I did what I had to…to survive. Mom wasn't…" I cut myself off. It was all too much effort. I summarized those years with a shrug and mumbled. "I had to eat also."

He nodded again. "Very well, then. So what made you join the Corps?"

Christ, *that* age-old question? Why does every officer want to ask you that, whether it's their goddamned business or not? I helped myself to some water, though not too much: I feared sending it back up again. I just had to do *something* about the cottonmouth the anesthesia left behind. Colonel Ross was waiting. He really did want an answer. "I figured I might as well do it right and become a marine. I'd had shit my whole life—pardon my French—and just wanted to be part of the best, for a change, sir. If I stayed around Brackard's Point, I'd be fixing cars…building houses…something. It'd keep me there until I was an old man and I'd have never gotten out of there…" Christ. I was babbling, and mumbling, too. Was he *really* that interested or was he trying to gauge me for something else. This was starting to sound like a job interview. I wanted to ask him if it was, but feared doing so would prolong the conversation.

"So you saw the Marines as your ticket out of Dodge, then."

"Yes, sir."

"Very well, then. Austin, I'm going to present you a rare opportunity. But you must decide quickly. You see this?" he held up a piece of paper. "Do you know what this is?"

"I can't see that far, sir; my eyes are still kind of wobbly."

"It's your death certificate."

"Sir?"

"The US Government needs men…good men. Great men. Now more than ever. The job will be dangerous—not that being a Marine in wartime isn't—and it'll be quite important. Of paramount importance. There are limits on

Marines. Limits of higher officers, of regulations and such. The US Government needs men to operate outside of these regulations. Men such as you. But you can't do it while you're a Marine, and you can't do it and go back to the man you were. You understand? If you take this opportunity, you'll be dead, for all official records. You'll be remembered in ceremony, died with honors as a Marine in combat here, in the first battle of a new war. But you must decide quickly. I realize you're groggy right now, so I'll give you until tomorrow. But don't dally. If we are to do this, we will have to have this signed by tomorrow. The official report will be that you lingered on, but ultimately died from your wounds."

Dead. I felt like death warmed over already. I didn't think that being officially dead—the doctor said I should be, the corpsman said I should be…last time I saw my mother, she said I was to her—was that a big of a deal. "What will I have to do, sir?"

"Become a ghost. Take the war to the enemy on fronts they never imagined."

"And I'll never have to go home again? Ever? What happens when the war's over?"

Colonel Ross looked at me. "If you take this job, there will *always* be a war for you to fight."

"I'm in, sir."

"Think about it some more. I'll be back tomorrow."

"I'm in sir. Have it signed now."

"I'll arrange transport for you. I'll be back at dinnertime."

This confused me. "Transport?"

"If you're dead, we can't have anyone that knows you from this base seeing you, now can we?"

"I suppose not, sir."

"Very well, then. Tell no one of this conversation. Am I clear?"

"Crystal, sir."

"And Austin, being as you're dead, thus, technically, no longer a marine, you don't have to call me 'sir' anymore."

"I think I will just the same, sir. For now."

He smiled. "You were a good marine, Austin."

"Thank you, sir."

I shut my eyes. Dead, officially. If I died today, I'd be amongst some fine men: that marine who carried in the sailor, and the one who kept emptying his pistol at the strafing Zeros. That group of sailors diving into the water to pull their burnt buddies out from the diesel fires, pulling them back from the flames. Yes, I thought, today was a good day to die. These were the kind of men with whom I'd like to be remembered.

My mother didn't care so if I may, I'll ask you to remember for me. Will you do that?—as a favor to an old combat-wounded veteran?

My name was Jack Austin.

I was a Lance Corporal in the United States Marine Corps.

I died on 7 December, 1941.

SPADES

"War is the remedy that our enemies have chosen,
And I say let us give them all they want."
—General William T. Sherman

Things happened quickly after that. I was loaded into a transport aircraft and flown away. I had no idea where I was. I asked someone, they said I was being transferred to a "secure hospital."

That hospital was damned secure. I couldn't tell you where it was. I never went outside. I saw no other patients. I think I was the only one there besides the three doctors and six nurses I saw during my stay and they wouldn't tell me anything. I went through some physical therapy to get myself back in shape, played a lot of solitaire. If it wasn't for a deck of cards I'd begged one of the nurses for, I'd have gone nuts.

Then, one day, Colonel Ross came to visit.

"I spoke with the doctors," he said. "Seems you're ready to be discharged. This is good, because we need to start your training."

"Training, sir?"

"Stop with the 'sir' bit, will you?"

"Yes, s—" I stopped myself. "All right."

"First bit of training. You need a new name. Pick one."

My mind froze. I'd always been Jack Austin, never thought of myself as anyone else. To alter that was a real challenge. I flipped over the top card. It was the king of diamonds. I didn't think King Diamond made for much of a name, so I turned over another. Nine of clubs. Three of diamonds. Eight of spades. Spade…that'd do. Now a first name. Ace? I snickered to myself.

"What's so funny?"

"I was trying to think of a first name," I said. "I figure 'Spade' is good for a last name, but I wouldn't think of a first other than 'Ace.'"

"It'd be your name so you'd have to live to it, but I don't think I could recommend that one. Sounds too fake."

Then it hit me. Back a long time ago, French playing cards—the face cards—had proper names. The spades were David, Pallas, and Hogier—down in order, king, queen, and jack. I started flipping those three in my mind, but they came out of my mouth as well: "Hogier Davidson…no…sounds too much like a motorcycle. David Hogier. Hogiers. Yeah, I like that better. Hogiers. Dave Hogiers. David P. Hogiers. Yeah, I think that'll do."

"Not bad," Colonel Ross said. "Dave Hogiers. Or do you prefer David?"

"I'm not sure."

"I think Dave works better."

"I do too."

"Very well, then, Dave. Come with me. There's someone you need to meet."

"Who's that?"

"Your instructor."

I followed Colonel Ross out of my room and down the hall I walked a million times before. We passed the nurses' station, then came to a door which had always previously been locked. Colonel Ross opened it with a key.

I stepped through and took my first breath of fresh air in months. The sun blinded me temporarily. I heard birds, smelled the grass, saw a bumblebee buzzing along the clover. Seagulls cried off in the distance.

"Where the Hell am I?"

"I'd suggest you concentrate more on where you're going," Colonel Ross said.

"And where's that?"

"Right now, to get trained. After that...I couldn't say for sure, but I'd bet it's someplace with slant-eyes armed with rifles."

"You're a cheery one, Colonel Ross."

"Don't mention it," he said, and led me to the car.

I hoped we would be going for a ride so I could—finally—figure out where the Hell I was by reading a sign, but as it turned out, the trip showed me nothing. We drove all of a quarter-mile, and hadn't gone off the complex. The building we entered was white, and bereft of any marking as to its purpose. It might have been a hospital, a school, an office building, a test lab...one couldn't tell. Now that I think about it, the building was all these things.

There was a brightly-smiling secretary sitting at the desk when we entered. She said, "And who do we have here, Colonel Ross?" in a tone so sweet, a damned-near fell in love. These feelings were only momentarily dashed when I saw her ring finger. I loved her voice, at any rate.

"David Hogiers," I said, trying my new name out. It seemed to flow naturally enough. Maybe I did like David better. Time would tell. "Pleased to meet you."

"And you too, Mr. Hogiers," she said. "Professor Gregori is expecting you."

"Who's that?"

"Why, he's the man you're here to see."

"Can't wait," I said.

She nodded toward the door. "You can go right in."

"Thanks," I said. "I'll see you around."

She laughed, a sound as sweet as her voice. "If you say so."

Colonel Ross waited by the door. "If you two kids are done with your flirting, we can get on with this."

"Good-bye, Mr. Hogiers."

"Good-bye," I said. "What's your name?"

"Nancy Ellensworth."

"Well, hello, Miss Ellensworth, and good-bye."

"Just Nancy," she said.

"Well, good-bye then, Just Nancy. Nice to have met you."

I followed Colonel Ross through the door before he blew a stack.

"You leave her alone," Colonel Ross said after we were though and the door had shut.

"Oh, what's the harm?" I said. I rather liked being able to respond to him as a civilian. As a Lance Corporal, I never could have said that.

"The harm is she's engaged to the son of a friend of mine, and you need to be concentrating on what you're going to do for us—for your country—rather than on someone else's fiancée. I can always pull you out of this program, Hogiers. And trust me, you wouldn't like where you'd end up if that were to happen."

"I apologize. But, sir, if I may ask, where *would* I end up if such a thing were to happen?"

"Nowhere you'd ever come back from, and nowhere you could ever tell a soul about this program."

"Dead, then?"

"Close enough to it to make the difference immeasurable."

"I see."

"Let's hope you do," Colonel Ross said. He stood by the door of a room. There were five other doors just like it down the hallway. "We won't be seeing each other again until you're done with your training. Good luck, Hogiers."

"Thank you, Colonel Ross. I won't let you down."

"I didn't think you would," he said, and offered his hand. I shook it. "Take care, now."

"You do the same. Sir."

He smiled and turned to leave. I opened the door and

entered professor Gregori's tutelage.

No training I had ever before received prepared me for this. The Marines shouted a lot. Drill instructors got in your face. They were stern, hard men and you feared them. You were piss-frightened not to succeed because to displease the DI was to displease god, and woe to any marine recruit who incurred their wrath.

Professor Gregori did not do this. He never shouted. He whispered. He whispered wisdom, he whispered madness. He whispered confirmation of fearful things, whispered the truth behind the myths. He whispered for months on end. He was whispering in my ear at night as I fell asleep and was still there whispering in the morning. He whispered all day long. I do not ever recall him not by my side. He must have, at some point gone to the bathroom to relieve himself, ate, or slept, but it seems that he was always there, always whispering.

I learned things. Lots of things. I learned about the borders between life and death, between past, present, and future. Learned how time was malleable. I asked if I really died in Pearl Harbor, and if this were all a dream, if I were a ghost, something kooky like that.

Gregori whispered that I was indeed alive, though Jack Austin was dead. "Though it is irrelevant."

"What is?"

"Jack Austin is. Forget him. You never knew him anyway."

"I don't think I can ever really forget him."

"Of course not. But put him out of mind for now, David."

"I'll try."

"You must."

I did.

Whispering, always whispering. He whispered questions without answers, whispered answers to questions I could barely understand. He taught me to read languages that were never meant to be spoken, to see the traces left behind of things passed on. He taught me to see with my eyes closed, to hear with my ears covered, to taste the difference between belief and truth, between belief in a lie and a lie to conceal the truth.

He was correct: Jack Austin was no longer relevant. Jack Austin could never have comprehended these things. Jack Austin was just a Lance Corporal in the US Marine Corps. I'd outgrown him. Transcended. Become someone greater. Something greater, and as I became, Gregori continued to whisper and I continued to learn.

I learned how to ask questions, learned that the most powerful words *were* questions. The answers were often secondary—it was the asking that held the importance. Whatever you knew was to be deconstructed as soon as possible, and only questions permitted this. The truth never set anyone free, the cliché a lie. Questions were the great liberators. The perfect answer was often silence.

One morning I awoke and Gregori was no longer there. On the table were a wallet, a bank passbook, a new deck of playing cards, a set of keys, and a note. It read:

Mr. Hogiers:

Here is your new life. Refer to your drivers license for your address (I do not know it at the time of this writing). The funds in the bank are available for immediate withdrawal, though I would suggest you first go to your new residence to see what it is you might need. Most things have been taken care of. There you will find clothes, food, and supplies, along with most of the trimmings of a modern household. The deed for your property will be in the safe in your study. The combination is in the cards. Your assignment is also in the safe.

Outside is a blue Ford. You will find the key for it on this ring. Please observe posted speed limits on your journey.

Best of luck to you.

The note was unsigned, but I knew it was from Colonel Ross. I glanced at the drivers' license. It was Hawaiian. They even had my thumbprint on there (you must remember: back then, Hawaii wasn't yet a state. Its drivers licenses had only the thumbprint of the holder). It looked legit. My address was in Pearl City.

Great, I thought as I walked out to the blue Ford in the parking lot. *Now how do I get there from here?*

I had an idea. I drove over to the hospital where I first stayed through my recovery and walked into the front desk. Just Nancy wasn't there.

The desk wasn't there.

There wasn't *anyone* there.

I wasn't surprised.

CLUBS

"This individual heroic stuff is a lot of crap.
The bilious bastards who wrote that kind of stuff
For the Saturday Evening Post
Don't know any more about fighting under fire
Than they do about fucking!"
—General George S. Patton Jr.

There was enough money in the wallet for my trip, and then some—almost a thousand dollars, which, in those days, was a *lot* of dough. The bankbook showed a single deposit of ten thousand dollars, on the day the account was opened: 18 February, 1942.

Jack Austin would have thought he had it made. A thousand dollars in his pocket, ten thousand in the bank, a house in Hawaii, a new Ford V-8…what else could a guy like him want? Women? He'd have his fill, with all the other men shipping out. Besides, he had ten grand, a new Ford, a house and both hands. He'd get by.

I opened the deck of cards, and remembered Gregori's whispers.

I shuffled, dealt myself a five-card hand on the hood of the Ford.

Jack of Spades was the first card to turn up, as I knew it would. Eight of clubs. Ace of Spades. Eight of Spades. Ace of Clubs.

Black Aces and Eights, Jack of Spades kicker: the Dead Man's hand.

I heard Gregori's whispered laughter. I joined him, then started the Ford and headed west.

I expected to come across a dusty New Mexico desert town. Instead, I came across a rolling sugar cane plantation. I pulled the Ford off the side of the road. I saw a Honeycreeper—an endemic Hawaiian bird. I was already in Hawaii. I should have known.

***

It took me a while to find my way to my new home in Pearl City. The house was larger than I'd never need, the lawn and landscaping perfect. There was a staff—a maid and a cook, a gardener and a butler—who all seemed to trip over themselves when I arrived. There were clothes in the closet, the study was stocked with books. I took inventory. Gregori must have had a hand in acquiring some of these. I smelled age, parchment and vellum. Some of them seemed to whisper. I had to block them out.

The safe was set in the floor. I grasped the large combination dial and spun it—one left, eight right, one left, eight right, eleven left. It clicked open.

Inside, as promised, was the deed to the house. There was also a note in the same hand as the first. It had only two words upon it: *Nan Modol*.

Nan Modol.

I shut my eyes.

Black basalt columns, floating islands made by man. The dominion of kings and gods, a civilization now lost. I knew the place. The Japanese were already there, but had not found what they were looking for. Not yet. They would soon, though. I was sure of that.

The Japanese High Command, like their allies, the Nazis, sponsored numerous archeological expeditions all over the Pacific Rim. They'd dug in Manchuria, Mongolia, and on many of their home islands. They'd sent divers into the waters off Okinawa, sent teams every place in the Pacific there was a site worth digging for. The Germans, in their digs, were seeking to support their "master race" theory, lend the Aryan myth some credit. Any findings went through the propaganda machine and were spewed out to the German citizenry. The Japanese, however, were being much more secret with their findings. They weren't parading skulls and pottery shards in front of a camera for PR.

I knew what they were after.

I gave in to the whispers, consulted the books.

***

Before recorded history had a chance to solidify, there were three continents now lost. The most famous was Atlantis. There were two more: Lemuria and Mu. Atlantis lies beneath the ocean that now bears its name—not *so* forgotten is it?— Lemuria lay at the bottom of the Indian ocean, and Mu, the Pacific. The warlike Atlanteans were masters of technology and, some say, black magic. The Lemurians were skilled in the arts of medicine and art. The farmers of Mu devoted their lives to nature. They could bring rain to their crops when it was dry, divert the wind to blow deadly storms offshore, beseech the earth to become fertile, or give up its rock for building homes, temples, or granaries.

Most sources blame the Atlanteans for the cataclysm, fooling around with technology—or dark magic—beyond their control. The world cracked. Not even the Mu could halt the rising seas. The low continents of Atlantis, Lemuria, and Mu sunk beneath the waves.

The few scattered survivors of Atlantis went to Egypt, and one of their descendants, Imhotep, became the architect of the first pyramid at Saqqara, then a god. The Lemurians were nearly all wiped out. A single pregnant Lemurian woman, Hariti, came ashore in India and was soon revered as a goddess and feared as a demon, with good reason for both.

The Mu were split between East and West. The eastern

Mu drifted eastward and found their way to South America. Their descendants, the Aztecs, became fierce warriors. Never again, would they permit an Atlantean-like civilization to bring doom upon them, and none did, until Hernando Cortez and the Spanish Conquistadores arrived and, like eons before, ended the reign of the children of Mu.

The western Mu also cultivated their warrior spirit, but, unlike their brethren, they did not completely ignore their naturalistic bent. They embraced it. They sought harmony with their new home, a land of volcanoes and earthquakes, of typhoons and monstrous tidal waves.

In 1281, Kublai Kahn tried to invade them. He came with four thousand, four hundred ships and a hundred forty thousand men. The descendants of Mu numbered only forty thousand. The Mongol horde would have most certainly wiped them out. They prayed to the ancient gods of air and sea and their prayers were heard: a typhoon smashed the Mongolian fleet for two complete days. The surviving ships limped home.

This storm, sent by the gods to save them, was what the Japanese—the children of Western Mu—called Kamikaze. The Divine Wind. And now that they were on the offensive, and digging on ancient sites, there cold only be one thing they were looking for: a way to control the elements by means more reliable than prayer. The Japanese, the naturalistic warriors, with the means to wage modern war, coupled with the ancient mastery of the weather, would be unstoppable.

They were doing it right, keeping it secret. I knew then we would eventually win the war with Germany. They were too much for the camera, too much for propaganda. The Japanese concerned me. Silence, that perfect answer, was their ally.

I had to reach Nan Modol. Quickly.

I shut the books, shuffled the cards, and called for the butler, whose name was Lazlow.

"Sir?"

"I work for a living," I said, a little bit of Jack Austin, Lance Corporal in the USMC showing through. "Please, call me David."

"I regret I cannot; it would not be proper."

"Call me anything but 'sir.' I hear that, I think I should stand at attention and salute."

"Mr. Hogiers, then."

"If that suits you, Lazlow, then by all means, refer to me as Mr. Hogiers."

"I think I shall."

"Fine. Are you a card player by any chance, Lazlow?" My question surprised me. Not that I asked it, but the manner in which I did. I thought it odd how a man such as myself—or what I assumed *was* myself, having not been in David P. Hogiers very long—could adopt a higher diction of speech so quickly.

"I have played some games, Mr. Hogiers, though I will not admit to being any good at them."

I didn't think he'd admit to being any good at them if he broke the bank at Monte Carlo. As he said before, it wouldn't be proper. "Well, then," I said. "Play a hand or two with me, will you?"

"I…I don't know, Mr. Hogiers. Not to insult you, sir, I just don't…think…"

He looked into my face and his arguments started coming apart. I shuffled, offered them for a cut. He tapped the top card, and I dealt them as is.

"What are we playing for, Mr. Hogiers?" Lazlow asked as he picked up the first few cards in his hand.

"To help me think, Lazlow. To help me think."

"I see," he said. By his tone, I thought he really did.

I glanced at my cards: Four of Clubs, Seven of Clubs, Nine of Spades, Queen of Diamonds, and, of course, the Jack of Spades.

"My I discard, Mr. Hogiers?"

"Of course."

Lazlow threw down three. I dealt him three more, then turned my attention to my own hand. I held onto the Queen and the Jack (for I could not throw myself out, could I?), and picked up the Six, Eight, and Ten of Diamonds.

Diamonds.

Fortune.

This was getting interesting.

Lazlow drew into three of a kind—Five of Hearts, Clubs, and Spades—with a Jack of Clubs kicker and a Deuce of Hearts below.

"It appears I've won, sir. Mr. Hogiers."

"So you have, Lazlow, so you have. A drink? And are there any cigars in this house?"

I played for thinking, then for drinking. As men are wont to do over cards, cigars, and whiskey, Lazlow and I talked. I admitted I'd never had a staff before. Lazlow said he could tell.

"How are you paid, Lazlow? I never did figure that out."

"You needn't worry about that, Mr. Hogiers. Sybil, Waldo, Edward and myself are all regularly—and, I might add, well—compensated for our services to you."

"But who does it?"

"Certain questions, Mr. Hogiers, I am not permitted to answer, and there are several I am not permitted to ask."

Colonel Ross, I figured. "So you all stay here during my absence?"

"Not in the house itself, sir. Our lodging is out back. They're quite comfortable. Of course, we do come into the house during the day, in case someone should telephone or come calling, but as of yet, no one has. A shame, really, for it is a lovely house, if I may say so, and should have the honor of regular guests, but I do understand certain things, and realize that, at present, this is not possible.

"Sybil busies herself cleaning and decorating—she chose the décor herself, sir. The directors—such is how I refer to them, for lack of a better term—gave her a generous expense account and let her buy anything she wished to decorate the place. Edward—he's the cook, and a fine one, at that—often says he's assisting Waldo, the Gardner, out on the grounds, but I've yet to see someone garden with a fishing pole in their hand."

"So Edward goes fishing?"

"You didn't hear that from *me*, sir, but if I may say so,

I think his small vice is forgivable when there is no one to cook *for*."

"You're probably right, Lazlow. I've done my fair share of worm-drowning on idle days."

"On Edward, I will say this, though, sir—when he returns from a successful 'gardening adventure,' he makes most excellent seafood dinners. One might say they're his specialty."

"Well, then," I said and dealt out a new hand. "It's all for the kitchen, then. If it makes him feel better to sneak about doing so, then perhaps we should let him continue, wouldn't you say?"

"I would most definitely, sir. I would hate to see him go. His seafood dinners and lunches are the best I've ever had."

I'd had enough. "I thought I told you not to call me 'sir.'"

"Forgive me, Mr. Hogiers. Habit, you know."

"Yes. I know," I said, thinking of my own trouble in adjusting my mode of address to Colonel Ross.

Lazlow sipped his drink and continued. "Waldo is rarely seen, but his handiwork is. He doesn't fraternize much with the staff, though I think he's spoken some with Edward—enough to offer an alibi for him when Edward's fishing, at any rate. While Sybil did the interior, Waldo did the exterior and the landscaping. He hired a few local boys to help with the heavier work and some of the things where it doesn't take much skill to do—cutting the grass, that sort of thing. He spends a lot of his time on the grounds, doing what, I couldn't tell you specifically, but the estate, in my opinion, looks wonderful. I saw him most often when he was working on the pond."

"Pond?"

"He's designating a water-garden of sorts."

"I'd like to see it."

"I could accompany you, if you wish, sir. I know the way."

"Stop with the 'sir,' already, Lazlow."

"Sorry. Habit."

"Besides," I said. "It's nearly dark. Perhaps tomorrow."

"Very well, then."

"So what about you, Lazlow? How do you occupy those idle hours?"

"Oh, Mr. Hogiers, I—"

"Come now, Lazlow. You mean to tell me you stand by the door, just in case someone should come by? Hover near the telephone in case it should ring while Edward's fishing, Sybil's decorating, and Waldo is doing god-knows-what?"

"I indulge my hobbies."

"Which are?"

"I make ships in bottles. I read. I take walks. Quite boring, actually."

"You do not strike me as a boring person, Lazlow. What aren't you telling me?"

"Reading occupies most of my time, Mr. Hogiers."

"What do you read that's so compelling?"

Lazlow answered in silence.

I understood.

"What, then, could you tell me about traveling westward?"

"That it's dangerous."

"I think I could gather that on my own."

"Tell me when you wish to leave, and I'll arrange transport for you wherever you wish to go. But I would suggest that you do arm yourself before departing."

"I was planning on that."

"I was told you were familiar with the operation of most arms currently used in the military, so I acquired them for you. Sybil suffers hoplophobia—the irrational fear of firearms—so I keep them under lock and key to placate her silly neuroses. Edward, Waldo, and myself all have access to them. They key ring with which you were supplied has a copy on there as well.

"Sybil refused her key, so we have one spare, which I placed in your top desk drawer. Of course, there is a pistol in your desk—the government model .45 I was told you're accustomed to—in the top right drawer. I think you would agree that no man should be able to be surprised in his own home. I assumed you'd be spending most of your time in the house in here, so this is where I placed it for you. If you wish, I could move it to another location, if you find the study uncomfortable, though, to be honest, if this was the case, I could have Sybil come in and redecorate for you. She'd be happy to do so, I'm sure, I'd merely suggest you keep the pistol out of sight and the desk drawer locked when she's in here, though."

"I don't think that'd be necessary, Lazlow. I like it in here just fine."

"Will you be leaving shortly, Mr. Hogiers?"

I shuffled the cards, chose the top one, said, "Apparently, so," as I returned the card to the deck.

Lazlow smiled, but in it was disappointment.

DIAMONDS

"Let's roll."
—Todd M. Beamer, passenger on United Flight 93, 11 September, 2001

Lazlow insisted on packing for me despite my objections of not being sure of what I would need. He gave me a look.

I relented. I would have to learn to let him do his job. It was not easy for me. I was used to doing everything for myself.

Sybil, whom I had barely spoken to in my time at home, looked heartbroken I was leaving so soon. I did remember to compliment her on the décor of the household, and she brightened somewhat with that. Edward forced me to eat a grilled Moi sandwich on homemade bread with fries before I departed (and Lazlow was right; after that one sandwich, I decided Edward may go fishing whenever he damned well pleased). Waldo was not to be found—it was speculated he was off collecting some things for the water-garden (which I had still not seen).

All told, I spent less than twenty-four hours in my lovely home in Pearl City. I hadn't had time to see the whole place. I hadn't even met Waldo, the gardener, or his staff of local boys. It was all quite bizarre for me. I'd not yet become accustomed to the lifestyle, and I was already leaving it for some half-forgotten ruins occupied by god-knew-how-many Japanese that'd be eager to slit my guts as soon as they saw me.

I had to be insane.

Gregori's whispered laughter in my ear did not assist in dispelling that thought.

I stopped at the bank, withdrew three thousand dollars more. In case I needed to bribe an official or two, I told myself, but part of me just wanted to be sure the money wasn't merely numbers on paper. I had no reason to doubt the bankbook's authenticity, but I felt better after verifying it for myself.

Lazlow arranged my transportation. It was a fishing boat/smuggling vessel called Ambrosia. Her captain, a Filipino named Queveco, was an acquaintance of Lazlow's during Prohibition (the way Lazlow stumbled over the proper term to call Captain Queveco hinted at much more than that, but I said nothing) and, Lazlow said, could be trusted to keep his mouth shut. His exact words were: "If the posters are true—that if loose lips sink ships—then the *Ambrosia* is unsinkable."

"That's what they said about the *Titanic*, Lazlow."

"The *Titanic* went down from an iceberg, Mr. Hogiers, not because of a secret someone unknowingly divulged."

"Perhaps, but I'm not so concerned with sinking as I am with being discovered, or sold out to the Japanese."

"Captain Queveco will tell the Japanese nothing in the unlikely event that you are boarded. As I've told you, Mr. Hogiers, the *Ambrosia* was a rumrunner. She's fast enough to outrun almost anything on the water."

"True as that may be, Lazlow, smuggling whiskey is one thing. Smuggling a man into enemy territory is something else entirely."

"Captain Queveco will not give you up."

"What makes you so sure?"

"He has no tongue."

Twenty-seven hundred miles, give or take, and my companion had no tongue. I hoped he played cards.

223

***

Captain Queveco was a hard, muscular little man whose numerous tattoos stood out in bold, sweat-darkened black as his skin glowed with the sun. Deep eyes, quick and violent, lurked under his hat brim. Around his neck, he wore a knotted necklace of macramé, from which hung a knife. A leather thumb break secured it in its sheath. On his hip, he wore a large-framed Smith & Wesson revolver in a drop holster, the end of which was secured to his leg by a similar macramé braid. His hands were crisscrossed with raised scar tissue. They appeared to be on the verge of bursting. Similar scars adorned his neck. I could easily determine the source of his neck scars: someone in the past tried to hang him.

The story was knotted into his necklace, but I had trouble deciphering the message. Something to do with piracy and whiskey, how they thought a short foreigner with illegal cargo would make an easy target. There was no mistaking the final knot of the sequence: such events could end only in death.

Captain Queveco knew I was studying his necklace… his past. He did not seem to mind—it was, after all, worn for those that knew how to read. He beckoned for me to remove my shirt.

Lazlow began to object, saying it wouldn't be proper, but I soothed him by saying: "Captain Queveco wishes to read my scars from the bomb blast. I see no harm in indulging him. It's the least I could do, considering he is offering me his most highly-recommended services."

The truth was I wanted the scars read. I did not know how to do it. I wondered what they said, and hoped that I could learn enough about the language of knots to understand by our journey's end.

Whatever Queveco saw must have been compelling. He traced the scars on my back for a long time with his raged finger. Lazlow must have been able to read them as well, for when I stripped my shirt, he too fell silent. Perhaps not, though: I'd seen them in the mirror, and they were impressive even if one could not understand their language.

I knew Queveco was done when he came around and faced me. His expression was curiosity, and a hint of fear. He bowed, slightly: a sign of respect. I returned the gesture.

"Well, then," Lazlow said. "Take care of him, Queveco, and please, get him below before the crew comes on board. May the seas favor your passing."

"Take care, Lazlow. I will return as soon as I can," I shook his hand.

"Good-bye, sir."

I did not have the heart to correct him.

* * *

Queveco showed me to my accommodations. He lifted the lid to one of the fish coolers, pushed the bottom panel down, then slid it sideways. Behind this panel was the entrance to my room. I had to crawl down a rope ladder to enter. Once inside, I could stand easily. My room—as it was—was an entire deck. He'd configured the *Ambrosia* to have a false hull. From the outside, in the water, it would be difficult to notice. Queveco followed me in.

Six waxed canvas bags, drawn tight with a string, as one might use in a counterweight system, rest on the floor to the side when I entered. I wondered about the nature of these for a moment, then tuned my attention to my—for lack of a better word—stateroom.

It was quite a contrast from the marble and oak of my Pearl City home. *Ambrosia*, obviously, had seen her fair share of illicit cargo since the Repeal of 1933. I knew not what she had smuggled and did not care to know, but suspected more than one man had traveled like this. The area had electric light run in—and Queveco did a fine job of concealing the wires— and a cot. There was a chair and a wooden spool that once held wire or tubing upended to serve as a table. Further off was another chair with a toilet seat attached and one of the bags suspended underneath. *Now* I understood their purpose.

All the furniture was secured to the floor to prevent it from sliding around in rough seas. The floor was covered in sawdust to prevent one's footsteps from resounding through the ship. When the secret door in the false cooler was closed, the light from the outside could enter, none from within could escape. Fresh air came in through a series of vents.

"This will do quite nicely," I said. "I have a lot of reading to do anyway."

Queveco nodded.

"Do you play cards, Captain Queveco?" I asked, and drew the deck from my pocket as I started for the table.

He shook his head and backed away from them, ran his mutilated fingers over the knots on his holster tie.

I put them away. I did not wish to offend him.

"May I?" I asked, and gestured to his holster tie.

He offered his necklace, angled it toward the yellowish light from the single bulb above us.

I read the knots. He had won the *Ambrosia* in a card game, but the previous owner felt cheated and tried to take the ship back. Queveco held onto the mooring lines as she pulled away from the dock, climbed the rope and boarded the ship. The previous owner rushed him with a knife, stabbed upward through the bottom of his jaw and, thinking the gout of blood was the end of Queveco, started to haul him overboard.

I stopped reading. "This is how you lost your tongue? And your hands?"

Queveco nodded.

"I'm so sorry, Captain Queveco."

He shrugged. *Not your fault.*

I continued to decipher the knots.

Queveco ripped the knife from his mouth and slashed out the man's eyes. Then tossed *him* overboard. A doctor saved his life by stopping the bleeding in time, but his tongue could not be reattached. The doctor said he was very, very lucky to be alive, that he'd lost an enormous amount of blood. Queveco agreed, and decided that Lady Luck owed him no more favors. He had his life and his ship.

I nodded, understood his reluctance: to play games of chance or cards would be to insult her. No sea-going Captain, especially a smuggler, wishes to offend Lady Luck. Sailors were such a superstitious lot.

"Is that the knife?"

Queveco's look made me wonder why I asked.

"When you have time, Captain Queveco, I should like to learn the story behind the revolver."

He nodded, and pointed to my scars.

"I'll be happy to tell you that story, sure, though it isn't very exciting."

He waved his hands, indicating that the story behind the revolver wasn't that exciting, either.

I doubted that.

ACE IN THE HOLE

"Alea icata est" ("The die is cast.")
—Gaius Julius Caesar

I intended to catch up on my research while we sailed, and I did, after a fashion. I believed I would spend the time reading, playing solitaire, doing daily exercises to keep in shape, and the first few days, I did.

The ingenious solution Queveco offered to the question of using the toilet took some getting used to. When the bag needed to be emptied, I simply opened the door and pushed it into the *faux* fish-cooler. Someone would come daily to remove the soiled bag and clean any residual mess. I never knew whom. It was difficult imagining Captain Queveco doing it himself, but I doubted he would permit any of the crew to know there was an illicit passenger on-board, either. Smuggling was a dangerous game. Smuggling during wartime even more so. If Queveco had been involved with illicit cargo since Prohibition, he had at *least* a decade of experience under his belt. I had little choice but to trust him.

I never saw the *Ambrosia's* crew, but I heard them. They were, for the most part, young Filipino men, some could more properly be called boys, but they seemed to know their jobs well. I began to be able to identify them by their footfalls, by their voices.

Their constant chatter lulled me into trancelike states at times. I would sit below, like a rat in the wall, and listen to them. I'd hear their conversations. Their questions. Many wished to know why they were not dropping the nets. Some speculated they had angered Captain Queveco, and he was taking them to a distant port and firing them—such concerns were mostly from the crewmembers with less experience, the voices barely past puberty.

Time passed and I listened. My tongue became numb, my body leaden, as I leaned against the wall and listened to the world outside. The ship's gentle rocking, the murmurs lulled me through the hours. Through days, perhaps. It was difficult to gauge time's passage. Hours passed by in eye-blinks. Days passed in seconds. Seconds took an eternity.

At some point in my trancelike state, I moved. I must have, because my things were all laid out in piles on the floor. My pens and compass. My maps. My clothes. Each card from my deck in a line down the center of the hold. I'd removed my bootlaces and laid them on the floor as well, perfectly straight. My .45 pistol had been disassembled to the frame. Every spring, every screw and every bushing, had been set down in a straight line in the sawdust. Each bullet from the boxes of ammunition Lazlow had packed for me.

I recalled doing none of this.

I released my clenched fists, and dropped sawdust from my fingertips. I do not know *what* my intent with it might have been, but suspected I would have tried to line up each shaving in a perfect line as well.

I picked up my things.

The boat rocked.

I listened to those I could not see, but not as intently as before.

***

Lazlow had packed two books for pleasure-reading. I ignored these. The serious reading material I had packed myself.

I was intent on learning all I could about the civilizations that came before us, of Mu, of Lemuria, and of Atlantis, but the language was archaic, the light dim, and the ship ever-rocking. Trying to read only made me queasy. I stopped before I retched, and gave myself away to those on the other side of the wall.

I played solitaire. Shuffle, deal, shuffle, deal. Soon, the cards were everything. I felt myself slipping into another trance-like state, but tried to keep myself aware this time, as one might when they knew they were dreaming.

I know not how long I played. My trance was broken when the steady rocking of the ship became violent, the crewmember's voices sharp, frantic, and urgent. Waves crashed against the hull with tremendous force. I became acutely aware that only one wall, a few inches thick, separated me from the unfathomable depths of the Pacific. Should it crack, the ship would likely stay afloat for a while, but as for me, I'd be drowned beneath them before too long.

Sunk beneath the waves, return to the depths. Perhaps my remains would find their way through the sea bottom silt and rest on ancient Mu. Perhaps I would be devoured by great creatures that lurked down below. I forced myself to think of other things. To try and read, to sleep, to study, but nothing worked. The cards called.

I dealt.

Time passed, and I floated along in semi-consciousness. I knew, outside, there was an ocean. I knew, outside, there was a war being waged. I knew we were in the enemy's ocean, in their front yard, and that good Captain Queveco and the crew of the *Ambrosia* were risking themselves to bring me here. What hold did Lazlow have on this man and his ship?

What did it matter? It did not. Only as a curiosity.

I unscrewed the light above, watched the darkness move, and listened to Gregori's whispers inside my head. It's always easier to hear silence in the dark.

***

I listened for days. Many eye-blinks. Many agonizingly slow seconds until I heard the screams.

Someone lit up a short burst from a machine gun. Then came pistol and rifle fire. I heard Captain Queveco's revolver blast off regular intervals of six shots with a pause to reload. Then the machine gun lit up again, swept the top deck of the *Ambrosia*, then started working on the hull.

No one returned fire after that.

I retrieved my pistol, jacked a round into its chamber, stood by the secret entrance and listened for anyone coming. Up on the deck, I heard orders barked in Japanese, the stomping of boots, the trashing of equipment, things being thrown overboard, and laughter.

It was the laughter that unnerved me. In that laughter, there was no humor. In that laughter there was no relief. In that laughter, there were dead bodies of good men that had kept me sheltered while bullets rained down. It sickened me to hear it. I wished death to those that laughed while I mourned.

I did not move until after the last one boarded their own vessel, and I heard the engine rev and face. Only then did I dare holster the .45, open the secret door and climb out through the *faux* fish cooler. I waited until the sound of the engine faced until I went above, and when I did reach the top deck, I kept low, lest someone be watching with binoculars… or a submarine periscope. I peeked over the railing and saw a large dredger-type vessel with two gunboat escorts.

The gunboats were little more than commandeered rich men's pleasure boats with a Nambu 92 machine gun secured to the foredeck. These were not ocean-going vessels: more the type used for day trips in sheltered waters. They had to have come from a nearby island.

Being confined to the secret hold the entire journey thus far prevented me from quickly calculating my position. I checked the cabin for a chart and the ships' logbook. I found the charts, but no logbook, only a length of rope.

I should not have been surprised. I didn't think Captain Queveco knew how to communicate any other way. As soon as my fingers touched the rope, the *Ambrosia* exploded.

The torpedo split her in two. The concussion knocked me against the wall of the cabin. I managed to clutch the rope in my hand as my ears rang and I blinked the white fire of the blast from my vision. I felt the water pouring in, the broken ship sinking beneath me as the Pacific claimed her due. The *Ambrosia* fell away, a few bubbles marking her descent, a slick of oil, some debris.

I swam over to one of the sawdust-filled bags that had bobbed up, wrapped my arms around it and took inventory. I had a gash in my forehead, but it did not appear to be serious. I had some minor burns which might blister, but otherwise, I was all right. I could feel the .45 in my holster, Queveco's rope in my hand. The seas were not rough, but the waves were still substantial enough so that the horizon dipped and rose, dipped and rose.

I felt Queveco's knots. We were a few hundred miles east northeast of Nan Modol. I wished I had the opportunity to grab the cards as well, but memory would have to suffice. I had the itch to draw a card, but they did not float.

It was only then that I felt the first twinge of despair. The second was short in following, when the gunboats returned to survey the wreckage.

I found myself staring into the hard eyes of Japanese sailors, and the black muzzles of Nambu machine guns. I thought they would shoot, as they had done before with the *Ambrosia's* crew, but they did not. Seeing I was an American, they pulled their boats alongside. One crew aimed rifles at me while the other picked me out of the water. My weapon was stripped away, my knees kicked out from under me so I was forced to kneel. I still held the rope, and gave it up only when the officer placed his pistol against my head.

They asked me questions. I answered in English that I did not understand their language. There was debate as to whether I was a spy, an officer, or just a ship's hand.

The officer decided I was to be taken prisoner and

interrogated. They would bring me to the island.

Someone hit me in the back of the head with a rifle butt, and I collapsed to the deck. The gunboat revved, the bow came up, and toward the island we sped. I had a gun barrel against the base of my skull and a foot on my back. I supposed that whomever was standing over me must be posing for his comrades. I wondered if any of them would flash for the camera. I hoped they would. Posturing for propaganda, like the Nazi excavations, was a hollow cause. It meant their belief was eroding.

No cameras clicked.

Not even when we came ashore.

***

I was shoved toward a command post, always with a rifle against my back or jabbing me in the ribs. My hands were interlaced behind my head, and lowering them earned me a blast to the kidneys. The Japanese knew how to administer pain. They were good at it. I think it gave them a thrill to inflict pain on an American, one who stood half a head taller than them, one who outweighed them by a great deal, even though my nutrition of late had not been excellent.

I was thrown into a pit, a bamboo trapdoor shut on top of me. I looked up into the faces of my captors. They hovered around the hole, grinning and congratulating each other, all the while making demeaning observations about me. They took turns spitting on me.

I spit back.

The man I hit shouldered a rifle, but his buddies got a kick out of it. He lowered his weapon and pointed at me. He said he would get even for the insult. I nearly responded in his own language, but instead smiled stupidly and gave him a mockery of a bow, just to get his goat a little more, make him question whether I really did understand him or if I was just being a cocky fuck.

I vowed that once I got a chance to start killing, he would be among the first to die. I did not have to say this. Not in my language, not in his, not in the speech of knots or cards or whispers. Any man could have seen the promise in my face and known it was sincere. He saw it, and welcomed the challenge.

I smirked. I'd made my first personal enemy from my country's enemy. Perhaps I'd save him for last. Just so I could have the time alone with him without interference or distraction. The more I thought on that, the more I smiled, and the more I smiled, the less the Japs watching me from above stayed around.

Soon, I was alone, and then, I started to laugh. Mine was unlike the laughter I heard on the boat in origin, but similar in that it contained no humor. My laughter was filled with relief, with rage, with a touch of madness. I laughed loudly, because I knew he was nearby. I wanted him to hear. I wanted them all to hear. Wanted them all to know that whoever they *thought* I was—smuggler, sailor, spy—I was not. Wanted them to question, because questions are unsettling to the unlearned: the ignorant prefer answers—and answers that confirm that which they already suspect, at that.

SHUFFLE

"The clever combatant imposes his will on the enemy but does not permit the enemy's will to be imposed upon him."
—Sun Tzu in *The Art of War*

It was only a matter of time before they came for me. The hatch lifted, two men hoisted me up. On the surface, two men with submachine guns flanked me. They had not been in long: for them, toting a submachine gun still held novelty, and from this they took enjoyment. I looked into their young faces and wondered how long it would take to pass. If they would live until then, or if they would die with their weapons in-hand, still reveling at the rate of fire even as blackness closed around them.

They thought I should bow to them. It did not occur to me that this is what they wished, so one of them drove the point home with a fist into my belly. I doubled over, more surprised than hurt. The one that had punched me lifted my chin and began yelling at me. He talked of respect for my superiors. I rolled my eyes and waited for him to finish. He hit me twice more, then led me toward the hut where I was to be fully interrogated.

He presented me to the officer in the hut, saluted and waited for orders. The officer returned the salute and dismissed him. Then we were alone.

I stood there as a civilian. If I were still a marine, I'd have stood at attention, so not to dishonor the uniform I wore, but I owed the uniform no such respects now, and certainly did not owe this Jap officer such an honor.

He rubbed his chin and walked around me. Then he sat behind the desk and motioned to the chair in front of him. "Sit down."

"Thanks," I said. It was only then that I realized he addressed me in English.

I pulled the chair up to the desk, saw my pistol and the rope sitting on it.

"So," he rubbed his chin again. "Your name. And rank."

"No rank. David P. Hogiers."

He wrote my answers down. "American, I presume."

"You got it."

"You'll address me as 'sir'. Understand?"

That "sir" shit again. This little prick demanding I use honorifics when I already told him I wasn't in the military. "Yeah, whatever. Sir."

His raised eyebrow was an unspoken dare to be so insolent again.

I played as if I had not understood the warning.

"Where are you from in America? Where is your family?"

"Pearl City, Hawaii. I have no family to speak of."

"I see." His tone was as if he disbelieved me, but he dutifully wrote down my responses anyway.

"So, Mr. Hogiers with no family from Pearl City, how did you get those scars?"

"Hunting accident."

"Hunting, you say. Very well, then: what animals leave such marks?"

"Backstabbing sneak-attacking purple-pissing Jap pilots."

I knew it was coming and did not try to block it. His fist connected with the left side of my jaw with such force, I nearly fell from the chair. My mouth tasted of blood. My instinct was to wipe my lip with my hand, see if I was truly bleeding, or just hated the taste.

I refused to do so on principle: the strike was not meant to hurt. Pain was incidental. Reacting to it was out of the question. The strike was meant to establish my role, as dogs nip at each other's heels and stand over each other's shoulders to display their place in the pack hierarchy. This little Nip was a lapdog in Imperial Japan's military.

I rose. Slowly. Not with timidity, but precision. I sat in the chair and locked eyes with him. He wanted deference. I gave him stone.

The little lapdog started yipping questions with implications. My answers refused to be manipulated. He started showing his teeth: shouting, smacking the table as he demanded information. I growled my responses into his face and always kept eye contact no matter how hard he hit me. He questioned David Hogiers, but kept bumping off the wall of Jack Austin, US Marine.

The little fuck couldn't figure that out after a couple of hours, so he led me outside. The four guards surrounded me, and two still quite proud of their submachine guns, and led me around the back of the building. They stripped my shirt, and whipped me with thin bamboo poles.

I bled, but the wanted me to scream. I shut my eyes and imagined cards. The deck shuffling. I dealt out a hand of solitaire and played until their arms grew tired.

Someone must have screamed—whether it was me, or the man I was, I do not know, but while I was trying to find a place to put a red five, my game ended and I was led back to my hole. It was dark. I don't think they had deigned to feed me. If they *did*, I did not remember eating. Then again, when my allotment of rice *was* dished out, it was done so in small portions and hardly worth committing to memory.

I drank rain that fell through the bamboo grate, let it wash the blood from my back. I slept in the mud, but did not mind. It felt cool on my raw flesh, increased risk of infection the price for minor relief: worth it. Dirt mixed with my wounds, mixed with my existing scars. Another chapter of my story, capture and interrogation, and the next day they had more to say.

I quit playing stupid. To do so was pointless now, I'd shown my hand the day before. I knew they wanted me to bow to them—and they knew that I was aware of this. So when they beat me this time, they did so with more gusto, as I'd transcended ignorance and willfully entered insolence. By the time I got to the interrogator's hut, I was already a bloody mess.

He wanted me to bow, too, and lower my eyes.

Dumb bastard.

"You will show me respect," he said.

"Then earn it."

"I have earned it already. By birth."

I locked eyes with him. Silence was my retort. It spoke volumes.

There was nothing he could say at that point, so the beating began anew. Fists landed. Ribs cracked. I swallowed a tooth. This, before they took me outside and whipped me with the bamboo again.

"Scream, damn you," the one guard said as he brought the cane down across my shoulders again.

He wanted it. He got it. I screamed for him, but instead of agonizing noises of pain, I put all the air my cracked ribs would allow into the Marine's Hymn. This angered him further, and the bamboo came down faster and more frequent. Soon, I was singing and shuffling cards in my head, listening to Gregori's whispers.

I remember laughing at the "halls of Montezuma" line in my head. Montezuma: Aztec: Mu. Japanese captors: Mu. Synchronicity. Gregori was pleased with my perception of the Marine's Hymn. I won the hand of solitaire. Shuffled again.

Blood and snot poured from my nose. I think that whichever one was punching me in the face again had broken it.

I shuffled. Dealt. Played, listened to whispers.

I awoke on the floor of the pit, to a soft voice calling from above. "Mr. Hogiers? Mr. Hogiers, wake up."

I groaned, raised my head and winced at the shaft of light driving in from above. I raised my hand to block the glare, and saw the speaker. It was the most beautiful woman I had ever seen.

"Come talk to me."

Aah...

I melted. The effect a soft voice and a pretty face can have on a man. I was covered in blood, mud, scabbed and scarred and wounded, but I still tried to fix my hair and wipe the crap off my face, stand up a little straighter when I saw her, heard her. I challenge *any* man not to have done the same.

The guards lifted me up, but in such a divine presence, even they were uncharacteristically gentle. They would not look at her. I could not help *but* look at her.

For an Asian woman, she was tall, came up to my nose. I'm six-one. Her eyes were the same shape as those that had shot at, torpedoed, bombed, kicked, punched, whipped, and bludgeoned me, but for the first time, I could look into them and find beauty. The men I thought of as having yellow skin. Hers was golden. What I loathed about the men, I found exotic and arousing about her. I can explain it no better.

Gregori whispered, but I could not hear him.

She held my stare.

"I've never seen an American face to face," she said.

I was unsure of how to reply, if an answer was required. She seemed to want none. I obliged.

"Come with me," she said.

"Where?"

She nodded up the path toward the water. "You need cleaning."

"They sent you to clean me?"

She chuckled. "No. 'They' do not send *me* anywhere."

Gregori whispered furiously in my head. The questions started to come. Women were not the equals of men in Japanese society. What was she doing here? If "they" did not send her anywhere, then she must hold some rank, some status, that transcends a few thousand years of tradition, and I was not aware of any such position in Japanese society. Not even the emperor's wife was seen in the company of men. So who was this woman?

My face showed my questions. She answered with a slow blink of her eyes. "Come, now," she said.

She stepped. I followed. The guards moved to flank me.

"Get away," she said. "He needs no guarding."

"We were to guard *you*," one of them said.

"I think you for your concern, your attention to duty, but I need not fear him. You may report to Lieutenant Muramatsu now, tell him I've dismissed you."

The guards looked at each other, unsure of how to proceed. Clearly, taking orders from a woman was an insult. Indignant rage boiled in their faces.

"Look at me," I said.

Ten eyes snapped toward me. "I am injured. Badly. I can barely walk. I'm hungry, malnourished and covered in mud made from my own shit and piss. You have riflemen all in this camp. I don't think we'll be out of range. I'm sure I make an easy target for a good shot with a scoped rifle, and I'm sure you'll have every one available trained on me, should something happen. And it won't."

Two of the men showed relief. The other two were obviously surprised that I spoke Japanese. I did not turn to look at her, but I suspect she showed amusement.

The senior guard nodded, and announced to the other three that they were going to take up positions with rifles and guard the priestess from a distance.

Then, he gave me the slightest of bows.

I returned it was best I was able.

"Lead the way, then," I said to the woman—priestess? She led.

I limped along beside her.

The guards' voices faded behind us as she led me to the water.

I turned to look at her. She was smirking.

"You know, Mr. Hogiers, you confuse them."

"That's been my intent."

"I'm sure."

"What are you?"

"I'll tell you later."

"Why not now?"

"Because you stink."

"You don't act like a Japanese woman."

"I don't need to. But you're starting to pick up some habits of Japanese men."

"How do you figure?" My response came swiftly. While she might be the most beautiful woman I'd ever seen, I didn't like being compared to her countrymen.

"Back there. You saved them face. That's important to them."

I knew that, but didn't want to admit it to her just yet. I wasn't sure what she was about, and did not trust her. Time to play dumb American: "I just figure that it's easier sometimes to convince people that they want to do what you want them to. Let them think it was their idea. They generally follow along better that way."

"Does all of America think this way?"

Now *there* was a question I expected. "I don't know. Haven't spoken to everyone in America about it."

"You don't trust me," she said, and did a fair job of looking hurt.

"Should I?"

"No."

We reached the water. There, in the sand, was a robe, a bar of soap, a razor, and a pistol.

She sat down, placed the pistol on her lap, and said, "Strip."

"Yes, ma'am." She was beautiful and armed. I was no fool.

QUEEN

"He who knows others is wise.
He who knows himself is enlightened.
He who conquers others has physical strength.
He who conquers himself is strong."
—Lao Tzu in *Tao Te Ching*

Two things kept biology from embarrassing me: the first was the sting of salt water on my wounds; the second was knowing at least four sniper scopes were trained on my genitalia should it try to make a move, with her pistol as backup. I got into the water as fast as I could. I could take a bamboo cane across my back and a foot to my ribs, but the thought of a vasectomy via bullet was not something I wished to test my manhood against.

I furiously ran my fingers through my hair and beard under water to try and shake loose flecks of foulness. When I broke the surface again, I felt nearly human despite the fire blazing across my wounds.

She handed me the soap and razor. My thanks were the most genuine I'd uttered since I'd left Hawaii. I remember thinking that, trust her or not, if she fed me a steak, I'd ask her to marry me.

No steak was forthcoming.

Just as well.

I must have bathed in the ocean for nearly an hour. She sat, watched in silence. Seeing a naked—albeit brutalized—man did not affect her. She was not demure, but she was not aroused, either. Impassive, but she did not take her eyes off me. Whether she found nothing better to watch or if it was to ensure I made no attempt at escape, I was not sure: another question she slipped into my brain.

She held up the robe.

Trust her?

Not a chance.

Lust for her?

Most definitely.

Sniper scopes and stinging salt water were losing their effect.

She did not seem to mind.

I did, and quickly tied the robe around me.

"I needed that. Thanks."

"I know you did," she said. "Sit."

I hesitated.

"You're afraid?"

I shook my head, though doing so was a lie. "Confused. From everything I know, you shouldn't be here. Who are you?"

"Sit. Then we'll talk."

I sat. "So, who are you?"

She shook her head at my lack of act. "If you don't know, it doesn't matter."

"What kind of answer is that?"

Since when do you care about answers?

I looked at her, more confused than ever. "You know."

She blinked, and in that second of silence there was everything.

"So, Mr. Hogiers—or do you prefer Jack?"

"Jack is irrelevant."

"Not so," she said. "He's quite relevant."

"Not to me he isn't."

"He's kept you alive."

"I think I could have done just as well."

"Are all Americans so arrogant?"

"Don't know. Haven't asked them."

"You're fond of that retort, I see."

I shrugged. "As you're fond of asking me of the habits of all Americans. So is that what this is? Is that how you work?"

"I don't understand."

"This. This whole thing. Beat the shit out of me for a week or so, then send some beautiful woman in here to get me clean, hope that in my desperation for contact I saw things to you that I wouldn't say to them? Is that what's going on here?"

241

"If you're asking will I tell them any information they're trying to gather, the answer is yes. But that is not why I'm here. As I told you before: they do not tell me to do anything. It's actually much the opposite."

She paused a moment to be sure I understood.

"I'm sorry you were beaten, Mr. Hogiers, but you did bring an amount of that on yourself. You *tried* to confuse them. And you know simple men get angry when they're confused. You also know they get angry when insulted. You've done both these things frequently."

"Wait, now, I—"

"I know. I know. It was to prove you could not be broken. That you would not submit and betray your cause. Yes. I understand that. But if they cannot break your spirit, they will break your body."

"No shit?"

There. I had finally crossed the line. This is where she looked offended and I was to apologize. Well, fuck *that*.

Should I apologize to some priestess because she *knows*? Should I apologize for living? Should I apologize for the Zero I missed? The marine with the pistol? The sailor with his flesh melting off? No. Perhaps the last two, for not knowing their names as I should, but no for all else. No. No apology.

Gregori started whispering, but I ignored him.

Should I apologize for the bombed and shot and drowned and torpedoed? For the *Ambrosia*, Captain Queveco and his crew? Should I apologize to my captors for making them beat me? For bleeding in a manner not to their liking? For the scars left behind, for the water-garden I'd never seen, for the neurotic maid and fishing cook, for "Just Nancy" who spoke into my heart then disappeared? For shuffling the cards, for reading the books, for Dad's pistol to his head, for mom's chief-of-police in her bed, for the food I stole as a kid and the crates of booze I helped unload for the rumrunners back when I was a boy?

Apologies: like opium, hard to stop once started. I abstained.

She was studying me.

"Go ahead," I said. "Ask if all Americans are so rude."

"I was going to ask if you were all so sarcastic."

"Same thing." The salt water was drying on my skin, drawing it tight. Whenever I moved, I felt it crack. It still stung and the pain must have showed on my face.

"Would you like me to take away the pain? Will you trust me a bit, then?"

"I thought you said I shouldn't trust you."

"No man should ever trust a woman entirely, no matter what her position: trust is for brothers and warriors in battle."

"Well said."

"My father's words. I heard them often."

"Aah," I said. "He was a soldier, then?"

"Of sorts," she said.

"I don't understand," I said.

"I think you do. Please, forget I mentioned him."

"I can't. It's all I know about you."

"Now that isn't true."

"Close enough to it," I said.

"Take your arms out of there," she said. "I'll get the salt out. You can leave it tied. I'm not here to seduce you."

"Pity," I said.

She laughed. "I expected another vulgarity."

"Do all Japanese expect such things?" I asked.

"I haven't asked them."

"*Touche.*"

***

She cleaned my wounds. I asked why she was doing this, if I was only going back into the hole whenever she left. She said I was not going back there.

"Where, then?"

"There's someone who wishes to see you," she said as she poured cool fresh water over the wounds on my back.

"You're reading my scars, aren't you?"

"Would you expect me *not* to?"

"Not really."

243

"So why ask?"

"Conversation."

"Conversation matters to you?"

"It's been a long time since I've had one," I said. "Lieutenant...what's his name?"

"Muramatsu."

"Right. Lieutenant Muramatsu's talks are stimulating, in one sense, but quite draining in most others."

"I'm sure," she said.

I got the impression that she really did regret my treatment at their hands. I changed the subject.

"So you're taking me away from here?"

"There's much hope in your voice, Mr. Hogiers."

"Sometimes, it's all a man has."

"Often, it betrays them."

"A warning?"

"An observation."

"So, despite your kindness. I should expect no better where I'm going."

"You call it kindness. You flatter me. And misunderstand."

"I'm being set up, then."

"You're a prisoner, Mr. Hogiers. You seem to forget that, at times."

"Lying on the beach with your hands on my back doesn't seem like prison."

"Then it's the best prison of all," she said. "The one from which you do not wish to escape."

"What's your name?"

"What does it matter?"

"So I know where I'm being held."

She laughed.

"What?"

"American men. Japanese men. You're both all so silly."

"Why's that?"

She did not answer, but it was not an answer of silence. Her smirk was far too loud.

"Oh," she said after a moment.

"What?"

244

Her fingers traced a shrapnel scar down my side. "Gregori taught you."

"You know him?"

"By reputation. Some refer to him as 'The Whispering Cossack.'"

"He was fond of the whisper. I did not get to know him well."

"I see," she said, but whether she saw from my words or from my back it was not clear. "He gave you the most basic of knowledge. That explains much."

"How so?"

"Why you do some of the things you do," she said. "When your training fails you as the card man, you fall back to your training as a solider."

"Marine, damn it."

She bent down, her face mere inches from mine. "Irrelevant?" She cocked her head to the side, and I felt the tickle-wisps of her long dark hair across my neck. She was close enough to kiss.

My back did not hurt anymore.

I was lying face-down. The sniper files had no effect.

I shut my eyes. Opened them. She was still there.

"You're being cruel."

"How?"

"Stop that. Playing coquette does you a disservice."

She backed her face away, but made damned sure her hair brushed against my neck again. I shut my eyes: bad move, visions flashed behind them. I opened them and watched the waves.

"Where will you take me?"

"You expect an answer?"

"Not particularly."

"Conversation again, then?"

"I guess."

"Soon."

"Soon, what?"

"You'll see."

***

Soon was, apparently, twenty minutes. The dredger vessel came around the point, the two gunboat escorts darting like hornets in its wake. I wondered if the submarine that torpedoed the *Ambrosia* still lurked under the waves. Probably.

She had said that she (and I assumed whatever sect she represented) did not take orders from the Japanese military—quite the opposite, in fact, Remembering this, and tallying the firepower surrounding the dredger added up far too quickly in my head.

The gunboats broke off to pick us up. The crew did not lay a hand on me this time. We were ferried to the dredger, climbed a rope ladder to board her. I presented myself on deck to my new captors, was surprised to see they were not all Japanese. There were Orientals, yes, but also Negroes, Mongols, Arabs and a handful of European descent. Each one had a handicap of some kind. Legs were missing on some, hands, arms, tongue-less mouths, eyeglasses strapped around the head, for the wearer had no ears. Their races diversified, their wounds united.

I wondered if these were the captors or fellow prisoners.

I asked, and was answered with stares and silence.

That solved that, then.

"Come," said one. He held out a hand I did not wish to take. "Come, face Kwan, and be judged."

"I'd rather not."

"Your preferences do not matter."

I refused to take his hand, but I did follow. I did not think I had a choice. The gunboats were well within range. I was outnumbered, if I tried to resist, and though they were handicapped, they were handicapped like Queveco: not at all. This is what I thought, though at the time it made little sense. As she said on the beach, I was still learning.

I looked for her. She stood watching by the top of the ladder. Her impassivity cracked for an instant, showed me pity, and she gave me the slightest of waves: *goodbye.*

246

I returned it. Connection made: an ocean separated our homes, a war separated our people, but there, on the deck of a dredger-ship, she and I had our moment.

I was taken below. The question I wanted to scream: *What's your name?* locked in my throat. If I voiced it, with the question would come sobs, for she was the only source of kindness—*you call it kindness? I do. I do.*—this side of Pearl City. Loss: it can come in an instant and overwhelm.

Gregori whispered. I think he tried to tell me it did not matter.

Fuck him: it did too.

ONE-EYED JACK

*"We can forgive you for killing our sons
—but we will never forgive you for making us kill yours."*
—Prime Minister Golda Meir to Anwar Sadat

Below decks, I was led to a room that I could only describe as a chamber. It belonged in an old forgotten castle. It belonged under the pyramids, in an Aztec temple. It did not belong on a ship. I was not sure it could have fit within the confines of the hull. Physics, natural law—they seemed to have an off-day. Either that, or here, in the dredger, they simply did not apply.

Shelves of books lined the walls, ladders on wheels permitted access to the uppermost volumes. A single wide, long table the color of dried blood stretched down the center of the room. High-back chairs with ornate designs were placed evenly down the span. At the head of the table, a lone figure sat. He was too far away for me to see detail, but even from this distance I could tell he wore white.

I was led to him. Unease strengthened with every step. He slowly came into focus.

Bald, save for the suggestion of a few white hairs. He sat hunched over, twisted in the chair. He did not look up at me, but rather down into his lap. Wrinkles creased his forehead. A scar marred his cheek.

247

"This is he," he said.

I thought he would ask to see my scars, but then I looked at his face.

He had no eyes. A single swipe with a knife had put them both out.

I shuddered. Queveco's nemesis: the one who had stolen his tongue.

He reached out. I shirked away from his hand, was shoved forward. He clasped my shoulder, then caressed my cheek.

"The marks of the traitors are on you. You know little and have seen too much. You must learn more or see less."

"Learn...from you?"

His mutilated eye-sockets regarded me. I knew he could see my expression. I was not fooled.

"Captain Queveco told me what happened to your eyes."

"Told you? He has no tongue. I took that from him. I needed the power to speak with the waters."

"He took your sight and used it to keep his shipments safe."

"But not you. You were aboard when we torpedoed the *Ambrosia*."

"Not me," I agreed. "You used deception."

"Everyone deceives. That's the language of war, of love, of friendship and hate. Deception is the only truth. We deceive because we are deceived. There. My first lesson to you: free of charge."

"I don't want your wisdom."

He made no answer, merely waved his hand.

My arms were seized and I was thrust against the table. Hands grabbed my throat, my chin, my shoulders. I lay looking at the ceiling that seemed to go on forever. His hideous face loomed over mine, scarred, sunken eye-sockets over a grinning mouth of yellowed teeth.

"Reject mine if you wish," he said. "But I want yours."

His hand came into view. The nails were long, flaking talons on the ends of fingers wrinkled with age, knobbed into arthritic hooks. His hands shook as they reached toward me.

Not the shaking of an old man struggling to move them as he wished: feverish anticipation. There was dirt under his nails, imbedded in his palms. Sweat—

I shut my eyes before his fingers touched me. Nails first, pushing up and around my left eyeball. I screamed, thrashed, but the hands holding me were too strong. The ones around my neck began to choke. I persisted, hoping to pass out from oxygen deprivation, rather than endure this, but my luck was in cards, my cards at the bottom of the Pacific. I stayed awake.

Shuffle.

Shuffle.

Sparks dotted my closed-eyed sight.

Deal.

Tugging.

Play.

The brightest flash of purest white.

Jack Austin howled, insults and agony, vulgarities and rage.

I did not want him to be alone.

I put the cards away, and joined him.

I must have opened my right at some point, because I saw my eye being sucked dry in a mouth of yellowed teeth that, when done, grinned and swallowed.

I wondered if murder was possible in war. Were we not all combatants? All casualties? All prisoners, from the halls of Montezuma to the shores of Tripoli?

Semper fi.

Amen.

***

It rained and the ocean threw me to and fro.

At first I hoped I had dreamed it all, that I was still floating from the wreckage of the Ambrosia, but hope is the second casualty of war: truth, the first.

I was getting soaked.

I tried to drink as much as possible, but salt water kept

249

getting in my mouth. I could not lay still and the rain refused to fall straight for me.

I thought the salt water on my back hurt.

Try it in an empty eye-socket. I dare you.

I kept wanting to touch the sunken lid, but the salt hurt too badly. The island was not far off. I could swim it, but then I'd be swimming back into Lieutenant Muramatsu's camp. Was there another choice? Swim to Nan Modol? Hardly.

I tried to envision the layout of the place in my head. The dock, the beach where She cleaned my wounds.

The task, the layout. The hole, the hut, the path. I could not remember how many buildings: I'd spent most of my time in the hole, or being questioned (beaten) by Lieutenant Muramatsu. The huts were all on the far side of the path leading to the beach and dock, the hole on the other. I'd come across it first.

I swam ashore, but did not swim to the beach: far too easy for them to spot me. Instead, I crept up between some large rocks and trees. The robe hung heavily about my shoulders and waist.

I removed it, but saved the tie. I wrapped one end around each fist, snapped it as tight as I could. It held: good enough.

I moved.

The first two guards I saw were the kids with the submachine guns. They were still proud of them. They were standing over another hole, one fifteen feet away from mine. Funny: I was so wrapped up in my own struggles I never once thought to look for other prisoners. They did not see me, but I did not attack them. While I would have liked to, prudence prevailed. I skirted around the camp toward the huts.

I snuck into the one furthest from Lieutenant Muramatsu's cabin.

There were sleeping quarters for four. No one was home: just as well. I found a pair of pants that fit well enough around the waist, but they were a bit short in the leg, but no shoes—they were all too small. I drank from one canteen, used another to wash out my empty eye socket. The other two I would take with me when I left: it would get hot during the day. Enshrined with some photos was a woman's fan and a silk scarf. I couldn't think of a reason to take the fan, but the scarf I fashioned into a bandage, of sorts, by wrapping it around my head lopsided so it covered my empty left eye. My half-hearted search for weapons came up with nothing other than a broken bayonet. They must keep the firearms in one central and well-guarded location. The bayonet could no longer attach to a rifle, but it was still a fine blade—the Japanese were fond of blades.

I think it has to do with their history. The shogun, the sword-wielding warriors of old. This is part of their culture. America, being far younger, is a nation of riflemen (or, at least, we *were*, before these moronic hoplophobes started popping up everywhere in the '60's). We make the best guns. They make the best blades. I kept it.

I intended to wait until nightfall, when I could use the blade's silence in the darkness to my best advantage. I was used to it: darkness was all I saw when I closed my right eye and opened my left. Gregori's teachings. The secret hold of the *Ambrosia*, the hole where I was held prisoner.

The Japanese said they were the land of the rising sun. I was going to use the night as an ally. This ought to be interesting.

Going through their personal effects, I found a deck of cards.

I grinned, and after holding it a moment, I was glad I could not see the mirror to my left: I'm sure madness glinted in my smile.

I shuffled, cut, dealt myself three. Ten of Clubs: *a gift*. I hefted the bayonet in my hand, thought: "Well, no shit." Deuce of Spades: *deceit*. Kwan's words drifted through my skull: "*We all deceive…*" Ten of Hearts: *good fortune*. I did not believe it: the Deuce told me otherwise. Trust, you see, dies before the war even starts. I put the deck in my pocket.

I wanted a rifle, a pistol, one of those sub guns the Nip kids were so proud of being issued. I wanted a grenade, close air support, a five-hundred pound bomb. Want into one hand,

251

shit into the other: tell me which fills up faster. I wanted these things, had a busted bayonet. It would have to do.

I left the barracks, stuck close to the wall. I feared a flash of sunlight—

(*Rising sun*)

—off the bayonet blade would find the enemy's eyes and alert them to my presence, so I kept the blade shielded between my arm and my body. The steel against my skin was unnerving. It should have given me comfort, but it did not—it reminded me that there was the very real possibility that soon there might be such a bayonet slammed between my ribs.

I slinked off into the jungle and waited for darkness.

***

Nightfall in the lower latitudes comes fast. There is no lingering twilight, hardly a dusk. The sea swallows the light, the diurnal creatures hunker down and the nocturnal ones awaken. The guard changes.

I struck.

The first man I saw with a rifle had no time to contemplate what was happening, much less shout. I clamped my hand over his mouth, yanked his head back against my chest, and slit his throat. The spray blew out of his neck and washed down his chest, over my arms, wrists. I smelled the blood in the air, on my hands, and as he twitched against me, I felt a surge of power. I held him as he died, but I doubt he took comfort in my embrace. No one had seen me.

No one heard except the insects and hidden creatures in the jungle.

I let him drop and tasted the blood on my hands. Tasted his pain. His confusion. His shock when he realized his moment had come and he could not react, his resignation to the dark numbing that seeped in from the tips of his fingers and toes, up his legs, arms, torso and collapsed his vision.

***

It is said that the first man you kill is the most difficult, after that they come easily. Perhaps there was something within me that prevented this cliché from ringing true. Perhaps it was those pilots I shot down that Sunday morning in December of 1941. I don't know. I do know that killing him was not difficult, the rest that followed were fairly easy as well. Some struggled more. One managed to get out a scream. Creeping with a knife soon became stalking with a submachine gun, and me raking fire into surprised groups.

I found my wallet, my .45 in Lieutenant Muramatsu's quarters. He had cleaned it well from its immersion in the salt water. I thanked him, then pulverized his back with bamboo canes. I did not stop hitting him when his skin split. I didn't stop hitting him until dawn. He must have died hours earlier.

When the sun rose on the camp of the Rising Sun, it was me and the corpses and the flies.

And one other.

I opened the bamboo gate of the pit.

She stared at me. I was drenched in blood. The scarf I'd tied around my empty eye was spattered with it. I was panting from my efforts, and my arm was sore from overuse.

Still, her face was impassive. "I thought it was you," she said.

"I don't know whether to drag you out of there or shoot you."

She closed her eyes, nodded once.

I offered my hand to help her up.

She took it, barely mindful of its condition. She looked me in the face as she ascended. Reached out and touched my empty eye with an insubstantial caress.

"I think you need to be cleaned," she said.

"I think you need to explain yourself."

"How so?"

"You lied to me."

"No I didn't."

"You were their prisoner and you were setting me up."

"No. They were mine, and I was setting others up."

"Who, then, if not me? Because I'm feeling really fucking edgy right now."

She looked me in the eye and was silent.

"I don't understand," I said.

She nodded. "I know."

I felt an inexplicable serenity. She was a priestess, or so I'd been told. Perhaps that was it—that she was the most exotic, incomprehensible woman I'd ever met was surely secondary.

She was leading me to the fresh water stores. She said I needed it to clean my face, to rinse my eye. With two steps, with a few words, she was back in control, leading me along. I wondered if I would lose another body part before this was over.

"What is your name?" I asked as she rinsed out my eye.

"Do you really wish to know?"

"Yes."

She leaned into my ear and whispered.

***

When we made love on the sand, I recalled the adage about all being fair, determined that it was not only applicable to love and war, but also to self-preservation and need. We whispered no promises to each other. We did not discuss the future, our dreams: for us, there was merely the moment, and we both knew it would soon be over.

For a few moments, she and I were merely and man and woman. Not Japanese and American. Not priestess and mercenary adept. Noting more than human: such recognition yanked on my heart when we parted and I went back amongst the animals.

My first challenge was to get off the island. I asked her to come with me, out of obligation to my values, but she refused, as expected.

"Will you be all right? Will someone come for you?"

"Anytime I wish," she said.

"I don't want to leave like this."

"You must, though."

Was there a hint of sadness? I thought I heard it. "This is not goodbye forever."

"No," she agreed. "I don't think it is. But it is goodbye for now."

"For now."

She turned away, her hand flashed across her cheeks. "The tide is changing."

"You're right," I said, but did not think she was talking about the ocean. I took her in my arms once more, kissed the tears from her cheeks. I held her and looked into those soft weeping eyes and said nothing, because she saw me breaking, too: the power of silence as an answer. When we separated, we did so reluctantly, her hands sliding down my arms, until we were joined at only the fingertips.

"Go," she said. "Go," and took her hand away.

My fingertips were cold without her touch. Another chill, deeper, that I tried to ignore.

I threw the pack of food and water into the gunboat and climbed board. I started the engine and turned to wave at her, but she was gone.

I screamed her name.

THE SUICIDE KINGS

"A brave man once requested me
to answer questions that were key
'Is it to be or not to be?'
And I replied, 'Oh, why ask me?'"
—"Suicide is Painless" (M*A*S*H Theme song)
Johnny Mandel/Mike Altman

The gunboat got me as far as I needed: another vessel. I came up alongside, let a blast of the machine gun across its bow. She tried to run, at first, but soon realized that unless they could get me into the open water, I'd run circles around them. A few of the more confrontational members of the crew tried to prevent me from boarding, but a submachine gun and a healthy dose of rage are usually more than sufficient to stop a couple men with pistols and flare guns. The three remaining crewmembers were too terrified to react. They held up their hands and backed against the railing. I asked for the Captain of the vessel. They pointed to one of the dead men on deck.

"Who's next in command, then?"

He did not want to say. His crewmates pushed him out of the line.

"We're going to Nan Modol," I said. "You're going to drop me off there. After that, this ship is yours. Understand?"

He nodded.

"Good. And I think you could figure it out, but I'll say it once, just so you can hear it, too: anyone—*anyone*—trying to screw with me, or mutiny, will be left for fish food. Are we clear?"

A few terrified murmurs, emphatic nods.

"Good."

We sailed.

A pod of dolphins tracked us, darted in and out of our wake. The sailors swore they spoke. Perhaps they did—only I could not understand. The dolphins' presence seemed to calm the sailors, and I was thankful to have them. If it weren't for the dolphins, I may have had to shoot someone else. And these men were not involved, other than peripherally. I did not wish to have them die, despite the crewmembers I shot as I came aboard; they were merely in my way. I had a place I had to go, and if I was going to take these men with me, I had an obligation—a duty—to keep them alive: it served my interests to do so. I could not run the ship by myself.

***

The problem with achieving power by force is the constant maintenance: rebellion is always imminent. Fear will gouge the track for the subjects to follow, but it will not ensure obedience. One in a position of seized power cannot expect much, and this is where most dictatorships fail. The tasks given must be simple, and the subjects must be granted certain rewards. I let them have double rations and to shirk some of the more tedious tasks. These, along with the companionship of the dolphins helped ease the immediate tension of the crew, but I still kept my gun at the ready.

I could not turn my back on them. I dozed on the bridge, but never truly slept. I spoke with the crew, but never really talked. They asked me questions to which they already knew the answers: dismal attempts at chit-chat.

***

I had many distractions: visions in my absent eye. Slaughter. Carnage. Impact craters of bombs, decimated bodies and buildings. Fish startled out of hidey-holes in coral, a wall of turbulent water rising up from the depths. Foul smelling mud bubbling to the surface, millennia of rot. The dredger ship grating the seafloor, divers retrieving pure platinum coffins, runes inscribed upon them that the divers could not understand, but the Kwan could—the Kwan, and the other mutilated men of the dredger vessel, Gregori and myself, Queveco, if he had lived long enough.

***

The visions faded when I became aware of the shouting—when the dolphins were being slaughtered.

I understood them now. Their cries of agony and fear—or was that the men?

I could no longer be sure.

Things were happening. Gregori's whispers flooded my brain. I saw through my absent eye and the one still intact. My scars vibrated and hummed, burned as they did when they were formed: with such intensity that my nerves could feel no more pain. Agony overwhelmed with an exquisite rush of endorphins and adrenaline. I squinted over the railing and saw the waves stained with viscera, floating white-yellow strips of dolphin flesh amidst dark clouds of red. Beaks and tentacles erupted from below, another dolphin caught, another scream as it met its violent end. The tentacles writhed up to embrace our ship. The men and I both scrambled for cover, trying desperately to get inside. One appendage smacked against the window. It was a grey-green color, with double rows of hook-tipped suckers that pulsed and drooled at the glass.

The men came undone, babbling prayers to gods their forefathers had created, and receiving no answer, no solace. They entreated to me to make this stop, to make it go away, but I understood what was happening little more than they did. I knew it had to do with Mu and Nan Modol, but the details of the connection were flushed from my conscious mind, replaced by the agonizing burn of my scars and a healthy dose of human fear, same as them.

I tried to offer words of comfort, but words are empty when a man's paralyzing fear and sense of self-preservation are at war. They need action, someone to think for them. Someone to be strong and stand up and fight: a leader, and I was the guy with the submachine gun.

I started firing controlled bursts at the larger tentacles, for they were the easiest to hit. I'd take aim, hold the trigger down for a second, and the Jap gun would belch out five or six rounds, and a section of tentacle fell on the deck. When the first fell, the tentacles as one began to draw back. Whatever creature was attached to these, it could feel pain. I shouted at the mate to get the damned boat moving. A few crew members, inspired by the submachine gun fire and withdraw of the tentacles, began hurling gaff hooks and harpoons—anything with a point or blade to keep the thing in retreat. As we pulled away, it slipped beneath the waves, pursuing easier prey, such as the remaining and wounded pod of dolphins, who cursed us in squeaks and clicks as their blood stained the surrounding sea.

The incident could have bound us together, the crew and I, but they were sailors, with the superstitions of their brethren from all over the globe. They thought the slaughter of the dolphins was an omen. I agreed that it was, but we spoke on different levels. They spoke of unknown forces and fears: I knew what was going on, but could not explain it to them.

Old things were awakening. Old magic calling them from the past to our time. The men of Mu had no machine guns, had no modern tools of survival and war. We were better equipped to deal with the henchmen of the coming apocalypse. They—the creatures, the beasts and the men, we could handle. A cataclysm such as the one that sunk Mu, Lemuria, and Atlantis, however, was still out of our realm. The only way to survive that was to prevent the mechanisms behind it from starting.

My fear was that, with the advent of the tentacled horror, that the old gears had already begun to spin.

***

The fears were confirmed when I came ashore. Nan Modol was a small island off the main island of Pohnpei. We did not go in there directly because of the six-inch shore gun batteries to discourage a direct approach as well as the Japanese forces buzzing all over the mysterious stones.

I was put ashore on Pohnpei, but the fishing village I entered was deserted. At first, I thought the Japanese had run off or killed the residents, but then I came to the town center.

Outside of the chief's home the entire village had assembled, waiting to hear words from their leader. He must have spoke, and his words were powerful indeed, for by the time I arrived, no other word was spoken in the village.

The only sounds were my own labored breathing and the buzzing of corpse-flies as they darted in the mouths and eyes of the men, women, and children laid out in neat rows. Each throat was slit, save one—the chief's.

A long dagger was thrust into his heart, his hand still on the pommel. He could not spare his people the horrors of what was to come, so he offered them up to their gods. I looked into his face. He was young to make that decision—perhaps only a year or two older than myself. His arm was stained red with the blood of his people whom he had slaughtered for a greater cause. I admired him for doing it himself before taking his own life, not relying upon a henchman, soldier, or servant to do the foul work of ritualistic murder. As much as I admired the chief, I admired the common folk of the village more for sitting in their neat rows as he walked amongst them with the blade, like a scythe through fields of rice.

I murmured some words of promise, shut his eyes with my fingertips.

I had to pass through three more scenes similar to the first on my way to Nan Modol, walked amongst a thousand or more corpses. Even the livestock had been slain: chickens and ducks, pigs and dogs. The heavy, meaty smell of death permeated everything in the thick wetness of the late morning. The early afternoon downpour cleaned nothing from my memory, though it drove almost all but the most persistent of the carrion-feeders away for a short while. A bird eating from the eye-socket of a little girl was not something I wished to carry with me in my head to the task at hand, but carry it I did. Carried it for all these years. This is the first I've mentioned it. God, I've tried too hard to forget that vision, but really, how could I expect to forget *that*?

How could anyone?

***

After the last village, I came to the far edge of the island. Nan Modol was faint in the distance. To the south, the huge dredger vessel loomed, its two gunboat escorts lazily circling like caged, fierce dogs. There were a few boats in transit out to the island city, with two more gunboats acting as escort.

Sneaking in there was looking impossible.

If I tried to swim it, I'd be spotted and mowed down. If I tried to hijack a vessel, I'd cause an alarm. I was looking pretty fucked either way.

The dredger churned. Her crew knew I was near. They saw me, as only the mutilated could see. They knew, as only they could know.

Cards shuffled in my head. I dealt.

Full house: jacks and sixes. Someone prone to believing the alleged mysticism behind the inept mathematics of early Christian scholars might see something dire, something unsettling in seeing their cards come up as 666. The number of the beast, they call it—which really makes me laugh. In reality, the number of the so-called beast is 616, but arithmetic obviously was not the strong point of the early Church—hell, they got their so-called lord and savior's birthday and year wrong (it was actually 19 April, 4BC), and forgot year zero. When you consider this, it's hardly surprising they didn't adapt well to numerology and the divination of their antithesis's name.

666: good enough for me.

DEAD MAN'S HAND

"The nation that makes a great distinction
between its scholars and its warriors
will have its thinking done by cowards
and its fighting done by fools."
—Thucydides

I'm surprised I didn't think of it before: it was right in front of my face the entire time. I studied it on the maps, knew about it before I even left Pearl City. Hell, even Lazlow knew about it.

Lazlow…I wondered if I ever would get to see that water-garden. I bet it was just swell.

The shore batteries were up on the top of a bluff over-looking Nan Modol. I could see the hill from where I stood—I could be there in half an hour.

The only thought in my head as I approached was how many Nip artillerymen were manning the guns. I figured about a dozen, by the time you got done with spotters, loaders, gunners, and radiomen, but it could be significantly more. Surely, there were no fewer than the twelve—if anything, they may have reinforced the battery with a squad of infantrymen.

The dredger vessel's horn moaned. Smaller ones answered: a mutant chorus of bleats, the sounds of wounded cattle.

I'd better count on the infantry being there: my luck would not permit another possibility. Figuring that if there were additional men, I could forget about taking the main thoroughfare up there: they'd surely have someone watching the approach. I'd have to go overland, through the jungle. That in itself was no guarantee of safety, but it was easier to hide in the wet green blanket of the foliage than it was trodding up the main drag.

I still had the Jap sub gun and the busted bayonet. My forearm muscle twitched at the thought of using them again. All the way up the hill it pulsed, an arrhythmic heart, beating on its own accord. The sensations spread to all my muscles, left me twitchy, cold despite the latitudes. Sneaking along became difficult.

It was hard not because the terrain was unaccommodating, but rather because I no longer wished to sneak along. I wanted to run in there, charge, screaming and look into their faces as I bore down upon them, see their flat, round, slanty-eyed expressions of surprise before I cut them down, but I could not: to do so would be beyond foolish—give in to a quick fix of bloodlust, but sacrificing the ultimate goal—which was so very close. I wasn't going to blow it now. Not after what I'd endured to get here.

So, despite my urges, I crept along. A white shadow. A ghost. I drifted through the brush on my approach, coming within feet of a four-man patrol.

I figured they would be there.

I stalked them as they ran their route, moving silent through the brush, keeping my good eye trained on them, using my absent one to search for a solution. They stopped. One of them had to take a leak. I was on the other side of the tree he pissed upon.

The bayonet blade flashed. He screamed, clutched for that which was no longer, chased it through the dirt with blood and urine-soaked fingers.

After he wailed, the others shouldered their rifles. I came low with the bayonet, slicing one's tendons behind his knees, riddled the others with the submachine gun. Three bursts and the mag was empty. Even as I pulled the trigger, I regretted it, because the gunfire would alert the rest that were surely nearby.

I debated for an instant: find and destroy the remainder of the additional garrison, or head directly for the guns. I heard men shouting as they approached, so I chucked the empty sub gun, grabbed one of the fallen soldier's rifles and found some cover.

The first one came into view about fifty yards away. By the way he was looking around, I knew my position was secret for the moment. I let him approach. Three others came closely behind him.

I started at the back of the group, taking the trailing man with a head-shot. As his skull erupted, the rest of his group paused, stunned, and began to look for cover. I tagged one more before they got there.

I was starting to like the odds—merely two on one—but more were coming to investigate. I'd blown the element of surprise. To make matters worse, that Jap rifle held only five rounds and when I grabbed it, I lacked the foresight to grab extra ammunition.

The Jap rifle, though, did have a bayonet attached. Two weapons for the price of one. Yes, the cards were right: there was a gift.

Lucky me.

I began to creep.

I saw where they ducked down. I looped around them. Halfway through I got a clear shot. The solider was scanning the brush where I used to be. I aimed, took him in the throat. There was not enough neck left to support his head. His friend turned toward me, cheek against the stock of his rifle, and almost had me lined up before I shot him in the chest. He still had some life in him, so I shot him again.

The approaching men were closer now, nearly in range. So I dropped the rifle I was carrying, picked up another and rummaged through the soldier's ammo belt. Finding what I was looking for, I headed back into the brush, but this time I was far enough up the hill where I could get all of them in front of me before I started firing. I'd have enough for four reloads—which ought to be plenty.

I found some cover and waited.

Below, I could hear the last moans of the man I'd castrated. I felt bad about that. No solider should have to die at the hands of an insult. I would have shot him, saved him some face if I'd had time, but such was not in his cards. I listened to him bleed out.

The next squad that came through I handled in much the same manner as the first: starting from the back, picking them off before they could locate my position. I had to reload the clumsy Arisaka rifle once, and used the bayonet on two of them that had ducked behind some rocks. My muscles sang and fluttered at the killing that was done, ached to do it again. The enemy's blood stained my hands, legs, chest and belly. Amidst the killing, I never felt more alive.

I headed for the gun emplacements.

Let me explain a few things about weaponry, for those of you that don't know. There is no "Perfect" weapon for every situation. Each has its advantages and drawbacks, uses where it's appropriate and those were it's not—but often, especially in war, we make do with what we've got available. Example: the marine plugging at the Zeros with his .45 pistol. Wrong gun for the job.

A rifle—particularly a bolt-action like the Jap one I was carrying—is great for long-range engagements—50, 100, 200 yards or longer. I'd be wary of a sub gun in close quarters, but out past 50 yards or so they tend to lose their accuracy rather quickly. A pistol excels at even closer ranges—25 yards or less, but even then, I'd still prefer the sub gun if it were around. When you're up close and personal, that's the realm of clubs, knives, rocks and bare hands. Like I said: you make do.

There's an old saying: "don't bring a knife to a gunfight." This is advice usually well worth heeding...unless you can change the gunfight to a knife contest. But in any armed conflict, there *is* one saying that keeps its appropriateness—get there first with the most.

The Japs were already there first. They had the most. I'm sure the artillerymen were armed with pistols, maybe a couple of sub guns. Their gun emplacements were dug in, offering excellent cover. I might be able to surprise one or two of them from a distance, but after that, all they'd have to do is hunker down, wait for me to try and rush them. Besides, with all the shooting and dying that had happened before, they were already alerted to my presence. And they had one weapon amongst them that could beat any gun anywhere: a radio, which I was positive they had already put to use. It wouldn't take long to surround this hillock, then put on the squeeze.

I had no time to fuck around, is my point.

The gun emplacements were in a line, each with reinforced concrete surrounding it on three sides. The only way to directly attack them was from the rear, and the land behind them was cleared. There was no place for me to lay down some lead out of their sub gun and pistol ranges—and that's where they'd be watching. So I approached them from the front.

I came in at an angle that would prevent the other two emplacements from getting a bead on me. The artillery crew had their backs to me. Two had pistols, two had submachine guns.

I crept over the wall, and slammed the butt on the Arisaka into one submachine gunner's head. I heard bone crushing. Before he hit the floor, I had rammed the bayonet into the other submachine gunner's back. The two with pistols backed up to get away from the blade, and started popping rounds at me. I felt two hit. I didn't care. I swiped the bayonet across one's throat, and went for the other, but he was out of slashing range by then, and was retreating to the next emplacement.

I didn't have to use my blind eye to see what would happen next. They would all pour out of their positions, start firing. If I survived that, they'd get me pinned. If I tried to move, they'd pop off more rounds to ensure I stayed put. Then, two men would circle around me, raise their weapons, and finish me off.

I wasn't finished yet, however, and if I wanted to keep it that way, I had to move fast. Ideally, I should move so they would have to pause to react, but I had limited options: either run out the back, through the clearing or out the front.

Through the clearing was damned-near suicidal, but it was the wisest option. If I could quickly get back to a rifle, I could open the round against them at a distance. The problem was, men who were shot did not move as quickly as required: I'd already taken two rounds.

Getting shot is not fun—ask anyone who's been unfortunate enough to experience it, and fortunate enough to live to tell you. You can feel the lead cooling inside you, the hole—even if it's only 8mm across—seems like the Grand Canyon. Blood comes out. Blood leaks inside, too. And it hurts like a son of a bitch.

The Type 14's 8mm pistol round is among the worst ever fielded. The Japanese viewed the pistol more as a status symbol than a true defensive weapon—unlike our .45 caliber pistol, which is a fighting handgun through and through. The 8mm round was decent enough out of a submachine gun, where extra velocity and high rate of fire could get the job done, but out of a pistol…I'm still here to tell you about it, and I'd taken two of them, which should speak volumes for the inefficiency of the cartridge.

It still hurt like Hell, and I was limping along from the holes in me. One was through my left side, unnervingly close to where I imagined my kidney must be. The other was in my upper thigh on my right side. I could feel it lodged in the muscle of my leg. It had not nicked the femoral artery near as I could tell—consciousness was a big clue, there.

Hitting a moving target, however, is not easy. More difficult still when you're moving yourself. These were the only things that kept me alive. Underpowered rounds or no, catching enough of them—or one in the correct place—

would do me in. They pursued, popping off rounds when they thought they had a shot. I kept moving, albeit not as quickly as I'd have liked, back down toward the men I'd encountered before—where there was cover. Where there were rifles. Where I could make a stand.

These men were not surprised. They knew who they were looking for, were ready to fight, and were confident in their numbers and my being wounded to play out in their favor. They came low, swiftly, fanning out to disperse their group. I could get no easy shot on several in a line and pare them down. These men were sharp—their officer was well-schooled.

And so, I found my first target. He was the head of this particular snake. The rest fell rather quickly after I took him out.

I stood amongst them, bleeding from my wounds. More scars added to my collection. The 6-inchers were mine. I limped toward them, stepping through the hands of the dying soldiers who clutched for my ankles. Some wanted mercy. Some wanted to bring me into death with them. They were both easier to ignore than you might suspect.

THE DEALER

"A human being should be able to change a diaper, plan an invasion, butcher a hog, conn a ship, design a building, write a sonnet, balance accounts, build a wall, set a bone, comfort the dying, take orders, give orders, cooperate, act alone, solve equations, analyze a new problem, pitch manure, program a computer, cook a tasty meal, fight efficiently, die gallantly.

Specialization is for insects."
—Robert A. Heinlein in *Time Enough for Love*

The first thing I did upon entering the gun emplacements was turn up the radio. A Japanese signal officer was desperately trying to make contact with the artillery crew. As I listened to him repeat his requests for a status report that was not forthcoming, I raided their first-aid kit and tended to my wounds, quenched my thirst from a canteen. These were the only luxuries I had time for: the signalman was becoming more anxious. Reinforcements were surely being dispatched, if they hadn't been already.

I approached the nearest gun and opened the breech. She was empty, as I suspected. They couldn't have made things easy for me. So I grabbed a shell, loaded it into the chamber, and locked it closed. I did this twice more, working my way up the line. At the last gun, I got a visual on the dredger. I watched her for a moment, figuring her speed and course, and aimed the gun well ahead of her. Working my way back down to the second, I did the same thing, but with less of a lead. Back at the beginning, I took advantage of a spyglass. The spotter wouldn't be using it anymore. I looked through the spyglass and saw her.

She was standing on the deck, leaning on the railing, looking up at me. I blinked, wished her away, but when I opened my eye again, she was still there. She waved.

"Goddamnit, get out of there," I said under my breath. I know she heard me.

She closed her eyes, breathed deep, as if I were testing her patience, and then affixed me with the look all women have employed against a particularly tiresome man.

In my head, Gregori whispered. My mind began to shuffle its deck. My scars started to burn. The radio continued to squawk Japanese.

"MOVE, damn you!"

She blew me a kiss.

I wrapped the lanyard that would fire the gun around my left hand. "Don't make me do this," I pleaded.

She closed her eyes, bowed her head.

I think her sorrow was genuine.

I pulled the lanyard and screamed my apologies. The gun boomed.

I ran to the next one, sighted it, looked through the spyglass. The mutilated crew ran about the deck, waving their stumps of arms, telling the mute, the blind, to secure hatches, to douse flames. The shell impacted against the hull. The hole was above the waterline by a few feet and billowed thick, black smoke. The gunboats buzzed—one toward Nan Modol, the other toward me. I considered taking aim at them, but they were too small, too fast, and I was not an experienced gunner. I kept the barrel trained on the dredger.

She was still on deck. Still in the same place. Still looking at me. She seemed disappointed.

"You're going to make me kill you, aren't you?" I said in a voice I could barely hear—the gun's deafening report sent my ears ringing.

She gave me the look again.

I felt like vomiting, felt like crying. Felt like dying. Felt like Death. In my mind, I pleaded with her to save herself. Get on a lifeboat. Jump overboard. At least cover your face with your arms, get your head down.

"Damn it, don't make me do this. Not you. Not this. Please…"

I heard her sigh.

I fired the second gun.

I was becoming more proficient—either that, or luck guided the second shell. It hit the dredger aft, a bit lower than the first. There was a massive explosion onboard. The ship heaved, lurched to one side. I knew it was in trouble. I must have hit the boilers, judging from the damage. I could see through several decks. Water poured in as flames rose on the upper decks. The dredger was burning and sinking. Its bow was already beginning to rise.

And still, she had not moved.

The deck beneath her feet tilted, she leaned to keep her place at the railing. Men jumped overboard to her left and right, but she paid them—nor the sinking vessel—any mind. She continued to look up at me. Her beautiful face hovered between sorrow, loss, impatience, and understanding.

I mounted the third gun.

Before I pulled the lanyard, I said: "I'm sorry."

I could not bring myself to look through the spyglass afterward. I feared what I might see, but my blind eye showed me anyway. I have lived with such visions for so long. So very long.

I have replayed that moment in my head countless times per day. I've told her I'm sorry so many times and begged for her forgiveness. I've begged for it while on my knees, cringing into the face of memories, while screaming at the sky and cursing that which I have become. She has forgiven me; she *had* forgiven me even as it happened. I just cannot forgive myself.

She was the closest thing to kindness and peace I have ever known. The closest thing to love. To redemption. And—so help me—I pulled the lanyard.

***

The dredger went down quickly. It was nearly out of sight as I approached the beach. Only the topmost rigging and a burning slick of oil remained.

The gunboats were searching for survivors, pulling rescue duty. Other, smaller boats in the area were doing the same. The docs were a flurry of activity as soldiers commandeered fishing boats to pick up the wounded and drowning.

If I tried to commandeer a vessel myself, I'd be spotted and shot. That much was assured. I looked out across the waves. The mutilated and scarred were swimming as best they could everywhere.

Then it occurred to me.

I too was mutilated. I too was scarred. And seeing a Caucasian amongst so many men of different races in the water would not be suspicious. Out here, with a pistol in my waistband, a submachine gun in my hands and a rifle slung over my shoulder, I was a target.

I stripped, saving only the bayonet from the rifle, and entered the water, heading toward those I'd placed into the sea. I swam past bodies floating face-down. I swam past debris from the wreckage. A particularly large piece of wood—probably from the top deck—floated past me. I grabbed for it, held on to catch my breath for a moment, then leaned over the top of it and started paddling and kicking, as others around me were doing. I floated past the wounded, the blind, the burned and the scarred. I looked for only one face. I did not see her.

I was still looking for her when a boat came alongside me. A Japanese solider was leaning over the deck. He offered his hand to pull me from the water. I glanced quickly at the boat. There were three of the Kwan aboard, huddled together, drenched and dazed, the Captain of the craft, and another solider. I made a pronounced effort to each for his hand as I gripped the bayonet with the other. He leaned further. Then I grabbed him.

I pulled him toward me. Off-balance already, he pitched into the water. I started shouting for help. The other soldier was laughing at the apparent clumsiness of his comrade. He found it so funny that he did not notice the guy he was laughing at was already dead, a bayonet wound in his neck. I don't think he even realized it when I pulled myself aboard. He figured it out only a fraction of a second before the bayonet was imbedded in his neck, and blood burbled past his lips. He died in confusion. The witnesses stared at me, open mouthed.

"This boat is full," I told the Capitan. "Set course for Nan Modol, pick no one else up, and if you shout to any soldiers, you'll wind up as dead as those two. Understand?"

I'm not certain he understood my words, but he could have figured them out. The three members of the Kwan mumbled amongst themselves, but none dared to meet my gaze. I didn't figure they would.

We put ashore near the rest of the boats coming in. The three members of the Kwan and I had to wade in. The Capitan was already backing away as soon as the last man's foot was clear of his railing.

"It was you," one of the Kwan said.

"No shit."

"Do you have any idea what you've done?"

My mind flashed to her face. "Yes," I said.

"I doubt that," said another.

"I don't care what you doubt. Or, for that matter, what you think."

271

"As well you shouldn't," said the third.

I was momentarily surprised. Was that admiration in his tone? I wasn't sure, but didn't feel like conversing with the others to find out. I had somewhere I had to be—in amongst the stones.

***

Nan Modol was—is—hauntingly beautiful. Strange and ominous. Black prisms of basalt just out of the water to form man-made islands, upon which sat the ruins of courtyards, temples, and palaces. One of the larger islets had several soldiers—engineers, armed with shovels and picks as well as rifles—and Kwansmen milling about. This was their primary dig site, in the ruins of the palace. Something important was happening there; if it weren't, the shelling of the dredger and the drowning of their Kwansmen would have taken precedence.

Perhaps I was too late.

Perhaps they'd found what they were looking for.

I watched them some more. POWs were doing the actual digging. Soldiers guarded. Kwansmen observed. They could not have found it yet—this dig was still active—but they must be close, have unearthed enough evidence to warrant their inaction toward the ship. Like gamblers, they could see the payoff. If they sat for only one more hand…

One of the Kwan turned and faced me with sightless eyes.

The old man grinned, teeth yellowed with age, abused wisdom, stolen sight. He beckoned. I hesitated. The sinking feeling in the pit of my stomach told me I had been set up.

He beckoned. I looked out to the sea, where the ruins of the dredger still floated. Somewhere, her body was amongst them.

I closed my eye. He beckoned. I told myself I had no other choice as I stepped forward, that I'd done everything I *had* to do.

(*Everything I* had *to do?*)

272

Even then, it sounded like a lie. I stepped forward to greet him. My feet against the stones sounded like the shuffling of a deck.

THE HOUSE

"I must study politics and war
that my sons may have liberty
to study mathematics and philosophy."
—John Adams

No one made a move to halt me as I approached, or to disarm me of my blade. It was as if I were expected, that any intent I had to kill The Kwan was insignificant. Their supreme confidence unnerved me. I was certain I was walking into my final moments, that, on some negligent hand gesture by The Kwan, the lot of soldiers and Kwansmen would commence a vivisection, dispersing my limbs and organs amongst them. I wondered who, after devouring pieces of me, would hear Gregori's whispers, who would feel the loss of my priestess, who would bear my guilt. My remorse.

The Kwan greeted me as if I were one of his own, which served to heighten my already skyrocketing apprehension of the affair. Figuring death was imminent, I said what I believed were to be my final words:

"I loved her, you son of a bitch."

The wizened, blind face turned toward me, his mouth and cheeks in a maddeningly neutral, maddeningly calm expression. I wanted to shove the bayonet into his throat.

I wanted to, but didn't. He knew I wouldn't. He knew that all he had to do was sit there in silence for a moment, and—damn him—I would wait to hear what he had to say.

"Loved her. Ah, love. Yes. Yes, you did. You did love her."

I thought that was all. I was going to respond, but before I could, he continued:

"You loved her and you had her in the sights of the gun. You loved her and you shot at her. You loved her, yes. You

273

loved her even as you fired the shell that ended her life. Blew her to bits. Only the smallest of fishes could make a meal of her now. The rest...the sharks will get some. But not her.

"Such is your love. Your love is death. Your love is violence. Your love is the fight. Would you have loved her if you didn't at first view her as an enemy, as an adversary?"

The question was rhetorical. I knew the answer as well as he did—better, even. I remained silent.

"I do not doubt your love for her. And no—put that matter out of mind. She didn't doubt it, either—even at the end when she knew you were going to destroy her. That is what you do. That is what you *are*. This is what you epitomize. You were born a fighter. You wished to die a fighter. There's not many like you. Not many at all. Of all the millions at war today, there's only a few who wish for war in the future. They tell themselves they're fighting for peace, even as they line up the sights on a rifle and place a bullet in another man's chest. This war is a personal sacrifice for them. They hope they are enduring the trials of combat so that their sons will not have to do so. A few have found their element—found something at which they excel—tacticians and strategists, the ability to lead, the ability to follow. They will take these skills learned in war and apply them to their lives outside of it. But not you. You're the rarest breed, because war has become your purpose, your *raison d'etre*..."

You don't know how bizarre it was to hear a shriveled old prune of an Asian man peppering his speech with French phrases. The contrast nearly bowled me over, but I let him continue uninterrupted.

"...your first and last thought. Your essence. Your soul. The tools of war have become your left arm. Your stance— even now—is battle. Your lust for violence...a red flag which you carry before you. You *are* the standard to which men will rally. You are the sweat. You are the blood slamming through arteries and spilling from wounds. You are the heartache, the grief. You are the exhilaration. You're the bomb blasts and the moans of the wounded civilians. The grimaces of both hate and pain. You're the love of your enemy, for they give

274

you purpose, and the love of your brothers-in-arms, for they lend you strength. You'd kill those you loved to ensure the success of your mission. You *have* killed them. We commend you for it."

His congratulations were genuine; not a trace of sarcasm entered his voice or his mannerisms. My hand still twitched with the urge to spill his entrails.

"So now I'm here. Why so smug?"

"Position permits me luxuries. Conceit is one I occasionally permit myself to indulge."

"Self-preservation, I would think would be a large incentive to curb your urge."

"As if I've anything to fear from you."

"I killed her—and I loved her, damn it; for you…I hold no such emotion."

Kwan laughed, a hacking wheeze of derision. "You're here, but you don't even know why."

"To stop you from whatever you're doing here."

"Oh," Kwan said. "I see. Please, enlighten me from your perspective as to what we are doing here; it always amuses me to listen to the paranoid delusions of the ignorant."

Ignorant, he called me. I took offense. I'd read the books. Endured Gregori's whispers. I knew what lay beneath this ruin of black stone. "You seek the magics of Mu—to control the earth, the wind, the sea…just as they did millennia before—and use these as a weapon."

"This is my point, Jack. Oh, excuse me. David. Whatever you choose to call yourself. This is my point. Everything to you has military purpose. Everything."

I didn't understand, but I'd be damned if I admitted it. I began to feel as though I was a pawn in a covert chess game, when I believed I was more significant piece…but then again, don't we all?

Though blind, he saw my confusion.

"We're here for the magics of Mu, yes. But not those magics. Those we've already learned. We could drown Japan and the united States both if we so chose."

"Wait, what do you mean? I thought you were working

with Japan…" My worldview was becoming undone. And as it fell, Kwan smiled. I hated to look at it; his smile was not the prettiest of things.

"We are 'working with' Japan. Just as we are 'working with' the United States. And Britain. And Germany. And China. And Russia. And Canada, France, Belgium, Romania, Australia, Holland, Poland, Norway, Brazil, Tibet, The Congo and The Vatican. We're 'working with' everyone. Everywhere. All the time. We have been 'working with' them before this war started—before, even, your United States was founded—and will be 'working with' them well after this little war is over."

"So who's side are you on?"

"Oh," Kwan said as if he were wounded. "Oh…come now. Come Please don't waste questions on such inane details, especially when the answer you already know!"

If he expected a response, he wasn't going to get one.

"No one's *side*," he scolded. "We're on our own side, as we always have been and forever shall be. This war between these countries interests us only as other wars have in the past: for the knowledge. If you must, in your black-and-white-brain, place us on a side, think of us as on the side of understanding. The side of learning. The side of the Ultimate Question, if you can comprehend that.

"War is a great impetus for men to think, a great obstacle for which ingenious solutions must be devised. We're on the side of the thoughts, the ingenuity…the ingenuity more so than even the solutions. Every invention, every scientific advance permits more questions…and these we must ask, until we've exhausted them all."

"And then what?"

If Kwan had eyes, he would have blinked at me stupidly. "The Ultimate Answer, of course."

"It's nothing. The best answers are always silence."

"So I suspect it is, myself. But we'll never know for sure if we do not ask…and it is in the asking that the power lies, not in the answering. The Ultimate Answer, I think, is out there, in the future…a half-second after the end of time."

"No silence could be more profound, surely."

"You see? You *are* on our side. And this is why I've nothing to fear from you."

"You set me up. Used me."

You came willingly. You wished to die amongst those mortal men who are remembered as heroes. A warrior's death. We provided you the means to do so."

"Colonel Ross?"

"Ours."

"Muramatsu, too, then."

"Of course."

"So what was the point of all my journey to get here? Why the torture? Why the death? Why kill Queveco? Why did you make me kill HER, you SON OF A FUCKING BITCH!"

"You are death. Shatterer of worlds."

"Fuck you and your Hindu scripture. Quotations are beneath you."

"A compliment in your criticism; I thank you."

I nodded instead of snapping his neck, and no one uttered a word of congratulations for my restraint. I was disappointed.

"Death follows you. Violence follows you. War follows you. You came of your own accord, and everywhere you went, the toils of war came soon after. Queveco knew this as he took you aboard; he read your scars…you never did ask him what he saw, because you thought you knew. You thought you knew so much, but you were deceived…as Sun Tzu said (if you will deign to forgive the reference, however relevant), war *is* the art of deception. So, even to your military brain, it fits, if one thinks hard enough."

"This has all been a bad dream I'm going to wake up in a Pearl Harbor Hospital."

"If ever you set foot in Pearl Harbor again, war, violence, bombs and death will come soon thereafter. Unless you wish that on your homeland, I suggest you never step foot on American soil again."

I understood his suggestion, but as angry as I was

right then, I considered doing just that—booking the next available passage to Washington DC, sitting down in President Roosevelt's office and asking if he was up for a game of five-card draw. One-eyed Jacks. Suicide Kings. The thought made me snicker.

"You laugh, but it's an awesome responsibility. Awesome power. The lives—and deaths—of millions, nay, of *all* men are at your whim."

"Forgive me if I seem under-whelmed. I don't care about all men right now. Only two. And one woman."

"She's…waiting for you." His voice was almost consoling. For an instant, he appeared almost human.

I nodded. "I know. I can feel her in the silence."

"And it is there she waits."

I could not help but look to the western horizon, the setting sun. She was in there, over there, somewhere. I could feel her. In the silence, I could almost hear her whispering. I whispered back: "…A half-second after the end of time." It was a statement, but in it was a question.

Kwan was silent.

I had my answer.

***

The silence was shattered by screams echoing from the dig. Even Kwan himself turned toward them. He smiled at the sounds. I knew the reasons behind them, then, were as ugly as his yellow-toothed grin.

I walked over to the edge. They'd bored through the basalt logs, down under the waterline, through muck and silt, and had kept going. Large hoses pumped away the water as it seeped in. An assembly-line of workers scrambled over themselves to escape the confines of the pit. They had found that which they sought.

The coffin was platinum. The lid was cast aside. It was empty, though its former occupant was easy to pick out. He was the one with the helm and breastplate, a severed head on the end of a spear, the one with fury in his sunken eyes, a sword fused to his arm. He pointed up at me with the sword and beckoned with his spear-hand.

Come. Fight.

I looked at him, this ancient version of myself. Wondered what he'd do if I were down there, if he were up here. He'd probably leap down and engage me hand to hand, sword vs. sword, spear vs. spear. I had only a bayonet, and my name, David, was assumed...I'd not win against the Goliath.

The more I hesitated, the more worker POWs fell. His attention was fully on me. He slashed and stabbed them as reflex. They fell as the same. With each drop of blood, he seemed to grow in strength. The more he used his weapons, the more deadly they became.

"He's yours, too," I said to Kwan. "You don't need me."

"No," Kwan said. "He is not ours. He's no one's. Not anymore. He's an anachronism. For him, for his Mu, Atlantis, and Lemuria...time has already ended."

"You should have left him alone."

"We couldn't. We needed you—one of ours—to continue his mission."

His sword arm was still pointed at me.

Come. Fight.

"He thinks I'm going to climb in there and duke it out with him."

"Thus, the anachronism."

"Sad, really," I said. I grabbed one of the soldier's rifles and lined the ancient warrior up in the sights. He looked at me, perplexed, but unafraid. He'd never seen a rifle before. Had no comprehension that I'd already won the battle before it was even engaged. He could not wage modern war. He'd been out of the game too long, already served his purpose and sank the old world from which he came. His final battle was ages ago, and has been resting since.

As my finger caressed the break point of the trigger. I knew this would be a mercy killing.

As the trigger broke, and the shot fired, I knew I could never perform this act again. Not until *my* final battle.

Not until I faced the end of time.

279

After the echo of the gunshot, there was silence.

In it, I heard her. It sounded like she sobbed.

She would have to carry the grief for the both of us. Until next time I saw her, and took my share back, a half-second past the end of time.

CUT

"Si vis pacem, para bellum." ("If you want peace, prepare for war.")
—Flavius Vegetius Renatus

That was how it started. How I became what I am today. I know too much. I've seen too much. Shed too much blood. Each drop makes me stronger. Each drop breaks my heart.

Since that day in 1942, I've traveled the world. Japan (I found Muramatsu's family was from Hiroshima—whip *me*, will you? Suffer *that*, bastard.), Korea, Vietnam…Look through recent history. You'll see my footprints.

I've always avoided coming home. I remembered The Kwan's words too well, but my loneliness grew too great. I had to see my mother's grave, just once, so I could make my peace with her. I spit on it one Tuesday morning in September of 2001. You know the rest.

I'm not the reason every man takes up arms against another—don't fault *me* all of humanity's violent tendencies, don't you dare. I'm just the important ones.

I try to help. I do. I steered well-clear of both the USSR and the USA while they had nuclear holocaust on-call. I could not permit that.

Don't thank me, though: I didn't do it for your sake, or for the sake of the millions that would have suffered in the ensuing nuclear war. Remember: mercy left me in 1942, with a single gunshot.

I had my own reasons. Armageddon is mine, not some bastard politician's. I didn't want them stealing my one chance to see her again. What good would the final battle be if there's no one left to fight it?

I close my eye, I see the carnage. Around me, men die. Sometimes I help them along, sometimes not. Often, I sit and play solitaire.

Every hand I deal myself wastes time.

Brings me closer to the end of it, where she waits.

I miss her so.

Shuffle, shuffle, cut.

***

My name was Jack Austin. I was a Lance Corporal in the United States Marine Corps.

I came alive on 7 December, 1941.

***

...I miss her so.

Soon, I tell my heart as I shoot another stranger. *Soon*, as I draw three cards. Them with understanding know the number for which I draw.

Soon, I tell myself as I look to the setting sun, as night falls, as time ticks by. Soon I'll find the end of it.

...and smile one half-second after.

Soon.

STORY NOTES

Aaah, yes…the story notes. This is the part where you, the reader, if you care, get a bit about each piece from the writer —a bit of backstory here, an opinion there…that kind of thing.

However, before we begin, I'd like to thank you for making it this far into the book in the first place. I hope you've enjoyed the stories, and am honored you'd venture to gain more knowledge on them. Truly, I'm humbled by your interest.

There's been some question as to whether this collection marks a return to the game for me …if I'm back on the writing grid. As was said in so many of the stories, and, indeed, the title of the collection, my answer can be only one thing…

The Questions of Doves
Synchronicity. I'm going through a similar situation now as I was when I wrote this. The experience and years don't make it any easier. Go figure.

There are questions we ask, and there's nothing wrong with the asking. Expecting answers is often futile, however, and serves only to drive you batfuck crazy. The problem is, once an unanswerable question is asked, it persists for eternity as it most often seeks to confirm that which we suspect—and fear—is true.

Dogs don't have this problem.

Incentive No. 43.
Personally, I think there's better stories in here, and in Brackard's Point in general –but this was one of the first, and several point back to it, so it's got relevance, even if it lacks style and skill. The idea was to show how much we don't know about our neighbors—which still rings true.

Bleed With Me
Some have referred to this as an erotic story. I guess that's in the eye of the beholder—it wasn't designed as such. I believe that which draws people to each other is feeling as though the other actually understands, and that's really what this is all about. If that gets you all worked up…outstanding. Sally forth and fuck someone.

Gethsemane (Reprise)
Standard horror tropes dictate that something bad happen to the punks messing with the old man, who was just trying to keep the ghosts at bay. Reality is: shit ain't like that. The other reality is: if it ain't like that, you've got to write a damned good story…a fact I was ignorant of at the time I wrote this. Heh. Despite the clumsiness of this story, Richard Laymon found it worthy to be in his anthology, *Bad News*, an honor for which I will be eternally grateful.

Mo 3:16
Religion doesn't factor much into my work because it is illogical. Here, however, it's the backdrop. Go figure. Don't think I have much more to say on the whole judeo-christian myth. That said, I do kinda dig this piece. It's been reprinted a few times and is probably the easiest of my old stuff to find.

The character, Mo, was named after a white RX-7 I used to burn up asphalt in Southwest Florida…made it from Ft Myers, FL, to New York in 17 hours in that car.

Badgetree
I'd forgotten about this piece, honestly. The last I glimpsed this story was on publication. Re-reading it for the first time since, today (5th May, 2012), it gives me a couple of giggles. My first draft of the story note here explained in great detail WHY I was giggling, but after careful consideration, I've decided…nah.

Latex: Like a Glove
Someone asked a group of us that were all hanging out, "Flash horror? Come on. How nasty could you really get in under 750 words? I mean, seriously…" This is my answer, at 549.

The Sheriff of Pensie Avenue
An old story—one of the oldest in the book here—and one of the first where something actually clicked. Reading it today, it's amateurish and clunky and goofy and embarrassing. I wrote this two lifetimes ago and a billion miles from here.

Turning Leaves (An Autumn Romance)
Yes, my first divorce fucked me up. I'm sure you get that by now. And yes, I'm still that '71 Ford pickup, but with more miles and even more badly misaligned. And not for nothin', but the second time around, divorce still ain't no peach.

For Whom We Mourn
I was actually starting to get good here…hitting my stride, so to speak (As much as I ever did). But at the same time, I was burning out. I've developed this concept further ("One-Eyed Jack."). and have attempted to play with it since, but to no avail—again, see "One-Eyed Jack." This piece debuts Gustav, a character with whom I've become a bit enamored. He's pretty cool for an evil son of a bitch, and makes for a good protagonist. He'd do just as well as an antagonist—which I think is the mark of a worthy character, personally, but what the Hell do I know?

MHz Minus Infinity
Despite accusations to the contrary, I do not drink, do drugs —not even the occasional beer or group-shared joint. Reading this story probably brings these facts into question, but hey…

Strangers: Good Friends and a Bottle of Wine
Eh. I've done better.

The Missive
There are a few stories a writer will remember where they were and what they were doing when the thought hit them. For me, this is one. This piece came to mind while grilling burgers on Matt Johnson's deck and discussing Japanese porn with Edward Lee. Because burgers and Japanese porn ALWAYS makes you think of Mars, and the possibility of a colony lost in time. Hey, what can I say? Matt made really good burgers.

Between its original publication and its inclusion here, this story got a major overhaul. I wanted to nix the entire thing, however, at the urging of Brian and Jesus, I re-worked it instead. Its previous incarnation was a work of metafiction, which they thought was wicked cool. I thought it was wicked pretentious, so I spent three weeks unfucking it.

I'm much happier with this version.

Jolerarymi's Rose
Oh, yes…this old thing…a young author's homage to (pastiche of) Clark Ashton Smith. Debuted in a chapbook, *Two From Zothique*, at World Fantasy, 1998, alongside the legendary David B. Silva. This was the promotional chapbook for the (then) forthcoming anthology, *The Last Continent: New Tales of Zothique*, which was my first appearance in an actual book with pages and a spine and everything.

One-Eyed Jack
Again, we visit the Kwan, and the whole alternate reality/modern sorcery/whackoweird shit, with a side order of conspiracy theorem and a dour reduction of loss, first visited in "For Whom We Mourn," above. This was fun stuff to play with, but hardly fit the short forms, and kept wanting to be longer and longer. For some, that might mean, "well, let it be a novel, then." To me, it meant: "too large to be manageable."

What you, the reader, may find mildly interesting is that each time the character practiced cartomancy (divining the future through interpreting playing card draws), the cards he drew, and the inferences made, were the cards I drew from a deck of Bicycle playing cards on my desk, with consultation of reference material. The two exceptions were the aces and eights—perhaps the most famous hand in history—and the jack-six full house... included because it was so pertinent to the story. Personally, I place cartomancy up there with tarot, astrology, and faith-healing as complete bullshit, but it was mildly entertaining to see what hogwash would turn up, and then write about it.

This is my personal favorite in the book, and I hope you enjoy it if reading here for the first time.

Bios in third person always sounded pretentious to me. I'm unsure why this became the preferred form, but I AM sure I'm not going to bother with it. Fuck tradition.

My name is Geoff Cooper. I'm a paramedic in a town much like Brackard's Point: corrupt, bankrupt, and riddled with decay —condemned buildings, necrotic souls. When not at work, I design and build rockets with —and for—my children. I also enjoy target shooting, cigars, coffee, music, and time with my friends. At current, my household has forty-two legs and forty-four eyes, but twenty of the legs and ten of the eyes live outside.

deadite press

"WZMB" Andre Duza - It's the end of the world, but we're not going off the air! Martin Stone was a popular shock jock radio host before the zombie apocalypse. Then for six months the dead destroyed society. Humanity is now slowly rebuilding and Martin Stone is back to doing what he does best-taking to the airwaves. Host of the only radio show in this new world, he helps organize other survivors. But zombies aren't the only threat. There are others that thought humanity needed to end.

"Tribesmen" Adam Cesare - Thirty years ago, cynical sleazeball director Tito Bronze took a tiny cast and crew to a desolate island. His goal: to exploit the local tribes, spray some guts around, cash in on the gore-spattered 80s Italian cannibal craze. But the pissed-off spirits of the island had other ideas. And before long, guts were squirting behind the scenes, as well. While the camera kept rolling...

"Wet and Screaming" Shane McKenzie - From a serial killer's yard sale to a hoarder's hideous secret. From a cartoon character made real to a man addicted to car accidents. From a bloody Halloween to child murder as a means for saving the world. The rules of normalcy and society no longer apply - you're now in a place of cruelty, terror, and things that go bump in the night. In Shane McKenzie's first collection - he explores the horrific, the grotesque, the perverse, and the downright bizarre in ten short stories.

"Suffer the Flesh" Monica J. O'Rourke - Zoey always wished she was thinner. One day she meets a strange woman who informs her of an ultimate weight-loss program, and Zoey is quickly abducted off the streets of Manhattan and forced into this program. Zoey's enrolling whether she wants to or not. Held hostage with many other women, Zoey is forced into degrading acts of perversion for the amusement of her captors. ...

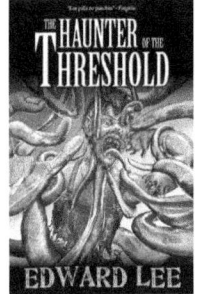

"The Haunter of the Threshold" Edward Lee - There is something very wrong with this backwater town. Suicide notes, magic gems, and haunted cabins await her. Plus the woods are filled with monsters, both human and otherworldly. And then there are the horrible tentacles . . . Soon Hazel is thrown into a battle for her life that will test her sanity and sex drive. The sequel to H.P. Lovecraft's The Haunter of the Dark is Edward Lee's most pornographic novel to date!

"Boot Boys of the Wolf Reich" David Agranoff - PIt is the summer of 1989 and they spend their days hanging out and having fun, and their nights fighting the local neo-Nazi gangs. Driven back and badly beaten, the local Nazi contingent finds the strangest of allies - The last survivor of a cult of Nazi werewolf assassins. An army of neo-Nazi werewolves are just what he needs. But first, they have some payback for all those meddling Anti-racist SHARPs...

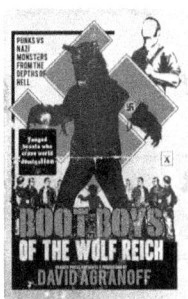

"The Dark Ones" Bryan Smith - They are The Dark Ones. The name began as a self-deprecating joke, but it stuck and now it's a source of pride. They're the one who don't fit in. The misfits who drink and smoke too much and stay out all hours of the night. Everyone knows they're trouble. On the outskirts of Ransom, TN is an abandoned, boarded-up house. Something evil happened there long ago. The evil has been contained there ever since, locked down tight in the basement—until the night The Dark Ones set it free . . .

"Genital Grinder" Ryan Harding - *"Think you're hardcore? Think again. If you've handled everything Edward Lee, Wrath James White, and Bryan Smith have thrown at you, then put on your rubber parka, spread some plastic across the floor, and get ready for Ryan Harding, the unsung master of hardcore horror. Abandon all hope, ye who enter here. Harding's work is like an acid bath, and pain has never been so sweet."*
- Brian Keene

AVAILABLE FROM AMAZON.COM

www.ingramcontent.com/pod-product-compliance
Lightning Source LLC
Chambersburg PA
CBHW052017020726
47501CB00004B/1099

* 9 7 8 1 6 2 1 0 5 1 9 6 1 *